SECRET OF THE

WHITE ROSE

ALSO BY STEFANIE PINTOFF

A Curtain Falls
In the Shadow of Gotham

SECRET OF THE
WHITE ROSE

Stefanie Pintoff

Minotaur Books
New York

This is a work of fiction. All of the characters, organizations, and events portrayed in this novel are either products of the author's imagination or are used fictitiously.

www.minotaurbooks.com

The Library of Congress has cataloged the hardcover edition as follows:

Pintoff, Stefanie.
  Secret of the white rose / Stefanie Pintoff.—1st ed.
      p. cm.
  ISBN 978-0-312-58397-2 (hardback)
  1. Police—New York (State)—Fiction. 2. Judges—Crimes against—
Fiction. 3. Upper West Side (New York, N.Y.)—Fiction. 4. Terrorists—
New York (State)—New York—Fiction. 5. New York (State)—History—
20th century—Fiction. I. Title.
  PS3616.I58S43 2011
  813'.6—dc22

                                                              2011001291

ISBN 978-1-250-00166-5 (trade paperback)

First Minotaur Books Paperback Edition: March 2012

10 9 8 7 6 5 4 3 2 1

For Craig and Maddie, always

ACKNOWLEDGMENTS

It is a tremendous pleasure to work with everyone at Minotaur Books, and I owe many thanks to my wonderful editor, Kelley Ragland. Thanks also to Andrew Martin, Matt Martz, and everyone else who has played a role in bringing this book into print.

I want to thank, as always, my agent, David Hale Smith, whose friendship and encouragement are invaluable.

Thanks to all family and friends for their unwavering support, with special mention to Natalie Meir, Mackenzie Cadenhead, and Mark Longaker for always helpful feedback.

To D. E. Johnson for explaining the appeal of the electric motorcar, and to Julie Cameron for arranging my personal tour of Gramercy Square Park. Thanks also to the staff and holdings of the New York Public Library and New York University's Bobst Library. Among the resources I found invaluable in writing this book, none was more so than Alex Butterworth's *The*

ACKNOWLEDGMENTS

World That Never Was: The True Story of Dreamers, Schemers, and Secret Agents. His depiction of the rise of anarchism and nihilistic terrorism in the late-nineteenth and early-twentieth centuries offers a comprehensive overview of how noble ideals were transformed into violent acts.

Most of all, thank you to Craig, whose partnership and input I rely on absolutely.

SECRET OF THE

WHITE
ROSE

PROLOGUE

Monday, October 22, 1906

Judge Hugo Jackson was on edge—and had been, ever since the trial began.

He was not alone. From the financial magnates of Wall Street to the ordinary shop workers at Macy's, bond brokers at Bankers Trust to grocery clerks at Wehman's: everyone was unnerved by *People* V. *Drayson*.

The difference, of course, was that Jackson was the presiding judge.

He felt nothing but revulsion for Drayson, who by neither word nor sign had shown any remorse for the lives he had taken. But this defendant would get a fair trial. It was the judge's sworn duty, after all. Not to mention the fact that he didn't want to give Drayson grounds for appeal.

Still, he remained unsettled.

Maybe it was Drayson himself—for it was disconcerting the way the defendant with the overgrown hair and beard sat mutely, staring at the judge day after day from behind thick wire-rimmed glasses. That sensation of being watched stayed with him for hours after he left the courtroom—though every time he turned to look behind him, no one was there. His wife would say he was growing dotty in his old age.

All around him, crowds of people anxious for the latest news grabbed their copies of the *World*, the *Tribune*, and the *Times* straight out of newsboys' hands before the ink was dry. They would read the details of how the defense had rested. Jury deliberations would begin tomorrow, and Drayson's fate would be determined. Outraged by his crime, the public condemned the man as a monster and waited with trepidation for the guilty verdict that was sure to come. The verdict that *must* come if any justice was to be had in this world.

At least, that was how most people felt. But as the judge knew too well, there were others. Even Drayson had his supporters.

When the judge arrived at his staid red-brick town house at 3 Gramercy Park West nearly half an hour later, he found his mail neatly stacked in a pile on a silver tray atop the entry hall table. He shuffled through the letters, pausing at one.

Not again.

He tore it open and glanced at its contents. Instinctively, he reached to loosen his necktie, which seemed to have constricted around his throat. He took a deep breath to steady himself. Then, without a word to his wife, he stuffed the entire stack of letters into his overcoat pocket, grabbed the large iron key that always hung by his front door, and crossed the street to the locked wrought-iron gate leading to the park—for only owners of those homes opposite the park had access to the small private oasis at the foot of Lexington Avenue.

His hands trembled as he lifted the key and turned the lock.

Cursing his raw nerves, he shut the gate behind him, and for just a moment he felt he had closed out all worldly evils. This was his private Eden: a place of peace and beauty. He walked the length of the park, past nannies pushing prams and gentlemen reading newspapers on the benches that lined manicured walking paths.

Finally, he chose his favorite bench, one near the stone fountain at the western entrance. Its gurgling waters soothed his raw nerves, and he breathed more easily. His composure restored by the calm of the park, he brought himself to review the rest of his mail.

It had to be done. Eden had never been immune to the presence of evil.

This afternoon's delivery had brought even more hateful, threatening letters. The first two he opened were filled with angry accusations that he was too sympathetic toward Drayson. Yet another proclaimed Drayson to be a martyr to the cause and threatened the judge's life.

He sighed, knowing he would have to call in the police. Again.

Why did everyone attempt to influence him with regard to this trial?

Drayson was a self-declared anarchist, but that fact alone was not responsible for the way New York City's population was captivated by the events in his courtroom.

No, Al Drayson was different.

At precisely four o'clock on the third Saturday of June, he had allegedly planted a dynamite bomb in a horse-drawn cab. His target had been none other than Andrew Carnegie, a wedding guest at the stately brick and stone town house at 115 East Forty-seventh Street. Yet from the outset, Drayson's plan was badly conceived. Carnegie was a poor target—for however angry Drayson may have been about the treatment of workers at Carnegie's U.S. Steel, the tycoon himself was now viewed largely as a philanthropist. He had vowed to give away his vast fortune before he died, and his endowments to Carnegie Hall and the Hero Fund suggested he was serious.

"I acted for the good working people." Since his arrest, Drayson had uttered those seven words and nothing more.

But five innocents had died when his bomb exploded: the wagon burst apart in a conflagration of fire, wood, and nails, causing glass windows to shatter and bricks to crumble. While a number of wedding guests suffered abrasions and cuts, Drayson's weapon wrought its most horrifying devastation on the street.

A dynamite bomb is an instrument of death both indiscriminate and savage; mere words cannot convey the carnage it creates. In just a moment's time, it transformed a pleasant June afternoon into a scene that more properly belonged on a battlefield, so great was the destruction of life and limb. The wagon's horse lay dead in the gutter, his hindquarters blown off by the blast; a woman was slumped against the town house stoop, both of her arms gone; and a man with seared flesh sprawled awkwardly on the sidewalk. Drayson had wanted to champion his cause by striking a blow to the capitalist system, but by killing innocent people with ordinary lives, he was forever damned in the court of public opinion.

Then, of course, there was the child.

The four-year-old boy had been walking home from church with his grandfather when the dynamite exploded. One of his shoes had been propelled onto a second-floor window ledge by the force of the explosion. It was the only intact reminder of the boy, and its image—a solitary child's shoe, made of black leather and buttons, dangling forlorn on that ledge—served as a poignant reminder of what was lost that day. It circulated in all the major papers and entered the public consciousness in a way more graphic photographs never could have, had they even been permitted to run.

And so Drayson, the man who wanted to be celebrated as a revolutionary, instead was reviled as the worst kind of common criminal: a child-killer.

For that reason, the spectacle outside the courthouse had for weeks been nothing short of a circus. Many wanted to see Al Drayson convicted, and they came every day—often carrying photographs of the victims. Some carried newspaper clippings that pictured the child's shoe. And the anarchists came, too, including the notorious Emma Goldman. Drayson had made mistakes, she argued, but the general goals of the anarchist movement remained sound. She succeeded in riling the crowds—sympathizers and detractors alike—with her incendiary speech.

The judge was being scrupulously careful in the Drayson matter, which only made the threatening letters that much harder to swallow. He was tired of the shenanigans that tested his courtroom authority, and the politicizing of this trial—by all sides—strained his patience.

The judge gathered his mail and returned home from the park, barely taking time to hang his overcoat before retreating to the library.

He reached for the telephone. He needed to make two calls. The first was to a man he had known and trusted for years.

"I received another letter."

"Like the others?"

"Yes."

"Well, then. It is as we expected." The voice on the other end of the wire was tired.

"What should I do?" the judge asked.

"The same as before. Just decode the message and follow the instructions."

"This cannot continue," the judge said, his voice shaking. "We must figure out who learned our code. It's been years since—"

"Quiet."

They were silent for some moments. Then the voice continued in calmer tones. "We'll figure out a way to stop it. But right now, just do as you're told."

There was no choice, so he would. For now.

He placed the black telephone earpiece onto its candlestick base. Almost immediately, he picked it up again and gave the operator the number for New York City Police Commissioner Theodore Bingham. As he waited for the connection to be made, he resolved to be careful.

Prudent—and always careful.

PART
ONE

Things fall apart; the centre cannot hold;
Mere anarchy is loosed upon the world,
The blood-dimmed tide is loosed, and everywhere
The ceremony of innocence is drowned.
        —W. B. Yeats, "The Second Coming"

Tuesday, October 23, 1906

Detective Simon Ziele

CHAPTER 1

171 West Seventy-first Street. 1:30 A.M.

Despite my best intentions—not to mention an excellent cup of French roast—I had fallen asleep from sheer exhaustion. Lying on a gold and green paisley sofa, halfway through W. D. Morrison's treatise *Crime and Its Causes,* I was startled awake by a ferocious pounding at my door. I bolted upright—causing Morrison to tumble to the ground, followed by my now empty coffee mug.

I fumbled for my battered pocket watch. *Half past one.* At such an ungodly hour, most people would telephone. Thanks to the modern black and brass Strowger dial telephone installed in my new quarters here last month, I could be reached at any hour. That was a mixed blessing, of course—but I'd already come to appreciate the telephone as a more civilized method of interruption than the incessant knocking that disturbed me now.

Why the devil was someone determined to wake me in person?

I walked barefoot to the door over newly varnished hardwood that was cold and smooth against my feet. As I drew close, the pounding stopped, but an urgent voice called out my name.

"Ziele! Open up."

I turned the lock and withdrew the chain. By the flickering light of the gaslight lanterns that lined my hallway, I recognized my friend and colleague: criminologist Alistair Sinclair.

The normally poised and garrulous professor staggered into my living room, collapsed onto my paisley sofa, and looked up at me helplessly. "Ziele, I need your help." He managed to rasp the words, before he succumbed to a fit of coughing.

"What's happened?" After I closed and locked my door, I lit the additional oil lamps in my living room, then surveyed Alistair closely for signs of an injury. I saw none.

Not once in our acquaintance had I ever seen Alistair in such a state. His dark hair, heavily lined with silver, was not smoothly coiffed; rather, it stood up on end as though he had run his hands through it repeatedly. His expensive cashmere-blend coat was torn at the sleeve and splattered with mud. But most disturbing was the blank expression in his blue eyes when he looked at me. Clear as ice, and always too cold for warmth, his eyes normally blazed with intelligence—yet tonight all I saw was emptiness.

I brought him a glass of water. He accepted, saying nothing.

The lanterns flickered, the result of a draft that perpetually ran through the room, and I pulled my dressing gown tighter. Then I sat in the overstuffed green armchair opposite Alistair.

My professional demeanor was carefully practiced for times

such as these, so my voice was calm when I asked him what had happened. But my manner belied my deep private concern—for whatever had undone his usual composure had to be significant. My immediate worry centered upon Isabella, Alistair's widowed daughter-in-law who assisted him in his research into the criminal mind—and who preoccupied more of my own thoughts than I usually cared to admit.

"A man was murdered tonight," he finally managed to say. "Someone I once counted among my closest friends."

"I'm sorry," I said, and meant it.

We were silent for several moments while he composed himself.

"Who was he?"

"Hugo Jackson. He'd gone to Harvard Law with me, class of 'seventy-seven." With a quick, wistful smile, he added, "We'd not spoken in years, but we were close once. In fact, he was the best man at my wedding."

"You had a falling-out?"

He shook his head. "Nothing like that. We simply drifted apart. We made different friends, developed varying interests, saw each other less often . . ."

"You're certain it was murder?" Now wide awake, I crossed my arms and regarded him soberly.

"Without a doubt. His throat was slashed from ear to ear."

"If you weren't close, why are you among the first to know?" A long-ago relationship of the sort he described wouldn't merit his involvement. Or explain why he was so broken up about it.

"Our wives had developed a friendship that lasted through the years, even as our own waned. In part, that's why Mrs. Jackson called me immediately."

"And the other part?" I asked, knowing that what Alistair didn't say was usually more important than what he did.

"There were unusual circumstances." Alistair lowered his voice instinctively, though no one was here but us. "Mrs. Jackson found him in the library, slumped over his desk in a pool of blood." He frowned and grew silent, lost in some thought of his own.

"Go on," I urged.

He passed me his water glass. "You don't have a stiff drink, do you, Ziele? Something to buck up our strength?"

All I had was the Talisker single-malt scotch that Alistair himself had given me for my birthday last summer—a souvenir from a recent trip to Scotland's Isle of Skye. I poured him a generous glass, neat, then waited for him to continue.

He swirled the tawny mixture, seemingly more content to smell its earthy essence than to drink it.

"There was a Bible next to his body—not the family Bible but one his wife had never seen before. And my friend's right hand was resting on top of it," he said at last.

I tried to envision the scene as Alistair described it. "Like the way you take an oath in court?"

He nodded, adding, "My friend was a judge."

"But don't judges usually administer oaths, not take them?"

"Exactly." He gave me a meaningful look. "And, given it was a Bible unfamiliar to his wife, we might presume his killer brought it with him to the crime scene."

His hand trembled, forcing him to put his drink on the table.

I leaned in closer, more concerned now. I'd never seen him so shaken up.

"We are," I reminded him, "discussing a crime scene neither

one of us has actually seen. But you already believe it signifies something of importance?"

"What do you think, Ziele?" he said, bursting out with an exasperation suffused with grief. "Have I done nothing this past year to convince you of the importance of crime scene behavior?"

He was right: it had been nearly a year since the Fromley case, when he first waltzed into my office and announced that he could use his knowledge of the criminal mind to help me solve a brutal murder. He had not been entirely correct, of course. But as he himself would say, knowing the criminal mind is as much an art as it is a science—and I never doubted that he understood more about criminal behavior than I ever expected to.

He shook his head. "There's more: a single, white rose was placed next to his hand."

"A *white* rose? Like a bride's?"

He nodded sagely. "I know. Hard to come by this time of year."

"The color of purity, innocence," I added, thinking of brides I had seen with such roses on their wedding day.

"Sometimes it is." He paused. "Other times, it's the color of death—usually associated with betrayal. During the War of the Roses, a white rose was given to traitors who had betrayed their word. It warned them that death was imminent."

"So you think—"

He cut me off. "I don't know what to think. But I want you involved."

"Where was Judge Jackson killed?" I glanced at him with skepticism.

"Gramercy Park West."

"That's in the Thirteenth Precinct; not my jurisdiction." I

was now working as a detective under my longtime friend Captain Mulvaney of the Nineteenth Precinct.

"I've seen you help out other precincts."

"This new commissioner is a stickler for protocol." Police Commissioner Theodore Bingham didn't want officers straying beyond their jurisdiction, absent specific orders from him.

"I can make the necessary connections," Alistair said, getting up and crossing the room toward my Strowger telephone. "May I call a cab?"

He picked up the receiver and spoke into it. "Operator, yes, telephone twenty-three eighty Columbus, please."

While he waited for the connection to be made, he spoke to me again. "My friend was an eminent man. Your police will be under significant pressure to solve his murder quickly."

I was obviously going to have to accompany him downtown. I got up and started toward my bedroom to get dressed. But his mention of the police brass triggered something in my memory. "What did you say this judge's name was?"

"Jackson. Judge Hugo Jackson."

My brow furrowed as the name he had just mentioned stirred a flicker of recognition. The name registered, and I spun back around toward Alistair. "Not the same judge who is hearing the *Drayson* case?"

"Of course." Alistair held up a finger as he spoke into the telephone once again. "New York Transportation? Yes, I need an electric automobile at Seventy-first and Broadway, please." He then hung up, grim-faced as he turned back toward me. "The jury was to have begun deliberations today. Now? There's a strong chance a mistrial will be declared."

That changed everything. The death—the murder, even—of

the judge presiding over the most controversial trial the city had seen in years would set off the worst unrest imaginable.

Like everyone, I had been following the trial with great interest—more so because I'd known men like Al Drayson. They grew and flourished in my native Lower East Side neighborhood, where new immigrants weary of hardships in their adopted country were sympathetic to those who championed their rights. Most were idealists who wanted only better working and living conditions.

But I'd seen the way some men's eyes fired with passion when they discussed their cause, lit with an enthusiasm I could not comprehend. Not when their talk turned to guns and dynamite. Not when they showed no regard for the human lives they destroyed. It made no sense to fight one injustice by creating another. I understood the devotion and sacrifice men might feel for another human soul.

In my experience, even the loftiest ideals were often twisted for individual profit and ambition.

Real good rarely came of it. The worst sort of evil often did.

CHAPTER 2

2:30 A.M.

I dressed in haste, gathering those supplies I brought to every crime scene—a notepad, pencil, and cotton gloves to protect anything I touched from my own fingerprints. We waited at my second-floor apartment window overlooking West Seventy-first Street until the electric cab pulled up in front of my building. We hustled down the stairs, through my courtyard, and into the cab itself—where we settled onto black leather seats. Alistair was in no condition to drive his own car, but his choice of an electric cab rather than one of the new, faster gasoline cabs seemed an unnecessary extravagance. Alistair swore that they were more reliable, and no doubt they appealed to his luxurious tastes. For my part, I considered them impractical and slow-moving, given their eight-hundred-pound batteries. The subway was my preference—where a five-cent ticket carried me uptown or downtown, faster than any other mode of transportation.

Alistair gave the driver an address in Gramercy Park, and we were whisked south along the Boulevard—which was how most people still referred to the part of Broadway north of Columbus Circle. The streets were deserted, and wrought-iron gaslights cast murky shadows against buildings that still slept. I liked this part of the city—the Upper West Side—where row houses and apartment buildings were springing up as fast as architects could design and build them. While the construction had its drawbacks, on the whole I liked being part of a neighborhood that was constantly changing. My own sublet apartment on West Seventy-first and Broadway was among them, built just two years ago. Normally I'd never be able to afford a one-bedroom in a new luxury building on a detective's salary. But a friend of Alistair's had moved unexpectedly abroad and wanted his apartment cared for in his absence: I'd be doing him a favor, or so he'd said. I wasn't sure about that, but I'd moved in the third week of August and returned to my career as a detective in the Nineteenth Precinct, which my former partner Declan Mulvaney now commanded. And so—after two years in Dobson, a small village just north of the city where I'd enjoyed a respite from the city's corruption and violence—I once again called the island of Manhattan home.

Alistair sat beside me, silent and preoccupied as our cab continued downtown. We passed through the Theater District in the west Forties, where along the Great White Way electric billboards made the streets shine bright as day—even at this wee hour of the morning. It was also the site of Alistair's and my most recent case together, when last spring a deranged killer had targeted beautiful young actresses. I had always enjoyed the theater on the rare occasions I could afford it, but I had not yet returned to a show. The Broadway murders had—at least temporarily—impaired my appreciation of the stage.

Faster than I had expected, the driver turned left onto West Twenty-third Street and we drew closer to Gramercy. The area swarmed with police officers, but the driver pulled as close as he could manage to the western edge of Gramercy Park. Alistair paid the exorbitant six-dollar fare.

The judge's home at 3 Gramercy Park West was typical of all those surrounding the park: a four-story red-brick town house surrounded by a two-and-a-half-foot wrought-iron fence. I immediately recognized men not just from the Seventeenth Precinct but also the Thirteenth and the Eighth.

I also recognized a reed-thin man with graying hair and hunched shoulders who hung back from the crowd. "Harvey," I said, "good to see you again."

He started in surprise but then broke into a smile and reached out to pump my hand. "Ziele. I heard you were back in the city. But you're with the Nineteenth now, right? Have you guys been called in on this one, too? It's chaos. Seems like the mayor's got every detective in the city working this case." He indicated the men in blue spilling out into the street.

I managed to say something noncommittal before I briefly introduced Alistair and asked, "Who's in charge? Not the General himself?"

Harvey shook his head and flashed a grin. "We got lucky: he's out of town, in Boston with the missus. Though I'd say the judge's murder will scuttle his plans and bring him home early." He nodded toward the commotion indoors. "Meanwhile, Saunders is running the scene."

Learning of Saunders's presence I breathed a sigh of relief. "The General" was Police Commissioner Theodore Bingham himself, a former military man who had brought forthrightness to his job—but also a stubborn belief that he alone knew the right answers. He had been commissioner for almost a year and was already deeply unpopular within the ranks. I had not yet crossed paths with the city's top police official, but I could not imagine he would be pleased to discover an ordinary detective attempting to insert himself into an investigation. Grandstanding, he'd call it—and not one of Alistair's connections would be sufficient to salvage my reputation.

Alistair brightened upon hearing the name. "Do you mean Deputy John Saunders?"

After Harvey confirmed it, Alistair explained how he had met Saunders, one of the comissioner's many deputies, earlier this year when he was in meetings at police headquarters. "Like me, he's interested in how new methods can help combat violent crime. I've suggested several ways they might incorporate my own research into their efforts."

I knew that the top brass had so far responded to Alistair's proposals with skepticism at best, and sheer mockery at worst. Most policemen, myself included, were not averse to trying new techniques that had been shown to work reliably in the field. But most of Alistair's ideas were textbook only—untested and untried.

I watched Alistair hesitate for just a moment at the door's threshold. Then he set his shoulders and walked squarely into the home of his old friend. I followed him through the foyer toward the library at the rear of the first floor where a cluster of men, Deputy Saunders among them, waited somberly just outside the door. The reason why was immediately apparent: two junior officers emerged from the room bearing a wooden gurney on which, covered by a thick white sheet, was a large form we knew to be the judge. We watched in silence as he was carried from his home for the last time.

"Wh—?" Saunders swallowed his words the moment he recognized Alistair. He held out his hand. "Professor. This is unexpected. I'm afraid you can't be here tonight. While I'm aware of your interest in such matters, this is a sensitive crime investigation, you understand—restricted to official personnel only." He gave me a hard look. "And restricted *only* to those precincts from which we've requested assistance."

Alistair fixed Saunders with a cold icy stare. "You'd better check with Mrs. Jackson. When she specifically requested my help, of course I came—and I insisted upon Detective Ziele's joining me."

Saunders stopped and looked uncomfortable. "I understand Mrs. Jackson is upset and thinks her friend—one who just happens to be a criminal scientist—will help matters," he said. "However, those of us investigating this case must be able to do our job without unnecessary interference."

When we did not move, he added, "That means I need you to leave."

"But *I* need him to stay."

The words, spoken with authority, came from an imposing woman with gray-silver hair that swirled round the top of her head. A black shawl covered most of her dress, and her face was pinched with grief. Mrs. Jackson, I had no doubt.

Close behind her was a tall, handsome woman with olive skin and black hair pulled into a tight bun. She wore a formal housemaid's garb of starched black and white, and carried a silver tray filled with coffee and small cookies.

"You may take that into the parlor, Marie," Mrs. Jackson directed coolly. "Men, please help yourselves. I know the hour is late."

"Mrs. Jackson," Saunders said, "I apologize, but you need to trust me to handle your husband's death according to protocol."

"My husband's *murder*, you mean," she said tartly, mincing no words. "Professor Sinclair is a family friend and an eminent criminologist. I have requested his help in the investigation"—she paused as her eyes rested upon me—"as well as that of whomever he trusts to help him."

When the deputy commissioner began to protest yet again, she silenced him. "I trust you do *not* wish me to telephone the mayor and inform him of our disagreement."

"Very well, madam," he conceded, and I immediately registered both the importance of the man who had been killed here tonight and the power of his family's connections. I would later learn that Mrs. Jackson herself had been born a Schermerhorn—one of the city's oldest and wealthiest families, whose influence within political and social circles remained strong.

Mrs. Jackson came forward to grasp Alistair's hand, and for the first time her voice trembled just slightly. "It was good of you to come."

"Gertrude," he began, "I'm so very sorry—"

"Of course." She was brisk once again. "The important thing is that justice be done. I need you to promise me you'll make sure of it. Now, come."

As she turned toward her husband's library, Alistair placed his hand on her arm and gave her a look of searching concern. "Are you sure?"

She gave a terse reply. "My avoiding this room will not change the fact he was killed here tonight. Might as well face up to it."

I exchanged another glance with Alistair before we followed her into the small library. I had seen many different types of grief in my years of murder investigations—but admittedly, never a reaction as fiercely stoic as Mrs. Jackson's.

I drew myself up, forcing myself to breathe slowly the moment I detected the sickly-sweet scent of blood. I had an unnatural aversion to it—a distinct liability in my profession that I tried to keep hidden. Most of the time, I succeeded—but only because of sheer willpower. My stomach lurched and a wave of nausea forced me to swallow hard.

Saunders hung behind us, keeping a discreet distance yet watching us closely. The other officers stayed in the hallway as we entered a small room filled with dark walnut bookcases stuffed to capacity with legal tomes. There was a mahogany desk by the window, littered with papers and books—all of which were now drenched from the dark pool that overran the desk and continued to drip slowly onto the floor. The judge had lost a tremendous amount of blood. I noted the black-leather-bound Bible Alistair had mentioned as well as the long-stemmed white rose— now heavily stained—lying at the center of the desk.

Mrs. Jackson circled behind the desk and leaned against her husband's burgundy leather chair, while the rest of us purposefully refrained from staring at the pool of blood on the desk itself.

"He came in here just after dinner," she said. "I had hoped he would retire to bed, but he insisted on reviewing his notes. Stubborn man. He had terrible insomnia. The case, you understand." She shuddered. "He was handling *Drayson* the best he could, but there's no pleasing some people."

She took a deep breath and addressed Alistair. "Hugo couldn't have been alone in here for more than an hour. It was just past nine when I came to insist that he go to bed. Instead, I found him. Dead." She gestured to her husband's blood.

We remained silent, none of us knowing quite how to proceed.

"People said the most vile things," she continued to say. "And they sent horrid threats. He received letters from those who had the audacity to support the child-killer." Her voice was cold with anger as she turned ever so slightly toward the window. "He received equally terrible letters from men who felt he was too soft on Drayson. He was a fair and just man," she said, clutching at her heart, "but emotions are running so high . . ."

I waited ten seconds in deference to Saunders, who stood apart from us at the door. When he did not speak up, I asked her, "You said he came in here at eight o'clock, and you found him shortly after nine. You had no visitors this evening?"

She shook her head. "Not one. I would have heard the bell. As we've told the deputy commissioner and his men already, neither Marie nor I saw or heard anything unusual." She gave Saunders a pointed look.

"Send for the maid, please," Saunders said, instructing one of his deputies who was standing in the hall.

"Who else was home with you tonight?" Alistair asked.

"No one. Charles, our driver, had the evening off. And our cook went home once she cleaned up after dinner—which would have been right around eight o'clock. My husband had checked all the doors before retiring to his office, as was his habit. Each one was locked."

"So how did his murderer get in?" Alistair asked, walking toward the window. It was locked.

"Were your doors unlocked earlier in the day?" I asked.

"Of course, in the afternoon," Mrs. Jackson replied. "We have too much help coming and going, between the deliveries and the shopping."

Alistair and I exchanged a look. It certainly raised the possibility that the judge's killer had entered his home earlier in the day and hidden—lying in wait.

The maid reappeared, closely flanked by one of Saunders's men. "You asked for me, sir?" Her voice was soft, but she remained composed, even when she realized all eyes were centered upon her.

"How long have you worked in the Jackson home, miss?" Saunders asked.

"Going on five years, sir."

"Marie is one of my best helpers, Deputy," Mrs. Jackson answered with a smile meant to reassure her maid. "Reliable and a good worker. I don't know what I'd do without her."

"And did you notice anything amiss earlier tonight?" Saunders gave the woman a hard stare.

"No, sir," she answered with confidence. "The judge and the missus had dinner. Then he went to read in his study and I didn't see him again. The missus and I were going over preparations for a dinner party planned for next week, then I started my evening cleanup."

"And you heard nothing unusual?"

She shook her head.

"And the doors were locked?"

"Yes, sir. I locked them myself."

"Gentlemen," Mrs. Jackson said with renewed determination. "I've already told Deputy Commissioner Saunders and his men all the details of my husband's routine this evening. It will be in his report. I asked you here tonight because of these."

She reached for a pile of letters from the desk—and though they were on the far corner, away from the bloody pool, they were still heavily splattered with the judge's blood.

Saunders gulped. "I'm sorry, Mrs. Jackson, but that's police evidence."

She forced a brittle smile. "Yes, Deputy Commissioner. That is why I am giving this evidence to a policeman. Specifically to . . ." She gestured toward me.

"Detective Simon Ziele," Alistair supplied.

"Yes, exactly. I would like Detective Ziele and my dear friend to have these letters for a brief period of time," she said. "When they have finished, you may take them."

And so when I had hoped only to help out a friend in need, I found myself in exactly the place I had wanted to avoid: the crosshairs of a political disagreement. It did not bode well for my future with the New York City Police Department.

Mrs. Jackson turned to us with instructions. "You'll find privacy in the upstairs parlor. And of course you may look at these other items if you like. I assure you they were not here earlier tonight." She indicated the black-leather-bound Bible as well as the long-stemmed white rose—also bloodstained—lying at the center of the desk.

"We don't need that nonsense," Saunders said with a dismissive glance as he stalked from the room. "Gentlemen, you may have twenty minutes with those letters—under official supervision."

He went into the hallway, and we overheard him instruct one of the officers to keep tabs on us.

"I believe the rose and the Bible are more important than the deputy commissioner thinks," Alistair said in a rush. "May we borrow them for a few days?"

She agreed, and so I wrapped both the Bible and the rose in a clean cloth and laid them gently just inside my satchel, where they were protected yet hidden—lest the deputy commissioner change his mind.

"Those items are indeed bizarre, but your best clues will be in those letters," she said. "Hugo has been receiving death threats ever since the day Al Drayson set foot in his courtroom. He saved them all." She took a deep breath. "Please, Alistair," she said, and for the first time tonight her eyes softened and filled with tears. "I need your help. I'm counting on you to do whatever is necessary to find the monster who has taken Hugo from me."

"Of course," he said. "We'll make sure the police get it right. I promise you."

But such promises, while well-meant, were often hard to keep.

Within moments, we were in the upstairs parlor under the supervision of Harvey, the officer I had recognized upon entering. He seemed as uncomfortable in his role as we were in ours—so he kept a discreet distance near the doorway. The parlor itself, obviously reserved for Gertrude Jackson's use, was a formal ladies' room of rococo rose wallpaper and blue floral furniture. We pulled two chairs near a small table at the window, where the rising dawn cast a faint pink light through the window. There, we read the letters and drank the hot tea that Marie had brought up.

Mrs. Jackson was right: many of the letters contained vile threats that must have shaken the judge throughout all the weeks of this trial. Each one was markedly different in grammar and style, handwriting, and even paper choice. The authors themselves were split among Drayson's enemies and his fellow anarchists: the former believed the judge was being too lenient with Drayson; the latter just the opposite.

"We don't want no judge who lets child-killers go free," read one letter.

But another countered: *"If you send Drayson to the chair at Sing Sing, he'll become a martyr to our cause. More of us will rise up, throwing bombs and raining hellfire on this modern-day Sodom. We'll kill all capitalist scum like you. Your death will be just the beginning."*

"The judge couldn't win," I said, shaking my head. "He was damned if he did—and damned if he didn't."

Alistair's reply was thoughtful. "Hugo tried his best to be a fair judge. He always sympathized with the prosecution, for he believed that every victim's story should be heard. Yet last week he also allowed the defense team to present mitigating evidence about Drayson's childhood during the pogroms of Russia—before his family escaped and came here."

I remembered the news reports summarizing that day's testimony: Drayson had witnessed unspeakable horrors as a child. But the press had not been kind; rather, their coverage had emphasized that, despite his Americanized name, he was not a true American. They painted him as the epitome of a Russian Jewish immigrant anarchist.

We continued reading. One writer used pencil and cheap notebook paper to threaten: *"Why don't we stick dynamite into your mouth and send you into eternity with Louis Lingg? You're no better than these damn anarchists."*

Alistair's brow furrowed. "Lingg was one of the Haymarket anarchists who killed all those policemen and was sentenced to hang, I believe. Specifically the one who committed suicide by dynamite the day before he was to die. So the letter-writer remembers; he got that part correct. Though it was in Chicago twenty years ago."

Of course I knew Haymarket; it had been our country's most violent anarchist attack to date.

There were plenty more letters, but the threats ran together. One that contained no verbal threat was perhaps the most disturbing: inside an envelope, we found the single picture of a child, an adorable little girl of about six with ringlet curls and a gap-toothed smile. Underneath the picture was an address on East Sixty-sixth Street. It was attached by paper clip to the popular newspaper clipping that depicted only the child victim's shoe.

Alistair grew positively white when he saw it.

"But Drayson's child victim was a boy . . ." I said aloud.

Alistair swallowed hard. "I believe this is a photograph of the judge's own granddaughter, together with her address. The implied threat must have wounded him deeply."

"Surely he went to the police with these letters," I said, spreading my hands wide over the table. "Why didn't he receive protection? He should have been given an escort to and from judge's chambers, as well as a police guard here at his home."

Alistair's face filled with regret. "He likely reported all threats. But Hugo Jackson was an independent man, loath to accept help from others. And that was how he would have seen police protection."

I passed him the final letter, marked by finer quality paper than the rest.

Alistair turned it over twice, noted its lack of a postmark, and then frowned.

A look of amazement spread over his face.

"What is it?"

Stunned, he seemed not to have heard me. I moved my chair closer, peered over his shoulder, and saw—music.

He handed the sheet to me, still lost in thought.

It was a musical score of four bars, written on thick cream paper. The bars of the grand staff as well as the individual notes were handwritten with precision.

"The judge was a musician?" I asked.

"He played the piano. This was likely mixed with the others by mistake."

Alistair stood. "We'd better return these letters to the deputy commissioner, and we'll request copies. I'd like to keep this one, though." He motioned to the musical score, adding with a sideways wink, "I daresay he'll never miss it."

I groaned inwardly, for Alistair's willingness to bend the rules of procedure always sat uneasily on my conscience.

I grabbed the letter, saying only, "For this one, it's easy enough to get permission."

I approached Harvey, assuming my most confident manner. "Say, would it be all right if we kept just this?" I flashed the letter in front of him. "We're returning all the others, but as you can see, this one is unrelated."

He eyed me warily weighing his decision. "Are you officially part of the case now?"

"As soon as the paperwork is signed in the morning," I said to reassure him, adding, "If you prefer, I can ask Mrs. Jackson or the deputy commissioner for permission."

His eyes flickered with doubt. He had witnessed the deputy commissioner's disagreement with Mrs. Jackson earlier, and fortunately for me, he decided it was not something he wished to risk repeating. If he incurred the deputy commissioner's censure, it could derail his career entirely.

"If it's just music, then I guess it won't make a difference," he said finally.

I smiled broadly. "We'll return it to Mrs. Jackson when we finish with it."

I watched him breathe a sigh of relief, since the final disposition wouldn't involve him. I stuffed the letter into my pocket and motioned to Alistair, and we left in haste before Harvey could change his mind—or Deputy Commissioner Saunders could intercept us.

As the pink glow in the eastern sky announced the dawn of a new day, we found a public hack to carry us uptown to a change of clothing and breakfast before our investigative efforts truly began.

It was only once I was home, unpacking the items Mrs. Jackson had given us, that I noticed something unusual about the music.

I frowned. It was odd that Alistair had missed observing it himself—or had he? Of course, Alistair had not been himself last night.

At the bottom of the score on the last bar, where the bass clef normally appeared, was, instead, a different image: a solitary white rose.

CHAPTER 3

The Nineteenth Precinct, West Thirtieth Street. 8:30 A.M.

"If it isn't himself, sure as the devil. Not like you to sleep half the morning, Ziele." A man with a smile as broad as his six-foot frame and a thick brogue turned in surprise as I walked into the over-crowded and dilapidated precinct station house on West Thirtieth Street.

Declan Mulvaney, the burly Irishman who had been my part-ner when I was a patrolman on the Lower East Side, was now my captain here at the Nineteenth Precinct. And while official department hours started at nine, he knew that I usually arrived at my desk well before seven each morning.

"If you consider half past eight to be late, you can take it out of the overtime I never put in for," I returned good-naturedly.

As was typical, Mulvaney was not shuffling paperwork in his cramped office just off the entrance; instead, he circulated

throughout the main room, arranging patrol duties and check-
ing with each of his officers on the status of open cases. By now,
Mulvaney had no doubt finished a meeting or two, completed
a half-dozen telephone calls, and downed at least three cups of
coffee.

And coffee was what I required, after a late night with little
sleep. I must have looked as exhausted as I felt, for Mulvaney
flashed me a wicked grin.

"I suppose there's no chance you were out 'til wee hours
with that lass you fancy, is there?"

I followed him into his makeshift office, ignoring his obvious reference to Isabella Sinclair—Alistair's widowed daughter-
in-law, with whom I had settled into an easy friendship that
defied all norms of social convention. Like me, she was rebuild-
ing her life following a devastating loss: in her case, her husband, Teddy; in my own, my fiancée, Hannah, who was among
the thousand victims killed in the *General Slocum* steamship disaster of 1904. Now Isabella assisted Alistair with his crimino-
logical research.

And if I enjoyed her company more than I should, I remained
mindful of the vast difference in wealth and class between us.
The Sinclair family, with its impeccable social pedigree, counted
themselves among the Astor Four Hundred. I, on the other hand,
had grown up in a derelict tenement in the German immigrant
section of the Lower East Side. The Sinclairs had a passionate
interest in the criminal mind that drew us together when there
was a case to investigate. But I was not one to forget the pro-
nounced differences between us when there was no investigation
at hand.

"Have you seen the latest drawings?" Mulvaney momentarily

switched topics, handing me a large blueprint plan. "Our pro-
posed new building. They say we're going to be the first precinct
to have an all-automobile patrol. See"—he pointed to a large
archway near the main entrance—"the vehicles will come and go
through here." He chortled. "'Course, I'll believe it when I see it."

The plans Mulvaney had just shown me—for a new, modern
station house to be built across the street from our current one—
had been subject to one delay after another for so many years
that most of us no longer truly believed new quarters would ever
be built. No precinct needed space more than we did: Mulvaney's
station had jurisdiction over an area running from Fourteenth
Street all the way to Forty-second, stretching from Park Avenue
to Seventh Avenue. We were responsible for the Tenderloin as
well as a tough area of Sixth Avenue dubbed Satan's Circus—
and our jurisdiction competed with the Lower East Side for the
dubious honor of being the city's most crime-ridden neighborhood. But crime here took a form I understood. The robberies,
killings, kidnappings, and rapes might be brutal and ugly—but
the criminal motives behind them were simple to understand.
Greed and anger didn't require much analysis.

Unlike the murder scene last night.

"I was out late on a case," I said, taking the wooden chair opposite the massive oak desk covered with papers. "Unofficially, of
course."

Mulvaney raised his eyebrows.

"It will be all over today's papers. A judge was killed. And
not just any judge: the presiding judge of the Al Drayson case."

Mulvaney whistled under his breath. "You don't say. And
why did they call you?" He put out a hand. "No—let me guess. It
had to be Alistair."

"It was," I admitted. Alistair had a talent for involving himself in the more controversial and baffling cases of the day. Though, to be fair, during our most recent case investigating a series of theater murders, I'd been the one to involve him. His understanding of the criminal mind was unparalleled—a resource I had learned to take advantage of when more traditional methods of investigation failed.

"Alistair always ends up stuck in the middle of some controversy. So do you, apparently." Mulvaney didn't miss a beat. "I got two calls already this morning: one from Deputy Commissioner Saunders, then another from Commissioner Bingham himself."

I shot him a look of annoyance. "So you already knew about the judge's death last night. When, exactly, were you planning on telling me?"

"Sorry," he said with a rueful smile. "I wanted your version of it, not what the big brass have to say. Their primary concern is the threat of a larger anarchist plot. You're going to be working under the man himself."

"You mean Bingham?" I was incredulous. It was a dubious honor, for Bingham was notoriously difficult to work with. But I wasn't blind to the fact that this presented a rare opportunity to work with the city's chief officer.

Mulvaney put it more bluntly. "This opportunity with Bingham will either make or break your career—and you've got no choice in the matter. In fact, you've got a meeting with him this afternoon at one o'clock."

I stared at him blankly for some moments before recovering myself.

"I knew Alistair planned to make my involvement official," I said in a low voice, "but not at this level."

Mulvaney chuckled. "Your professor has his share of influence, I'm sure. But he isn't responsible for your current predicament. You've the judge's widow herself to thank for this."

"But I barely exchanged a word with her last night," I said with a frown.

"Then you otherwise made an impression—or Alistair secured her request. I take it they're acquainted."

"Alistair went to law school with Judge Jackson. I understand they grew apart over the years, but their wives remained friends."

"Alistair's wife?" Mulvaney's eyes widened. "I thought they were divorced."

"I don't think so," I hastened to say. I knew little of Alistair's estranged wife, except that she now resided permanently abroad—and had, ever since their son Teddy was killed while on an archeological expedition in Greece three years earlier. Though I wasn't privy to the details, I knew it wasn't uncommon for the loss of a child to cause an irreparable rift between the parents. I also suspected that Alistair's womanizing had something to do with it.

"Is the Nineteenth going to be involved in some capacity?" I asked.

"Not yet. The commissioner hopes it will be a simple case, since the judge had more than his share of death threats on record—many of them from known anarchists. He believes that with enough men making the necessary inquiries, the judge's murderer—and any anarchist conspiracy—will readily come to light."

"Maybe."

"You're off to a good start on this case, if you already disagree with the commissioner." A look of exasperation crossed

Mulvaney's face. "Out with it, Ziele. Either something you learned last night troubles you—or else you're being hoodwinked by your professor's malarkey."

I smiled, knowing that Mulvaney never had much tolerance for Alistair's criminal theories. Alistair believed we needed to understand why particular criminals behaved as they did if we were to apprehend them more efficiently—and ultimately rehabilitate them. Once we understood more about the criminal mind, Alistair argued, then we would solve crimes faster—and one day stop them altogether.

But for the more pragmatic Mulvaney, the *why* was unimportant; what mattered was ensuring that the criminal couldn't strike again. And he believed that was best accomplished by jail cell bars—not education and understanding.

Once, I had been of the same mind as Mulvaney. But time— not to mention a handful of tough cases—had taught me to recognize there was value in understanding the enemy we faced. I'd learned that the behavior criminals exhibited at their crime scenes revealed important information—sometimes with more clarity than traditional clues. In two very different cases, I had made use of Alistair's teachings to solve a brutal crime—and if I wasn't a true believer in criminal theory, I at least considered it one of many valuable tools at my disposal. What I'd learned was that few people—however well educated—had all the right answers. Success hinged on formulating the right questions.

And I had many questions about Judge Jackson's case.

I briefly filled Mulvaney in on the crime scene at the judge's home, sharing all the relevant details about the Bible and the white rose found by the judge's body. "Plus, there was a rose drawn on a sheet of music found among his death-threat letters.

I think Alistair saw the rose, too," I said, "and is holding back what he knows." I had an uncomfortable sensation in the pit of my stomach as I said it.

Mulvaney chortled. "That's nothing new." He leaned back in his chair, flexing his fingers. "Why don't you just ask Alistair about the symbol drawn on the music? I've no doubt he'll have some fancy explanation for it. Do *you* really think the rose is important?"

"Maybe. I'm not sure."

He ran his fingers over the stubble covering his bald head. "Look, this case is going to be politically complicated—no argument there. But as a murder inquiry, it should be cut-and-dried. This judge presided over the most controversial anarchist trial New York has seen since President McKinley was assassinated. So you've no need to look beyond the anarchists." He made a noise of disgust. "They come to this country with their talk of violence and bloodshed. I say, if they don't like it here, why don't they go back where they came from?"

He paused a moment, struggling with his emotions. Mulvaney had made something of himself from the worst of beginnings—eleven siblings and only their widowed mother to support them—and he had little sympathy for those with a lesser work ethic.

"My point is," he said, leaning in, "don't get distracted by some fancy symbol or strange Bible you think you've noticed. These items were planted there by a man . . . by an anarchist. You've just got to find him."

"I know it was a human hand that killed the judge; I don't forget that for an instant. Yet we both know that often the simple solution is also the wrong one."

There was an uncomfortable moment between us. Just this past spring, Mulvaney had made such a mistake—and it had caused the only rift between us in our ten-year history.

"Look, Ziele," he finally said, his eyes meeting my own, "I brought you back to the city to work with me because you've got better skills and instincts than any detective I know. Focus on the real threats that surrounded the judge—and that continue to surround all of us in this city." He spread his hands wide. "They call themselves anarchists. What kind of people are they, that they value their ideas more than human life? That they'd plant a bomb to take the life of an innocent child?"

"I don't understand men like Drayson," I said. "But you also know they're not all like that. Remember Samuel Lyzke from the old neighborhood? He joined the anarchist circles to fight corrupt government. He was just an ordinary man who wanted better conditions for working people."

Mulvaney's expression softened. "Sam is one of the good ones."

I remembered Sam as a peace-loving idealist. And I knew his weapon of choice would be words, not dynamite—for he was a dreamer, not an actor.

"It's not their *ideas* I have a problem with; it's their violence and killing. When they take a human life," Mulvaney was saying, "damn their ideas. They become no different from an ordinary killer. They deserve what's coming."

The official response would be to hunt down every anarchist in the city—of that I was well aware. Yet this killer had eschewed the anarchist weapon of choice—dynamite—in favor of the knife. He had quite possibly sent personal threats to the judge, and then left the ambiguous symbols of a Bible and a white rose by his handiwork. Perhaps these acts had some meaning within the anarchist community. Mulvaney was right. The threat of further violence was real.

I looked up and saw Mulvaney was regarding me with sympathy in his deep blue eyes. "You're in the thick of it now. Let me know how I can help you."

I gave him a smile of reassurance. "It's an opportunity like no other, right?" Then I checked my watch. "Can you arrange for me to get into the Tombs to see Drayson before I meet with the commissioner?"

Mulvaney's eyes widened. "You want to talk with that bastard now?"

I nodded. People already suspected him of orchestrating the murder from his jail cell—and before I could begin to come to grips with this case, I needed to see him for myself. And I wanted Alistair to come with me.

In a matter of minutes, all the arrangements were made. I left Mulvaney and headed downtown to the Tombs—into the bowels of hell itself.

CHAPTER 4

The Tombs, Centre Street. 10:30 A.M.

There was no place in New York more repulsive than the Tombs, the city prison where Al Drayson was being held in a solitary basement cell. It was a new building, constructed just four years ago on the same site as the original Tombs prison. In fact, from the street, it was almost a thing of beauty—a majestic French chateau dominated by a handsome stone turret. But for those of us who had seen firsthand what lived within, even the fanciest exterior made no difference. The misery of those incarcerated within seemed to permeate its very walls and become palpable— even before a visitor like myself entered from Centre Street through the eight-inch-thick iron-and-wood door. In reality, it wasn't misery I sensed—it was the smell of unwashed bodies as well as vomit, feces, and urine. The putrid odor was unmistakable, even at the entrance door.

I presented my credentials to a dour-faced guard dressed entirely in black. He admitted me with a terse nod, saying only, "Jenkins will take you down."

Upon hearing his words, a hunched older man rose up from a wooden stool, jangling his large ring of keys. His voice was a hoarse rasp when he said, "Come."

I followed him first through the main hall, where prisoners convicted of relatively minor crimes were housed. The Tombs was divided by level, with criminals placed according to the severity of their crimes. Those here on the first floor enjoyed the relative comfort of the single wood-burning stove in the center of the room. Most of them regarded me silently as I passed by— though no end of catcalls came from the levels overhead. Buggerer. Twat. Nancy-boy. I'd learned to ignore the curses and name-calling during my visits here, so the words that followed me down the hall were nothing to me. What I had to steel myself for was the basement—an area marked by the most miserable of conditions and reserved for the most depraved of criminals.

The moment I descended the stairs, I was overwhelmed by the rancid smell of rot. The Tombs had been built on swampland, a legacy that gave its porous stone foundation a perpetual wetness. And so the stench of feces and urine mingled with that of the damp, which created a vile stink that threatened to overpower me with each succeeding step. The bowels of the Tombs were fit only for the rats . . . one of which scampered in front of us, so close that Jenkins nearly kicked it. Jenkins cackled—a hoarse noise that sent more of a chill down my spine than either the fetid smell or the vermin had already done.

By the time we were halfway down, I heard voices from the cells below. Alistair was here. I had asked him to give me fifteen minutes alone with Drayson before he joined me; I should have known he would be too impatient to honor that request. But when Jenkins and I reached the bottom floor, it was not Drayson with whom Alistair was engaged in animated conversation.

Alistair stood before the cell of a gaunt man with deepsunken eyes. The man was mesmerized by Alistair's words—or perhaps, instead, by Alistair himself. A bath and a few hours' sleep had restored Alistair's composure entirely; he was now dressed in his usual impeccable fashion: a fine gray wool suit complemented his black cashmere-blend coat and paisley scarf, and he carried a satchel made of the finest leather and brass. He took notes in a matching leather-bound notebook using his new Waterman fountain pen—the kind that contained its own ink.

The imprisoned man gawked openly at Alistair. "So all I gotta do is answer some questions and you'll help me get a new trial?" He was hopeful and incredulous at the same time.

"I'll do what I can," Alistair answered in his calmest voice. "It will be up to the judge, of course, but I can make sure your argument is at least heard."

The prisoner made a hoarse guffaw. "That's just a fancy way of sayin' you'll try. Guess it's better than my good-for-nothing lawyer did first time round, though."

Alistair smiled and jotted something down in his notebook. "I just need to double-check your story, Mr.—?"

"Hayes. Rawlin' Hayes." The man clenched a fist with grimy fingers around the bars that separated him from Alistair and leaned his face in. "Just ask around in Five Points and anybody'll tell you: I didn't commit no attempted murder. 'Cause I never attempt to kill nobody." His lips spread into a wide grin that revealed a mouth almost wholly devoid of teeth. "If I want somebody dead, there's no attempting about it."

No wonder he appeared not to have eaten in months: if prison fare wasn't bad enough, he had no teeth with which to eat it. In fact, I wouldn't be surprised if poor health ended up cheating Alistair from whatever he wished to learn from this particular prisoner. The foul air and bone-chilling damp made for deplorable living conditions—ones that even healthy men would find a challenge to survive. And I suspected that Rawlin' Hayes had not been a picture of health to begin with.

Alistair, now aware of my presence, glanced toward me and nodded slightly before returning his attention to the prisoner.

"Thank you, Mr. Hayes; I promise you I'll take a look at your case."

Alistair turned toward me, and even in the dim light, I noted that his cheeks were flushed despite the cold. He was in his element, almost entirely unaware of our grim surroundings—including Jenkins, the guard who hovered over us, anxious to move us along.

"You boys ready?" Jenkins asked. "No need to stick around in a place like this."

At my sign, he led us down a hallway that grew even darker as we approached the end. This is where prisoners sentenced to solitary confinement were held; with windowless cells and thick wood-and-iron doors, there was no light whatsoever but for the feeble glow of Jenkins's lantern.

When we came to the last door, Jenkins took out his large key ring and—with his bully stick in his left hand, poised to strike—undid the double padlocks on the door with his right hand. It swung open to reveal a frail, thin man with a dark beard and wire-rimmed spectacles, wearing a standard prison-issue gray uniform. He sat in a chair that more closely resembled a medieval torture device—for his hands and feet were shackled, and there was a leather strap across his chest. I'd not seen one in years, but I knew what it was: a "restraint chair," usually reserved as severe punishment for the worst offenses. It was so uncomfortable that previously sane men could be driven crazy after too much time in it.

Al Drayson showed signs of repeated physical beatings. The entire left side of his face and nose was crusted with dried blood, the eye swollen shut. And even in the low light, a variety of bruises—colored blue, purple, and yellow—were visible on the lower portion of his arms.

Drayson didn't react to our entry. His head lolled to the right and his good eye remained closed.

"This is unacceptable." Alistair's voice was sharp as he turned to Jenkins. Alistair deplored the use of such devices in any prison, for any criminal—even for a child-killer like Drayson. "We don't better ourselves by mistreating the most depraved among us," he said.

Looking at Drayson, I had to admit I agreed. I'd never been of an "eye for an eye" mentality. Drayson was already locked up in this fetid place and certainly on his way to the electric chair. It seemed a severe enough punishment.

Jenkins only grinned. "Don't blame us; we're not the ones who beat him up every day. That's the work of the crowds. They assemble outside, just lyin' in wait for him, soon as he's brought back here from the courtroom."

"And your men can't manage to keep them at a safe distance?" Alistair asked.

"There's too many of 'em. And they hate him."

"What about the restraint chair?" I asked.

Jenkins shrugged. "Complained about his cell last night, 'e did. Said he was tired of living in his own excrement and threatened to throw shit at us jailers."

Alistair drew himself up, giving Jenkins a severe look. "Well, we cannot talk with him like this. You'll have to unbind him."

Jenkins looked to me.

"This man may have important information," I said. "We would like to speak with him freely—without his fetters." And I bit my lip, hoping I'd made the right judgment.

Jenkins frowned, then reached to the wall for a key—which he handed to me. "You gotta do it yourself, then. I don't touch scum like him."

With keys in hand, I took a step closer to Drayson. I breathed through my mouth, trying to avoid the worst foul odor of his body. They had not moved him in hours, and he had urinated on himself—probably more than once. He did not attempt to open his eyes.

Before I touched him, I spoke as though he would understand me. "My name is Detective Ziele and I'm here to ask you some questions today. But first I'm going to undo these restraints, starting with the one across your chest."

I unbuckled the leather belt that cut too tightly across his upper torso. He wheezed the moment its pressure was released— then drew the first of a series of jagged breaths, trying to make up for the amount of air he'd not been able to breathe before.

"Now your feet," I said, and leaned down to undo the iron chains at the base of the chair.

For a split second, I was afraid he would kick me—but he merely stretched his legs to their fullest extension.

"And hands." I circled behind his chair, leaned down, and undid the chain and lock binding his arms.

Just as I was about to stand up and circle round him again, I felt his wiry hand clench my right arm—gripping so hard that I winced in pain. I was surprised he had such power in him after having been chained for so long—but then again, my right arm was an easy target. It hung limp, almost useless, and in chronic pain—especially in the damp or the cold. That had been the case ever since the day of the *General Slocum* steamship disaster when I had worked to rescue as many victims as possible and been rewarded with an injury that was a permanent reminder of the day. As if I needed any reminder at all.

I wrenched my head toward the door. Jenkins appeared to have deserted us entirely, leaving us to the results of our folly.

"Let go of me." My voice boomed loud and menacing as I delivered a sharp punch with my left fist to his head.

Drayson winced in pain, but his grip on my right arm grew even tighter. I jabbed him again, this time with my left elbow.

"Who're you to tell me what to do?" Drayson hissed.

"I'm someone who has the authority to release you from this awful contraption. But you'll find yourself right back in it if you don't let go of my arm now."

At that, the viselike grip relaxed . . . and I freed my now-aching arm, rubbing it as I walked over to Alistair.

Drayson's eyes followed me with a gaze in which I saw both steely resolve and pure calculation at play. "You said you were a detective. Why are you here?"

"I have some questions for you about Judge Jackson's murder."

He raised an eyebrow. "Is he a detective, too?" His eyes flicked toward Alistair.

"He is a professor of criminal science who is assisting me," I replied.

Drayson's mouth formed an odd smile as he mocked us. "Well, this is a first. I've never been interviewed by a professor before." He drummed his fingers against his knee. "And is criminal science interested in me—or in my cause?" he asked Alistair.

"I'm interested in what draws you to your cause," Alistair said, determined to take no offense. He obviously wanted to win Drayson's cooperation—for our purposes today as well as in the future. I knew that the question "why?" was ingrained in Alistair—and it became a virtual obsession when the answer eluded him.

"If you'll use your influence to educate the masses," Drayson said with an oily smile, "I'll answer any question you want."

"Ah," Alistair said, beaming, "education is truly the answer to almost everything, isn't it? I have always—"

I cut him off. The foul air was making me light-headed, and I had no patience for Alistair's theoretical discussions right now. "First," I said to Drayson, "we understand you're Russian."

"Yes," he said, "I come from Gdansk. My family came here to escape the pogroms—and we found a hell in America to rival the one we thought we had left behind."

I swallowed hard and held my tongue. I'd read about the horrors of the pogroms, and whatever injustice Drayson had encountered here, it was nothing compared to the violence wrought by the Cossacks. Of that I was certain.

"When you came of age, you joined the anarchist movement. I believe that now—together with Miss Goldman—you're the leader of the New York organization."

He spat on the ground. "Not together with Emma Goldman. I am the leader—and have been, ever since her pansy Berkman landed himself in jail. No one's authority supersedes mine. Not Baginski, not Abbott, and not Goldman herself."

"As their leader, what is your goal?" Alistair asked.

I knew what Alistair was doing: before we asked Drayson about the judge specifically, he was building a rapport and encouraging the man to be comfortable talking with us.

Drayson looked at us as though we were daft. "Justice, of course. We work to protect the working people from exploitation by the capitalist government. You see," he said, leaning in close enough that I recoiled from his foul scent, "we all came here for opportunity. America is the land of opportunity, we heard. But we got here and found no work. Nothing to pay us a living wage and allow us to support our families. So our every act is intended to focus the public's attention on the plight of working people."

He slammed his fist against the restraint chair, looking up at us with fury. "That is all I want: to teach the public to see the injustices they are blind to. So we tell them about the crowded tenements where we live in despicable conditions. We open our doors and permit Jacob Riis to take our photographs. We show other muckraking journalists the factories where we toil long hours for not enough pay—while the capitalist scum make a fortune off the sweat of our brows. But none of this has any effect.

The government and the banks and the factories continue to exploit us all. We pretend we have a democracy in these United States, but only the rich have a voice."

"But you planted a bomb," Alistair said. "You took innocent lives. That's a far different matter from asking the world to notice the injustices you suffer."

Drayson shrugged. "Not really. No one was listening, so we were forced to move to the next stage: limited attacks on the worst capitalist offenders. Men like Carnegie and Vanderbilt. Even that did little good, so now we must embrace approaches that are even more ruthless—actions that will make the world sit up and take notice."

"What do you mean by that?" I asked, my voice guarded.

"We've sent numerous warnings to the government and industries that have been ignored. We've tried to be careful to avoid injuring ordinary citizens. But these soft methods are not working." He leaned close and grinned, and it was all I could do not to flinch. "Our country is filled with stupid people, Detective. They do not learn. If the world doesn't act now, we will be forced down this path of no return."

"Meaning you will kill more innocent people," I said bitterly. "First, the child. And now, Judge Jackson."

He pressed his hands together. "The child was a martyr to our cause, if you will. But I had nothing to do with killing this judge, however much he may have deserved it for supporting the capitalist policies that hurt us."

"*This* judge?" I asked, and my voice rose in anger. "Judge Jackson was *your* judge. You've stared at him every day for the past two months. He was the judge who would have sentenced you to die. As you yourself said, your power over the anarchist movement here is absolute. Any one of your followers would have obeyed your command."

"He did not die by my hand." He smiled. "Do you really think this is about any one man alone?"

In that moment, I realized that he had every intention of talking circles around us for however long we would let him. He enjoyed spouting his propaganda, and he took a perverse pleasure in denying us real information.

"Tell us the truth about Judge Jackson," I said heatedly. "We just need a name. The name of whatever follower you tapped to kill him last night—in the nick of time before your case went to the jury."

Drayson closed his eyes and did not answer. We remained silent for several moments—not yet ready to give up and leave empty-handed.

"Do you not care how the world sees you, Mr. Drayson?" Alistair finally asked. "You are going to be put to death, branded a child-killer. If you were to talk with us . . . tell us the truth . . . we could help you achieve something better than that."

"Mr. Sinclair," Drayson said, opening his eyes and folding his arms together. "You must remember: beauty is in the eye of the beholder. To the oppressed working people, I am a savior, a David fighting the capitalist Goliath for the people's rights. If I am to be martyred by my oppressors, then what can I do?"

"Nothing," I said bitterly. "There's clearly nothing we can do here." I turned to Alistair and jingled the keys to Drayson's cell. "Come. We've spent enough time in this godforsaken place."

And so, despite Alistair's petulant stare—and his obvious

willingness to continue to talk with Al Drayson—I got up and walked out of the room.

I waited until we were far away—not just from the Tombs building but even its shadow—before I asked Alistair, "What did you think?"

"He's not our killer." His voice reflected no indecision whatsoever.

"But he is a killer. And he certainly will benefit from the mistrial that's likely to be declared now—when a guilty verdict was all but assured."

"A jury is a wild card you'll never want to bet on. And that's not the reason why I'm convinced Drayson played no role in the judge's killing. Here," he said, gesturing to a bench near a small green space across from City Hall, "let's sit a moment."

He pulled a cigar from his satchel, offering me one. I declined, and we sat in silence, with Alistair puffing perfect O-rings for some moments before he continued talking.

"Drayson is the leader of a group of intellectual, rational people who kill in the name of a cause. To put it another way, Al Drayson's anger is fierce—but it's a controlled anger directed toward capitalist targets. Not a judge like Hugo Jackson."

"But half the letters Judge Jackson received described him as 'capitalist scum.' That sounds a lot like Drayson to me."

A thoughtful expression crossed Alistair's face. "True—and I don't think Drayson would have had any issue killing Hugo if it fit his larger goals. He would do anything to further his cause. But, you see, his cause is what motivates him; he doesn't care about the outcome of his trial or even whether he lives or dies. He wants to strike targets where major casualties will result—

and where the newspapers will cover the damage, creating a news frenzy." Alistair shrugged. "Killing one lone judge with a knife? It's just not something Drayson would do."

"He tried to take out Andrew Carnegie," I reminded him.

"Carnegie together with an entire wedding party," Alistair said. "And he would have succeeded, if the driver's bomb hadn't exploded prematurely."

My gaze wandered to the street across from us, filled with myriads of people rushing about. The sky above us had grown dark with threatening clouds, and everyone was in a hurry to reach their destination before the sky opened.

"If Drayson didn't kill Judge Jackson, then who do you think did?" I finally said.

"We must return to the crime scene," Alistair said, not unkindly. "Remember, criminals reveal themselves through their crimes. So I ask myself: What kind of killer has chosen not just to kill but to kill in this particular way? Why use a knife? Why leave the judge with his hand on the Bible and a white rose nearby? These choices signify something important. Something personal."

"You haven't mentioned the music," I said.

A perplexed look crossed his brow. "The musical score among the judge's papers?"

I nodded, watching his reaction.

He laughed, then slapped me on the back, beaming. "By golly, you noticed it. You've got quite an eye for evidence, ol' boy. I figured I was going to have to explain it to you and convince you of its significance."

"If it's important evidence," I said, "we might have discussed it last night."

"Yes, but what's to discuss? It's part of the puzzle, to be sure. But I can't make sense of it at the moment."

I stood, straightening my coat and hat. "I've got to get to the commissioner. We'll talk later."

"Let me know what the commissioner thinks. I don't envy you: having to describe this complicated body of evidence and explain why Drayson is not the killer we seek."

I gave him an incredulous look. "You expect me to tell Commissioner Bingham all this today? I'll be kicked off the case, no sooner than I'm on it."

But Alistair merely smiled, saying dryly, "If anyone can handle the commissioner, Ziele, it will be you. I've always admired your remarkable ability to sidestep the pitfalls of police politics."

"Much the same way I marvel at how you've inserted yourself into the heart of the city's most controversial criminal investigation in years."

"True," he said, adding, "though in this case I was brought in by the judge's widow." He caught his breath. "Good luck with the commissioner."

Good luck, indeed. I'd need more than luck to keep my job after the grilling I was sure to get from Commissioner Theodore Bingham and the top police brass if I so much as hinted that the man they were certain was our killer—incidentally, the most reviled man in this city—was in fact as innocent of the crime as I was.

CHAPTER 5

Police Headquarters, 300 Mulberry Street. 1 P.M.

The chauffeured black touring car parked in front of 300 Mulberry Street signaled that Commissioner Theodore Bingham was in the building. I raced up the brownstone steps, entered the dilapidated lobby, and made my way to the third floor. The door to the conference room was closed. I pulled out my pocket watch to check the time. Ten till one. In my haste to get here, I had managed to arrive early.

The largest part of the third floor was occupied by the Bertillon Room—luckily empty at this moment, so I entered and looked around while I waited. It was named after the European scientist, Alphonse Bertillon, had insisted that criminals looked different from law-abiding citizens. Though most of us no longer believed that the size of a man's head or the shape of a woman's ear revealed anything about their propensity for criminal

behavior, Bertillon's standards for measuring and photograph-
ing criminals had proven useful as a system for identifying and
cataloguing them. Now, as a result of his legacy, criminals were
routinely photographed upon their arrest, face front as well as in
profile, according to uniform standards.

We called the photographs "mug shots"—and many of them
were displayed on the walls throughout the Bertillon Room.
Dubbed the "Rogues' Gallery," its pictures featured the city's
most notorious criminals, from Scar Face Bill Stinzensky, who
had robbed and tortured his victims with a blade, to Harry
Thaw, who had murdered the architect Stanford White just this
past May. Of course, Al Drayson, the most notorious of them all,
was front and center.

Five minutes later, I returned to the conference room where
this afternoon's meeting would be held. Two other men now
waited outside the door, deferring to a rule that was no less strict
because it was unwritten: meetings with the commissioner began exactly on time—never early, never late. I had always supposed it was because of his lame leg, an injury caused by a falling
derrick when he was a brigadier general in the army. Now, his
arrivals and departures from official meetings were carefully
choreographed, for he was a proud man who didn't care for the
world to observe his weakness.

A man with oil-slicked black hair pulled out his gold pocket
watch. "It's time," he said with a grim nod. I recognized him as
Tom Savino, a serious, hardworking man I'd met when I first
started at the Fifth Precinct.

I took a deep breath and entered with no small amount of
trepidation. The commissioner—or the General, as he preferred

to be called—was, by all reports, not an easy man under the best of circumstances. And I had the distinction of being the one detective in the room not of his own choosing. Mulvaney had said this opportunity would make or break my career. At this moment, the latter seemed a real possibility.

General Bingham sat at the head of the massive oak table that spanned the length of the room. He was a distinguished man with sandy gray fringe on the sides of his bald head, a handlebar mustache, and piercing blue eyes behind wire spectacles. Surrounded by his deputies and favored advisors, he appeared almost regal in the wheelchair that might have been his throne.

"Damn foreigners," one deputy said. "They'll destroy this city if we let them."

"Which is exactly why we've gotta stop 'em," boomed a man with a loud bass voice and a large gut. I recognized him as Big Bill Hodges—the officer credited with breaking up several gangs, including the notorious Eastman gang.

"Yeah, but there's too many of them," said another man with a high-pitched twang. "If it's not the filthy Italians throwing dynamite, it's the Russian Jews." He made a noise of disgust.

General Bingham cleared his throat before speaking. "Gentlemen, I tell you: they're responsible for eighty-five percent of the crime in this city."

"We oughta just ship 'em back to where they came from," Hodges groused.

I took a seat at the side of the table next to Howard Green, another officer I recognized from previous cases. He caught my gaze, leaned in close, and muttered, "It's like they don't know they're talking about us."

Tom Savino, overhearing, turned to give him a scathing look. "Don't be ridiculous. We're Americans, now."

Except that we weren't. Men like Savino might choose to deny it, but the reality was that our immigrant past stayed with us—and the General's words only reflected broader department policies. There had yet to be a police commissioner or top deputy who wasn't of English or Irish background—and I doubted there would be in my lifetime. Men like Green, Savino, and me were here only because of President Teddy Roosevelt's efforts when he was New York City's police commissioner ten years ago: he had implemented the entry exam now required of all new patrolmen, replacing the old patronage system that had relied upon bribery, connections, or both.

General Bingham fancied himself a reformer, too—but he was no Teddy Roosevelt. The General's manner was brusque, his speech was blunt, and he lacked the unique blend of enthusiasm and discretion that had enabled then Commissioner Roosevelt to accomplish sweeping changes. The others might be angry that Roosevelt's successors hadn't done more, but I'd decided long ago that resentment accomplished little—and I didn't care to waste my own efforts on what couldn't be changed. Life never would favor all of us equally. And the crime victims I encountered through my job were a frequent reminder that the common goal I shared with my fellow officers—that of solving violent crimes—was far more important than the differences that separated us.

A slight man with hunched shoulders scurried into the room and took the seat beside me, glancing nervously at his pocket watch. The General addressed him loudly. "Couldn't make it on time, Petrovic?" He fixed an icy gaze on the latecomer.

"Sorry, sir," the man mumbled in embarrassment.

"We've got important business this morning." The General's speech was clipped, and he almost swallowed his every word. Pounding his fist on the table with such energy that his wheelchair spun back at least two feet, he said, "Last night, an esteemed judge—an honorable man—was brutally murdered in his own home. We needn't look far to find a compelling motive. Judge Hugo Jackson was presiding over the Drayson trial. In fact, many of you here in this room were involved in the aftermath of the bombing Drayson is accused of orchestrating."

Comments like "damn anarchists" reverberated throughout the room as several heads nodded.

"Judge Jackson was on the verge of sending Drayson to the electric chair—a powerful motive for Drayson to orchestrate the judge's murder from his very jail cell. Of that, I have no doubt." The commissioner paused dramatically. "The challenge for us will be to round up those anarchist scum who are helping him."

"Round up?" Big Bill Hodges arched an eyebrow. "No offense, General, but when these men know we're looking for them, they disappear. Think how long we've been trying to arrest Max Baginski. The worst of 'em all, and we can't catch him."

"That's why we need a different approach," the General responded with a broad grin. "It's why you men are here." He turned his icy blue stare toward the four of us. Was it my imagination, or did it linger just a moment too long on me?

He turned to the deputy on his left. "Bring in the boy."

The deputy disappeared, returning moments later with a young man of about seventeen, his hair a tangled mass of straw curls. He came to stand awkwardly beside the General, hands shoved deep into his trouser pockets.

"This is Oliver," the General announced. "We recruited him

last summer after the bombing—and I'm pleased to say that he has successfully infiltrated a group of anarchists who meet regularly at Philipp Roo's beer hall. He's got names for us." He clapped the boy on the back. "Specific names. And if we can't find the men who are named, then we're going to target their families. We'll make their lives a living misery till the men we seek turn themselves in."

The tall deputy beside him looked troubled. "General, with due respect—I'm not sure I'd put it quite like that."

"Balderdash," the General replied. "You forget that I am the law in this town. I don't mean anything beyond what the law allows. But we can put them under surveillance. They won't make a move without our watching them. We'll be outside the businesses they run, making note of their customers," He grinned. "That'll hit them where it hurts. They'll see how many patrons want to shop when they're watched so closely." His eyes narrowed. "Then if they know where our wanted men are, they'll give them up."

"You mentioned you had names, sir?" Savino asked quietly. "Men you want us to follow?"

"Not follow," the General blustered. "I want you to hunt them down like the animals they are. Boy, write the names on the board and tell us about them."

"I—I can't," Oliver stammered.

"I forgot. You're illiterate. But you're street-smart, not like the fat and stupid boy I hired last time."

Oliver flushed a deep red, as Bill Hodges grabbed the chalk and addressed us. "We called you four detectives here because of your connections to our prime suspects."

The hackles on the back on my neck were immediately raised.

"Connections, sir?" The question burst from me before I was aware of it.

"That's right, Detective . . . Ziele, I believe? Each one of you has some connection to the men we seek today." The General turned toward me with a penetrating stare. "I won't deny that I was annoyed when the widow first insisted you join my case. I don't care who her family is, I don't like people interfering with how I do my job."

"No one does, sir," I replied evenly, still on my guard.

He smiled. "Well, sometimes Providence has a strange way of looking out for us, Detective. I discovered you're actually the perfect man for this case. A necessary Fourth Musketeer, so to speak. Oliver will explain."

I said nothing more but looked warily at Oliver as he began to talk. I noticed the three detectives who had joined me seemed equally ill at ease. Now it was clear to me why the top brass had so readily agreed to Mrs. Jackson's request to involve me in the case: my background—a childhood spent living in the tenements of the Lower East Side, the breeding ground of criminals and anarchists alike—had suited their purposes. Apparently, one of my boyhood associates had grown into a man now suspected of this crime. I realized with a pang of disappointment that it wasn't quite the opportunity that Mulvaney had thought. Still, perhaps that was for the best. Too much personal interaction with the General himself was not necessarily something I desired.

"I've been going to meetin's at Philipp Roo's since August," Oliver said haltingly. "I told everyone there 'bout how my mother died of overwork in a factory, and that I wanted to do my bit to improve working conditions. Now I hear 'bout all the latest news, including when and where meetin's are planned and who's leadin' them."

He fell silent, uncomfortable with being the center of attention.

"Go on," Hodges encouraged him.

"The radicals who meet at Roo's talk a lot about revolution, not to mention women's rights and free love," he continued, flushing with embarrassment. "They all worship Emma Goldman and want to write for her new magazine, *Mother Earth*."

"Magazine?" Hodges scoffed. "You can't be serious. By God, we're talking about murder here—"

"And we all know how Emma Goldman's words have led men to act," the General cut him off. "After all, she inspired her lover to try assassinating one of the world's richest business tycoons."

I knew that he meant Alexander Berkman, who had served fourteen years for attempting to murder Henry Clay Frick. Berkman had been released just this past spring.

Oliver continued to talk. "There's two men who are clear leaders. They've got direct access to Red Emma herself, and the mass of 'em don't lift a finger without gettin' say-so from one or t'other. So there's no way Judge Jackson was murdered by anarchists without these men knowin' 'bout it." He looked to Bill Hodges, who stood ready, chalk in hand.

"Jeremy Wesson is one," Oliver said.

Hodges wrote the name in block capitals on the board. It meant nothing to me, but I saw that Howard Green had begun to sweat profusely.

"I believe this is your cousin, Detective Green," the General said, then shook his head in mock pity. "Someone oughta do a report sometime about how one half of a family can turn out decent and the other half scum. Happens more often than not, from what I can see."

"Jeremy's not—" Howard began to sputter.

The General cut him off. "Don't even try to tell me he's not involved in the anarchist movement. All of us know better. We've got proof. So instead of trying to defend your family's honor, I want you to use your family connection to find out what Jeremy knows."

"I haven't spoken with Jeremy in over seven years," Howard finally said, his voice flat.

"Then I'd say it's the perfect time to renew your acquaintance." The General's voice was not unsympathetic, but he was all business. "You're one of us, now," he reminded Howard, more gently this time—and the turn of phrase made me wonder whether he had overheard our comments earlier. "Your allegiance is to me. Not to whatever black sheep are in your family—and we all have them," he finished, looking roundly at the rest of us in the room.

But he would not find any with mine—at least, not anymore. My father had followed my mother to the grave six months ago—and with him, so too lay buried any claim my family had to unrespectable behavior. He could not gamble from the grave, and my sister was a respectable matron in Milwaukee. There was no one else.

"Petrovic," the General said, "you will assist Detective Green. You look the part of an anarchist if any officer does."

Petrovic flushed but said nothing. Not every anarchist was a Russian Jew, but clearly the General was more interested in stereotypes than actual facts.

Hodges began writing the second name on the board—and at first, I couldn't make it out, for his large frame completely blocked the chalkboard from my perspective.

The General's words alone brought the name home to me. It was one I'd neither heard nor thought of the past two years. I physically winced the moment I heard it, so sharp was the pang of the memory it caused.

Jonathan Strupp. *Hannah's brother.*

"Jonathan?" The name erupted unbidden from my dry mouth.

When I had known him, he had been a serious boy in wire spectacles, always wrapped up in a book. Since he was four years Hannah's junior, I hadn't known him well. And I'd not kept in touch with the Strupps . . . no, not since the early weeks following Hannah's death. It had been selfish, of course—but I hadn't been able to bear the look of sad reproach I imagined I saw in her mother's eyes. "You were there," she seemed to say, "and yet you didn't bring her home." It was true: I'd helped save many lives the day the *Slocum* burned, but not that of my own fiancée. And the injury I still bore—my weak right arm that had never healed from an improperly set fracture—was a constant reminder of that failing.

"I gather he wasn't a card-carrying anarchist when you knew him?" The General's lips curved into a sarcastic smile. "People change. He's in a position of authority now—and if Drayson directed the hit on the judge, then Strupp participated in it."

He turned to Savino. "I believe you and the Strupp boy were schoolmates. If Ziele has no luck, I'll ask you to follow up."

Tom Savino nodded unhappily but asked only, "How many men are we looking for?"

The General drew his hands together. "Gentlemen, I believe we're on the trail of the largest anarchist conspiracy this city has seen. We will start at the top, with Wesson and Strupp—and work our way down, till we've caught all the minions who were helping them."

I cleared my throat. That was when the enormity of what the General had in mind hit me. This was to be a witch hunt focused on two men, and driven by a belief in guilt by association. He was prepared to arrest numerous men—and to mistreat a family who had already suffered enough—in the name of targeting two men against whom there was absolutely no hard evidence.

"Sir, I grew up among many men who now call themselves anarchists," I said. "Most of them are all talk and no action."

"In the beginning, perhaps, Detective," the General said, fixing me with a stern look. "But Oliver mentioned the magazine *Mother Earth*. It reminds us these vile acts start somewhere. I believe they start with ideas and idle talk."

"Even if you believe that, General, these men's families are not at fault—"

He cut me off abruptly. "I don't care. I'll use whatever means are at my disposal to apprehend those responsible." He pounded his fist on the table again, this time leaning in so his wheelchair did not move. "These are not men that we seek. They are scum—vermin of the earth who pollute everything good with their vile words. Then they kill good men—children even—in the name of their godforsaken cause." He caught his breath, and the words that followed were barely audible. "Men like Drayson don't deserve the protection this fine nation's laws would give them."

"Of course, General," I said, with as much politeness as I

could muster. "But do you have proof—by which I mean hard evidence—that Jeremy Wesson and Jonathan Strupp are actually involved?"

He grew red in the face, and I knew I was walking a fine line between my duty to this investigation and outright insubordination. "I've got all the proof I need," he roared. "These anarchist scum draw support from their own communities—from ordinary citizens in the beer halls and saloons, their libraries and even their churches. They're all to blame," he said, pounding his fist, "every last one of them. That's why I've sent spies like Oliver to go undercover into places like Justin Schwab's Beer Hall and Fritz Bachmann's Teutonia Hall. A boy like him keeps his ears open." He gave me a hard look. "I don't care what connections you have, Detective Ziele. I'll not have you tell me how to do my job. My leg is lame," he said, tapping his wheelchair, "but my mind is sharp. I'm in charge of this city for a reason."

I stiffened. "I mean no disrespect, General. I only want to emphasize that as we search for the anarchists responsible, we shouldn't ignore standard investigation protocol. After all, it is possible that Judge Jackson has been killed for reasons other than a top-level anarchist conspiracy." I took a deep breath, and when he did not interrupt me, I continued. "At the crime scene last night, there were indications that the judge's killer may have had a unique motive."

"Are you suggesting it wasn't an anarchist?" Bill Hodges sputtered, aghast. "Drayson's trial is the biggest thing this city has seen in years."

"No," I replied evenly, "but we should consider the possibility that someone—very likely an anarchist, I agree—had a more personal motive for murdering the judge. Many anarchists may

have wanted to free Al Drayson. But only one of them was motivated to kill the judge in this particular way."

I continued, emphasizing the bizarre elements that no doubt
the official reports had glossed over. I'd spoken up out of concern for the Strupps, but now, I believed my own words.

The General's blue eyes were alert behind his wire-rimmed
spectacles, and though his words continued to be abrupt, there
was now genuine curiosity behind them. "I understand your point.
But no one has a more personal and compelling motive than
Drayson. Good God, man—his very life is at stake."

"Yes," I replied calmly, "but the problem is: Drayson doesn't
value his own life."

"What do you mean?"

"I interviewed him this morning, sir. I admit, it's hard for
rational men to understand—but I believe he's prepared to die
for his cause. In fact, he *wants* to become a martyr—as he puts it."

"This city is happy to oblige him," the General groused.
"That doesn't mean his followers don't want to save him."

"They may," I agreed. "But you've seen the crime scene report, General, and I've explained my own concerns. You have to
admit that your typical bomb-throwing anarchist wouldn't have
gone to the trouble of leaving a Bible or a white rose behind."

"But our informant has told us that he personally overheard
talk by those who would rescue Drayson from jail." The General
looked approvingly at the boy.

"With due respect, sir, I believe you pay your informant by
the tip," I said delicately.

"Why, I oughta—" Oliver bolted out of his chair, but the
General silenced him by placing a firm hand on the boy's arm.

"You may go now, Oliver," the General said.

Oliver stumbled out of the room, giving me a final, sullen glance.

"Why would an anarchist—or anyone, for that matter—care about a Bible or a rose?" he demanded.

"I don't know," I said. "But the judge's hand was placed on the Bible, as though he were swearing an oath. Maybe his murder was retribution for breaking one?"

"You . . . you can't possibly say that Judge Jackson was derelict in his duty in any way." The General now sputtered in anger. "He was one of the finest judges on the bench. To suggest otherwise is the worst tomfoolery I've ever—"

"General, the truth isn't what's important here. It's what the killer *perceived*—in his own, tainted view of the matter." I watched as the General visibly relaxed. "With your permission, sir, it's something I'd like to explore further. I believe the crime scene offers leads that are ultimately more promising than anything we may learn from hounding the families of two known anarchist leaders."

The General drew himself up. "Detective, I promise you we won't ignore any good leads. But as your commissioner, it's my decision to focus on the anarchist leadership. I believe they will lead us to the killer responsible for Judge Jackson's murder—and a whole lot faster than this gibberish about Bibles and white roses."

He paused for several moments, looking me up and down.

I waited. Was he going to take me off the case?

Finally, he said, "Look into your theories all you want, Detective. But on your own time—and not at the expense of my direct orders."

"Of course, General."

"I'll be watching you," he said with a stern look as he dismissed me. "Help me solve this case quickly and I'll see you promoted. But interfere with my commands, and you'll suffer the consequences."

He didn't have to spell it out. At best, I'd find myself on desk duty filing paperwork; at worst, I'd never work as a policeman again. I was walking a fine line, indeed.

The General smiled, and stroking his handlebar mustache, he dismissed us all. "Get to it, gentlemen. Make me proud of what we can accomplish when we set our minds to it. My goal is to arrest those responsible for the judge's murder within forty-eight hours."

As I walked out, I tried to steady my nerves. *Focus on the victim,* I told myself. That also reminded me that anything I risked professionally or personally was nothing compared to what the victim had already lost: his very life.

CHAPTER 6

The Dakota, 1 West Seventy-second Street. 3:30 P.M.

"You've come in time for fresh-baked blueberry scones, Detective, just served in the music room with afternoon 'tea.'" Mrs. Mellown made an exaggerated sniff of disapproval as she let me in the door.

Alistair was no doubt having scones with a stiff drink instead of tea—much to the chagrin of the matronly, gray-haired woman who served as housekeeper of Alistair's eighth-floor apartment at the Dakota building. For over twenty years, she had organized Alistair's home and attempted to bring general order to his life—albeit with mixed success and much exasperation.

I greeted her warmly, handing over my hat and wool plaid scarf, then my coat. She hung them on the coat rack as I removed my shoes at her request. Though I knew the way, she always insisted on showing me in properly. I followed her down a hall-way that would have been the envy of any art collector—for it displayed artifacts, paintings, and tapestries from Alistair's ex-tensive travels. The plush red and blue Turkish carpets, finely detailed oil portraits, and Chinese silk paintings always made me feel as though I had entered a museum, not someone's pri-vate home.

As we drew closer, I was surprised to hear Alistair's voice, angry and loud.

"There's no room for error. Too much is at stake!"

Another voice, rough and deep, thundered in reply. "Do you think I'm unaware of that?"

I hesitated—but Mrs. Mellown did not break her step, though her right hand reached down and jangled the key ring tied to her apron to signal her presence.

She stopped next to the open French doors with polished brass handles that led to the music room, turned her head, and gave me a knowing smile. "An old friend of the professor's stopped by for a visit. It's good that you'll be joining them."

So I was to play peacemaker—but more interesting to me was why Alistair would be exchanging heated words with his guest.

Mrs. Mellown preceded me into the music room and for-mally announced me, adding, "Will you be needing anything else now, Professor?"

I entered in time to observe Alistair recompose himself, but the placid expression he arranged on his face could not disguise the telltale red flush that burned on his cheeks. He had been arguing with his guest for some time—not just in the moments I overheard.

"Yes, would you bring us another plate of scones, please," he said, giving Mrs. Mellown a boyish smile. Then he turned his attention to me. "Come in, old boy. Glad you're here. I'd like you to meet a friend of mine, Angus Porter. Detective Ziele, Judge Porter."

I reached to shake the hand of the man who stood to greet me. Judge Porter was a short, portly man with a gut that almost burst out of his buttoned white shirt. His wide chin was covered with gray stubble, and though his general appearance was unkempt, his bloodshot hazel eyes were alert with intelligence.

"Angus was at Harvard Law with me," Alistair said. "He remained friendly with Hugo Jackson through the years."

"Hugo was an honorable man and a good friend," Judge Porter said, sinking once again into a plush green sofa.

"His death is a great loss," I said.

Alistair indicated that I should come sit beside them, pointing to the small paisley chaise longue across from the judge. I sat, realizing that I had never spent much time in Alistair's music room before. More so than the other rooms in his expansive eleven-room apartment, this one seemed designed for comfort: we sat at the back of the room, near the floor-to-ceiling window looking into the Dakota's interior courtyard, in a cozy arrangement of overstuffed sofas and wood-framed chairs. A black Steinway piano dominated the front half of the room, next to a wall of bookshelves filled with musical scores, histories, and biographies of famous musicians. The remaining walls of the room displayed paintings of other musical instruments, from flutes and violins to mandolins and harps.

There was even a new elegant mahogany floor-cabinet Victor-Victrola phonograph, its horn folded down into a cupboard below that Alistair used to control the player's volume: open for loud music, closed for muted sound. Next to it was a bookshelf containing numerous Victor phonograph records and an extra supply of spear-shaped needles for playing them. I knew no one else with such a machine—but Alistair made a practice of acquiring the latest inventions. Today, the soft baritone of Enrico Caruso was just audible from behind closed doors. I recognized his voice; he was Alistair's favorite opera singer.

"Join us for a glass of sherry, Ziele?" Alistair asked as I helped myself to a scone. He added ice to their glasses before refilling them with a pale amber liquid. "Harveys Bristol Cream." He sniffed its aroma with satisfaction. "Unlike other sherries, it's best enjoyed chilled, on the rocks."

"No, thanks. I've got another late night." Though I wouldn't have minded a glass of Alistair's favorite sherry, I needed to be alert for tonight's visit to the Strupps.

Alistair took a sip from his glass, then poured me a cup of the hot tea Mrs. Mellown had brought in with the scones. "Then we should get down to business. I asked Angus here today because he knew Hugo Jackson so well. In fact, he was Hugo's confidant on matters relating to the Drayson trial."

Following Alistair's train of thought, I turned to Judge Porter. "Why did Judge Jackson want your advice?"

"To ensure he was being fair." Judge Porter spread his hands wide. "It was tough with the Drayson case. Hugo bent over backward to be impartial, but he hated Drayson. It wasn't just what Drayson had done, killing innocent people, especially the child." He leaned toward us confidentially. "He had nightmares because he believed Drayson was threatening him."

"*Threatening* him?" I raised an eyebrow.

The judge nodded sagely. "No matter what testimony was

presented at trial—no matter who was being questioned—Drayson's eyes never left Judge Jackson. Hugo found it tremendously unsettling. He'd even begun to dream about those eyes watching him from behind wire-rimmed spectacles."

I could well imagine. I recalled from this morning's interview how Drayson had a penetrating gaze—the kind that seemed to see through you and past you, all at once.

"Did he have other reasons to believe that Drayson meant him harm?" I asked.

The judge shook his head. "No. Not physical harm, at least. He thought it was a strategy on Drayson's part to unnerve him."

"Did Drayson seem to be in communication with anyone in the courtroom?"

The judge shrugged. "Nothing that Drayson initiated. But his sweetheart tried to pass him messages in court. The judge intercepted a number of them: love notes, really—not anything sinister."

I put down my cup of tea and pulled my small leather-bound journal and pencil out of my breast pocket. "I didn't know he was sweet on any girl. Do you know her name?"

"Of course." His eyes flickered with amusement. "China Rose."

"Not her real name, I presume."

"No, her real name is Guo Mei Lin."

"Where can I find her?"

"She works in her parents' Chinese restaurant on Mott Street."

"Any idea how long he's known her?"

The judge's mouth curved into a wry smile. "You give me

too much credit. I'm just repeating what Hugo told me about disruptions in his courtroom."

"So he mentioned nothing else that was significant?"

"Only the usual crowd who assembled each morning outside. Over half were citizens hoping to tear Drayson limb from limb. The others were anarchists spouting their drivel about reform and workers' rights. Emotions ran high at court, every day, and if your downtown policemen hadn't done their part to maintain order, the crowds would've torn each other apart."

I'd heard something similar from within the ranks.

Alistair had been sitting back for this part of the conversation, reviewing his private notes, but now he rejoined us. "What about earlier cases?" he asked. "Are you aware of any other recent case on Hugo's docket—other than Drayson—that might have led someone to wish the judge harm?"

"Absolutely not." Judge Porter's voice was tinged with defiance.

"No other anarchists?" I asked.

"Not that he mentioned to me," the judge said.

"Nonetheless, we ought to check Judge Jackson's recent docket." I looked to Alistair. "I can obtain it through official channels, but it may be faster if you request a list of his recent cases from Mrs. Jackson."

"Of course," he said with a nod.

Judge Porter pushed his glass of sherry aside impatiently. "You wanted to talk about the symbols—"

"Yes, we'll get to that." Alistair cut him off. "First, let me quickly share with you the results of the autopsy conducted on Judge Jackson."

"How did you . . . ?" I stopped myself before I finished the question. I had no doubt that Alistair's connection to Mrs. Jackson was the reason—and he immediately confirmed it.

"Of course, the judge's widow wanted me to see it right away," he said, passing a sheaf of papers across the coffee table to me. "It supports what I had thought."

"Which is?" I raised an eyebrow.

"That Judge Jackson's killer was supremely organized and capable; his preparation cannot be faulted."

"And *that* is stated in *this* autopsy report?" I tapped my fingers against it.

Alistair smiled. "Not in so many words. But if you look at the notes made by the coroner's physician, you'll see my point: this killer knew exactly what he was about."

I scanned the report, focusing on the most pertinent sections. Judge Hugo Jackson had died due to exsanguination, bleeding to death after his throat was slit from ear to ear. The incision was nine inches—both long and deep enough to cut both carotid arteries and the jugular vein. Alistair was right: the report noted that the injury had been inflicted in such a way as to ensure almost immediate death. The judge's head had been pushed forward into his chest, bringing the jugular and carotid arteries together.

An amateur might have leaned his victim's head back, better exposing the neck to his knife—but, in the process, risking that the knife would miss the major arteries. By sliding his knife under his victim's forward-leaning neck, the murderer had exhibited confidence and knowledge. But what amount of strength had been needed?

I skipped through additional pages, but there was nothing

on that subject. "Either the killer was strong enough to subdue Judge Jackson—or he took him by surprise."

"That's my theory, as well," Alistair said. "Either way, it was carefully planned."

"And he wanted to kill the judge efficiently; he had no interest in making him suffer by prolonging the process," I added.

"What does that tell us? This autopsy is no help." Angus waved away the report that I offered him. "And all your talk of how well this murderer planned his kill doesn't take you even one step closer to solving this crime."

"Which is why we need you, Angus." Alistair then turned to me, saying, "I asked Judge Porter here today because he is an expert symbolist."

"A *symbolist*?" I gave them both a quizzical look.

"It's my hobby," Angus said with a grin, "and has been, since my college days." He and Alistair exchanged a look before he continued. "It was an outgrowth of my studies in Greek, for Greek letters are often used as symbols. Slowly, I came to appreciate that we have symbols all around us, and my interest spread to all forms of symbolism." He shrugged. "I suppose I like the challenge of unlocking secret, private meanings."

"The symbols at the crime scene, I believe, are the key to identifying Judge Jackson's killer," Alistair said. "You see, in terms of method, he was the model of expediency: he entered and exited the judge's home without anyone noticing, and he dispatched his victim quickly, without so much as a sound." He paused, looking both of us full in the face. "This behavior is entirely at odds with what we see when we consider the symbols he left behind. He risked precious time he might have used to escape by choosing to leave the white rose, and by making the effort to place the judge's left hand upon the Bible. The question becomes: Why were these symbols important?"

I spread my hands wide. "The Bible could signify any number of things . . . how can we determine one meaning from among many possibilities?"

"Because only one meaning will make sense in context," the judge explained. "Hugo's killer used more than one symbol, which is to our advantage: it means he meant them to work together."

"Was Judge Jackson religious?" I asked.

"He attended church with his wife most Sundays," the judge said with a bland smile. "Religious affiliation was important to him."

"So he liked socializing at church," I said.

"That's actually a good way of putting it," Judge Porter said, nodding. "He was socially religious."

I helped myself to another scone. "Then it's unlikely that the Bible is meant to suggest anything about Judge Jackson's personal religious practice?"

"Highly unlikely." Judge Porter's reply was decisive.

"So we are left with my initial thought—that the Bible signifies something about his professional life. Every time he swore in witnesses at trial, he would have instructed them to raise their right hand while placing their left on the Bible. Am I correct?" I looked to both of them for my answer.

"You are," the judge said.

Alistair added, "And Hugo would have taken his oath of office in exactly that manner, too—affirming his loyalty to the law and his commitment to upholding it."

"Do you know the oath he would have taken?" I asked.

"I took it myself, just two years after Hugo joined the bench,"

Judge Porter said good-naturedly. He recited from memory: "'I, Angus Jervis Porter, do solemnly swear that I will administer justice without respect to persons, and do equal right to the poor and to the rich, and that I will faithfully and impartially discharge and perform all the duties incumbent upon me under the Constitution and the State of New York. So help me God.'"

"And it was the judge's *left* hand that was placed on the Bible, correct? As though taking an oath?" I did my best to mimic the gesture, trying to copy what I'd seen time and again in courtroom testimony.

Judge Porter jumped and made a move to disagree but was silenced when Alistair gave him a stern look—something I couldn't let pass.

"What is it?" I asked the judge.

The judge coughed to clear his throat. "It sounds like overreaching to me. Just because Hugo's hand ended up on top of a Bible doesn't mean the killer *intended* it."

Alistair, more diplomatically this time, said, "I know you've got doubts, Angus. But I need you to trust me on this one: nothing we discover in a crime scene like Judge Jackson's is unintentional." He turned to me again. "Yes, the judge's left hand was positioned on the Bible as though taking an oath. And that *is* the meaning I believe the killer intended."

"So you believe the killer is gesturing to a failing in office . . . some abrogation of judicial duty?" I asked.

Angus interrupted with a sharp reply. "No one can accuse Hugo of being derelict in his duty—in fact, to the contrary. He was one of the most esteemed members sitting on the bench in this city."

"No one is saying otherwise," Alistair said. "Remember, what we are discussing is the killer's own flawed perspective. Not your usual standard of a reasonable person."

The judge grumbled some more but seemed mollified. "Don't forget: even if we believe Hugo's killer was making a point about the judge's oath of office, there is another important symbol we've not yet discussed." He leaned forward and looked us both full in the eye. "I mean, of course, the *rosa alba*. The white rose. You said one was left on the judge's desk, next to his corpse."

I confirmed it.

"Assuming it was left by Hugo's killer, then it is of the utmost importance. To clarify, however—is there any chance that Hugo could have picked it up himself, as a gift for his wife?" The judge looked first to Alistair, then me.

I could only respond with what seemed to be common sense. "In that case, wouldn't he have given it to her right away, the moment he arrived home? It seems unlikely he would have delayed."

I didn't mention it yet, but I was also thinking about the symbol of the rose that appeared in the musical score.

"Angus," Alistair said, chiding him gently, "you of all people know the meaning the white rose has accrued over the years."

Angus blanched, and for a moment I thought he would be ill. "Another refill, please," he said, holding up his glass.

Alistair poured more sherry, almost emptying the glass decanter, while Angus's jaw worked back and forth—as though he was trying to say something but couldn't manage it. Then he took a large swallow of his drink, gathered his courage, and began to explain.

"The rose itself is a flower that symbolists have imbued with multiple meanings over the ages. But of all roses, the white rose is invested with the most complicated of meanings. The easy meanings are the ones you will know: purity and innocence."

"Like a bride," Alistair said.

Angus nodded. "Exactly. It can also be a symbol of remembrance or honor. White roses are often displayed at funerals."

"So it *could* be a sign of death, like at a funeral. Nothing more." I looked from Alistair to Angus, watching their reaction. Both appeared unsatisfied.

"Certainly it *could*," Alistair said. "But given that the killer planned the murder so well, the fact that he included it at the crime scene—"

"Means it signifies something more." I finished his sentence for him.

He nodded.

Angus let forth a deep sigh. "One of my favorite stories surrounding the white rose comes from Greek mythology. Aphrodite gave a white rose to her son, Eros, who in turn gave it to Harpocrates, the god of silence, as the price of hiding her indiscretions."

"So another reading that points to a misdeed," I said.

Angus agreed with a vigorous nod. "Exactly."

The symbols were beginning to make some sense to me now, especially when I thought of the Bible as representing the judge's oath.

"Just to make sure we're not missing anything, is it possible that the rose signifies a different kind of religion? Like the Rosicrucians, perhaps," Alistair said.

"What are Rosicrucians—some kind of secret society?" I asked.

Angus chortled. "My sister is a practitioner. Or was. She got caught up in their promises of secret knowledge. They believe their followers can unlock the secrets of everything from reincarnation to astral projection!" He laughed again. "Next, she drifted into an even more bizarre movement—Spiritualism—and now she spends her days trying to communicate with our dead mum. Nothing but malarkey, I say." He coughed loudly. "And no, I don't think *this* rose is connected with the Rosicrucians. Their rose symbol is always entwined with the cross."

We sat in silence for some moments, just thinking.

I turned to Alistair. "You mentioned something earlier about the white rose in the War of the Roses—that it was given to anyone who betrayed his oath as an omen of death."

"Yes. I meant the *sub rosa:* death to him who under the rose's secrecy betrays his oath," he replied.

Angus gave us both a stern look. "It's just another line of thought about a betrayed oath. But this symbolic meaning is given to us by literary writers, not historians. That means it's the stuff of legend, not necessarily truth."

"Does it matter *how* the meaning of the symbol is established?" I asked.

"I suppose not." Angus leaned back, his gut practically bursting out of his shirt. "You recall that the War of the Roses was a civil war fought over the British throne, pitting descendants of Edward III, or the House of York, against descendants of Henry IV, or the House of Lancaster. Much later, Renaissance writers like Shakespeare depicted noblemen as choosing sides by plucking a white or red rose from the garden. White represented the House of York and red the House of Lancaster."

Alistair beamed. "'This brawl today . . . shall send, between the Red Rose and the White, a thousand souls to death and deadly night.' You may recognize it from Shakespeare's *Henry VI*."

I swallowed hard, forcing myself to follow their argument. It was hard not to feel completely out of my element—for my brief stint on scholarship at Columbia had given me little of the knowledge these men took for granted. I'd wanted an education, thinking it would guarantee me a life different from the one I'd known growing up. But when family obligations intervened, I had to abandon those plans.

"It wasn't just a matter of choosing sides," Angus added. "Those who betrayed their loyalty to their chosen house, be it York or Lancaster, were considered traitors and put to death. But according to legend, they always received fair warning first: the delivery of a single, white rose."

"So the judge could have been a traitor in the killer's view: someone who had to be put to death for betraying his oath," I said.

"I think so. An oath on the Bible implicitly invokes God as our witness, to judge and avenge us if the person taking the oath doesn't stay true," Alistair said.

"So the judge was a traitor—but to what cause?" I asked. "Earlier, we talked about his duty to the law. But what if his killer is thinking of a different duty? I'm struck by the fact that we're talking about a number of closed societies not unlike the anarchists—from the Rosicrucians to members of the House of York."

Angus gave me a severe look. "I'd not go that far. The anarchists are like no other group. They've no positive goals. They want to overthrow church and state—in short, everything good, hardworking men have tried to create."

"Only because they feel they'll never be treated fairly as our society currently exists," I responded. "I can see how someone from their cause might believe the judge had betrayed some higher duty to the working man in general—or to the defendants in his courtroom, particularly."

"Careful, Ziele," Alistair said, eyes twinkling, "you'll make me think you've become an anarchist follower."

"Hardly." I smiled in return. "But that doesn't mean I don't understand—and even sympathize—with the sources of their discontent." And my smile disappeared when I thought again of this morning's meeting with the commissioner.

"If images of betrayal—and specifically betraying one's oath—are repeatedly associated with the white rose," I continued, "then this fits with how the killer posed the judge's hand on top of the Bible. But is there anything in this to help us identify the judge's murderer?"

"We must look to the remaining piece of the puzzle," Alistair said, his voice sober. "Ziele, I know you noticed it, as well: the white rose symbol that was embedded in the musical score we found among the judge's papers. Did you bring it?"

I nodded as Judge Porter nearly choked on the scone he was eating. "Alistair, you said nothing about a musical symbol."

"I'm mentioning it now," Alistair said, as I passed the copy of the musical score to the judge. "It's not a musical symbol per se. Rather, the white rose substitutes for the bass clef symbol in the last bar of the page."

The judge looked at it for some moments, then held it high in

the air toward the light. Finally, he put it down on Alistair's coffee table with a grunt.

When he finally spoke, his voice was rough. "When did
Hugo receive this?"

"It was among the letters delivered the same day he was
killed," I answered. "Do you have any idea what it means?"

Alistair shook his head. "Hugo appreciated fine music as
much as anyone, but he only dabbled with the piano. I can't
imagine why anyone would send him a musical score." He took
back the copy of the score and crossed the room to the piano.
"I wish Isabella were here. She is far more accomplished than
I am."

It would have been easy enough to invite her, for she lived
across the hall—in the same apartment that she had occupied
since her marriage to Alistair's son. But Alistair sat down, opened
the piano top, and began to hunt for various keys. It was now
obvious to me why Alistair had chosen this room for today's
meeting, rather than his library—which, with its sweeping views
of Central Park, was normally his favorite. When he finished
the score, he swiveled the stool back around to face us.

"Well?" He gave me an expectant look.

I shrugged. "It's a nice melody but nothing catchy or memo-
rable."

The judge was deep in thought for some moments. "You've
played it in its entirety," he finally said, "and it means nothing to
me. Let's try something else: Where the last bar shows a white
rose instead of the bass clef, can you play that section alone?"

"All right." Alistair obliged, saying the notes out loud as he
played. "Low A, E, E, high E, G, E, middle C—"

Angus interrupted him. "Say, is there a rhythm to that?"

A look of annoyance crossed Alistair's face. "I'm playing it exactly as written. It's just a mix of quarter notes and half notes."

"Can you try it again?" the judge asked.

Alistair shrugged and played the notes again, careful to follow their rhythm. It didn't improve the melody at all.

"The rhythm leads me to believe the melody is unimportant," the judge said, thinking aloud. "Do you have a blank sheet of paper?" Then, after draining his sherry, he began working out something on the coffee table. Alistair and I watched, mystified, until Angus finally leaned back with a look of smug satisfaction.

"It's a musical cipher," he said.

"A what?" I asked.

"A cipher—a code that conceals a secret message," he explained patiently. "Specifically, the writer of this code"—he tapped at the musical score with his forefinger—"used Porta's code, where musical notes represent letters of the alphabet."

Alistair's eyes lit up. "Giovanni della Porta?"

"Who?" I asked, puzzled.

It was Angus who responded. "Porta was a Renaissance man with many interests, and his code became famous. It was used widely throughout the eighteenth century and later adapted by others. Most musicians knew of it; many amused themselves by using it for secret communications with one another. I suppose it makes sense," he added, eyes twinkling. "After all, many believe that music is the one, true universal language. Schumann wrote his *Carnaval* Opus Nine based on a cipher, and Brahms and Bach embedded names in their music. But I digress . . ."

He drew a musical bar on a new blank sheet of paper. "You see, in Porta's cipher, every note has an alphabetic correlation. So the half-note value of A-below-middle-C corresponds to the alphabet letter *A*. But A-above-middle-C corresponds to the letter *H*. And so it continues till you reach high E . . . then you descend the staff, this time with quarter notes to show the difference. You finally end with low A again, this time representing *Z*."

"So let's work out what this means." Alistair leaned in, making some notes with his own pen.

Angus nodded. I couldn't quite decipher the odd expression with which he returned Alistair's gaze. I felt as though they understood something that had eluded me.

When Alistair finished, he turned the paper around so the judge and I might read it. "Do I have it right?" he asked.

"You do." The judge confirmed it, then read the full message aloud. "'Leroy avenged.'"

"Leroy avenged." I echoed the words, then looked at Alistair and the judge. "Al Drayson was never known as Leroy, was he?"

The judge shook his head. "Not to my knowledge. But we should double-check records of his middle name as well as any nicknames he may be known by."

"Now the list of the judge's former cases becomes even more important," I said. "But if this is correct—"

The judge interrupted me. "It's correct. I'm certain of it."

"Then we've just found our killer's motive," I said.

Identifying the killer himself, of course, would be far more complicated. But Leroy, assuming he was not a clue planted only to lead us astray, now held the key to the case. Judge Hugo Jackson had somehow injured a man named Leroy. Who was Leroy?

And what person in Leroy's life wanted this wrong—whether it was real or perceived—avenged badly enough to kill for it?

The timing suggested a connection to Drayson. After all, this killer had struck on the eve of jury deliberations in Drayson's trial. And while that might be a simple coincidence, I was coming around to Alistair's view that little in this crime scene could be characterized as "coincidental." There must be some relationship between Al Drayson and the Leroy named in the musical cipher, some as yet unknown link that would lead us to Judge Jackson's killer. And given Commissioner Bingham's and the police department's unwillingness to entertain any leads that would not cripple the underground anarchist network, uncovering this connection would rest squarely on my shoulders alone.

CHAPTER 7

The Dakota, 1 West Seventy-second Street. 6 P.M.

"What's going on? And why are none of you dressed for dinner?"

I caught my breath when I looked up and saw Isabella standing in the doorway—wearing a yellow dress, her chestnut hair done up for the evening. Her brown eyes sparkled as she regarded us all.

Alistair visibly relaxed the moment he saw his daughter-in-law, though he approached her with an apologetic smile. "I'm sorry, Isabella. We were so caught up in discussion, I completely forgot."

A look of disappointment crossed her face, though her eyes were warm as she greeted me first, then Angus Porter. Had she been looking forward to their dinner—or was she sad to have been excluded from the afternoon's discussion? My bet was on the latter.

Alistair pulled out his pocket watch and frowned. "Past six o'clock already. Angus and I still have things to discuss; I'll have Mrs. Mellown put together dinner for us here." He turned to me. "Ziele, why don't you take Isabella out for dinner and fill her in on this case? Take my automobile, even, if you like."

Caught off guard by this unexpected display of generosity, I gave him a questioning look. Not only was it unlike him to offer me the use of his most prized possession—a 1905 Ford Model B motorcar—but I also knew that he regarded the friendship I had developed with Isabella with no small measure of suspicion.

"Alistair," I said, "you know I've never driven a motorcar before."

His expression remained bland. "You've watched me often enough. It's not difficult."

"No, thanks all the same. A hansom cab will suit us fine." I'd been a passenger in Alistair's motorcar many times, but I knew I lacked his skill in navigating roads filled with horse-drawn carriages, trolleys, and pedestrians. Not to mention his patience in hand-cranking the engine whenever the motor sputtered to a stop.

I exchanged a brief good-bye with Judge Porter as Alistair walked Isabella down the hallway. It was almost as though he couldn't be rid of us fast enough—and I wondered what he wanted to discuss privately with the judge? Since our first case together last year, I'd learned that Alistair was often less than forthcoming; in fact, it was his habit to withhold information he didn't consider relevant to the case—never mind that I might disagree.

Then again, I didn't want to judge Alistair harshly. He and Angus Porter had been schoolmates with Hugo Jackson; I supposed it was natural for them to spend time alone reminiscing about their friend.

"Here," Alistair whispered to me in parting as he handed me a small packet. "These are copies of the letters Guo Mei Lin wrote to Al Drayson. I thought you might want to review them over dinner."

"How did you get these?" I asked, my voice rough.

"Connections, my friend," he answered with an enigmatic smile.

"And why didn't you mention these earlier?" I pocketed the letters.

He shrugged. "I didn't think Angus needed to know. Enjoy your night."

Once we were settled into our cab heading downtown and I had given the Chinatown address to the driver, Isabella gave me a curious smile. "Are we going to Mon Lay Won, Simon?"

I shook my head. She referred to the restaurant we'd frequented with Alistair in the past, known as the Chinese Delmonico's, the usual choice of New York's elite because it was said to be to Chinese food what the famed uptown restaurant was to fine cuisine. "Tonight I have a less fashionable Chinese restaurant in mind. We're meeting a woman there."

She looked at me askance. "We made dinner plans not fifteen minutes ago."

"I didn't say the woman was expecting us."

"Then you'd better tell me quickly about this latest case of yours—and how she figures into it," she retorted, gripping the sides of her seat as our wagon jolted suddenly to the right.

I filled her in as the cab took us downtown at a rapid clip, over cobblestones mired in sludge, and who knew what else, jockeying for position with motorcars and trolleys and other horse-drawn wagons, splattering mud on those unfortunate pedestrians who drew too close.

Isabella was a quick study, so it took little time to explain how Alistair had pulled me into this case—involving a prominent judge, a controversial trial, and a crime scene riddled with symbols. After I had filled her in on the background, I returned to China Rose and our purpose this evening.

"Her name is Guo Mei Lin," I said, following the Chinese convention of pronouncing the surname first. "She's also known as China Rose—and apparently she is Al Drayson's sweetheart. She attended his trial every day and attempted to pass him love letters. I just received copies of two of them." I gestured to the brown satchel at my feet.

"And you think she is somehow involved in Judge Jackson's murder?" Isabella asked.

"Given the timing of his murder—and the notoriety of the Drayson trial—it seems likely that an anarchist was involved. If she wasn't involved herself, then she may know who was."

A perplexed look crossed Isabella's face. "I wonder why she was never written about in the papers. I've followed the trial and read the news just like everybody else; Drayson has been vilified by everyone from Hearst and Pulitzer to Ochs. I'd have thought the yellow rags at least would have picked up the story." She turned to me and laughed. "I could practically write the headline myself, based on what you've told me: 'The Devil and His Chinese Paramour.'"

She had a point. "I'm not sure why," I said. "Maybe because she's Chinese?"

"Emma Goldman is Russian, and they write about her all the time." She jutted out her chin.

"She's also a prominent anarchist."

"Yet you suspect China Rose to be just as active, if not as prominent."

I gave up, laughing. "You're right—and I don't have an answer for it. It may be nothing more than a favor called in by the police, who have found controlling the crowds outside the courtroom to be a challenge. One of the commissioner's deputies may have promised full access to Drayson after the trial in exchange for restraint during it."

She looked at me closely. "Something else troubles you. You keep wrinkling your brow, the way you always do when your evidence doesn't quite add up."

Her lips curved into a smile when I nodded. She was coming to know me too well.

"It's possible that the judge was killed merely to derail Drayson's all-but-certain conviction," I admitted. "But because of the symbols found at the crime scene—and the message 'Leroy Avenged'—I believe the killer could be motivated by something in the judge's past that the Drayson trial has brought to the surface."

The hansom cab lurched to a halt—for we had arrived at our destination: the corner of Bayard and Mott.

"In other words, you think it's more complicated than just anarchist support for Drayson?"

"I do. Come." I paid the driver and helped Isabella out of the carriage. "We'll talk more over dinner."

Once we were on the sidewalk, I paused for just a moment to take in the unique odor that was Chinatown—always an olfactory sensation that overwhelmed me. This evening, the smell of the day's fish from competing markets mingled with the pungent aroma of cigar stands and tea shops. Their scents were so strong that they generally masked the odors emanating from the mass of humanity around us—from sweaty laborers returning home to perfumed women headed out for the evening. And the din was terrific, as people shouted in all different languages: Mandarin and Cantonese dialects, mixed with Korean and Japanese as well as English. I could speak only my native tongue, but I could generally distinguish among the others if I listened to their tones.

The crowds jostled us as we descended into the street and made our way onto the sidewalk. Chinese laundrymen passed us, carrying bundles of clean clothes on their heads; women bumped us with baskets filled with meats and vegetables; young men jockeyed their way into saloon doorways; and the occasional patrolman on his evening rounds made a pretense of keeping order, stopping at various places of business to talk with the shopkeepers.

"You like tour? Only fifteen cents for half hour." A lobbygow, or tour guide, came up to us. "Then I take you to a restaurant with exotic cuisine."

"No, thanks," I said, taking Isabella's arm. I had no need of a guide; I knew this area well, thanks to a boyhood spent just blocks north of here. And during my own father's frequent absences, Nicky Scarpetta, the gruff owner of a saloon around the corner on Pell Street, had served as a surrogate of sorts—helping my mother when the rent money was missing, and looking out for me in ways I appreciated only now that I was grown.

We continued down Mott Street, past several Chinese restaurants that competed for business on this block alone: the Imperial, the Port Arthur, and the Tuxedo.

"Which one are you looking for, Simon?" She pressed her hand into my arm as a basket of fish—seemingly suspended in air, so tiny was the person behind it—materialized from nowhere and bumped into her.

"The Red Lantern, just ahead." I pointed to the yellow awning that showed Chinese characters only, next to the drawing of a simple lantern on a red flag.

I pulled Isabella toward me, out of the way of a man who staggered near us haphazardly, no doubt having spent too many hours this afternoon in one of Chinatown's opium dens or saloons. Some advertised openly; others could be found only in the upstairs rooms of certain restaurants, hidden from general view. Their presence had given respectable Chinese restaurants all over the city a bad reputation—with the result that few survived in neighborhoods outside Chinatown. New Yorkers associated Chinese restaurants with these disreputable haunts, but, in fact, most degenerate patrons and owners were Irish or English, German or Russian. Anything but Chinese.

We eventually made our way to the corner, where the Red Lantern had a menu displayed in its front window. We ascended two steps, entered through red curtains that passed for a door, and found ourselves immediately greeted by a pretty, petite woman in a blue silk robe, or hanfu.

"Ni hao ma," she said with a polite smile. "Good evening."

"Hun hao, xie, xie. Table for two, please."

"Of course." Her second smile was broader, revealing yellow teeth that ruined the otherwise pleasing effect. I presumed she was a heavy user of tea, tobacco, or both—for there was no other explanation why her teeth would be so heavily stained.

We followed her into a small dining room filled to capacity; she led us to the one free table at the back. The other patrons stopped eating to stare at us—for we were the only non-Chinese diners in the room, and Isabella the only woman, save an elderly lady dining with her son.

When we were seated at a small wooden table in the back, our hostess addressed us again. "We have Chinese language menu only. You read Chinese?"

"E dien dien. Maa Maa dei," I replied, trying two different dialects and probably bungling both. *Only a little.* I'd learned some Mandarin characters, enough to differentiate noodle dishes from rice, but nothing more.

She nodded. "I help you then."

"Mei Lin!" A voice called out from the kitchen, followed by something in Chinese.

"Sorry," she mumbled as she turned. "One minute."

The moment she was out of earshot, Isabella leaned in to me, saying in a whisper, "She doesn't look like an anarchist to me."

I could only shrug. Bertillon may have been wrong when he argued that criminals had different features from law-abiding citizens, but he had one thing right: we all tended to expect a criminal to look the part of a villain. It was human instinct— and I recalled how, just this morning, I had searched for some telltale sign of evil in Al Drayson's eyes. Of course there had been none. The worst sort of evil was invisible; it slept in the heart and mind.

We waited several moments, but Mei Lin did not return.

"If we order standard fare, chances are they'll have it,"

Isabella suggested. So we decided on our order: a pot of Long Suey tea, fried lobster in rice, and vegetable chow mein with a side of bok choy. I gestured to a male waiter who came over, introduced himself as Charlie, and wrote down our choices on his small tablet.

I kept an eye out for Mei Lin as I talked with Isabella, explaining my concerns about the case, including the central dilemma I now faced: how best to handle General Bingham's impossible demand that I investigate Hannah's brother by bringing pressure to bear on the entire Strupp family.

"I'd not met the General before this morning," I explained. "He's got a reputation for being too blunt and never listening to anybody. But I hadn't taken those complaints seriously; men in the field all think their superiors know less than they do." I made a wry face.

"And now you agree with them: you don't trust the commissioner."

"His approach is completely wrong," I said, reaching for the teapot to refill both our cups. "The General is a military man who thinks he can bulldoze his way through all problems to a quick conclusion. But people—especially those caught up in an investigation—don't respond well to orders or brute force. It's better when you can persuade them to think as you do."

Isabella was honest, as usual. "The commissioner's approach is one thing; your own is another. That leads me to wonder: Is your real objection here to the commissioner?" she asked between slow sips of tea. "Or—are you simply looking for excuses to avoid the Strupp family?"

"Both," I admitted. "The General's methods may tip off our best suspects—and if they go to ground, then our investigation is doomed. But you're right: I've no desire to see any of the Strupps—especially not to discuss Jonathan's anarchist involvement." I paused a moment. "Not that there's any particular reason to avoid them. It's simply a connection, now closed, that I prefer not to reopen."

Isabella waited, silent, until I continued.

"I don't believe Jonathan had anything to do with the judge's death. Whatever position of leadership he now holds, he cannot have been an anarchist for long. It's been just over two years since I last saw him. And if I'm correct, the person involved in Judge Jackson's murder has harbored a grudge for a very long time."

"Two years can be a long time." She gave me a pointed glance before she refilled her cup of Long Suey tea. "Long enough for people to change. Were you close with Jonathan before?"

"No. He was a timid, reserved boy when I knew him, interested in books and science experiments, hoping for a college scholarship like I'd been given. That didn't materialize, so he went to work for his father."

The dishes we had ordered arrived on steaming platters. We were silent as the food was served—and I noticed that Mei Lin was back. She greeted customers, served them drinks, and then managed the cash box for dinner receipts.

"What about Mr. and Mrs. Strupp?" Isabella asked.

I struggled with my chopsticks, which seemed ill-suited to my plate of lobster fried rice. "I got along well with them, certainly in the beginning. They approved of me when I was a student at Columbia, aspiring to be a lawyer. But they became concerned after I abandoned my studies and joined the police force." I made a wry face. "Policemen, you see, earn a steady and reliable income but there's a potential on-the-job risk to life and limb. And since most of my earnings went to support my mother and sister, they despaired, I think, of my ever being in a position to marry their daughter. I understood and didn't blame them for it; they were simply looking out for Hannah's best interests."

"How long has it been since you've seen them?"

"It's been since the weeks following Hannah's funeral," I admitted, struggling for words. "It was too difficult . . . and I only made it harder for them." *And I felt they blamed me for not saving her,* I silently added.

She considered for a moment.

Finally she spoke. "I think you need to see them, Simon. Because it's the right thing to do—not just because the commissioner has ordered it." Her brown eyes looked full into my own. "The commissioner will send someone else to the Strupps, if you do not go. And his next choice is unlikely to be as sensitive to their concerns as you will be." She took a deep breath. "It will be good for you, too."

She was right: it had to be done. But it was a task I'd have given a good deal to avoid.

The evening had grown late, and now only a handful of diners remained at the Red Lantern. Charlie, our waiter, brought over our bill and a dessert of star fruit.

"When the young lady is free, could you please ask her to come speak with us?" I handed him the three dollars that would cover our dinner.

He raised his eyebrows but agreed.

I glanced again at the remaining diners. Though under normal circumstances I would seek greater privacy for my conversation with Mei Lin, it appeared they did not speak English well enough to eavesdrop.

Some moments later, Mei Lin joined us at our table, her brown eyes pools of suspicion.

"Your dinner was fine?" She forced a smile.

"It was. *Xie xie. Mh goi.* Thank you," I said, mixing dialects again. I wanted to be polite, and I was unsure what Mei Lin preferred. "I'm hoping you may be able to help us with a different matter. I believe you are Guo Mei Lin—sometimes known as China Rose."

Her eyes widened, but she neither confirmed nor denied it.

I went on to introduce Isabella and myself, explaining that we were investigating the murder of Judge Jackson.

She responded with a blank stare. Had I not conversed easily with her just minutes before, I would have been concerned about our language difference.

"We are searching for his killer, and we need your help," I repeated, not unkindly.

"You have wrong lady, Detective," she finally said, her voice defiant. "I work here." She gestured around the tired red-wallpapered room. "Long days, like my parents. I know nothing about dead judge."

"Maybe," I replied carefully, "but you found time to attend the trial he most recently presided over—that of Alexander Drayson."

She scowled and was silent again.

"How did you meet Al Drayson?"

"I do no wrong. I don't have to talk to you." She shoved her chair back and stood; it seemed she was challenging me to stop her.

I reached into my satchel and slowly drew out my copies of the letters she had written to Drayson and had attempted to hand-deliver at his trial. "The police know all about the letters you tried to send Al Drayson," I said, keeping my tone friendly. "They've sent me to talk with you—but if you refuse, they will send others. They're also likely to station a team of officers outside your restaurant to watch your every move—which no doubt is not ideal for business."

She blanched, gripping the back of the chair. "My parents know nothing about Drayson."

"I believe that's true. Our interest is in you—and your connection to him."

She was silent, deep in thought.

Isabella broke in with a charming smile. "We just need you to answer a few simple questions."

Mei Lin stared at Isabella for a full moment. She finally sat, but at the very edge of her chair.

"When did you meet Al Drayson?" Isabella asked.

"Last year," Mei Lin answered reluctantly. "He eat in our restaurant. Invite me to meeting."

"There aren't many anarchist meetings in Chinatown," I observed mildly.

Her voice was flat as she agreed. "My people too busy. Everyone here," she said, gesturing to the restaurant and beyond, "we all work hard, long days in restaurants and laundries. And for what? Even other immigrants hate us. They say we *all* make nothing because the Chinese work for nothing. But we have no choice. We need work to survive." She was speaking rapidly now, with bitterness.

She pulled out her cigarette case. "Got a lucifer?"

I shook my head, but Charlie—who had been observing our conversation from the other side of the room—came forward with a box of matches. He immediately retreated, but his point was made: he was watching over Mei Lin.

She took a long draw, savored it, then spoke again. "Your government give us permit we have to carry. They pass laws to keep us out—mainly women. Only Chinese men, no women here. Because of Exclusion Act. It's no wonder the men look elsewhere. My own brother has Irish wife and red-haired son."

She grinned, showing her heavily stained teeth yet again.

"Is that why you joined the anarchists?" Isabella asked. "To make things better for the Chinese people?"

Mei Lin nodded vigorously. "Yes. Just like Italians and Russians and Germans. They work hard to make things better for their people, too."

"Then your relationship with Al Drayson became more personal. He trusted you," Isabella said gently. "We're told you tried to pass him notes during the trial. Love letters, I believe."

At this, she laughed—with more volume than I would have expected from a woman of her diminutive size. "That's what you supposed to think. Drayson would be proud."

"What else should we think?" I demanded.

She shrugged. "I didn't write those messages. Only deliver them."

Now she had my full attention.

"Who gave them to you?" Isabella asked.

"I never knew. They come inside boxes of mooncakes, deliver here, to the restaurant. What I receive at night, I take to court next morning—or try to."

"Who gave you instructions?" I asked. Obviously if Mei Lin

was telling the truth, then she was merely a delivery girl; the real person of interest was the anarchist instructing her.

"Mr. Strupp," she said simply.

Jonathan. Hannah's brother.

"And what did he tell you?"

She shrugged. "Only what I tell you. That when letter arrives with mooncakes, to deliver to court next day."

So was Jonathan the person of interest I sought? Or merely another player in a larger conspiracy? Either way, I now had no choice in the matter: I would need to visit the Strupps tonight.

Isabella had been temporarily distracted, reading the notes. Now she turned to me with a frown. "Did you look at them yet, Simon?"

"Not closely," I admitted.

"All these hyphens," she said. "The words make sense—sort of—but it's odd how the words are put together. See."

She passed me the letter and I read:

"Alas my great-love unless-we-meet-soon and rekindle-passion's-flame die close-to-you I guess-my-fate."

"Did you understand what you delivered?" I asked Mei Lin.

"I understand what I need to," she replied with an enigmatic smile.

It was an answer that conveyed nothing. I continued to prod her, reminding her that only her full cooperation would satisfy me. "Otherwise, they'll send someone else."

Her nostrils flared with anger, but she finally answered. "It's a code. That's all I know."

Isabella's brow furrowed. "Let me see that again. I've always been good with word puzzles." She took the paper from me and began working, pencil in hand.

"Do you know what any of them said?" I asked Mei Lin.

She shook her head—but almost immediately, Isabella looked up with a satisfied smile.

"I've got it. It's the most basic of ciphers. Do you have a new sheet of paper?"

I obliged her, pulling my notebook from the back pocket of my leather satchel.

"It's known as a null cipher," she said, "because the coded letters aren't obvious—they're disguised by the hyphens. But look: they're just trying to tell Drayson they've smuggled him cigarettes."

I stared again at the text. "So what's the code?"

"The first letter of each word," Isabella replied. "Then the message changes from a half-literate's love ramblings to something else. See?"

We looked again, and my mind's eye transformed the lettering:

"**A**las **m**y **g**reatlove, **u**nless-we-meet-soon **a**nd **r**ekindle-passion's-flame **d**ie **c**lose-to-you **I** **g**uess-my-fate."

Isabella wrote it down, then turned her paper around toward us with a satisfied smile.

A.M. Guard Cig.

"You tried to alert him that the next morning's guard would offer a gift," she said.

Mei Lin nodded.

"But why was that even necessary? He would have gotten the cigarettes, anyhow," Isabella said, curious.

A droll smile crossed Mei Lin's face. "The messages were good preparation for the day we had an important message to send him. If the authorities saw these love letters as nothing special, you see . . ." She broke off, but we could finish her thought. The less important messages were paving the way for a real message to get through.

Remembering my own altercation with Drayson, I added, "Also, I can't imagine Al Drayson was a cooperative prisoner, especially if a guard approached for no good reason. The message would have smoothed their interaction."

Another thought nagged at me. "Why you, though?" I asked.

"Maybe," Mei Lin said, her face deadpan. "I am just stupid Chinese girl who cannot write well. What can you expect, right?"

Now I understood. "People would assume you were not educated. They wouldn't question the hyphens. Still, Drayson never received your messages," I said.

She shrugged. "He was unlucky man."

"Yet you sympathize with him . . . approve of what he did?" I asked cautiously.

A flash of anger crossed her face as she ground the remains of her cigarette into an empty saucer. "I don't like violence. No one does." She cocked her head back. "But people don't listen. If they fear us, maybe they pay attention to us."

"Were you aware of a plot to kill Judge Jackson?" I asked.

Her eyes were serious when they met my own. "I know no one planning to kill a judge. Why would they?"

"It might create a mistrial that would free Drayson—or, at the least, prolong his life by delaying his date with the executioner."

"But he no longer matters. His work is done."

Now I was genuinely puzzled. "You think even if he lives, he can do no more? Isn't he one of you—of use to your cause?"

She shrugged. "No more than anyone else. Others take his place. He not so special."

"Perhaps others think differently," I said, watching her reaction closely.

But she was noncommittal. "They might. But why waste effort on just one man?"

Someone shouted in Chinese from the kitchen.

Mei Lin sighed. "I need go. Have I answered your questions, Detective?"

"For now, yes," I said, and thanked her for her time. "If you think of anything—or hear anything—please let me know." I passed her my card with the Nineteenth Precinct telephone number, knowing she would never call.

"Do you believe her?" Isabella asked the moment we were out of earshot, even before the restaurant door closed behind us.

"It's hard to say." I shepherded her through crowded sidewalks toward Canal Street, where we would have better success finding a hansom cab. "What she told us makes perfect sense— and yet I believe she is fully capable of spinning a good tale. To her credit, precisely because she seems smart, I believe she would not have told us about her cipher messages to Drayson had she truly been involved in the judge's murder. And had she known about the musical cipher at the murder scene, she'd never have acknowledged writing any sort of cipher."

"Yet it's a coincidence that may point to someone within the anarchist organization."

"Exactly. It's a solid link between the anarchists and the judge: someone is behind this who is a code writer."

We continued north on Mott Street, stepping around garbage that had simply been dumped on the sidewalk. It felt more deserted than usual; with tonight's damp chill in the air, the outdoor vending stands that typically lined the street were empty.

"Would you mind if I took the cab with you only partway?" I asked.

"You'd like to get your conversation with the Strupps over with," she said. "It's fine, Simon. I understand." She placed her leather-gloved hand on top of my arm for the briefest of moments.

We hailed a passing cab, I helped her in, and she arranged her voluminous skirt onto the seat, making room for me beside her.

"There's a workers' demonstration backing up traffic in the Bowery ahead," the cab driver called back to us. "May take an extra few minutes."

After I assured him it was fine, he swung his horses to the east, toward the river, before cutting north on First Avenue. The neighborhood deteriorated over the next few blocks as the saloons and gambling dens of the Bowery gave way to block after block of abandoned buildings and street beggars—many of them mere boys of no more than eight or nine. The cab drew near Third Street and we were in what had been Little Germany—a place at once strange and oddly familiar.

Isabella had been gazing out the window intently. Now, she turned to me and spoke as though she knew my thoughts. "This was your neighborhood, wasn't it, Simon?"

"It was," I said stiffly. A lifetime ago.

The neighborhood was a ghost town now, for most survivors had done as I had and left. Most had gone to the Upper East

Side; others went to Astoria or the Bronx. The schools and shops I had known were now closed—and though new children and merchants had slowly arrived to take their places, the neighborhood neither looked nor felt the same.

Every block was marked in my memory. We passed the building where Andrew Stiel had lived with his wife and four children; he took his own life after his family was killed aboard the *Slocum*. Fifth Street was where the Felzkes and the Hartungs had lived; the *Slocum* had wiped out those families, as well.

Then I saw it: number 120 First Avenue. One of the more rundown tenements on the street, it was where I'd grown up— and a reminder of the vast divide that separated me from Isabella, a chasm of class and upbringing that seemed insurmountable. Her eyes seemed to widen as she took in the sight.

My onetime home was a brown box of a building, the most basic of brick structures unmarked by any detail of note. This evening it was nearly obscured by the vast array of laundry that seemed to connect each window. Those inside had needed to do their wash, and all manner of shirts, trousers, and bedclothes remained strung on the wire lines, despite the damp.

I leaned forward to speak to the driver. "Would you stop here, please?"

Then Isabella turned to me, her face sympathetic. "May I see it?"

"Of course," I said, giving her a reassuring smile. "Just not tonight."

I exited the wagon and handed the driver sufficient fare to take Isabella home. I tipped my hat to her and, as the driver started his horses, crossed to the other side of First Avenue and my former building. I looked up to the fifth-floor window overlooking the street. That had been our flat—a fifth-floor walk-up of the most miserable kind. Three rooms—a back room, front room, and kitchen—had housed the four of us. Three of us, really—for my father was rarely there. My mother had done her best to decorate it. She'd placed mantel scarves on all our shelves and displayed her dishes. She'd painted our back room walls green and put up a red paisley wallpaper in the front room. But all the colors and scarves hadn't obscured what was a meager existence. And it was likely just as squalid an existence inside as it had ever been. I'd managed to escape all that—and I'd no desire to go back, even for the most fleeting of moments.

But tonight, I must.

Hannah's building was the one next to mine—only slightly less decrepit and forlorn. With a deep breath, I steeled myself, entered, and ascended a narrow wooden staircase that reeked of urine.

On the third floor, I turned toward the Strupp apartment—number 3C. Perhaps they had moved, I thought for a fleeting second. But no—I smelled the odor of fresh-cooked brisket, which had been Mrs. Strupp's speciality.

It had to be done. Waiting would make this no easier.

I knocked.

It seemed several minutes—but was in fact only seconds—before the door opened. A petite woman no taller than five feet two inches stood before me. Her jet-black hair, now heavily streaked with gray, was pulled back tightly into a bun, and her olive skin was heavily wrinkled from worry and age.

She opened her mouth—and suddenly her eyes registered a spark of recognition.

"Simon," she said with a sigh of relief. "You've come."

And before I could say a word in answer, she had enveloped me in a tight hug.

CHAPTER 8

120 First Avenue, Apartment 3C. 8:30 P.M.

The living room was as I remembered it: crammed from wall to wall with broken-down furniture and smelling of beef and potatoes. I had spent so many wonderful evenings here with Hannah and the Strupps, my surrogate family at the time, that I could describe the apartment with my eyes closed. Nothing was noticeably different since my last and final visit here two years ago. Yet the surroundings were drabber, the furniture more threadbare than I recalled. I wondered what had changed more: this third-floor tenement flat that was the center of my life just a few short years earlier—or myself, now that I had left this existence behind.

The Strupps had never boasted much in the way of material possessions. Hannah's father, who owned a drugstore on the corner of East Ninth Street and First Avenue, was too kindly a man to run a successful business. He would extend his neighbors' monthly accounts as a matter of course, with the inevitable result that some took advantage of his leniency and never paid at all. "You need medicine more than I need money," he'd tell his elderly customers—even as Mrs. Strupp complained under her breath that "you'd think we were running a charity, not a pharmacy."

The realization that Mrs. Strupp was talking to me shook me back into the present.

"Sit, sit," she urged.

I complied with an awkward half-smile, taking a seat on a sagging orange sofa that was riddled with stains.

"I've made a fresh batch of knoephla soup. Please, have some."

She beamed in anticipation. Knoephla soup had always been her specialty, and she prided herself on the light, fluffy dumplings that filled it.

"I just finished dinner," I replied, shaking my head. But the moment I saw the disappointment that filled her eyes, I added, "But I'll taste a small bowl. I haven't forgotten how delicious your dumplings are."

She was all smiles again as she stepped into the small kitchen just to the room's left. I heard the sound of a metal ladle clanging against a pot as I surveyed more of the room: the coat rack with Mrs. Strupp's thick green shawl flung across it; the peeling floral wallpaper, once red but now faded to the palest pink; the simple gaslights on either side of the sofa that provided some light to the room. That was when I saw the table, nestled behind a rattan chair. In dim gaslight, I had missed it at first. There, to the left of the window, placed so as to be protected from the rain—and it was covered with photographs. Unable to help myself, I drew nearer and saw Hannah: first as a budding beauty at sixteen with a winsome smile; then in our engagement photograph, me beside her, stiff and self-conscious yet beaming with happiness. I looked absurdly young: another man, living a life that was no longer my own.

I had returned to my seat by the time she appeared with two bowls of soup, handing one to me and placing another on the table.

"For Hans," she explained, indicating her husband. "He will be home any moment."

I glanced at my watch. It was half past nine—which meant he was working late hours at the pharmacy, a fact she soon confirmed.

"Times are tough," she said. "So many neighbors have left since . . ."

She didn't finish. She didn't have to. I knew better than anyone how many, like me, had chosen to move away in the months that followed. I'd certainly found my own grief easier to bear when it wasn't mirrored in the faces of everyone around me.

"Hans works hard yet brings home less than ever," she said, her eyes clouding with worry.

Then just as suddenly, she brightened and asked, "But tell me about you, Simon. Are you still working up north?"

"Up north" meant Dobson, the small village in Westchester County just fifteen miles north of Manhattan where I had spent two years forgetting my life in the city—or certainly trying my best to do so. I knew that for the Strupps, anything north of Fourteenth Street was uncharted territory—so from their perspective, my move to Dobson had taken me beyond the pale. I had often wondered why the same people who possessed enough spirit of adventure to come to America in the first place chose to limit their existence to a few square blocks once here. The Strupps had done just that—and they certainly were not alone.

"I just returned," I said, explaining to her between spoonfuls of soup that I was a detective working for Declan Mulvaney, now a precinct captain.

"Ah my." She clapped her hands together in delight, for she had known Mulvaney well when I first joined the force and he was my partner on patrol in the Lower East Side. Her expression turned wistful as she added, "You boys have come far. As I always knew you would."

What remained unspoken was her hope—now forever lost— that I would take Hannah with me.

A key turned in the lock and a tall man with gray whiskers, a thick handlebar mustache, and gentle eyes came into the room.

"Hans," she whispered, "look who's here."

He came farther into the room, turned to me—and his look of surprise was almost immediately replaced by a broad grin as he came over to pump my right hand vigorously. I managed not to wince, though the shot of pain that raced up and down my arm was terrific. He had forgotten my injury—and that was a good thing.

As he ate his soup hungrily, the three of us talked of the past two years, focusing on mutual acquaintances and changes in the neighborhood. Neither of the Strupps showed any sign of resentment or anger toward me—a fact that did little to assuage my own sense of guilt. What we avoided was any mention of

Hannah, for my own presence here after two years' absence was more than reminder enough. In this room where time seemed to stand still, her ghost hovered around me, threatening to take hold of my long-fought-for sanity.

"What brings you here tonight, Simon?" Hans Strupp finally asked. He gripped the sides of his chair, bracing himself firmly, and I realized they both probably assumed I was here to tell them I was engaged to another woman—or similar news.

Wanting to spare them that at least, my words tumbled out of my mouth in a rush. "I came because of your son. Jonathan is in trouble."

Mrs. Strupp's face collapsed, but it was Mr. Strupp who answered.

"Has he been arrested—or hurt?" He phrased it as though those were the only alternatives—and it was clear that he was resigned to either one, for he had apparently been expecting bad news about Jonathan for some time.

"As far as I know, he's fine right now," I said, quickly reassuring them. Then I paused, knowing that once they had been regular readers of both German and American papers. "I'm not sure how closely you've been following the news, but a judge was killed on Monday night."

I saw the flash of recognition in Hans Strupp's eyes. "The judge in the child-killer case," he muttered.

I confirmed it.

His face went white. "They think the anarchists are involved, don't they? Is Johnny . . . ?" He couldn't bring himself to say the words.

"I need to talk with him," I said. "I understand that he's involved with the anarchists—that he's in a position of authority
within the New York organization."

Hans Strupp balled his right hand into a fist, gripping it
with his left. "It's true."

"From the beginning, we've tried to stop him. We've told him
he'll come to no good with that group," Mrs. Strupp said, her
expression pained.

I pushed my half-finished bowl of soup away from me and
took my notebook and pencil out of my satchel. "Can we start at
the beginning? I need to know how Jonathan came to be part of
the anarchist movement."

Half an hour later, we were still talking—mugs of coffee in hand.
The Strupps still favored Lion's Coffee, a brand that unabash-
edly targeted German-Americans with the slogan "All Germans
Like It." It was once a favorite of mine, and I was surprised by
how bland it tasted now—lacking the rich, deep flavor of the
Italian brands I'd come to prefer.

They told me all about how a Czech man named Paul Hlad
had befriended Jonathan—first pretending to share Johnny's
scientific interests, then encouraging him to attend anarchist
meetings at various German beer halls in the city, and finally
convincing him that, when put to use, the anarchist ideals would
allow him to avenge his sister's death. Still, I remained puzzled.

"Johnny was a scientist," I said. "All he talked about was
Svante Arrhenius and Marie Curie, as well as college and the
scholarship he hoped to win."

I searched their faces for some sign, some explanation—but
none was forthcoming.

"He changed," Mr. Strupp said, twisting the button on his left shirtsleeve. "One day, he talked of nothing but Pierre and Marie Curie and what they did for chemistry . . . then the next, he was raving about the capitalists and how they killed his sister." His voice, bitter, choked when he added, "You know the charge as well as we do: how greed led the *Slocum*'s owners and captain to cut corners on safety and bribe the inspectors." His button snapped, flying across the room. "Would it have cost them so much to buy new life vests when the old turned to dust? Hundreds might have lived, if only—" He broke off, unable to continue.

Countless others, and perhaps Hannah among them, could have been saved. But the steamship's owners were focused solely on profit, not safety, and so they had set out that day with rotten life vests that drowned those they should have saved—not to mention lifeboats that had been painted and wired onto the decks so that no one could detach them. The owners of the *Slocum* as well as the inspectors who had taken a bribe were equally at fault, but only Captain Van Schaick had been made to answer for this negligence with a ten-year prison term. The owners and managers of the company had escaped charges, untouched by the disaster that had killed so many.

Mrs. Strupp silently crossed the room and searched for the missing button as her husband continued to talk.

"Well over a year ago," he said, "when it seemed no one responsible would see jail time, Johnny became obsessed with how none of the ship's owners had to face up to their misconduct. He started spouting nonsense about the evils of capitalism, and how that was what killed Hannah. No individual person, see—but 'the system.' He started going to workers' meetings regularly. He made new friends . . . and abandoned his old ones entirely."

I was silent for some moments. I had been angry for a long time, too—but my own rage centered on those individuals who had made bad decisions. Their judgment—or lack thereof—had cost over a thousand people their lives. That was human error, not the capitalist system. And yet Johnny, feeling similar emotions, had come to a different conclusion.

"The anarchists focused Johnny's anger and gave him a target," Mrs. Strupp explained. "Now it's all he does. We barely see him anymore."

"So he doesn't live here?" I asked.

"Hasn't for over a year," his father responded.

"How often do you see him?"

"He came for Hans's birthday in August," Mrs. Strupp said, her voice dull. "We've not seen him since. Only the occasional letter, sometimes with money."

"He has regular work?"

"No." Hans Strupp shook his head. "I think he lives off what the membership contributes. He's high enough up that they pay him. Or maybe he just takes what he needs."

"Do you know any of his associates other than Paul Hlad?"

"A few. We can give you their names," Mr. Strupp offered.

"If you would," I said. "Do you have any idea where I might find him?"

The Strupps exchanged a look but were silent.

"The commissioner has asked me to talk with him." I continued to press them, slightly annoyed that they were holding something important back. "But if I don't, someone else will come looking for him." I let the implication linger.

Finally, Hans Strupp cleared his throat. "We have an arrangement, but for emergencies only."

"Your son is a suspect in a high-profile murder case. If that doesn't constitute an emergency . . ." I trailed off, mincing no words.

Mr. Strupp, with a guilty look, apologized. "We will contact him for you. Ask him to meet you at a specific time and place."

He was about to continue when a loud wail came from the back room. With a start, Mrs. Strupp got up and scuttled across the room.

I raised my eyebrows, giving Hans Strupp a searching look. He stared down at the floor.

"You have a baby here?" I asked, knowing it was a stupid question.

He remained silent, at a loss for words, while my mind raced through the possibilities. I had just settled on the most likely possibility—that Mrs. Strupp had taken work as a baby nurse to earn extra money—when my answer arrived in the form of a small bundle, swathed in pink and cream, nestled in Mrs. Strupp's arms. The baby, now content, clutched at an earthenware feeding bottle. Mrs. Strupp brought the baby closer.

She hesitated, then spoke—her words coming out in a rush. "I was thinking, Simon. Maybe it's not too late for Johnny."

"Too late?" I repeated, wanting to follow her.

"When you meet him, you can try to bring him home," she pleaded. "He always looked up to you. Maybe you can convince him there's another way."

"You want me to convince him to leave the anarchists?" I said, knowing what she asked was futile.

But she nodded. "He still thinks of you as a big brother. He'll *listen* to you. I know he will."

I wasn't so sure, but I promised to try.

I glanced at the baby, who sucked at the bottle in grasping, hungry slurps. She had rosy pink cheeks and delicate features; Mrs. Strupp was clearly taking good care of her. It no doubt brought back happy memories, now that her own children were no longer with her.

I had grabbed my coat and was preparing to say good-bye when I looked at the baby again. Now done with her bottle, she regarded me with sober brown eyes.

Hannah's eyes.

I took two strides closer and stared, then swore softly under my breath.

Startled, Mrs. Strupp took a step back, and the baby's dark-skinned face wrinkled up as if to cry. Mrs. Strupp offered the milk yet again, which worked as a distraction to grab the baby's interest.

"Hannah," I said stupidly. "She has Hannah's eyes."

Mr. Strupp cleared his throat. "And that's what we call her. Our Hannah. Johnny has rejected everything we believe, but he named her according to our customs. I believe that secretly he still believes; he wants his sister's spirit to live on in his own child."

"His child," I repeated.

"Born six months ago," Mrs. Strupp explained. "We've cared for her from the beginning. He claims he's still close to the mother, but I have no idea. We've never met her. I suppose he's embarrassed to bring her by. Though it wouldn't matter to us."

"So you've no idea who she is?"

"No, though . . ." She paused a moment, her voice cracking. "Though it would be nice to have some connection . . ."

That was when a host of realizations came to me, all at once, jumbled together, with only two facts clear. Jonathan Strupp was a father, and his child was now being raised in Mrs. Strupp's care.

Little Hannah—with jet-black hair and my own Hannah's eyes—stared up at me. It was too much.

I passed Hans Strupp my card and asked him to call me when he had contacted Jonathan. He would waste no time, I was sure.

My heart was pounding. It was all I could do to manage a formal good-bye before I raced down the stairs and into the night, my feet carrying me farther and farther away from the long-buried, heartrending memories this night had reawakened.

Wednesday
October 24, 1906

CHAPTER 9

The Nineteenth Precinct Station House,
West Thirtieth Street. 8 A.M.

"Looks like you could use some help," Mulvaney said, casting a skeptical eye at the ten brown boxes stacked haphazardly behind me. Piled high, they created a makeshift wall between my own desk and that of Tim Gallagher, my neighboring detective. Each box was chock-full of documents from Judge Jackson's trial docket over the past five years—and I'd made little progress, though I'd been working diligently since just past five o'clock this morning.

I'd had no more than a few hours of restless sleep after last night's visit to the Strupps, for it had reawakened emotions that I'd done my best to suppress the past few years. Finally, I had surrendered to my insomnia and decided to get a head start reviewing the cases Judge Jackson had presided over in recent years, in hopes that I might learn something—anything really—to provide a connection to Judge Jackson's murder.

As promised, Alistair had used his influence to secure the judge's case files and have them delivered to my office. While sifting through their contents was certainly a long shot, I believed it would be more productive than Commissioner Bingham's efforts to round up New York's anarchist leaders. After all, my training as a detective had taught me to focus any murder investigation on the victim—so with the exception of tracking down those anarchist suspects the commissioner had ordered me to find, that was exactly what I intended to do.

"I'm not even sure what I'm looking for," I said, adding with a grin, "except that I feel confident I'll know it when I see it."

I brought Mulvaney up to speed on the case, explaining how the commissioner had wanted me on his team, not for my skills or expertise but instead because of my relationship with Hannah's brother, now a prominent anarchist. "Remember Tom Savino? He was at the meeting, too. It seems he has a connection to another anarchist suspect—a link that General Bingham wants to exploit."

Mulvaney, shaking his head, looked concerned for the first time. "You'd better be careful. The General may think the both of you would make useful scapegoats if someone isn't arrested soon."

He glanced at his beaten-up gold pocket watch, then pulled Detective Gallagher's chair over and sank into it. "I've got half an hour to spare. Can you give me a little more detail as to what I should be looking for?"

"All cases associated with known anarchists," I said, passing him a stack of files, "as well as anything that strikes you as unusual."

"Unusual, how?" He shot me a skeptical look. Mulvaney liked specifics, but today I had none to give him. It was pure gut instinct that I was relying on now. And though some called it nothing more than dumb luck, I'd learned that I had an uncanny knack for uncovering hidden facts, a sixth sense that led me to discover answers in places more straightforward methods would never take me.

Giving it some more thought, I replied, "I guess I'm looking for cases where one party harbored an intense anger or a particular grudge, directed toward Judge Jackson."

He gave me a look of disbelief. "*Any* losing party carries a grudge."

"True, but not the kind I'm looking for," I said. "I told you about how Jonathan Strupp's outrage toward the *Slocum*'s owners had developed into an intense hatred of our capitalist society as a whole. I'm looking for that kind of anger. Maybe it starts small, from some injustice that isn't fully addressed—but it grows into something larger, perhaps leading to murder. And when we find it, we may see a reference to the name Leroy."

Mulvaney's eyes grew wider when I went on to explain the cipher embedded in a musical score sent to Judge Jackson. "But we have no idea who Leroy is—or even whether the name is a real one. It's possible the case we seek doesn't mention him at all," I said.

Mulvaney shook his head. "I still say you're talking about half the cases in New York City. And it's got to be asked: How come you're convinced young Jonathan himself isn't involved?"

My reply was abrupt. "I'm not. In fact, it's *likely* that he is involved in some way—and I am worried that I won't be able to spare the Strupps yet another heartbreak. But right now, I have nothing to tie him—or any other suspect—to Judge Jackson."

Mulvaney's eyes finally lit with understanding. "Be careful. Your judgment may be easily clouded by your sympathy for the Strupps."

"Let's just see what we find." I gestured toward the untouched pile of papers in front of him—which after a moment's hesitation, he began to tackle with a grunt.

As precinct activity swirled around us, we worked for the better part of the next two hours—long past the time Mulvaney promised to help me—making notes of certain cases to look into further. Then I found a case of exactly the sort I'd been searching for.

"I've discovered a possible link," I said, my voice sober. "It seems Judge Jackson is no stranger to controversy where anarchists are involved. He is on record as calling for the deportation of all alien radicals." I tapped my finger against a folder containing the Bisso case.

Mulvaney was all ears. "When was this?" he asked.

"Three years ago. He was presiding over the case of Louis Bisso, a fishmonger who repeatedly called for the violent overthrow of the government—even in Judge Jackson's courtroom. Bisso was accused of robbing the payroll department of a shirtwaist factory."

Mulvaney interrupted me. "Shirtwaist factory? I don't understand. I thought the anarchists wanted to help the working people at factories, not steal the wages they earned through backbreaking labor."

I shrugged. "I'd say they wanted to hurt the capitalists who own and manage such factories. Plus, when the anarchist movement needs money, its members aren't particular about where they get it. From what I can tell, most anarchist trials don't involve bombs and dynamite; they involve basic robbery charges."

Mulvaney brought his hands together, thinking. "So the judge made comments during the trial about how Bisso should be deported?"

"Not exactly," I said, passing him the exact transcript to read. "It looks like he spoke during Bisso's sentencing phase, when information that had been inadmissible at trial was finally allowed to be presented. To prove that Bisso was a hardened criminal who deserved the stiffest penalty the law would allow, the prosecutor submitted evidence of Bisso's background. And that's where I've found my link."

"To the anarchists," Mulvaney said, his eyes moving rapidly over the lines of the transcript.

"And particularly, to Jonathan Strupp."

He put down the pages he held and stared at me. "Are you sure?"

I swallowed hard. "Louis Bisso regularly associated with Henry Tractman and Paul Hlad—two anarchists with extensive and troubling criminal records. Tractman, in fact, is spending the next twenty years at Sing Sing because of his role in a mass-poisoning plot. And Paul Hlad has written and dispensed a variety of manuals on bomb-making."

"I still don't understand: How do any of these men implicate Hannah's brother?"

"Paul Hlad is the man responsible for Jonathan joining the movement—and he is now Jonathan's closest friend."

"As though that family hasn't suffered enough. A terrible thing, isn't it? Sometimes I don't understand what this world is coming to." Mulvaney shook his head. "The dawn of the twentieth century and you'd think we'd have gotten beyond all the hating and killing. It's the same all over the world: the anarchists assassinated President McKinley, just like they did the Austrian empress and Italian king. And back in Ireland, the troubles continue—" He broke off, shaking his head yet again.

I got up, pushing in my chair. "I'd better visit the Strupps again and see if they were able to contact Jonathan. I see now that it's not just the information he may have—it's the other anarchists he may lead me to."

"Assuming he cooperates," Mulvaney reminded me as I gathered my things. "He's no doubt changed a good deal since you last saw him." He glanced at his pocket watch. "I'll see you out. I've got a meeting downtown at noon, or else I'd go with you."

But neither Mulvaney's meeting nor my own interview plans were to take place—at least, not that day. As he was about to return to his office, after wishing me luck with an encouraging clap on the shoulder, his secretary's voice called out to us, rising above the noisy din in the precinct room.

"Hold on a moment," Mulvaney directed me.

And so I remained by the precinct entrance, watching as Mulvaney's long stride allowed him to cross the room to his secretary's desk in only a few steps. They exchanged words—after which Mulvaney looked in my direction, long and hard. Had there been another attack? The young man handed Mulvaney a paper; and this time, donning his own coat and scarf, Mulvaney rejoined me.

He handed me the paper, swearing under his breath. "Your goddamned professor has done it again."

I glanced at the white scrap he had given me, confused. It read: *"Judge Angus Porter. Breslin Hotel. Twenty-ninth and Broadway."*

"Judge Porter." I repeated the name with surprise. "That's the name of Alistair's friend—the one I met yesterday who decoded the musical cipher."

Mulvaney had a strange look on his face. "I believe you also mentioned that Alistair intended to spend the evening with him last night. Do you know what they had planned?"

I thought, trying to remember. "Dinner at Alistair's home, I believe; he asked his housekeeper to prepare something as I was leaving."

"Let's walk," he said abruptly, continuing to mutter under his breath something about "damned meddling."

I caught his arm instead. "Not until you tell me what's going on. What does Judge Porter have to do with anything? He's not part of this case."

Mulvaney gave me a hard stare. "He is now. They just found him—murdered—at the Breslin Hotel. There was a white rose and a Bible in his room, next to his corpse. And given that your professor was perhaps the last person to see this judge alive, I'm wondering what he knows right now that we don't."

"Judge Porter?" I asked, my mind awhirl, unable to take the news in. I had spoken with him just yesterday on matters of codes and ciphers, Bibles and roses. It was unthinkable that he had fallen victim to a similar murder, an identical scenario.

"He was killed late last night," Mulvaney said. "We'd best get to the crime scene now. Then, I'd say we have some tough questions for Alistair Sinclair." He looked me full in the eye. "Are you sure he's helping you as much as you think? That he's told you all he knows?"

"He brought me into this case, remember?" I retorted. "His friend was murdered. He's got nothing to gain by keeping me in the dark."

But Mulvaney's reply unsettled me more than I'd have expected. "Two friends murdered," he said flatly. "Sounds like an odd coincidence to me."

And the moment he said it, I knew it could be no coincidence at all.

PART
TWO

Anarchy is no more an expression of "social discontent"
than picking pockets or wife beating.
> —President Theodore Roosevelt,
> State of the Union Message, 1901

The People—the toilers of the world, the
producers—comprise, to me, the universe.
They alone count. The rest are parasites,
who have no right to exist. But to the People
belongs the earth—by right, if not in fact. To
make it so in fact, all means are justifiable;
nay, advisable, even to the point of taking life.
> —Alexander Berkman

CHAPTER 10

The Breslin Hotel, Fifth Floor,
1186 Broadway at Twenty-ninth Street. 11 A.M.

The area where the Breslin Hotel stood had once been the center of New York's theater and entertainment district, but now the area was filled with more ordinary businesses: dressmakers and milliners, dentists and doctors. As a result, the magnificent brick and terra-cotta hotel, built just two years earlier, competed with its more established neighbors—the Grand and the Gilsey—for an ever-dwindling supply of customers.

"They had only fifteen guests last night," Mulvaney was saying as we crossed a sumptuous lobby of red and gold. "At least we have a limited number of people to interview."

I caught our reflection in the floor-to-ceiling brass-framed mirror at the back of the lobby. Instinctively, I ran my fingers through my hair and straightened my tie. I expected that I might see the commissioner upstairs, and while I knew it probably wouldn't make a difference, I wanted to appear at my best.

We approached the iron-cage elevator, and the attendant, a young man with pale skin and hair so blond that it was almost white, closed the door behind us.

"Where to, gentlemen?" he asked. His voice was lilting, with the soft tones and broad vowels that I had come to associate with Scandinavian countries.

"Fifth floor, please," I said.

He turned the crank and initiated our ascent—all the while staring at the floor, deliberately avoiding our gaze.

"There's a lot of commotion here this morning," I said, keeping my voice friendly. "Did anything odd happen during the night shift?"

"I wasn't there," he said. "But you can ask the night man yourself. You guys didn't let him go home. You've got him locked in a room upstairs." His eyes darted back and forth between me and Mulvaney.

I knew that he didn't truly understand what was going on. It was unlikely that the elevator attendant from the night shift was "locked up" anywhere in this hotel, though it was true that he wouldn't be permitted to leave until he had been interviewed. But a small army of police had now invaded the Breslin; it was no wonder that this man was unsettled and confused.

We reached the fifth floor, and in response to the operator's movements, the elevator doors parted with a screech to reveal a hallway lined with police officers. The room nearest the elevator bank had been transformed into a waiting area; hotel employees and last night's guests alike—some crying, others staring silently—

were lined up to be interviewed by the multitude of police officers that had taken charge of the Breslin.

Mulvaney whistled under his breath. "Looks like General
Bingham called in the whole city for this one."

By rights, this case should have been Mulvaney's to lead, for
the Breslin Hotel was solidly within his precinct's jurisdiction.
But because someone recognized that another high-ranking judge
had been killed in unusual circumstances, the call had gone directly to the commissioner's office. I found that fact puzzling in
itself; who would have taken it upon himself to notify the commissioner before the precinct captain had arrived on the scene?

The officers in the hallway made way for Mulvaney—a gesture that was an acknowledgment of his rank. A lanky junior officer stepped forward hesitantly. "Excuse me, Captain," he said,
his manner bashful. "You just missed the commissioner, but he left
a message for you. When you're finished here, he'd like to have you
report, in person, at his office downtown."

Mulvaney stared wordlessly at the junior officer, then shook
his head in exasperation. "The General wants a report and I
haven't yet laid eyes on the crime scene. He's got no patience."

The junior officer gave a sympathetic smile. "You know the
commissioner."

"Let's see what we're dealing with." The door to room 503
was partly closed, but Mulvaney opened it wide and soldiered
into the room. I followed close behind, steeling myself to encoun-
ter a scene similar to that at Judge Jackson's Gramercy town
house.

Almost immediately, the sickly-sweet odor of blood filled my
nostrils and clung to the air. Two officers near the door, charged

with protecting evidence at the scene, were smoking cigars—no doubt in an attempt to camouflage the stench of death that permeated the room. But there was no disguising it; I remained aware of its distinctive smell, and as my stomach lurched in response, I vowed not to be sick. I couldn't be—especially not in front of so many fellow officers who had been called to this case. But what stemmed the wave of nausea that threatened to overwhelm me was not my own willpower but rather Mulvaney himself.

He stopped short. "What the hell!"

I immediately moved to the left of his large frame, which had blocked my view of everything save the cigar-smoking officers guarding the entrance.

I drew a sharp breath the moment I saw the judge. He lay in front of me—his short frame stretched out on top of the bed at the center of the room, its luxuriant white sheets now saturated with red blood. He was naked, with his hands tied together on top of his bulging gut.

This crime scene looked nothing like the first. Except that there—on the mahogany nightstand next to the bed—I saw a black leather Bible and white rose.

I drew closer, struck anew by the fact that I had spoken with Judge Porter merely hours before. My mind filled with questions for which I had no answers. Had he confronted a suspect and suffered these disastrous consequences? Or had he himself been a target? But my mind also filled with questions for Alistair the moment we had finished our examination of this crime scene. There was much that Alistair Sinclair needed to explain, and I did not intend to waste any time in obtaining the answers only he could provide.

Death had rendered the judge almost unrecognizable. He had been shot at close range, and the left side of his head was split open, leaving a gaping wound ringed by telltale traces of gunpowder.

I focused on breathing through my mouth, for the odor from the blood-soaked bedclothes was almost unbearable.

On the chair beside the desk, the clothes that the judge had been wearing were carefully folded. "Black evening dress," I observed. "He must have gone out after meeting with Alistair."

"The question is, was he undressed already when his killer surprised him? Or was he forced to disrobe?" Mulvaney pointed to the judge's tied hands. "Looks like the killer restrained the judge with his own cravat—or ascot—or whatever those fancy things are."

"You're right." I inspected the dead man's fleshy wrists. "There is no chafing or bruising; no sign that he struggled against his restraints. This would lead me to suspect that the killer tied his hands after the judge was shot. But that makes no sense, unless he was trying to stage the murder scene, somehow sending a message to us."

"I'd be careful not to read too much into it," Mulvaney said, sounding a note of warning.

"Let me guess: you want to know when he was killed." The door leading to the hotel room's bathroom opened, and Jennings, the coroner with whom I'd worked many cases in the past, ambled into the room, wiping his hands upon a thick, plush white towel. He placed his black leather supply bag at the foot of the bed and turned to greet Mulvaney and me.

"Of course. How have you been, Jennings?" Mulvaney clapped the short, rotund doctor on the back.

"The same. But I'm getting old. Aches and pains are worse than ever." Jennings rubbed his lower back. He had agile hands and a keen mind, but his body itself was almost as oversized as the bloated form on the bed. I was not surprised it gave him trouble.

He turned to me. "Glad you're back in the city, Ziele."

I nodded. "The message we received said the victim was killed sometime last night."

Jennings grunted. "The muscles are stiff; rigor mortis has taken hold. So he's been dead more than three hours but less than twelve. Officially, that would put it between approximately midnight and eight o'clock this morning. I incline to say closer to midnight, however. His body has cooled significantly. He was a large man, and let's be frank: an obese corpse typically takes longer to cool. But in this case, with his body exposed to the air, lacking clothing or covers, the process has gone faster than I'd normally expect." He coughed. "With your permission, I'd like to move him now."

Mulvaney turned toward the cigar-smoking officers, still standing at the rear of the room. "Lads, have you gotten the necessary photographs?"

"We have, Captain," the taller one answered.

"And you've dusted the room for prints?"

"Yes, sir."

"Very well. Let's move him," Mulvaney said.

Jennings whistled, and two of his assistants materialized. It took them only moments to place Judge Porter's massive corpse onto a stretcher, cover it with a clean white sheet, and remove it from the room.

"You'll have my autopsy report tonight," Jennings said as he made his way slowly to the door. "But this one seems pretty straightforward, medically speaking. A gunshot at close range means he was killed almost instantly. He never had a chance."

No, he didn't—at least not once he found himself in tight quarters with this killer. But why had he been here? And had the killer followed him—or met him here by arrangement?

"Let's gather the evidence to take back to the station house— and with luck, we'll find something I can tell the commissioner about," Mulvaney said.

I put on my cotton gloves and went over to the nightstand. I examined the rose and Bible but found nothing out of the ordinary. In every respect, they were exactly like those found at Judge Jackson's home early this week.

I again regarded the bed where the judge had breathed his last breath. "His killer had nerves of steel," I remarked. "Looks like he was shot while lying on his back, facing up. It takes a steady hand to look your victim in the eye before killing him."

Mulvaney nodded in agreement.

I bent down, leaning over the swath of red, mixed with a gray substance I knew to be brain. It formed a giant balloon shape on the bed, at the center of which a small brass item glinted in the morning sun.

The bullet.

"Do you have the tool kit?" I asked Mulvaney. Wordlessly, he brought it over and I chose a pair of long metal pincers.

Gingerly I grabbed the bullet with the metal pincers, then held it up to the light. "It's a standard thirty-two caliber. It could have come from any number of automatic pistols on the market . . ."

"Let's bag it and I will take it by Funke's after I meet with the commissioner," Mulvaney said. A. H. Funke was a gunseller on Chambers Street who often helped us make sense of cartridges and pistols, not to mention the criminals who used them. "I've seen enough here. We'd best get downtown."

But I stood at the bed, shaking my head. "Why was he shot? The Bible, the white rose—" I broke off, nodding toward the items now in my satchel as evidence. "It's just like Judge Jackson's murder. Except most killers don't change their methods so radically. Why kill one victim with a knife, the next with a gun?"

Mulvaney appeared annoyed. "You trust too much in what your professor says. And who's to say he knows what he's talking about, any more than the rest of us? Half the time his nonsense sounds no better than witch-doctor mumbo jumbo to me."

"Maybe," I admitted. "But even if we discount his theories of criminal behavior, he was the last person we know to have seen Judge Porter alive last night. I need to talk with him as soon as possible."

"If it's an anarchist plot," Mulvaney mused, "then several of them could be in on it together. Perhaps we're not looking for just one killer but a team of them."

I agreed. But thinking of Jonathan Strupp, I hoped Mulvaney was wrong.

As we made our way down the hallway toward the elevator, I stopped by the room that had been transformed into temporary interview space; here, a handful of senior detectives would speak with every employee of the Breslin. Mike Burns, a detective I knew, seemed to be organizing the junior officers.

"Say, Mike," I called out, poking my head into the room. "Have you found out yet when Judge Porter checked into room 503 last night?"

He looked over with a smirk. "Well, if it was Judge Porter,

he didn't use his real name. He—or somebody else—signed into the room as a Mr. Sanders. Gave his address as 3 Gramercy Park West. I've got the register right here." He held up a thick sheaf of papers.

I caught my breath. "That's Judge Jackson's address," I told Mulvaney as I walked across the room to take a closer look at the register.

"You've got to be kidding me." He stared in disbelief.

"And it raises the question: Who called in Judge Porter's murder? The staff here would have known him as Mr. Sanders," I said.

"The killer may have made the call. Or one of his anarchist conspirators."

"Exactly. Where did Mr. Sanders sign?" I asked Mike.

"Let's see." We waited a few moments as he ran his finger down to a signature near the bottom of the page. "Here it is. He listed his first name as Leroy. Leroy A. Sanders."

I drew in a sharp breath—but I thought only of the message contained in the musical cipher that Judge Porter himself had decoded just last night.

Leroy avenged.

And my mind was so consumed with this chance discovery that it was not until much later that I realized that the elevator operator who took us back to the lobby was not the same man who had taken us up to the murder scene earlier.

CHAPTER 11

The Lawyers' Club, 120 Broadway. 1:30 P.M.

"Do you think the Moody pick stands any chance of passing?" A man's voice, loud and obnoxious, filled the stately marble lobby of the Lawyers' Club.

A different man, with long silver hair, the kind that just reached his collar, answered in soft, cultured tones. "William Moody's Supreme Court nomination will spark no end of controversy, but don't count him out just yet. He's the President's choice, and as you know, Teddy Roosevelt never backs down from a fight."

The first voice emanated from a sturdy fellow with a ruddy complexion and close-cropped brown hair. I followed him into the elevator. "Top floor, please," I instructed the attendant.

After I left Mulvaney, I'd placed four telephone calls to

track down Alistair here at his favorite club, where Mrs. Mellown had assured me I would find him. Presumably, he was unaware of his friend's brutal murder.

My companions continued to talk.

"The only complaint against Attorney General Moody is that he's a Massachusetts man. Why should it matter that two men on the court are from the same state?" asked the stocky man.

"I'd say the geographical question only matters if you're a Southerner or a Westerner. It smacks of favoritism—especially after the President packed his Cabinet with New Yorkers. Still, if anyone can push the nomination through, it's Roosevelt." The silver-haired man smiled.

The second man clutched at his brown felt fedora. "I support the President, but even so . . . I'm not sure I like having a judge on the court so completely in Roosevelt's pocket."

"He has the chance to create a legacy that will endure long beyond his term. We should all be so lucky as to have such influence . . ." Their voices trailed away as the elevator lurched to a stop, the attendant cranked open the doors, and they entered the club room ahead of me.

"Sir?" A maître d', crisp in both manner and dress, approached me expectantly.

"I'm here to meet with one of your members, Alistair Sinclair," I said, with more confidence than I actually felt. It was a private club—and while flashing my police credentials might have gained me entry, they would not necessarily inspire his cooperation.

"He's expecting you, Mr. . . . ?"

"Simon Ziele."

He ran a pencil down his list of reservations.

"He may have forgotten our plans," I said, forcing a rueful smile, "but I'm sure if you reminded him?"

"Of course, sir," the maître d' said. "Just one moment."

The man disappeared, leaving me standing at the entrance to the large room that was nonetheless intimate: the warmth of plush red carpets and gold-patterned draperies contrasted with the dark lustrous wood that enveloped the room from beamed ceiling to paneled walls. The centerpiece of the room was a large fireplace decorated with intricate wood carvings. The room itself was infused with the smells of alcohol and cigars—the residue of decades of lawyers' traffic.

I had never been to the Lawyers' Club before, despite Alistair's long tenure as a member. Perhaps he thought it was too exclusive for my taste; he and I had our differences in that respect, for Alistair was at ease in diverse parts of New York society in a way I was not.

"The professor is expecting you. Please follow me, sir." The maître d' issued his instructions with a stiff nod.

He ushered me past the large stained-glass window, beyond half a dozen tables of men having hushed conversations, and into a secluded alcove at the back of the room, where Alistair sat with a copy of the *World*, sipping a single-malt scotch.

I took the seat opposite him and ordered a coffee, black, from a waiter who materialized the moment the maître d' left. "It's not like you to follow the yellow papers," I said, observing him carefully. Alistair normally looked to the *New York Times* or the *Tribune* for his news, not the sensationalist *Journal* or *World*. Although none of them would have news of Judge Porter's murder in this afternoon's issue, I was sure. Still, I watched Alistair for any sign that he knew.

There was none. He laughed as he flipped the paper to show me. "For news coverage, never. But the Sunday comics are another matter. Someone left a copy from this past weekend, so I decided to check on this week's yellow kid."

I half smiled, knowing he meant *Hogan's Alley*, one of the *World*'s popular color comic strips—and no doubt one of the few nonacademic topics that captured Alistair's attention.

"If you're here, you must have uncovered something interesting," he said, showing no sign of worry or concern. I was relieved that he did not yet know about the judge's murder—but that feeling was immediately tempered by the realization that now I would be the one to tell him.

For his part, he ordered another single-malt scotch, neat. Then, after pushing aside his paper and a half-eaten serving of baked salmon, his eyes caught my own—and immediately widened with anxiety.

"What is it, Ziele?" he asked, his voice steely but quiet.

"About what time did you finish with Judge Porter last night?" I watched for any hesitation or other sign that he was lying.

But we had come to know each other too well. Something in my voice or manner betrayed me.

"Why do you ask?" Now his voice was laced with ice— though from fear or worry, I did not know.

"I need to know when you last saw him," I repeated.

"Blast it, Ziele!" He pounded his fist on the table, rattling the dishes and silverware. "You might behave like a friend and not a policeman."

Several heads turned toward us.

"Quiet," I said, and my own voice was brittle. "The fact is, I can't tell you more until you answer my question. I need to know where—and when—you last saw Angus Porter."

Alistair's breath caught sharply. "Your question can only mean one thing. My friend is dead. And *this* is how you tell me?"

Now we had the full attention of most surrounding diners. I forced my own voice into a low whisper when I said, "You're not letting me tell you anything—much as I want to. Please—just let me know where and when you left the judge last night."

"He left me," Alistair said without emotion. "We talked until near midnight. Mrs. Mellown was still up, tidying the kitchen. She saw him out, as I'm sure the elevator attendant and man downstairs did." He shook his head. "Now for God's sake—"

I interrupted him as his voice rose again. "Judge Porter was shot in the head last night in room five hundred three of the Breslin Hotel. His hands were bound tightly together, and there was a Bible and a white rose on the nightstand next to his corpse."

Alistair froze. "Damn." The word, loud and anguished, was wrenched from somewhere deep inside of him.

The waiter who resurfaced to bring his scotch and my coffee gave us a worried look. "Please, gentlemen," he reminded us. "Remember our other members this afternoon."

Alistair seemed not to have heard, though he took the glass the waiter offered. The slight trembling of his hand made the caramel liquid slosh, though it did not spill. He raised the glass to his lips and took a large gulp; then just as abruptly, he placed it on the table. All blood drained from his face, and just as I thought he might become ill, he excused himself.

I finished my coffee and waited several anxious minutes for him to return. I had handled it badly—and yet, there was no good way to deliver terrible news like this.

"I'm sorry," I said, more gently, when he returned.

"He was a good man." Alistair wiped his face with his napkin, then took another sip of his scotch.

"What did the two of you talk about last night?" I asked.

His ice-blue eyes seemed fixated on a point in space just behind me. "We talked of Hugo and old times. Nothing more."

"You must have discussed the case," I said, pressing him.

"Not after you left." He took a sip of his drink.

I looked at him sharply. "You mean to tell me that Judge Porter didn't discover anything new? Something that might have led him to confront someone or go somewhere—"

"Of course not," Alistair cut me off roughly.

"How can you be so certain?" I said. "He was murdered within a couple of hours of leaving you, and his crime scene is almost a perfect replica of Judge Jackson's." I leaned in closer. "There has to be a reason why . . ."

"You said he was shot," Alistair said, after a moment of silence, with his head held in his hands. "That his hands were tied. Those are important differences. I've told you time and again," Alistair said, his face growing red, "that killers tend not to vary their methods. Method is *everything*." His voice began to rise again. "Vidocq was correct when he showed us that every criminal has a certain behavioral pattern—or style—that remains consistent throughout every crime he commits."

I leaned back in my chair and looked at him askance. "Exactly. That's the difficulty here. Nothing about the crime scene matches up. Except that when I see a white rose and a Bible in the room of a dead man, I see something too remarkable to be a coincidence."

Alistair shook his head. "The gun is a very different weapon from the knife. It takes one kind of personality to hold one's victim close while slicing his throat. A gun appeals to another sort of person entirely: it requires less strength, only the ability to shoot straight."

I shot him a look of disbelief. "You, of all people, can't be telling me you don't believe these murders are linked. Angus Porter was Hugo Jackson's friend and colleague—not to mention the fact that he was advising us on this case. If you are suggesting that there are two separate killers at work, then the only argument that makes sense is that those two killers were motivated by the same cause and they endeavored to deliver the same message."

"You mean, two different anarchists?"

"It would explain the difference in weapon. I'll grant you that. And the fact that Judge Porter counseled Judge Jackson on Drayson would account for his being targeted. But the coincidence is still too much."

"Was there music?" Alistair asked, a worried expression crossing his brow.

"You mean at the crime scene?"

He nodded.

"I don't know."

"I let him keep the composition we found among Judge Jackson's papers," Alistair said glumly.

"No matter. You kept copies, I assume."

Alistair nodded. "Made them myself, by hand."

"The more important question is: Why did Judge Porter go to the Breslin after leaving you?"

"Again, I don't know." Alistair's voice was dull.

"Was there a lead there he hoped to track down? Or—I know nothing of his personal life—could he have been meeting someone?" I asked, trying to put it delicately.

"Angus was a confirmed bachelor," Alistair replied. "His own living quarters are on lower Fifth Avenue. Had he wanted to meet anyone at home, only his housekeeper would have objected. He didn't need to go to a hotel in the middle of the night."

"Yet, last night he did—right after leaving your home. He was registered under the name Leroy Sanders and listed his home address as Three Gramercy Park West."

"I don't understand," Alistair said.

"I suspect that either Judge Porter's killer or a co-conspirator posed as the judge at the registration desk. Judge Porter was later invited upstairs and killed—at which point his murder was called in to the commissioner's office, possibly by the killer himself. You see, the hotel staff would have identified him as Mr. Sanders."

"It must have been a trap. I'm only surprised because Angus was being careful."

"Stranger things have happened, Alistair," I said, "and we often know less of our friends' personal lives and secrets than we might think. But I believe that you know more about Angus Porter than you're telling me."

"I don't like your tone—or what you're implying." Now Alistair was almost shouting, and the movement of his arm overturned my half-drunk cup of coffee.

Our waiter hustled over to clean the spill, quickly joined by the maître d'. The latter spoke up. "Perhaps now that you gentlemen have finished, you might take your discussion outside. I'll put the bill on your account, Professor." When Alistair gave him a blank stare, he added, "The other diners are taking too much of an interest in your confidential conversation. I'm sure you understand—and would appreciate having greater privacy elsewhere."

I had been facing the rear of the room, looking into the kitchen, but now I turned and saw: every pair of eyes in the room was fixed on us, in rapt attention.

Alistair apparently noticed, too, for he rose, mumbled an apology, and staggered out of the room—leaving me to step awkwardly behind him, trying to catch up as all eyes followed me.

We rode the elevator to the lobby in silence, not trusting ourselves in front of the attendant.

Outside, we began walking south on Broadway, fighting against the crowds that swarmed around us. Alistair turned to me, and for the first time I thought I saw something that almost resembled fear in his eyes.

"I've got to get home," he said.

"We've got to get out of these crowds," I replied and, taking his arm, ushered him toward Trinity Church. I pulled him off the street and onto the quiet of the church grounds, finding a wooden bench under a sycamore tree, where I forced Alistair to sit.

The wind whipped above us, shearing the tree of its remaining leaves, and whistling around the belfry as the bells began to chime a hymn. Still, we took a moment to collect ourselves in the relative peace of the grounds—where a few yards over in quiet graves the dead slept amid the crowds and noise on the surrounding streets.

I spoke again. "I know you've lost two friends this week. And I know you usually prefer to share only the information you think is relevant to a particular case. But it's important for you to tell me *everything* here—whether you think it pertains or not."

Alistair was indignant at the suggestion. "I'm not hiding things from you, Ziele."

"Then you'll tell me more about your evening with Judge Porter."

He spread his hands wide. "There's nothing to tell. We drank, we talked." He shrugged. "Nothing more."

"Alistair," I said, more insistently this time, "less than two hours after leaving your home, Angus Porter ended up in a hotel room, shot to death. There is a reason for that. And if your conversation with him in the hours before his death doesn't hold the key—well, then I don't know what does."

"I am not Angus's keeper," Alistair said, his voice rising again. "I haven't socialized with him in years. I don't know what he did when he left me. I *assumed* that he went home."

"Then help me figure out what might have happened to intervene. Was he worried about anything? Did he have an idea on the case that he wanted to explore? Was there someone he wanted to confront?"

Alistair remained silent—and so we sat for some moments, facing one another, braced against the ever-growing wind.

"When someone is killed," I said, "there's usually a pivotal decision point. Something happens to make the killer decide that his victim must die now—not tomorrow, not next week or next year."

Alistair looked at me, his eyes clouded. "I don't know why Judge Porter was targeted last night after leaving me. I can't figure it out myself."

"That's why you need my help," I said, almost cajoling him now. "Tell me more about Leroy."

"I don't know," he said, spreading his hands wide. "I promise I'll search for his name in the legal archives."

"Did Judge Porter know the name 'Leroy Sanders'?"

"Of course not."

"I'm not sure I believe that," I said, looking into the bleak gray sky above. I chose my words carefully. "I think that both you and Judge Porter had your suspicions. And they were near enough to the truth that the judge was killed because of them."

"Don't be ridiculous," Alistair said, scoffing at my suggestion.

But by now, my own frustration was rising. "Look, Alistair— you brought me into this case. I'd never have been assigned to it otherwise; it wasn't within Mulvaney's jurisdiction, and I've no political connections of my own. But I'm in the thick of it now— and thanks to the commissioner's involvement, my very career is at stake. Meanwhile, two of your friends have been killed. You have to understand"—my voice broke slightly—"you *must* understand that only by sharing everything that you know with me, without reserve, will we be able to solve this."

Alistair only looked at me, his eyes unreadable. "You ask too much, Ziele."

"I ask no more than what you owe me." I stood, and when

I replied, my voice was bitter. "Sometimes, Alistair, I regret ever getting to know you."

I walked away, not once looking back, as the wind whipped through the trees and the bells of Trinity Church tolled their last chime of the hour.

CHAPTER 12

After an afternoon spent pursuing fruitless leads, I checked in at Mulberry Street headquarters, where scores of anarchist sympathizers were being interviewed. Mr. Strupp had left a message for me: Jonathan would meet me that night. Alone. While that meant no fellow policemen were welcome, I knew that I was on my own in other respects as well.

I walked the few short blocks to the Spring Street station, my resolve hardening with each step. For all the evidence we'd uncovered, I was missing something important: some crucial fact that would crack the case open. And despite his protestations, I believed that Alistair held the key to the solution. But whether because of grief for friends lost—or by virtue of simply being too close to the case—I could not convince him to cooperate with me. He had brought me into this case; now I'd have to finish it without him.

By the time I descended the stairs to the subway platform, my frustrations with Alistair were replaced by simple determination. I stood amid dozens of fellow passengers until a slight rumble and brilliant beam of light announced the next train. I entered, then watched as the guard threw the lever on the platform, which closed the doors and sent us rumbling uptown. Not fifteen minutes later, I reached my stop—Seventy-second and Broadway. I should have headed home, a block south of the station, but I found myself turning toward the Dakota.

The attendant downstairs, who knew me well by now, motioned for me to go up.

I shook my head instead. "Would you send a message to Mrs. Sinclair?" I briefly penned a note asking if she was free to come down—and waited while the young boy who ran such errands within the building took it up to her.

I paced back and forth between the two gaslight lamps at the building's entrance, uncomfortably aware that my desire to see Isabella tonight was not a wish but a need. There was no one else I could talk to about Alistair. No one else who could possibly understand.

To my immense relief, she came downstairs within minutes.

Her face filled with concern, she asked, "Simon, is everything all right?"

"If you're hungry, we could talk over dinner," I said, forcing a half-smile. I'd not been able to think of food since this morning's crime scene, but my pounding headache was a reminder that I should eat.

"How about Ma Pickett's?" She took my arm and we began to walk west toward Broadway.

The popular restaurant she'd just named was one of my favorites, but it would be too loud tonight. It was located in San Juan Hill, the area south of West Sixty-seventh Street that formed the largest African neighborhood in Manhattan, where most restaurants offered entertainment in addition to food. Ma Pickett's also had a small dance floor, and when the band played the new ragtime music that was popular among the San Juan Hill restaurants, the crowd's noise was nothing short of deafening.

So, I replied, "I need quiet so we can talk. How about—" I said.

"Not Shi Ling's," she interrupted, wrinkling her nose. I knew she disliked the Chinese restaurant near Fifty-ninth and Columbus Avenue, which did not allow Africans inside their dining room. Not unusual in this city, to be sure—but in San Juan Hill, it was an especially poor choice.

"Definitely not. I was thinking of Beau's." Beau's was a small café just off Sixty-sixth that served Caribbean food. Its small size—only eight tables—would mean there would be relative quiet, but there would still be a ragtime player at the piano to ensure that our conversation remained private. Not that I was overly concerned. In San Juan Hill, where African and Irish residents coexisted uneasily in derelict tenements, and ordinary laborers clashed with gang members and drug dealers, my true concern was in finding a restaurant shielded from the tense confrontations typically found in the rowdier establishments.

Isabella agreed with a smile—and we walked the few, short blocks making small talk, before eventually settling in at a table near the window. We ordered codfish and plantains, rice and peas, all the while listening to a piano man playing the syncopated rhythm of "The Black Cat Rag."

"You wanted to talk," she said, once we had settled in comfortably.

"I'm not sure what to do about Alistair," I admitted rather bluntly. I then set about briefing her on the day's events. With each new fact, Isabella's eyes got wider and wider, as she tried to absorb the shocking news of Judge Porter's murder and my subsequent conversation with Alistair. Summing up, I said, "I'm convinced there's something he's not telling me—though I can't say whether that's because he doesn't see it or simply because he doesn't see it as relevant to the investigation. If he would only talk . . ."

"You know," she reminded me gently, "usually he's in your position when he analyzes a crime: outside looking in, with scientific objectivity. This time, it's his friends who have become victims. And he *did* consider them both friends; Judge Jackson's death affected him deeply."

"Though he claimed that he no longer had close ties with either man," I said, thinking aloud.

Our plantain appetizer arrived, though I only picked at it. I had no appetite tonight, though the hot Jamaican coffee was a godsend. Just one cup took the sharp edge off my mood and alleviated the headache I'd battled all day.

"It's more than his personal grief," I said, suddenly convinced. "He's hiding something; I'm just not sure what."

She considered this for a moment. "Then you've no choice but to proceed without him. For his sake, as well as the success of your own investigation. What do your instincts tell you about this case?"

"It's possible that we're dealing with the work of more than one man," I said, explaining how the different murder weapons likely pointed to multiple killers. I finished explaining as our main courses arrived, saying, "The presence of the Bible and the white rose tells me there is a link—a similarity in message and motive—that supersedes those differences."

Isabella looked at me thoughtfully. "We talked about how Judge Jackson was likely killed for violating some kind of oath, as signified by his hand on top of the Bible. Judge Porter was also a member of the judiciary, but his killer didn't position him the same way. Tell me again what he looked like?"

In my mind's eye I still saw him. And as I began to describe how Judge Porter had lain naked, the answer suddenly came to me—almost too simple to be believed.

"Judge Porter was killed—literally—because his hands were tied. From the murderer's point of view, this judge's crime was one of omission." I watched for Isabella's reaction, aware that I also yearned to test my theory with Alistair, whose knowledge about crime-scene behavior was unparalleled.

"You know, Simon, I think you may be right," Isabella replied, after giving my statement careful consideration. "Was there music at the crime scene?"

It was the same question Alistair had asked.

After I assured her there was not—at least, not that Mulvaney and I had seen—she said, "Then perhaps there is something at his home. I'm wondering if there's another reference to 'Leroy avenged.'"

"And even if there's not," I added, "I forgot to mention that there's already a reference to Leroy at the crime scene. Whoever registered for the room in which Judge Porter was murdered signed in as 'Leroy Sanders.' "

Unconsciously, she reached for the strand of hair behind her ear and began to twirl it. "Did the clerk remember anything about who checked in?"

"Other officers were still questioning the night clerk when I left," I said. "I'll find out once I review the report in the morning."

"Meanwhile, why don't I visit the Jackson and Porter families tomorrow," Isabella said. Upon seeing my deep breath of protest, she added, "It will be a simple condolence call, as would be expected since Alistair was acquainted with both families. And my goal will be to figure out whether a man named Leroy Sanders means anything to either family."

I nodded. "I only worry about the danger to you—especially now that someone so close to the investigation has been killed."

In typical fashion, she brushed aside my concern. "Judge Porter wasn't killed because he was involved in the investigation," she said with conviction. "He and Judge Jackson were longtime colleagues. There must be some other connection."

"You're thinking of Leroy."

She nodded.

"Still, please be very careful. Although while you're there, perhaps you could try to find out whether Alistair may have had closer connections with Hugo Jackson and Angus Porter than he has intimated."

She almost said something, then hesitated.

"It's for his own good," I said. "I'm worried about him—but without understanding the true extent of his involvement in whatever I'm investigating, I can't help him."

I would have said more, but Lena, the owner and cook at Beau's, came over to our table. Tall, strikingly angular, and dressed head to toe in a vibrant yellow dress that reflected the fashion of her native Jamaica rather than of New York, she frowned the moment she saw my plate. "Don't you like my cookin' tonight, Simon?"

"Wonderful as always," I assured her. "It's my work, not the food."

"Hmph. You can't live on coffee alone—though if you could, I guess you'd do it," she said with a laugh. Then she turned to Isabella. "And where's your father-in-law tonight? It's usually the three of you."

Isabella gave a sad smile. "He's paying a condolence call."

For all we knew, it was the truth.

"Well," Lena said, giving us a wide smile in return, "tell him no excuses next time." And turning her attention to the next table, she motioned for the piano player to end his break, and soon the sounds of the "Maple Leaf Rag" filled the room.

Out of guilt, I ordered Lena's dessert special, a sweet potato pudding—and we sat in comfortable silence while listening to the music.

Glancing over at the other diners, I saw a familiar face: that of Mrs. Jackson's housemaid, Marie, enjoying an evening off. She and her companion—a large man with a wide, infectious smile— were sitting and laughing, appreciating the music. In what was probably her best dress, gazing with obvious affection at the man beside her, Marie was the picture of happiness. And I found my- self envying the close camaraderie that was evident between them.

Finally Isabella spoke again. "Are you going home now, Simon?"

I pulled my pocket watch out to check the time. Still an hour before I planned to visit the beer-hall meeting that Mr. Strupp had told me Jonathan would attend. "Not tonight," I said, clearing my throat. "I'm headed to an anarchist meeting, in hopes of learning something to help with the investigation and appease the General."

"Let me help you," she said earnestly. "I can pretend to be your assistant. And two sets of eyes are better than one."

I shook my head. "Not only are you far too well dressed, but I'm also meeting Jonathan there." I paused awkwardly, knowing she would recall the name of Hannah's brother.

"But you're going undercover, aren't you?" she asked. And upon seeing my look of confusion, she added, "I mean, you're not walking into an anarchist meeting and announcing yourself as a policeman."

"As I'd prefer not to be strung up by a mob tonight, no."

"Then I can help you to establish your cover," she said, raising her chin. "I want to be a full partner with you in this case, Simon. And don't even try to say you don't need me—especially without Alistair."

I realized there was going to be no help for it; she'd already determined to accompany me.

"Then we'd better get you home so you can change into your oldest, least fashionable dress," I said, keeping my voice light. "And even then . . ."

"I'll be fine, Simon," she said with a smile.

I managed to return a weak smile. We walked the few, short blocks uptown, my mind filled with just one thought: I was treading through dangerous territory, indeed.

CHAPTER 13

Charles Ehrhardt's Beer Hall,
405 West Thirty-fifth Street. 8 P.M.

The fetid stench of Ehrhardt's Beer Hall was nearly over-whelming: the smell of alcohol mixing with sweaty, unwashed bodies. The room was sweltering; there were simply too many people packed into too small a space. It didn't help that the windows were closed tight, covered with black ticking, so as not to attract the attention of the police—a naïve practice, for even in my precinct house, we received regular notification of when and where workers' meetings were being held. Rather than break up these meetings, as had once been our practice, the police had learned it was more productive to infiltrate them and obtain valuable information. At least, that was our practice so long as there was no fugitive anarchist in attendance, whose arrest would be a real coup.

Two men blocked the door to the beer hall, more interested

in their own conversation than in those entering the hall—though their job was to screen out uninvited attendees, like Isabella and myself.

"I agree with you on everythin' but the violence, Savvas," said a thin man with a scraggly red beard, shaking his head. "If you listen to Emma Goldman herself, she never talks about killing nobody."

"But how else is revolution going to come about? The capitalist scum don't care if we're cold and hungry. They fire us if we get sick. They're never going to give us better pay and working conditions out of the goodness of their hearts." Savvas, a short burly man with thick, curly black hair, beat his chest with emotion. "Not in our lifetime, Joe. We've got to force them."

"But now we got the union to force them," Joe said stubbornly. "The IWW. That gives us real power."

I tried to edge my way into the room past the two of them, protectively shielding Isabella with my body. Even in this environment, her touch electrified my injured right arm—a particularly odd sensation, given that I was unused to any feeling there other than pain.

Savvas blocked our way, so we stood awkwardly outside, under a poster advertising the IWW. It showed a man who stood tall, arms crossed, in front of a city skyline. A slogan underneath him read FIGHT WAGE SLAVERY.

"What is the IWW?" Isabella whispered.

"It stands for Industrial Workers of the World," I answered, quietly explaining that it was a new union founded by anarchists together with syndicalists and trade unionists. "Its leaders believe that it's large and well organized enough that it can succeed where other labor movements have failed. But its size also means that it's made up of members who disagree with each other about nearly everything."

She nodded.

The black-haired man was now speaking in mocking tones. "Did you see the latest issue of *The Liberator*? Filled with articles about women's needs. They *need* the right to divorce, they *need* access to birth control. Well, what about my rights and needs?"

The other man shrugged. "That's just because Lucy Parsons is the new editor. It don't mean the IWW ain't doin' grand things for us workers."

Savvas suddenly caught sight of Isabella. "What do you think about Lucy Parsons, miss? You think she's looking out for your needs?"

Isabella blushed a deep red. "I don't know Lucy Parsons, I'm afraid."

I waited a moment to see their reaction, almost afraid to breathe. Isabella looked the part for tonight, having exchanged her fine silk dress for a worn and tired black muslin. But she could not easily camouflage the well-modulated, educated tones of her voice.

Their focus turned to me.

"Haven't seen you around before, either." Savvas narrowed his eyes.

"Jonathan Strupp invited me," I said quietly.

"Yeah?" He raised a suspicious eyebrow before calling out to a burly man standing behind him. "Lukas, is Johnny here yet?"

"He's running late. Why—you worried this one isn't a true comrade?"

I felt a moment's flash of fear. What if I was revealed here as a police detective? Isabella would be endangered, as well. I'd counted on my past history with Jonathan to protect me. But—now that I observed the belligerent faces surrounding me—I realized that I may have underestimated the extent to which Jonathan's anger had changed him.

"Maybe." Savvas ran a hand through curly black hair, then stared at me curiously. "How do you know Johnny?"

"I was engaged to his sister."

His suspicious eyes came to rest on Isabella. "Then who—"

But he stopped mid-sentence, his eyes catching a signal from someone just behind me.

I turned to find a man standing there. He was a tall but slightly built man with well-defined Eastern European features: high cheekbones, dark blond hair, and a chiseled nose and chin. The way a shock of straight hair fell over his left eye—itself covered with a black patch—gave him a rakish look. But what was most striking was the quiet authority he exuded, though he had yet to say a word.

He stared at me a moment before he finally spoke in soft but clipped tones. "Johnny has told me about you. You are Simon." He took a step closer. "The Simon who would have been his brother, but for the filthy capitalists who mismanaged the *General Slocum*."

He held out a hand to me. I pretended not to notice that the last two fingers were missing.

His mouth twisted into something resembling a smile. "A necessary sacrifice to the cause, suffered while instructing a student in the art of bomb-making." Then he added, "And I'm sorry for your loss—one for which there's still been no justice."

"Only for Captain Van Schaick," I said. "If you consider ten years' time for criminal negligence to be justice. And that's assuming he ever serves a day of it." The captain whose fateful decisions had doomed over a thousand of the 1,300-something passengers that day had been convicted in court this January, but he remained free on $10,000 bail.

The blond man shook his head. "I wouldn't hold your breath. Judge Thomas is a tool of the capitalist system. And the officers and directors of the Knickerbocker Steamship Company—who so prized their profits that they wouldn't invest in the most simple of safety measures—will never see their day in court. What can you expect? The whole system is corrupt."

I knew I was being manipulated—and yet I almost couldn't resist agreeing with him, at least where the *Slocum* disaster was concerned. Was this how it had been for Jonathan? I wondered. For the first time, I understood how easy it might be to become seduced by the anarchists—surrounded by those who under-stood what it was to know unfairness, and who yearned for justice and a better life. It was their methods I took issue with, not their ideals.

"My name is Paul Hlad. And, comrade or not, I'm glad you are here tonight. Come—I'll take you both to Jonathan." He motioned for Isabella and me to follow him.

We made our way past men and women with their arms raised to cheer the speaker, who had just stepped in front of the podium. I caught sight of Mei Lin on stage behind him, clapping. I even saw my old schoolmate Samuel Lyzke. But there was no sign of Jonathan—not yet.

I held Isabella's hand tight so as not to lose her, glancing now and then at the railway worker who spoke of better wages and shorter workdays as the crowd cheered.

"The railroads are controlled by men like Jay Gould and

Cornelius Vanderbilt," the speaker said to gasps of disgust and mutterings of "dirty capitalists."

"Do you think they care if we have enough to eat? Or if we have a decent place to live?" the speaker asked, pounding on the podium.

"No," the crowd shouted back.

"Do they care if our children work all day in a factory when they should be in school?"

"Damn, no." Their second response was even louder.

He continued to talk, riling everyone in the room into a frenzy. But I heard no more, for we had approached what looked to be a concrete wall at the back of the room. I watched in amazement as Paul Hlad picked up a foot-long length of wire, inserted it through one of the cracks, and the wall magically opened.

We followed Paul inside to a smaller room. "How does that work?" I asked, surveying the large hinges on either side of the wall.

He shrugged. "Precision hinges. And a door faced with concrete slab."

"You always did have to know everything, didn't you, Simon?"

I turned sharply, for I had thought the room was empty. Was there another secret entrance to the back? Or had I somehow missed him?

Whatever the answer, I now found myself facing Jonathan Strupp for the first time in two years. His shock of auburn hair was a mirror image of Hannah's—but there, any resemblance between the two ended. Hannah had been happy, always ready with a smile. But Jonathan's face was pinched with anger, and his eyes glared at me from behind wire-rimmed glasses. He had become thinner; his clothes fit his slight frame so loosely that he appeared even younger than his twenty-three years.

"I'll leave you to your conversation," Paul said with a nod before he disappeared once more behind the mock concrete wall.

"Who is she?" Jonathan stared at Isabella. "My sister's replacement?"

Isabella took his rudeness in stride. "You may call me Mrs. Sinclair. Together with my father-in-law, I'm assisting Simon with an investigation."

"You're married?" He raised a skeptical eyebrow.

"Widowed." Her answer was soft.

"Perhaps we should sit," I said, gesturing to the table and chairs at the center of the room.

But Jonathan shook his head. "I've no need to sit. I've nothing to say to you. This meeting is merely to appease my father." His words were punctuated, almost staccato.

I took a seat, indicating for Isabella to do the same. I forced myself into a relaxed position, though I actually felt anything but. It was a strategy I'd developed for this type of situation—the more difficult the interview, the more I needed to appear at ease and in control. More often than not, it led to people divulging more information than they intended. "Your father worries about you," I said. "You might stop by more often to see him and your mother."

His laugh was harsh, guttural. "You're one to talk, Simon. You haven't stopped by in two years."

"I'm not their son," I said. But his words had hit their mark.

"You might have been."

"And now you have a daughter—a beautiful one with eyes just like Hannah's."

"Yes. My parents care for her better than I could ever hope to."

"Even though she's *your* daughter. *Your* responsibility," I said.

Angry eyes flashed at me. "My responsibilities are here. She's better off with them. She fills the void that Hannah left behind."

"I doubt that," I said. "What responsibilities do you have that are more important than your daughter?"

He said nothing, glowering at me.

"You also must have obligations to her mother. Who is she?"

"She is nothing to you. I warn you: do not get involved."

"Without a mother, all the more reason why your daughter needs you," I said, keeping a calm tone. "I, for one, know first-hand what happens to families without a father."

His face hardened. "That's because your father was a drunk and a gambler who thought only of himself. Except for the fact that you had to leave your scholarship at Columbia when he took off, you were better off without him. All of you."

Without warning, he took the seat beside us, shoving it with so much fervor I thought it would break. "My responsibility is only to make a better world for my daughter," he said. "One where she will not be forced to work in some rich lady's house, answering doors or scrubbing floors. One where she can work for fair wages and good hours. Where she will live in a good home. And her children will attend school and learn."

"As you once wanted to do." I released a deep breath. "What's happened to you, Jonathan? You've given up everything you once dreamed of—and for what?" I gestured to the room next door. "These people understand our society's problems, but they don't have the answers."

"You're right; they don't," he said, quieter now. "They think a few pennies more an hour will make things better. It won't. They talk till they're blue in the face and think politicians and journalists will listen. And they never will." He pounded the table with his fist. "So much talk. For what? Nothing's ever accomplished."

"So why are you here?"

"Because a select group of us believe in turning all this talk into action. We want to be free—though we'll never achieve that till all our oppressors are defeated and the capitalist lie is revealed for what it is."

"But who are your oppressors?" Isabella interrupted. "Besides employers who don't pay a living wage or provide decent working conditions?"

He made a brittle noise. "Our entire society is made up of systems that oppress us. Our religions force women into slavery through marriage. Our governments give the robber barons carte blanche to deny the workers of the world the most basic of human rights. Only by overthrowing it all can we start anew."

"When did you decide this, Jonathan?" I asked. "You had the makings of a great scientist. You used to think that scientific advancements would revolutionize the world."

"Science is no help when the working people can't make a living wage."

"That's not true," I replied. "Especially in medicine, we see science accomplishing great things for everyone, the working class included. I know you've been in a dark place since Hannah died. And men like Paul Hlad do you no service by involving you in things that are over your head."

His eyes flashed with anger. "I'm not in over my head. I hold a position of authority in this organization. Men answer to *me*."

I kept my voice even when I replied. "I don't care who answers to you. If you're involved with people who advocate killing and violence, then you're in over your head."

He returned my gaze with a belligerent stare.

"Did you have anything to do with Judge Jackson's murder?"

He was silent.

When I asked again, I was practically begging him. "Just tell me it wasn't you, Johnny. Hlad or Joe or Savvas, fine. But not you."

He gave me only a cold stare. "I have nothing to say to you. Please leave."

"Listen to me. The murder of Judge Jackson is the highest profile case I've ever seen. The commissioner is running this one himself and the public wants a scapegoat. They crave revenge. Whoever it is—or if it's friends of yours you want to protect— you need my help."

Jonathan stood, leaning on the table with a hostile expression. "You need to leave now, Simon. I have nothing to say to you. I never will."

"You're destroying your family," I said. "Your parents—and the daughter who needs you."

With a final, malevolent stare, he walked across the room and opened the concrete-plated wall. "Leave. Now."

I took Isabella's arm as we got up. And before we passed through the door, I turned to him one last time. "Hannah wouldn't have wanted this, Jonathan. She expected something different from you."

With a pointed glance at Isabella, he said, "I'd say she expected different from you, as well."

His face was pinched tight as he closed the door and followed us for a few moments before he disappeared into the crowded room. The speaker had finished, but most of the audience remained behind—drinking and talking.

"We may as well get out of here," I said loudly into Isabella's ear as I ushered her toward the door. Clearly I could expect no favors from Jonathan—which led me to feel decidedly less than comfortable here. And even worse, any hope I'd held that Jonathan was innocent of anarchist violence was now dashed. How was I to tell the Strupps that their only son might well be guilty of murder?

Thirty-fifth Street—at least this far west—was quiet with no one in sight. I pushed Isabella to walk faster, explaining, "I'll feel safer when we reach Broadway."

She shot me a puzzled look. "You don't think we're in danger, surely."

"I don't trust Jonathan" was all I said.

"They weren't what I expected," she said, shaking her head. "Paul Hlad especially. I'd not expected him to be so articulate."

"Don't tell me you believe everything you read in the papers: that all anarchists are crazy, dynamite-throwing immigrants?"

"Of course not. But I didn't expect them to sound quite so rational, either."

"Their arguments are solid," I said, quickening my pace. "Much of their talk is hopelessly idealistic, but it's rational."

I glanced behind us and saw three men in the distance. Had they come from the beer hall? I was uncertain but wanted to take no chances.

"Can you walk faster?" I asked Isabella. "We need to reach

Broadway, where we'll have more company on the streets and can find a hansom cab."

Another glance showed the men gaining on us. A look to the street showed no motor cars. I'd hire a cab if I could find one this time of night.

"I need you to hurry," I whispered to Isabella. We could now hear footsteps behind us.

Another backward glance.

They were now running, on the verge of catching up to us. If we split up, at least Isabella would be safe.

I could see the lights of Broadway just ahead. "They want me, not you," I said forcefully. "Keep going without me. Ask for help once you reach Broadway."

She gave me a panicked look. "Simon—I—"

"You can do it," I reassured her. "Get help right away. Find a night watchman. Or a hotel—anyone who has telephone service to call the precinct house."

As she ran ahead, I crossed the street, nearly tripping over a pile of muck in the middle of the road. She would be fine, I told myself.

The three men crossed, as well. Was one of them Savvas, the large Russian I'd encountered at the front door?

Bracing myself for a fight, I raced forward—but it was only moments until a violent thud felled me onto the sidewalk.

"We don't like pigs stickin' their nose in our business," a throaty voice growled.

Savvas.

I rolled over and kicked up. I hit him hard in the groin with every ounce of my strength; then he was on the ground, too. Another swift kick to his head and he didn't move.

But his companion, a stocky blond man I didn't recognize from the beer hall, came at me with a bully stick that I barely avoided.

I was outnumbered. Still, I was not an easy target. With a youth spent on the dangerous streets of the Lower East Side, I was no stranger to brawls and gang violence. I quickly took stock of the two remaining men. In addition to the man with the bully stick, there was a swarthy man who did not appear to be holding a weapon. Good. I had left my gun at the precinct, worried that I would be searched entering the beer hall.

Without warning, I dove at the knees of the blond man, knocking him off balance. As he fell to one knee, I chopped him to the throat with my good left arm. The man and his bully stick fell to the ground. Grabbing the weapon, I turned to the swarthy man.

"Who sent you?" I demanded. "Jonathan Strupp?"

The sole response was a grunt and a stream of spit sent to the street.

Realizing that I was not going to talk my way out of this predicament, I advanced cautiously, brandishing the stick.

But my advantage was short-lived. Savvas must have recovered from my initial attack. It was no use, I thought, as he sucker-punched me to the side of the head. The swarthy man then jumped on top of me. His breath was sour and stank of chewing tobacco as he held me down.

I thrashed, trying to knock him to the side. But out of nowhere came a thud to my head—and as white flashes danced in front of my eyes, all faded to blackness.

"Simon. Simon!"

I was vaguely conscious of Isabella's voice calling my name, each time more insistently. But when I opened my mouth to speak, no sound came. And though I tried to open my eyes, I could not.

"He's going to be all right. It looks worse than it is."

That was Mulvaney's Irish brogue, comforting Isabella. She was all right, then.

I felt her hand softly touching my cheek and the sensation of other hands lifting me, before I once again descended into a darkness that was a release from all pain and worry.

Thursday
October 25, 1906

CHAPTER 14

Fifty-seventh Street and Ninth Avenue, Hell's Kitchen. 9 A.M.

It was Bridget Mulvaney's voice that called to me, permeating the fog of my heavy slumber the next morning.

"I've got ham and eggs waiting on the table. You'd best get up before they're cold," she said tartly. "You'll find clean clothes on the chair. They belong to Declan's brother. He's much bigger than you, but I daresay they won't fall off."

I sat up slowly and tried to open my eyes, but heavy, swollen lids prevented me from managing more than the tiniest slit. I was disoriented and sore; the slightest movement sent fresh darts of pain throughout my body.

"Here." She placed an offering on the bed: a small brown towel holding a block of ice that I applied with relief to my eyes.

I managed to mutter a few words of thanks, but she brushed them off in typical style. "'Tis nothing. Mrs. Hart got an ice delivery this morning that she was happy to share. Her youngest, Annie, got married last month—and now it's just herself living downstairs."

After she left, I managed to get dressed. There was no mirror in the makeshift guest room where the Mulvaneys had put me—a corner of their main living area where they'd placed a mattress and hung faded red and white checkered curtains for privacy. But I knew what sort of shape my face was in.

I made my way to the round pine table off the kitchen where the Mulvaneys regularly ate.

Mulvaney was sitting down already, waiting. "Good night's sleep, Ziele? It should've been. The doctor gave you a heavy dose of chloral hydrate." He grinned. "Knockout drops."

"That explains how hard it was to wake up this morning," I said ruefully. It also explained my fuzzy head; my thoughts were slow to form and process.

I took the seat opposite Mulvaney. "How did I get here last night? I don't remember much."

In fact, I hardly remembered anything at all after my attackers caught up with me.

"Your professor's daughter-in-law ran straight for the precinct house after she left you. I was still there, working." He raised an eyebrow. "You gave her quite a scare; she thought you were going to be killed. So we sent a couple of young guys to scare off the thugs. Then I arrived with Tim Gallagher to take care of you."

He pushed a cup of coffee toward me. "I made it strong."

I took an immediate gulp; the heat and the familiar flavor provided both comfort and relief this morning.

"Of course," he said with a grin, "I also gave the order to break up that worker's movement meeting you attended. And since Isabella couldn't identify which men attacked you, we've got at least thirty anarchists holed up in a jail cell until you're well enough to make it downtown to formally identify your attackers and press charges."

"Is Jonathan among them?" I asked.

More soberly, Mulvaney nodded. "A damned shame, isn't it?"

"We can't be sure—" I started to say, but he held up his hand.

"Don't say it." He looked at me hard. "I asked Isabella to identify the man you'd spoken with earlier. She described how angry he was—and we believe that he is same man who ordered this attack. You show a lot more consideration for him than he has for you."

But I couldn't believe that Jonathan was responsible. It could just as easily have been Hlad or Savvas. Besides, it wasn't Jonathan that I worried about. It was his family.

"We'll ask you to identify the others later today. No rush, of course."

"No rush" meant that Mulvaney intended for all of them to spend the maximum amount of time possible in a holding cell before being released.

"Seriously, how are you feeling?" he asked with a sharp look. Either my appearance—or my black mood—had given him cause for new concern.

"I'll be fine." I shrugged. "Sometimes I think the commissioner is right: there's nobody but scum of one sort or another in this city. Everyone's out for themselves; those who get in their way be damned."

Mulvaney's face tightened. "It's not just here; it's everywhere, Ziele. And with a job like ours, we see the worst of human nature, don't we? Between the greed and the complete disregard for life . . ." He was quiet for a moment, then continued talking. "Last night I was still at my desk because a Black Hand operative was arrested. He was caught in the act—just about to light the fuse of his bomb in a tenement hallway."

"So he planned to destroy the tenement because the building owner wouldn't pay protection money?" I asked, shaking my head. "Never mind the cost to innocent lives."

"With them, it's always about the money—and keeping up the reputation of the Black Hand," Mulvaney said.

I pushed my plate aside; I had no appetite this morning. "The anarchists claim they're motivated by moral ideals. But I wonder: if they got what they wanted, would they turn out to be as corrupt and greedy and addicted to power as the men they want to destroy?"

"There's not much place for honor and decency in this city, Ziele." Mulvaney looked at me with sad eyes. "We only do the best we can—especially for those that deserve it. It's the only reason I can still work murder cases after all these years."

"Speaking of which, did you attend Judge Porter's autopsy last night?" I asked.

"Yes. Death by gunshot wound—pretty straightforward. But don't worry," he said, eyes gleaming, "we've still got one solid lead to investigate."

He reached into his pocket, pulled out his white cotton handkerchief, and placed it before me on the table.

I unwrapped it slowly to reveal the shiny gold object inside. "It's a bullet. The same one we found in the hotel yesterday?"

"It is. And Dr. Jennings has confirmed it's the bullet responsible for killing Judge Porter." He gave me a curious look as he passed me another handkerchief bundle. "Now, tell me if you think it's a match with this one. Use the magnifying glass." He gestured to a silver-rimmed glass on my left.

Through bleary eyes, I did my best to compare the two small brass .32-caliber bullets, focusing on the number of lands and grooves. There were distinctive marks on each that appeared similar, at least to my untrained eye.

"They look alike. Where did you get the second bullet?" I asked.

"Yesterday I visited Funke, the gun seller."

"And he just happened to have a spare bullet on hand that matches our murder weapon?"

"Even better," Mulvaney said with a self-satisfied grin. "He happens to have the murder weapon itself."

I was incredulous. "You can't be serious."

"Couldn't be more so. The killer—or someone helping him— returned it yesterday, claiming it was defective."

I could only stare at him.

"Finish your breakfast," he said. "We'll head down to Chambers Street so you can hear for yourself."

A. H. Funke's gun shop at 53 Chambers Street had proven indispensable to us time and again. There, Funke and his right-hand man, Sullivan, sold and repaired all manner of guns. Rumor had it that we paid dearly each month to keep them on retainer as police informants. But if their information wasn't cheap, it was at least good: the result of the fine line they walked between the legitimate firearm trade—and that which was decidedly less so.

The shop was small, with all manner of guns from rifles and pistols to shotguns hanging from its walls and ceiling. The smell of gun polish and cleaner was overwhelming as we walked in the door and were greeted by Sully's broad smile.

"Simon Ziele—glad you're back. It's been a dog's age, hasn't it? You ought to come around more often. I could've supplied you with something that might've chased off whoever took a piece out of you." He gave a pointed look at my swollen eye and bruised face, even more painful now that the doctor's sedative had worn off.

But I preferred not to carry a gun except in those rare instances where it was absolutely necessary. I didn't want to be tempted to use it.

"I'm all right, Sully," I said. "Besides, I hear you have a piece here in the shop that the captain and I are very interested in."

Sully's eyes, their color a match for the dark blue nickel guns on the counter in front of him, glinted with excitement. "I do." He pulled out a wooden box, which he placed on top of the glass display case.

"Yesterday the captain brought me a bullet from a murder weapon."

"That's right." Mulvaney nodded. "I have it here." He once again brought out the small brass ball that had taken Judge Porter's life.

Sully picked up the bullet and stared at it—a tiny thing compared to his broad fingers. "It's a .32-caliber bullet, obviously. And when I looked at these lands and grooves," he said, "I immediately suspected that it came from a Browning automatic pistol." He looked up. "You're aware that it's possible these days to match an individual bullet to the gun that fired it?"

"We are," I said. "Ever since Justice Oliver Wendell Holmes himself showed us how."

Years ago, Holmes had famously called a gunsmith into the courtroom to test-fire an alleged murder weapon. He then used a magnifying glass to compare the markings on the test-fired bullet to the bullet from the victim. He was satisfied. And after he showed the jury, they were convinced as well: they promptly convicted the defendant.

"So you're familiar with the method, too," Sully said with approval. "I test-fired an ordinary 1900 Browning automatic pistol yesterday for the captain. We examined the bullets afterward and they were similar—enough so that I would have told you with certainty that your murder weapon was a Browning pistol. But the marks weren't perfect enough to tell us that it was the same Browning model that had fired this bullet." He held up the brass slug once again, then tapped his head with his finger. "That's when something occurred to me. A similar Browning pistol was returned to the shop only yesterday. And I thought, why not test it out to see if the marks were closer? Sure enough, that Browning made marks identical to the bullet that killed your man. We're talking dumb luck. To identify the exact Browning model would have been the best we could have hoped for, but this . . ." he said, his voice trailing off.

He looked at me strangely. "Perhaps you'd like to see for yourself?"

I nodded to encourage him.

He smiled with anticipation as he opened the wooden box. Nestled inside was a small six-inch-long pistol, silver-colored, with a double-barreled silhouette and humpback shape. He looked at it with obvious satisfaction. "She's a real beauty: there aren't many of these nickel ones in circulation. More commonly they are blued." He picked it up. "And she weighs under a pound."

Watching him handle the gun with his bare fingers, I shot a look of concern at Mulvaney.

"I dusted it for prints personally when I first saw it yesterday," he said. "There were none. It had been wiped clean—though we don't know whether the killer was trying to avoid detection or was just cleaning his gun."

Sully looked at me. "Ready to test-fire?" He held an extremely thick wad of cotton in one hand, the Browning pistol in the other. He placed the cotton in a wooden crate, loaded the pistol with a new brass .32-caliber bullet, and fired. The loud crack reverberated in my ears for several seconds.

He lifted out the wad of cotton and passed it to me. Picking up the tiny brass bullet, I placed it next to our original, found at Judge Porter's murder scene—and the magnifying glass that Sully provided showed the truth, even to my swollen eyes: we now had in our possession three bullets with identical markings. There seemed little doubt that the shiny nickel pistol in Sully's hand was our murder weapon.

"Well, then," I said, placing the bullet on the glass counter. "We've found our murder weapon. What can you tell me about its owner?"

Sully gave me a sly look. "Assuming, of course, that its buyer and eventual user are the same."

"Assuming that, yes."

Sully was one of the sharper informants I'd ever encountered. I supposed that in his line of work, he had to be.

Mulvaney and I followed him as he crossed the room to a

small walnut secretary where he kept a ledger. He pulled it out and showed it to us; I was pleased to see that he kept notes organized by weapon, not by customer.

"See here." He pointed to a notation for a 1900 nickel Browning. "The gun came into my shop on Monday, September tenth, from my usual distributor. I cleaned and tested it; then it sat until a customer came in to inspect it on Thursday, October fourth. He was pleased, and purchased it the following day: October fifth. Then yesterday—Wednesday, the twenty-fourth—he returned to my shop. He complained about the recoil, said it was faulty." He sighed. "I knew he was lying to me; this little Browning is one of the finest that's ever come into my shop. And I normally don't take a return after seven days have passed. But in this case, I refunded his money and took the gun back—simply because I liked the pistol so much. I knew I'd have no difficulty finding a new owner—one who'd appreciate it."

"Did he give a name or address?" I asked.

"No address, but he gave his name," Sully replied. "Didn't the captain tell you?"

I gave Mulvaney a questioning look.

"You'll do better to ask for more information about what the buyer looked like," he said, his voice almost a growl.

"Why?" I asked, now suspicious.

Sully shrugged. "I can only tell you what I told the captain yesterday. He was a tall man with broad features. White-blond hair. He looked Scandinavian to me; my best guess was Swedish, based on his accent. But I'm no expert."

I immediately thought of our elevator attendant at the Breslin Hotel.

"A woman waited for him outside," he continued. "I didn't get a good look at her, but she was short. Petite, if we want to be polite. And exotic looking."

"Chinese?" I asked, for Mei Lin immediately sprang to mind.

"I dunno. Didn't get a good enough look."

"And you got his name?" I repeated the question to Sully and held my breath with anticipation.

But some sixth sense gave me his answer before he said the words.

"It was Sanders. He said his name was Leroy Sanders. See?" Sully pointed with heavily blue-stained fingertips to a different place in his ledger. "I made him sign."

I traced the signature lightly with my own finger. And I'd need no handwriting expert to tell me what I clearly saw with my own eyes: the signature perfectly mirrored the one made in the hotel register. The signer at the Breslin—and the purchaser of this Browning pistol—were one and the same.

CHAPTER 15

Holding Cell at the Tombs, Centre Street. 12:30 P.M.

The main holding cell on the first floor of the Tombs was typically filled with a motley assortment of drunkards and thieves, but today it was filled to capacity with the thirty-some men—all anarchists—that Mulvaney had rounded up at the beer hall last night following my assault.

The junior officer in charge had been expecting me.

"You came down quicker than we thought," he said with a grin. "No rush to press charges if you'd like to keep them in the cooler a bit longer."

"Not that some of them don't deserve a stay at the Tombs, but I'm hoping you have one man in particular," I said. "Tall and broad shouldered with white-blond hair and other Scandinavian features. Possibly a Swedish accent."

"I'll check," he said, leaping to his feet. "Meanwhile, why

don't you and the captain make yourselves comfortable in the viewing room."

The viewing room was a chamber just off the main hallway, characterized by a small slit in the wall that allowed a view of the holding room while still providing some measure of privacy as the potential convicts were paraded in front of it.

Mulvaney, keeping his frustration barely in check, exclaimed out loud, "It makes no sense. Who is this Swedish man who is killing judges in the name of Leroy Sanders?"

"I agree. Leroy Sanders must be the key. We find out who he is and we're on our way to solving these murders," I said. I was about to continue but was interrupted by the officer from the Tombs. "Here they are," he said.

A lineup of six blond men passed in front of the window, standing alternately face forward, face left, and finally face right.

"Second from the left was one of my attackers last night," I said to the officer, pointing out the stocky blond who had carried the bully stick. "You can book him formally on charges of assault. But he's not the man we're looking for."

"We have a few more in the pen who may interest you," the officer replied. He stepped outside to direct those men handling the lineup. Five of the men followed one policeman to the left to be released; my attacker was led to the right for booking.

A parade of several more lineups passed in front of me, and I was able to identify Savvas and the swarthy man with sour breath as my other attackers. But I saw no sign of the elevator operator from the Breslin Hotel.

After the junior officer retreated to help book my assailants, I turned to Mulvaney. "You put Mike Burns in charge of interviewing everyone at the Breslin; he must have a lead on our Swede. Where can we find Burns?"

"The commissioner has been breathing down my neck for any leads from the Breslin murder. While I don't typically like my men going around me, I told Burns to report his findings directly to the commissioner. He's one of my best men and he knows how to handle sensitive information. I knew I would be tied up with you all morning," Mulvaney said. He pulled out his pocket watch and checked the time. "Almost one o'clock. I daresay we can catch him. Besides," he added more grimly, "the commissioner's certain to learn of the beating you took last night. He may as well hear it from you."

My stomach clenched, even though I recognized the truth in what Mulvaney said.

We stopped by police headquarters at 300 Mulberry Street only to learn that the commissioner was taking lunch at Lombardi's on Spring Street.

I was famished, having been unable to eat Bridget Mulvaney's hearty breakfast, so Lombardi's was almost music to my ears. "May as well join them for lunch," I muttered, as we retraced our steps downtown again—not bothered in the least.

Lombardi's was packed when we arrived. Several construction workers were lined up outside the door, waiting to buy as much of a tomato pie as two cents would get them.

We made our way past the line to the dining area, where two rows of red and white checkered tables were packed with diners. We found General Bingham sitting in the rear next to the large brick oven that encompassed almost the entire back wall. The General was helping himself to a large tomato pie slice. Mike had apparently finished; he was now surrounded by papers and talking to the General at a rapid clip. He didn't notice our approach, but the General did.

"Captain. Detective. Sit and join us." He wiped his gray handlebar mustache with his red napkin. "We've got plenty of food; help yourselves."

Mulvaney and I each took a slice of tomato pie and gratefully accepted the glasses of water that a waiter brought over. And while I typically would have had a hard time eating anything under the commissioner's stern gaze, I had no problem with a Lombardi's slice under my nose.

"You came to report progress," he said, turning a careful eye to my injuries. "Progress that came at some personal cost, at least to the detective."

"Aye," Mulvaney said, "we have something to report—as well as to check. You see, we believe Detective Burns may hold the key to unraveling our case. We've found the murder weapon that killed Judge Porter. And we also have a good physical description of the man who purchased it at A. H. Funke's. We hope that the detective's interviews at the Breslin may have yielded the man's identity."

The General laughed, loud and deep. "And Burns was just telling me that his interviews yielded no information whatsoever."

Mike Burns flushed in embarrassment. "This is news to me, General." Turning to Mulvaney, he asked, "What type of man are you looking for?"

Mulvaney and I took turns filling him in as to this morning's progress. When we had finished, I said, "So, based on the gun shop's description and the matching signatures, we're looking for the Breslin's day elevator operator who took us upstairs the same morning Judge Porter's body was discovered. We saw him with our own eyes—and I'd recognize him anywhere."

"But he wasn't among the anarchists you rounded up after last night's beer hall meeting," the General said thoughtfully.

I indicated that he was not.

Mike Burns gave us a bewildered look. "But I interviewed all three elevator operators who work at the Breslin. Not one comes close to matching your description."

A sick feeling took hold of my gut. "You're sure they have only three operators?"

"I'm sure," Mike replied. "You're welcome to look through my notes." He passed the stack of papers to Mulvaney, who immediately began flipping through them. "I've got names, addresses, and physical descriptions of everyone we spoke with. And I definitely remember the elevator operators: I spoke with each of them extensively about each person they took up and down in the hours before the murder."

"But no one mentioned a man with blond hair?" I demanded.

He indicated they had not.

"Then how do we account for the fact that he operated our elevator that morning?" Mulvaney asked.

Mike shrugged. "Maybe he took advantage of the regular guy's five-minute break. Maybe he had to retrieve something left behind. Or maybe he simply wanted to see how the investigation was coming along. All I can tell you is that nobody mentioned him. No one else even saw him."

"But we did," I said. "And a man matching his description signed for the weapon at Funke's." I pulled the register Sully had given us out of my leather satchel. "Here: put this into evidence.

And when you check it against the hotel register, you'll find that his signature is a perfect match."

"But you think it's a false name?" Mike asked.

"We don't know," I said, shrugging. "I can't find any reference to Leroy Sanders."

"Get our newspaper contacts to search the name," the General instructed gruffly. "And, Mike, run it past our embedded anarchist spy. I want him pulled in anyway."

We were silent for some moments, watching the General finish. When he at last pushed his plate aside, he spoke.

"Gentlemen, I fear we may have a modern-day Haymarket Conspiracy on our hands—right here in New York, twenty years after the first. Perpetrated by men who will use any means of violence to disrupt all we hold dear. These men aim to martyr our city's protectors of the law. Our esteemed judges. Our hardworking police officers," he said with a pointed look to me.

He was overreaching, but this was not the time to point out that I was in no danger of becoming martyred. Certainly not like those policemen who were killed in the violence of the Chicago Haymarket riots that followed a factory workers' strike gone wrong. During a demonstration that followed, a pipe bomb had been thrown into police ranks, killing seven officers and injuring over sixty others. A group of anarchists had later been convicted of conspiracy to commit murder; some were hanged, others pardoned, and most people believed that the true perpetrators of the violence had escaped justice.

"I fear we are dealing with a larger conspiracy than we first imagined," the General was saying, his face drained with worry.

He was a hard man to like, but in that moment I felt sorry for him: his responsibilities were a heavy weight to carry.

He folded his napkin. "Have you gentlemen finished eating?"

Without waiting for us to answer, he backed up his wheelchair and motioned for Mike to assist him in getting out. Mulvaney managed to take a final bite of lunch as Mike stepped behind the General's chair and pushed him carefully through the restaurant; there was just enough space between the rows of tables to accommodate the wheelchair's width.

"I want to prosecute those men who attacked Detective Ziele to the fullest extent of the law," the General said when we had reached the street, Mulvaney and I walking alongside Detective Burns as he pushed the General. "And arrest those anarchist leaders responsible. Charge them all with attempted murder."

"But General—" I began.

He cut me off. "We'll reduce the charges later. But right now, I want the full attention of all the papers. Let them whip the public into a frenzy of anger."

I refrained from saying that more angry people was the last thing this city needed. Emotions already ran hot, too close to the surface.

"Captain, I also want you to be sure to tell the press that our fine officer was assaulted because we're on the murderer's trail and getting close to the truth." The General stopped his chair and turned round to face Mulvaney. "I'm counting on you not to fail."

"We won't, General," Mulvaney said. His voice brimmed with a confidence I did not share. Then again, he was playing a political game that I wanted no part of.

We had reached Houston Street; headquarters were just ahead.

"Carry on, gentlemen." The General waved us away.

Mulvaney shook his head the moment the General was out of earshot. "He's intent on brewing a tempest, isn't he? And we've no choice in the matter; we've got to follow his orders."

He paused, looking uncomfortable. "There's one more thing, Ziele."

I looked at him, surprised by something in his voice.

"It's Alistair. He was the last to see Judge Porter alive. Yet, by your own admission, he has told you nothing. I'm going to have to bring him in."

I stopped short. "To the station house for questioning? That won't work, and you know it. He has powerful connections at every level in this city. You'll not get him to say a thing he doesn't want to—and ruin any chance of his cooperation."

"What choice do we have?" His voice was rough. "Why won't he talk to you? He claims to be your friend."

It was the same question that troubled me.

"Give me one more chance," I said. "Now that the shock of the judge's death has worn off . . ."

Mulvaney shot me a dubious look. "All right. But we need real information from him, not academic theories."

"Understood," I said. "I'll try to catch up with him now."

I left him to make my way uptown, thoroughly afraid. Afraid of what Alistair might tell me—and equally afraid of the consequences if he once again refused to come clean.

CHAPTER 16

The Dakota, 1 West Seventy-second Street. 3:00 P.M.

I had just arrived at the entrance to the Dakota when I saw a man in a dark trench coat jump into a hansom cab.

Alistair.

"Going somewhere?" I called out.

He did not hear me. The carriage door closed behind him, and I quickened my pace. The driver, a heavyset man with gray stubble covering his chin, grabbed the reins to start the horse.

"Stop!" I sprinted the last few paces, grabbing my badge out of my pocket and holding it high.

The driver hesitated—and relaxed the reins. His horse snorted, pawing at the ground, impatient to leave.

"Hold up! I need to speak to your passenger." I ran to the carriage door and pounded on it, hard. "Open up!"

"Hey—watch yourself," the driver said, looking down at me

with an expression of annoyance. "Give the gentleman a second. That latch can be tricky."

I watched as the door opened a crack. I grabbed it—and pulled it the rest of the way.

Alistair sat inside, his face ashen and lined with worry. His trench coat had been removed, and I saw that he had dressed in haste. His shirtwaist was untucked, not fully buttoned; his hair was uncharacteristically mussed.

"I was coming to see you," I said. "We need to discuss Judge Porter."

He managed a faint smile. "Not now, Ziele. I'm on my way out."

I held the door. "This is important."

"Can't do it now. I've got an appointment." His right hand, trembling uncontrollably, reached for the door.

I raised a skeptical eyebrow. "The appointment can wait. This is a murder investigation—one that *you* insisted I join and that has now claimed the life of two of your friends."

"I know, Ziele." His eyes had a vacant expression as he repeated it. "I know."

"What is wrong with you?" I asked, my voice incredulous. "Good God, man. I've put my career on the line for you. I need your cooperation."

He covered his trembling right hand with his left.

"I know you were shocked and in no condition to answer questions earlier. But I can't put off getting a formal statement from you."

"I've nothing to say."

I made a noise of exasperation. "You've no idea how much I'm trying to help you, do you? How much I've protected you?

You were likely the last person to see Angus Porter alive before he was brutally shot to death. You certainly were the last to spend any significant time with him. And your conversation during those hours just may hold the key to identifying and apprehending his killer. Yet what do you tell me? Absolutely nothing." I shook my head in disbelief. Alistair's stubborn refusal to cooperate infuriated me.

"You're not an ordinary policeman. You're my friend. You ought to believe me when I say I have nothing to add to your investigation."

"Don't you understand that it's not just me? This is a city-wide investigation led by Commissioner Bingham himself. I answer to him as well as to Captain Mulvaney—and both are men who demand results. They want you to answer important questions."

"Just let them try . . ."

"No one is looking to threaten you; we just need your cooperation."

"I have no help to give you, Ziele," Alistair said with some measure of contrition. "I don't know why Angus was killed within hours of leaving my home."

"We might figure it out together if you'd talk to me," I said.

One of the lobby attendants from the Dakota came up behind me, interrupting us. "Professor, the electric motorcar you ordered for your trunk just arrived. Since you hadn't left yet, I thought I'd better ask if you wanted to go with it." He paused when he noticed Alistair's blank stare, adding, "I've got another lady waiting for a cab. She'd be happy to take this one."

Alistair came to himself again. "Thanks, Tom," he managed to say, "but I'll travel separately. Please send the trunk ahead."

I was dumbfounded. "Where are you going, Alistair, that you require luggage?"

He stared at his right hand, which had begun to tremble again.

"Alistair, answer me!" I said, becoming alarmed now. "What's going on here? I need the truth—the whole truth that you've kept from me."

A dark shadow clouded his face. "I'll telephone you later." He reached outside with his umbrella and tapped the roof, calling to the driver, "Let's go."

I thrust half my body into the carriage. "Not until you talk to me."

"Unless you're prepared to arrest me, Ziele, step out of the cab and let me go."

"Don't force my hand."

Our eyes locked and held—and I saw the flash of naked fear in his eyes.

"Simon!" Isabella's voice called to me from the Dakota's Seventy-second Street gated entrance.

I glanced backward, and she called out again, insistent.

"Stay here," I said to Alistair. "I'll be right back."

"Simon," Isabella said as I approached, "I've found something important. Can we talk?"

It was rotten timing.

"Of course," I said in a rush, glancing behind me, "but I need one more minute with Alistair. Can you wait here?"

"Of course." She gave me a puzzled look. "That was Alistair in the cab?"

"Yes. I'll only be a moment."

"But—" She bit her lip and her eyes widened.

I turned in an instant—only to watch Alistair's cab race away and disappear down West Seventy-second Street.

"Where is he going?" Isabella asked, her face pinched with worry.

"I don't even know," I said, feeling as though I'd just been sucker-punched in the gut. "I'll ask one of the attendants."

"It's not like him to leave like that."

"Something's wrong," I said, watching as Tom, the attendant who had helped Alistair, unloaded an elderly lady's packages from her cab. "Would Alistair have left you a note?"

"Maybe." She sounded doubtful.

"Come, sit a moment," I said, leading her back into the court-yard to the wooden benches where residents waited for cabs or for their cars to be brought up.

"Mrs. Sinclair, do you need a hansom cab?" Tom raced over to ask.

"No, thank you," she replied, her voice clear. "Tom, do you know where the cab with Professor Sinclair's luggage was headed?"

"I assume the train station, madam. But the professor made the arrangements himself."

"I see. Thank you."

The attendant bowed stiffly before he disappeared. "Of course, madam."

The moment he was out of earshot, she spoke again, her voice hurried. "This afternoon I visited both Mrs. Jackson and Miss Porter, the spinster sister who often visited Judge Porter. What I've learned makes me concerned."

"Go on." I watched as two porters helped another lady into a waiting cab.

"The two judges were close friends—and together they were far more involved in the anarchist trials than we've been led to believe. Judge Porter advised Judge Jackson in chambers almost daily, discussing the Drayson case. And Simon," she said, her breath catching, "Alistair had been joining them in recent months."

"Are you sure?" I sat up straighter.

"I have it on authority from both women. In fact, Miss Porter let me borrow her brother's appointment book." She reached into her coat pocket and passed me a small black leather-bound volume with "Angus Porter, Esq." in gold letters on the cover. "Look here." She directed me to the morning of Monday, October 22. "The three of them met the day of Judge Jackson's murder."

Alistair's voice echoed in my mind from that night he'd brought me into the Jackson case. "We'd grown apart," he'd said. "Haven't seen him in years, though I think Angus has kept up closer ties."

"I'm worried about Alistair," she said. "He knows something he's not sharing. And I don't understand why."

I flipped through the pages of the book; Alistair's name was used many times.

Why had he lied?

"Judge Porter fully expected to be asked to take over the Drayson trial—or, rather, to preside over a new trial in the likely event of a mistrial," she said. "In fact, with official permission, he had already brought much of the trial material into his chambers for review."

"They were more worried than they wanted to admit, then. But especially after Hugo Jackson's murder, they ought to have shared this information." I rubbed my forehead. "Alistair wanted the police—and specifically *me*—kept out of it."

"Also, Angus Porter was hiding a cipher that he had received," Isabella said. "I left it where I found it: at the back of his appointment book."

I turned to the final pages in the book, where among blank pages meant for notes, there was a thick, cream envelope addressed to Angus Porter. It bore no postmark—only the judge's name, written in a thick, black script I recognized from the musical cipher that Hugo Jackson had received. I opened it and found a musical score.

"It's not the same one . . . ?" I looked at her with curious eyes.

"No. See—there's a white rose in the staff, just like the one sent to Judge Jackson. But it's in the first bar, not the last."

Sure enough, the hand-drawn image of a white rose was there, this time replacing the opening treble clef.

"Avenge Leroy, again?"

"I don't think so. I didn't decipher it, but the melody is entirely different."

"Did the name Leroy Sanders come up during your visit to either man's household?" I asked with renewed interest.

"Not unless it's in the message contained there," Isabella said, indicating the composition score I was holding.

So Judge Porter had received a musical cipher of his own in recent days. And yet he had not mentioned it during his final meeting with Alistair, when we had discussed and deciphered its twin. Why had he kept it a secret?

The only answer that made sense involved the Drayson case. If he wanted the case for himself, he may have feared sharing anything that would be considered a conflict of interest—for then he would have been compelled to recuse himself and send the case elsewhere.

That might explain why Angus Porter had hidden the extent of his own preexisting involvement with Hugo Jackson and the Drayson trial. But it shed no light on Alistair's secretive behavior.

"You still have the key to the cipher, right?" Isabella asked.

I nodded, placing the black appointment book and letter in my own coat pocket. "But not with me. I'll have to decode it later."

I managed a reassuring smile for Isabella as I bid her goodbye, promising to stop by to give her an update tomorrow. Meanwhile, I needed to find Mulvaney. He ought to know that I'd failed with Alistair—as well as news of these other developments.

"Be careful, Simon," she said with a wistful smile, reaching up with her hand to touch my bruised cheek. "This is a dangerous case."

Her hand lingered just a moment too long—and instinctively I took hold of it. For a minute we stood in silence, until I let go, saying roughly, "I'll see you tomorrow."

As I walked down Seventy-second Street, I was increasingly troubled. The big question remained: Who was Leroy Sanders and how was he connected to the murders of two prominent judges? I could have used Alistair's help, which wasn't forthcoming.

Had I only imagined the expression of fear I'd seen in his eyes?

I would stop by home to make some telephone calls. One

way or another, I'd find out where he went—and bring him back.

What sort of game was Alistair playing? I wondered. And as my thoughts returned briefly to Isabella, I faced an even more uncomfortable thought: What sort of game was I?

CHAPTER 17

Outside the Tombs, Centre Street. 4:30 P.M.

"What the hell do you mean, he went to Boston?" Mulvaney thundered, pacing back and forth on the sidewalk off Centre Street in front of the Tombs as we awaited the commissioner's arrival.

"That was the message he left with the law school office at Columbia. He said he was going to Boston for a few days to present a paper."

"This is a murder case and your professor's a material witness. I can bloody well bring him back." Mulvaney stopped pacing, turned, and gave me a look of reproach. "How could you have let him go?"

"What did you expect me to do—arrest him the moment I saw him? He left when my back was turned. I didn't expect that. Not from him."

"I won't blow this investigation because of your professor." Mulvaney gave me a hard look. "My own job is on the line now, thanks to him. And if you could hear the way the commissioner's been ranting this morning, you'd know it's only a matter of time before—"

"I understand," I said, interrupting him. "This case isn't moving quickly enough—not for you or me or anyone. And you're not going to like this, but I've just come into more information that Alistair has been holding back from us. We now have a real motive for Judge Porter's murder."

There were few passersby on the street this morning, but I lowered my voice so no one could hear and briefly filled him in as to all Isabella had learned from the Jackson and Porter households.

Mulvaney set his jaw. "So Judge Porter would've been Jackson's replacement; that firms up the anarchist link. We can use that to our advantage—especially now that we've got a whole wing of the Tombs full of them. We'll take 'em out one by one for interrogation, and I guarantee the weaker ones will break." He sighed. "The commissioner himself may want to question even the low-level anarchists."

I raised an eyebrow. "I thought the General was planning to supervise interrogations of only the highest-level suspects?"

"From our slow progress, he seems to believe we're incompetent to handle even the smallest of tasks," Mulvaney said with a tight grimace. "If he doesn't fire the lot of us, then he will at least make our jobs a living misery."

"Have you personally interviewed—"

I stopped talking mid-sentence because of a prickling at the back of my neck, the result of some sixth sense that detected a change in the atmosphere. I turned to find Mrs. Strupp staring at me, her face lined with anguish. With her thick black woolen shawl drawn close around her, she was a picture of grief itself. She must have just exited the building, where she'd no doubt visited with Jonathan.

"What have you done?" Her voice was a charged whisper. "The last time I saw you, I lost my daughter. Now, the moment you finally return, I suffer the loss of my only son." Her breath came faster now, in ragged bursts. "I asked you to save him. And now he sits, rotting in a filthy cage that's not fit for an animal." Her final words disintegrated into a sharp, keening noise.

"I'm sorry," I said. "I talked with him—but he wouldn't listen."

"You might have tried harder," she said with a look of reproach. "You could have refused to give up."

I didn't bother mentioning that Jonathan had given me no opening whatsoever—that, in fact, he had betrayed me by revealing my identity and setting his anarchist thugs on me.

"I can still help him, if he'd let me," I said. "But he couldn't get rid of me fast enough the other night."

The tears she had been holding back now streamed down her face. "My only remaining child is locked away. They won't let him go free for years; I know it. His child will grow up not knowing her father. She'll have no one to raise her except for me." She clutched her stomach as she doubled over, stricken with grief.

I stepped forward awkwardly to catch her—feeling my stomach churn as I thought of the devastation wrought on the Strupp family and Hannah's niece. It was exactly what I had warned

Jonathan of, to no avail. And it did no good telling myself that Jonathan's choices alone had brought on their troubles; I regretted my own involvement. Not to mention my helplessness, for I could do little but watch as the Strupp family continued to suffer.

We were interrupted by a series of raucous shouts from somewhere behind the building.

Mulvaney, who had stepped back during my exchange with Mrs. Strupp, now spoke. "Drayson's got a court hearing this afternoon. The officers planned to sneak him out the back, but it looks as though the crowd figured that out."

"Let me take you home," I said to Mrs. Strupp; she was in no shape to travel alone, especially with an angry mob nearby. I would be late for our meeting with the commissioner—but I trusted Mulvaney to make it all right.

He nodded, his eyes sympathetic, before he turned and walked alone into the Tombs.

I took Mrs. Strupp's arm and escorted her across the street. "I promise I'll look in on Jonathan. And I'll see if there's anything I can do to make him more comfortable. . ."

Her crying had stopped and she followed me, though she gave no indication that she had heard either my words or my directions.

We had made it to the other side of Centre Street when, out of the corner of my eye, I noticed a brilliant flash of light—one that caused me to stop and turn.

I was just in time to see a plume of white light surrounded by thick black smoke; it rose slowly above the stone towers of the Tombs. An arc of light flashed inside the building as well, shades of orange and white just beyond the point where I had last seen Mulvaney's tall frame.

The sound of the explosion itself was delayed, coming what seemed like minutes later—though it could only have been a fraction of a second. The boom was deafening—and the ringing that echoed in my ears drowned out even the sound of Mrs. Strupp's horrified screams beside me.

A powerful aftershock followed. We felt it even across the street: the cobblestones shook underneath us, causing Mrs. Strupp to stumble to the ground. Even as I knelt to assist her, I couldn't look away; I suppose I was attempting to make sense of a sight unlike any other. The building now sparkled—and not just the building but the very air, for even the dust and the black smoke had begun to shimmer. Thousands of small, glittering rays of light danced up and down the building. And it was only when I heard the tinkle of tiny bells that I realized what I had seen. Most of the windows in the mighty Tombs had broken and were now falling in shards of glass to the ground.

Those men who were unhurt in the blast were running from the building—ordinary men, transformed by the dust into gray ghosts.

How many more had been hurt or—

I was superstitious enough that I didn't dare form the thought. Not with Mulvaney inside.

I searched wildly for any sign of him near the entrance to the Tombs. But he had disappeared—into the thick smoke and acrid fumes that choked us into unseeing oblivion.

CHAPTER 18

Centre Street—After the Explosion

Just ahead of me, a newsboy scrambled to his feet, chasing his papers, which had fallen to the ground and were now blowing away in the brisk afternoon breeze.

It didn't matter. An explosion had just ripped through the Tombs. Everything had, in a matter of seconds, become stale news.

I righted myself and called to him. "Can you help?"

"Sir, is she hurt?" He ran over to where I was attending to Mrs. Strupp. She was insensible to everything around her as she stared, openmouthed in horror, at the smoking building.

"Only shocked, I think," I replied. I helped her to her feet, then reached into my pocket for several coins. "I'm needed inside." I motioned across the street to the Tombs. "Could you please see that she gets home safely? One twenty First Avenue."

"Yes, sir," he said, pocketing the money and taking Mrs. Strupp's arm.

She balked, not wanting to leave the area.

"You need to go home," I said, helping her move forward and continuing to reassure her. "I promise to stop by later. I'll check on Jonathan and make sure he's okay."

She didn't respond, but this time she allowed herself to be led away.

With my anxiety mounting, I hurried across the street, determined to find Mulvaney.

The acrid stench of smoke choked me when I approached the main entrance. *Nitroglycerin*. There was no mistaking its pungent smell—one I'd learned to recognize when the city first used dynamite to create the tunnels that would house our new underground subways.

Struggling for breath, I covered my mouth and nose with a cotton handkerchief as I made my way through the chaos: officers and guards shouting as they checked injuries and prisoner locations, smoke and dust obscuring everything. Mulvaney must have been walking toward the cell that housed the anarchists when the bomb exploded. That area, at the rear of the main floor, had received the brunt of the damage. The massive stone wall had crumbled in portions, and several men were pinned underneath the rubble; their moans and curses filled the air, mingling with the cries and shouts of prisoners.

A handful of uninjured guards stood awkwardly, surveying the carnage yet doing nothing. It was the shock of it—they couldn't conceive what to do. I'd seen it before when the *Slocum* burned: able-bodied men became paralyzed with shock, unable to

think or act. Once someone told them what to do, they'd galva-
nize into action—but not before.

One man, a guard I recognized, was now pinned under a
collapsed portion of the wall. He grabbed at the leg of my pants,
wailing in pain. "My foot . . . I'm pinned."

I called to the man standing nearest me. "Come. If we work
together, we can free him."

The guard I'd spoken to seemed not to have heard.

I reached and touched his shoulder, forcing him to look at
me. "Help me," I said. "The stone's too heavy for me to move by
myself."

Soon the others joined in, and we freed five or six men before I left them to their task; I'd still not seen Mulvaney.

The men I passed were injured but alive. I continued down
the hallway, assuring each one that more assistance was coming.

I'd nearly reached the end when I finally heard Mulvaney:
he was unfurling a litany of curses in his thick Irish brogue. He
sat in the middle of the corridor, grimacing in pain—with his
left leg stuck at an odd angle. When he saw me, he spoke with
relief. "About time you got here, Ziele."

I knelt to examine his leg.

"Don't bother. It's broken, and I'll not be leaving here till a
doctor helps me out. I need you to take care of them." He pointed
not to the other injured officers but rather to the cell some ten
feet down the hall where the anarchists were being held. The
wall to their cell had also been damaged—and a group of them
who saw an opportunity were working feverishly to create an
opening wide enough to allow their escape. Jonathan Strupp
was among them—which at least would allow me to reassure his
mother that he had been unhurt in the blast.

"I'll stop them from the outside," I said, giving a last anxious look at his limp leg.

"Go," he said with a grimace of pain. "I'll be all right so long as none of those damn anarchists get away."

As I retraced my steps through the Tombs, I recruited a handful of men to help me secure the small opening in the wall where the anarchists were attempting their escape. I knew additional police reinforcements would be on their way—but until they arrived, we needed to pin back the anarchists in their damaged cell. Despite the urgency of our mission, it took us several frustrating minutes to navigate the significant amount of debris that was scattered throughout the grounds.

We finally reached the crater created by the bomb. While it was not deep, its impact was widespread and had charred the stone wall almost up to the roof. Just as we arrived at the crater, two official-looking men began walking its length. To be here so rapidly, they must have been on the move the minute they heard the explosion. In any event, they were not bothered by the extent of the bomb's destruction, as they coolly exchanged comments without emotion.

"Must have been at least twenty pounds of dynamite." A short, heavy man wearing a black fedora chomped on a cigar as he surveyed the damage. Beside him, a younger man with wispy blond hair feverishly took notes on a clipboard. "And look," the short man continued, "they packed the bomb with these heavy metal slugs. They work just like shrapnel."

He ran his hand across one section of the wall, fingering small pockmarked dents. Then he bent to the ground and picked up one of the metal slugs responsible for the damage. "See? If the bomb itself doesn't kill you, this thing surely would."

"Any idea where it went off, boss?" A thin man with a tired expression called out from the far end of the crater.

The cigar-chomping man considered. "I think the bomb was in a bag planted right here by the wall," he finally said, gesturing to a crumbled area marked by heavy black charring.

"Maybe even garbage," his assistant added. "Just look at the debris."

The debris here was even more concentrated than in the area we had just passed through: all manner of trash—food scraps, cigarette butts and newspapers—was strewn throughout the crater and beyond.

"Did they really think they were going to blow up the Tombs?" The thin man gave a half-amused shake of the head.

"Maybe they just wanted to make a point." The heavyset man dropped his cigar butt and ground it into the dirt with his heel.

"Which precinct are you men with?" I called out.

"None," the cigar man answered. "Name's Burt." He walked over and held out his hand. "This is Sam." He nodded to the thin, lanky man at his side. "We're assistants to the General, based at Mulberry Street."

I introduced myself quickly and indicated that the guards helping me should proceed to the place in the wall where the anarchists were struggling to escape. I would follow, I hoped, with additional reinforcements.

"How did you get here so fast?" I gave them a puzzled look.

"We're bomb specialists," Burt said with a grin. "As luck

would have it, we were testifying in court when the bomb exploded. Court adjourned—so we walked across the street."

I'd heard that General Bingham had developed a bomb response team to deal with handling the evidence following a spate of Black Hand bombings. Unbelievable, really, that dynamite was a big enough problem in this city that we needed a special division just to deal with it.

Burt pulled a handful of pink flyers out of his pocket, some of which were half burned. "We found these blowing around. Damn anarchists." He held one up for us to read.

"*'Our acts of destruction will rid the world of your institutions.'*"

"Nothing's more institutional than jail," the thin man muttered.

The sound of tumbling rocks interrupted us.

"We'd better get over there. I think the anarchists are making progress," I said, adding, "The bomb created an opening in their cell wall where they're trying to escape."

Burt looked confused for a moment, but then grabbed his Browning pistol out of its holster. "Not if we can help it. You're all armed?"

The prison guards with me were—but I was not.

"Here, take my Colt." Sam, Burt's assistant, handed it to me nervously. "You'll make better use of it than me."

I took it and led them toward the broken wall opening where the guards were waiting. My thoughts turned to Jonathan, struggling to escape, and I certainly hoped no guns would be necessary at all. Stepping forward, I placed the gun barrel within the opening and called out in my most authoritative voice. "Move away from this wall now!"

In answer, a barrage of rocks was launched from inside the jail.

I nodded to Burt, who fired his own gun into the air. At the sound of his shot, the rock volley ceased.

"If anyone tries that again, we'll fire inside your cell. Now, step away from the wall," I commanded. I motioned for the other men to make a lot of noise as we set our position. It was enough to convince the men inside to cooperate.

And we held that position, keeping the jailed anarchists from making use of their escape route. We were still there—waiting, guarding—when our reinforcements from Mulberry Street arrived.

"We'll take over here, boys," a grim-faced man in a black bowler hat said. "You all need to report to your supervisors immediately for alternate instructions."

"Why?" I asked, my voice filled with suspicion. "It's an emergency situation here; I doubt we can be spared."

He shook his head. "We got a worse emergency now." He fixed me with a sober look. "It's Drayson. During the chaos, he killed two guards and managed to escape."

CHAPTER 19

Fifty-seventh Street and Ninth Avenue, Hell's Kitchen. 11 P.M.

"All that destruction and bloodshed so that one bastard can steal his freedom? There's no justice in this world, that's for sure," Mulvaney said, his voice rough.

We were sitting in the main living area of Mulvaney's flat, sharing a bottle of Bushmills Irish whiskey. While I sipped the whiskey in hopes of settling my nerves, Mulvaney was using the alcohol to dull the pain in his broken leg, judging from the overfull glass of tawny liquid in front of him. Assured that I would keep watch over her husband, Bridget had left to gather those supplies she felt would be required while Mulvaney was out of commission.

"Which doctor set your leg?" I asked, with a quick glance at his stiff limb, now propped up and surrounded by pillows.

"You think I'd let anyone but Jennings touch me after what

happened to you? I intend to have this leg back, good as new," he said.

"A simple break . . . will mend good as new." I'd heard that diagnosis myself, coming from the very doctor whose poor skills had doomed my right arm to a lifetime of pain and partial use.

"So the commissioner believes that the bomb was planted only as a diversion," I said, wanting to move on.

Mulvaney nodded. "The anarchists surely wouldn't have minded had more died. Or if any of their jailed comrades had managed to escape. But the point was to free Drayson when he was in transit and not as closely guarded."

"They say the bomb created even more damage than the anarchists expected. They didn't think the wall would crumble in parts."

"And two guards murdered by Drayson's hand," Mulvaney said, shaking his head.

"Any leads on who slipped him the gun?"

"Not one. No one even heard gunshots, there was so much noise and confusion from the bomb."

It was true; I had been just across the street.

"When are you back on duty?" Mulvaney shot me a worried glance.

"Five in the morning." Because I'd been at the scene of the bombing, I'd been granted a few hours' leave to rest before joining my fellow police officers in a full-scale manhunt for Drayson.

"Bridget made up the bed where you slept last night," Mulvaney said. "Why don't you get some sleep? I'll be all right out here."

"You sure?" I set my whiskey glass on the table. I was

exhausted—and now that Mulvaney mentioned it, sleep seemed like a good idea.

Clapping him on the shoulder, I said good night. And after making my way into the makeshift bedroom that Bridget had created for me the night before, I collapsed into a dreamless sleep.

The entire household was dark when I was awakened by the shrill ring of Mulvaney's telephone a few hours later.

It was Bridget who answered; I heard her brisk steps, then her voice, husky with sleep, followed by a pause as she waited for the operator to make the connection. When she spoke again, it was clear that something was wrong.

After a series of whispered words and the sound of awkward shuffling, Mulvaney's own voice spoke into the telephone.

"That's not even my jurisdiction!"

Another pause.

When he spoke again, he was more agitated—which always made his brogue thicker. "My resources are all going to Commissioner Bingham, as well."

He stopped, listening. Then he went on to say, "I'm aware that I command one of the largest precincts. I've got absolutely no one available. The Drayson hunt takes precedence."

After more silence, I heard him sigh and agree to send a man up.

I got up and sat on the edge of the bed when it became clear that he was shuffling in the direction of my makeshift sleeping area. Mulvaney's large, six-foot frame was simply not designed to move with only one good leg—and his walking stick wasn't tall enough to offer him real support.

"Wait." I rushed to meet him, and taking his arm, I helped him sit on one of the dining room chairs. "Careful," I warned, as he nearly knocked his broken leg into the table. "We'll find you a better walking stick today."

"There's got to be someone in this city who makes them for tall men," he said, grimacing with pain. "Blasted leg."

I waited, knowing that he would explain the telephone call the moment he could.

"I need you to handle a shooting victim uptown," he finally said. "Three eleven West 103rd Street—off West End. The victim's wife found him."

"Suicide?" His description—"shooting victim," rather than "crime scene" or "murder case"—made me think so.

Mulvaney shrugged. "I don't normally take the family's word for it, but that's what it sounds like."

I glanced at my pocket watch. It was nearly four o'clock in the morning.

"I'm sorry," Mulvaney said. "There's no one else. You know I've got every man on the search for Drayson."

"You'll make it right with the commissioner's deputy?" I asked. Saunders was running the Drayson manhunt, and he was not a man I wanted to cross.

"Of course," Mulvaney said with a nod. "Besides, I don't expect you'll find any complications. Sounds cut-and-dried. The sort of thing you can do in your sleep."

"I wish I could." Between my exhaustion and frustration, the last thing I wanted to handle was this case. The crime scene would be easy; the distraught family never was. But I had no choice. I got dressed and caught a hansom cab to 103rd and

Broadway, resolved to make quick work of the visit. With the manhunt for Drayson, my investigation into the murders of two judges, and Alistair's mysterious disappearance—I had far more urgent demands on my time.

Friday
October 26, 1906

CHAPTER 20

311 West 103rd Street. 4:30 A.M.

The gaslights flickered eerily on West 103rd Street, creating dancing shadows that half illuminated number 311, the middle row house in a line of red sandstone buildings. With a deep breath to steady myself, I ascended nine steep steps to the front door and lifted the brass knocker.

No one answered at first—which prompted my frustration to rise. Bad enough that I had drawn this assignment when more important work was being done downtown. Even worse if I had the wrong address.

I pulled a scrap of paper out of my pocket and read my hastily scrawled notes. *"311 West 103. Gunshot victim Allan Hartt. Found by wife Elizabeth."*

Reading the words, I felt a pang of guilt. There were two victims here: the man who had died and the family he had left behind. It wasn't their fault that personal tragedy had struck the same night that Drayson had broken free.

Glancing up, I confirmed that I was at number 311. I rapped the knocker again, more loudly this time.

"Coming," a woman's voice called out. A lock turned, the large wooden door swung open, and I found myself face-to-face with a heavyset woman in her late forties, far too well dressed to be a servant. She had a tear-streaked face, and a small child—a sturdy fellow of about three or four years old—clung wide-eyed to her skirt.

"Didn't they send more officers?" she asked, her eyes searching wildly behind me.

"Detective Simon Ziele," I said, presenting her with my credentials. She barely glanced at them. "I'm expecting two medical men to join me shortly," I finally added, putting the situation as delicately as possible. Dr. Jennings—not to mention every other coroner's physician—had been put to use treating victims at the Tombs. But his office retained men on staff who would operate the coroner's wagon at all hours of the day and night. They should arrive soon to take away this victim.

I regarded the woman for a moment when she remained silent.

"Are you Mrs. Hartt?" I asked. I would not have expected the victim's wife to answer the door herself tonight, but the child's presence made me uncertain.

To my relief, she shook her head. "I'm Mrs. Johnson—Mrs. Hartt's mother. My daughter is resting upstairs. She is overwrought; I'm sure you understand."

"Of course," I said with a nod. "May I come in?"

She picked up her small grandson, saying, "There are two

more children asleep upstairs." Then she stepped aside so I might enter.

I glanced around the entry hall, which was lit by gaslight sconces. Apparently the Hartts had not yet installed electric lights.

"I believe a patrolman is here?" I asked. I'd been told that a night watchman had called in the report of Allan Hartt's death.

"He's in the back parlor," Mrs. Johnson said, gesturing to the rear of the brownstone. Her lip trembled.

"You needn't go with me, if you'd like to wait out here," I said, indicating the front parlor to our right. "I won't be long, but I'll need to ask you a few questions momentarily. Probably your daughter, too."

She nodded mutely, and—still carrying the boy—she took a seat on a sofa that stretched the length of a long bay window.

Meanwhile, I made my way to the rear of the building. Was there no one here except the family? While it was obviously not as wealthy a household as the Jacksons', I'd still have expected such a large home to retain at least one live-in servant, if not two.

I started to push open the wooden door, but it opened from behind—and the night watchman welcomed me with obvious relief.

"Detective," he said, "I've never been happier to see a superior officer. My name's Will Blount." He held out his hand, and I introduced myself, as well.

The lad was probably twenty-one, but he looked much younger: he had hazel eyes, large freckles that lined his nose and cheeks, and thick uncombed brown hair. I suspected he usually stuffed the hair beneath his cap, but tonight it stuck out in all directions.

"The victim's in here?" I asked. It was a hint for the patrolman to let me by. In fact, the sickly-sweet smell of blood that dominated the room—an odor that never failed to turn my stomach—was all the confirmation I needed.

"Of course." He backed away from the door but continued to talk in a rush as I entered the room. "It's my first crime scene, sir. I've only been on the job for two weeks. And Frankie—that's my partner, who's been doing this for almost twenty years—had to pick this night to leave me on my own."

"Where is Frankie tonight?" I asked, walking toward the figure obviously slumped in a chair at the window.

"He's working downtown. Some emergency at City Hall," the youth said, twisting one edge of his coat.

He meant the Drayson manhunt, of course. Only rookie cops like the young man with me now were exempt. It was where I ought to be now . . .

With another pang of guilt, I pushed the thought from my mind.

I stepped to the window, cracked it open, took a deep gulp of fresh air to settle my stomach, and then turned to face the chair where Allan Hartt had taken his own life.

A blood-soaked pillowcase covered his head—a small mercy, I supposed, designed to protect the wife who would probably be the first to find him. I walked around to the left and saw the perfect hole in the pillowcase where the bullet had entered and ended his life, most likely immediately. His arms hung lifeless over each side of the upholstered green chair.

I stepped closer. I knew that we would have to remove the pillowcase—both to positively identify the victim and to ascertain whether he had suffered any other injuries before the fatal gunshot. I wasn't looking forward to this task and decided I would wait until the coroner's men arrived.

Looking down, I saw that the day's newspaper sections were scattered on the floor. Something was missing . . .

"Where's the gun?" I asked—for it should have fallen to the ground.

"I didn't think to look," Will said, flushing a deep red. "Probably under the chair—if not under some of the papers."

He got on his hands and knees to search while I continued to survey the scene.

"Maybe his wife moved it?" I finally suggested when he came up empty-handed.

"Probably," he said too readily. "She's distraught, obviously. And I don't know exactly how much time she spent in here."

"Couldn't have been long. Didn't she report it right away?"

"She ran screaming into the street when she found him. Luckily for her, I was just three houses away. It took me several minutes to calm her down enough to figure out what was wrong."

I turned, noting that the carpet in this room was threadbare, and the green upholstered chair was ripped. Mr. Hartt was obviously a man of some means to afford a brownstone of this size, but the interior did not match the grandness of its façade. Had they come into recent money troubles? This would not be an uncommon reason for suicide. And committing suicide at home, with a wife and children upstairs, suggested a severe desperation. Or callousness.

"Any neighbors hear? Someone must have come to help," I said.

"Can't imagine the neighbors *didn't* hear," he said, shaking his head. "But it was early this morning, and no one left their home."

"So you came inside and called for help?" I had begun to walk the length of the room, trying to learn something more of Allan Hartt. He seemed to be a historian by hobby if not profession, for several books on United States and European history lined the bookshelves.

"That's what I expected to do, but she doesn't have a telephone. I hated to do it, but I had to leave her for several minutes while I walked back over to Broadway. That's where I asked a cabby to go to the precinct house and tell them I needed help."

The simple walnut table that served as Mr. Hartt's desk was covered by a mess of bills and papers. I leafed through them quickly. He had been a frugal man, spending little—but no account appeared to be in arrears.

"Do you know what he did for a living?" I asked the patrolman.

"The missus said he's a teacher at Barnard College."

I nodded. It was a reminder that Mrs. Johnson had answers I needed.

"Stay here until the coroner's men arrive, and don't touch anything," I directed the rookie as I left.

"You don't want me to clean anything?" Will asked, obviously wanting something to do other than stand guard over this gunshot victim.

"Not now," I said. "You may want to open the other window, though. Sometimes the fresh air helps with the stench."

No doubt unhappy to be left alone, he complied—and I propped the door open as I made my way to the front parlor and Mrs. Johnson.

The front parlor was also sparsely furnished, but the sofa and chairs in the room were of a higher quality than the furniture I'd seen in Mr. Hartt's study. Mrs. Johnson sat in darkness on a paisley sofa by the bay window that overlooked 103rd Street. It was not yet dawn, so the room's faint illumination was provided by the street lamp just outside the window. At least her grandson was now asleep—stretched out beside her, head in her lap, as she stroked his hair gently.

I entered the room and sat in the gold-stuffed chair opposite her. "I'm sorry," I said.

She shook her head. "I just can't understand it," she said. "Roddy's birthday is next Thursday. He turns three. And what he wanted for his birthday was for my son-in-law to take him to see Barnum and Bailey's new elephant." She stifled a sob. "What kind of father would do this right before his son's birthday?" Then, a moment later, she whispered, "What kind of man would do this at all?"

Everyone suffered pain or desperation at times. But I didn't understand this: not the way he'd done it, not with his family at home upstairs.

"You mentioned earlier that your daughter has other children, asleep upstairs?" I took out a small notebook. I needed the details correct for my report.

"Ella, her oldest, is six," she said. "And Luke is not yet a year."

I nodded. "And how long has she been married?"

"Seven years. He was older than my daughter by a good deal, and thus was very anxious to start a family."

"He was a professor—an historian, I understand."

235

She gave me an awkward glance. "You may as well hear it from me; he was *her* professor. She met him while still a student, though he didn't begin courting her until her final semester."

"Forgive me, Mrs. Johnson, but it's my job to ask difficult questions. Was your daughter happy in her marriage?"

"Happy enough. And so was he—or so I thought."

"Any recent disagreements?"

"No." Her voice was firm.

"Trouble with money?"

Again, she said, "No."

"Had he been upset in recent weeks?"

At this question, she paused before shaking her head. It was a moment's hesitation only, but it led me to ask her one follow-up question. "Did you notice him behaving differently in any way?"

"It was just—" She stopped, biting her lip before continuing. "He was more forgetful and distracted in recent weeks. I'm sure it was nothing, but my daughter didn't usually have to remind him of things."

"Things?" I raised an eyebrow.

"Simple arrangements that are part of our weekly routine, like how I come every Thursday night for dinner or that Ella takes a piano lesson Tuesdays after school."

"But you know of no reason for this change?"

Shivering, she pulled the blanket that covered her grandson to the left, so that a portion of it reached her legs, as well. "I can't understand it," she said once again. "He has three small children. What's to become of them?" Her eyes welled up with tears.

Wordlessly, I passed her a clean handkerchief from my pocket and sat with her while she cried. I hated these cases, for there was never a good answer to the question "why?" And there were never words to help the family left behind.

"Your daughter must have household help?" I asked.

"Just a woman who comes in three days a week to help with the laundry and cleaning," she replied. "My son-in-law was both frugal and private. He never wanted live-in help—not even after my Elizabeth had their third child."

"There was plenty of room," I began to say.

"Of course," she said.

"So no one except your daughter and grandchildren would have heard the gunshot." I paused. "I need to ask her about that—as well as the gun itself."

She was aghast. "Not tonight, surely? Not after the ordeal she's been through."

I considered for a moment. Was my impatience to process this case affecting my judgment?

I decided it was not. I would be kind, but I had real questions for the widow that I needed answered. "I promise to be brief."

An infant's cry rose from somewhere upstairs—faint at first but quickly gaining volume.

"Excuse me," she said, rising with a start but first grabbing a sofa pillow to cushion her grandson's head.

"Of course," I said, getting up as well.

She had not been upstairs for five minutes before I heard the rumble of the coroner's wagon as it turned the corner and stopped in front of the town home. Soon, two burly men were at the door, accompanied by a third man who carried their supplies.

"You have what you need? We can move him?" A gray-bearded man I'd come to recognize asked permission before entering.

"Of course," I said. "He's right back here."

I led them to the back parlor. Mulvaney had been right: this seemed a cut-and-dried case. I needed only a few words with Mrs. Hartt and the doctor's formal autopsy to classify the death a suicide; then I'd write up my notes and close the case file. Mrs. Hartt had my deepest sympathy, of course. But there was nothing I could do to help here, whereas I was desperately needed in the manhunt downtown.

The moment Mrs. Johnson returned downstairs, I asked her to come formally identify her son-in-law.

She took a step back. "There can't be any doubt."

"It's a formality," I said, "but one that either you or your daughter must go through. I'd rather spare her the ordeal."

With that, she agreed. For their part, the coroner's men made the process brief; they had already removed the bloodstained pillowcase and covered Mr. Hartt with a thick white sheet. When Mrs. Johnson approached on unsteady legs, the older assistant took her arm.

"This will be quick," he said to reassure her.

And it was. The other two men lifted a corner of the sheet to expose the victim's face—lowering it the moment Mrs. Johnson nodded.

"It's him," she managed to say.

The moment she confirmed it, they escorted her out of the room—and swept Mr. Hartt's body onto their waiting gurney, re-covering him with a clean, white sheet. Within moments, they had him outside the house in their wagon.

The rookie's eagerness to leave mirrored my own. "We're done now, right?" he asked the moment we heard the wagon depart.

"Almost," I said. Passing my notebook to Will, I added, "While I speak with Mrs. Hartt, would you write up a simple statement of your part in tonight's events?"

He gave me a blank stare.

"Just a few sentences about what happened, as you experienced it," I said in exasperation.

Then I turned once more to Mrs. Johnson. "Would you like help getting your grandson upstairs?" I offered, gesturing toward the boy who still slept in the front parlor.

She hesitated a moment as though she weren't quite sure, but then finally declined. She picked up the boy, supporting his head as she cradled him.

"And I'm almost finished here, if you'd please ask your daughter to come down."

But another voice answered, husky with grief. "There's no need to ask me."

Elizabeth Hartt, a petite blonde in her late twenties, entered the front parlor. "I just wanted to check on Roddy," she said, reaching out her hand to stroke his head.

"I'll put him to bed, dear," her mother said, before leaving us with a final, worried glance.

"Please sit, Mrs. Hartt." I gestured to the sofa.

She took a seat wordlessly, grabbing the wool blanket that had covered her son and pulling it around her.

"I'm very sorry," I began—but then fell silent as her lip trembled and she struggled to retain control.

"It makes no sense," she said after a few minutes.

"Of course not," I said to reassure her. "I just have a few questions for you tonight."

I led her easily through a few, basic factual questions before asking what I most needed to know. "When you heard the gunshot," I asked, "do you recall what time it was?"

She gave me a blank stare before she shook her head. "I never heard anything. It must have happened when the baby was crying. That has to be why I missed it." She thought for a moment. "It was only after I put him down and looked for my husband that . . ." She stopped, choking on the words.

"I understand." I let her compose herself again. "Just one more question; the rest can wait. I need to know if you found and moved your husband's gun?"

She gave me a puzzled stare. "What gun?"

"I'm sorry, Mrs. Hartt. I mean the gun your husband used to end his life."

She flinched upon hearing the words, and I berated myself for not being more sensitive.

"I'd—I'd . . . I'd never touch any gun," she stammered, "much less the gun that killed my husband."

"Never mind. I made a wrong assumption." I stood. "Thank you for your time, Mrs. Hartt. I'll come back at a better time if I have further questions."

She appeared very small, sitting on the sofa.

I left her with a brief nod and returned to the rear parlor.

The rookie had simply missed seeing the gun; of that I was now sure. I should have searched the floor myself and not left the task to him. If I had, we'd be finished by now.

No matter—I'd find the gun now. The only other important evidence I'd need to close the file would come from Dr. Jennings's autopsy.

Back in Allan Hartt's office, Will was ready to leave.

"Just one last thing," I muttered, crossing the room to the chair. I first knelt down, then submitted to necessity and dropped to all fours. I crawled left, then right—lifting the edges of the carpet.

I frowned. There was no gun in sight.

"Did you move anything?" I asked Will, looking around the room.

"Nothing important," he responded with a shrug.

"What did you move?" I asked, immediately suspicious.

"I was waiting here a long time, so I neatened some books. But don't worry, they weren't near his body. And I threw out the flower, 'cause it was all stained with blood. I didn't think Mrs. Hartt would want it anymore."

No gun in sight. He'd thrown out a flower covered in blood.

I didn't like the prickling sensation that started at the nape of my neck, then continued down the length of my spine. "What sort of flower?"

"I dunno," he replied, flustered. "Like I said, it was covered in blood."

"Where is it?" I got up. My eyes darted left and right, looking for the wastebasket.

"There," he said, pointing. "Over by the desk."

I ran to the small waste can that was tucked under the table. Forcing a deep breath, I pulled it out—and shivered.

At the bottom of the can was a single flower: a solitary, bloodstained white rose.

I held it up with my left hand.

My voice shook when I asked him, "The books you straightened. Was one of them a black Bible?"

He nodded, now too scared to talk.

"Show me where."

Again, he said nothing but crossed over to the bookcase and pulled out a leather-bound Bible. Just like the others.

I stared at both the rose and the Bible for what felt like a long time but was probably just seconds.

"Sir," he finally said, "I'm sorry I put those things away. Is something wrong?"

Everything was wrong. The white rose. The Bible. And this dead man who, at least on the surface, appeared to have no connection whatsoever to the murdered judges, the anarchists, or the Drayson case.

Just when I was convinced that someone within the anarchist organization was responsible for the murders of Judges Jackson and Porter, the white rose and Bible—here at a history professor's brownstone—confused everything. How was Allan Hartt connected to the turbulent events that unsettled this city?

It seemed impossible that he was—and yet the bloodstained rose that I held in my fingers suggested otherwise.

I gave the rookie a sober look. "Will, I need you to return to your station house and get an urgent message to Captain Declan Mulvaney. I need two additional men here immediately with camera and fingerprinting equipment."

He stared at me, bewildered, but didn't move.

"This wasn't suicide," I said in exasperation. "Which means this room is a crime scene that requires a thorough investigation. Captain Mulvaney needs to get that message, now!"

Will's eyes widened, but he turned and scampered out the door.

And I was left alone with the rose and the Bible, the blood of Allan Hartt, and a case that made less sense than ever.

PART
THREE

Friday,
October 26, 1906

CHAPTER 21

Barnard College, 116th Street and Broadway. 8 A.M.

Later that morning, I searched Professor Hartt's Barnard office under the watchful gaze of Dean Laura Drake Gill. A determined woman with a round youthful face, she looked much younger than her forty-something years.

"You realize this is highly unprecedented," she said with a stern frown. "We don't normally permit searches of our professors' offices."

Isabella, who had accompanied me, immediately addressed her concern. "And we're fortunate that you understand the urgency of the situation, in light of Professor Hartt's murder."

It had been a stroke of genius to invite Isabella to meet me here this morning. Not only had she smoothed things over with Dean Gill—even deflecting questions about the colorful bruises on my face—but she had been able to elicit the basic facts of

Hartt's tenure at the women's college. Mulvaney had given me only until noon to produce some evidence linking Allan Hartt's murder to that of Hugo Jackson, Angus Porter, or both.

"I can't spare you, Ziele," Mulvaney had said with a sigh. "Besides, no one's going to believe that the Hartt murder is related, since there's no anarchist connection. Not after the attack on you outside the workers' union meeting the other night. Not after the bombing at the Tombs. And especially not with Drayson himself on the loose. No one wants to hear about roses and Bibles."

But my arguments had eventually prevailed over Mulvaney's concerns. "If you can find solid evidence for the commissioner— more than a flower, mind you—it wouldn't be a bad thing for either of our careers," he had grudgingly said. "Especially if it points to an even larger conspiracy."

The commissioner would certainly relish being the person responsible for taking down a large-scale anarchist conspiracy—if that was what this truly was. I had my doubts. Isabella and I had interviewed a number of Professor Hartt's colleagues. And nothing they said about the mild-mannered professor would indicate that he had any connection to the Drayson trial or to Judges Jackson and Porter. But I couldn't ignore the fact that the rose and the Bible indicated a link among these three men.

My thoughts turning to Jonathan, I wondered: Were most anarchists able to separate their personal lives from their political goals? For Jonathan, there was no separation. I had grave concerns that given the opportunity, he would murder the men directly responsible for the *Slocum* disaster—either Captain Van Schaick or one of the Knickerbocker Company owners—mingling his personal anger with political resolve.

Perhaps that was the sort of person we were searching for. I thought of the Swede, whom we had met in the elevator at the Breslin—as well as the other suspects who may have played a role. Strupp, Hlad, China Rose, the mystery woman at the gun shop, or Drayson himself—any one of them might harbor a personal motive, as yet unknown, that was hiding beneath the political fervor of their anarchist ideals. In fact, the more I thought of this angle, the more confident I became that I was on to something. The official focus on Drayson and his anarchist cronies was the perfect cover for a deep-seated personal motive. A personal motive that involved someone named Leroy Sanders.

I turned my attention back to Allan Hartt's office, which was almost as austere as his home. There were no pictures on the walls or the bookshelves; no personal letters or notes on the desk, not even a carpet on the wooden floor. Other than some academic treatises, only a stack of student essays could be found on the bookshelves. And Dean Gill had already assured us that Professor Hartt was a well-respected member of the faculty, with no complaints against him.

I sat down at the desk and opened the top drawer.

"When did Professor Hartt join your faculty?" I asked Dean Gill.

Her eyebrows knitted together as she calculated the years. "He joined us in 1885, when he was a newly minted Ph.D. from Columbia."

"I assume his specialty was European history," I said, having noted the contents of the bookshelves.

She nodded. "Must you really examine the contents of every drawer?"

I made a polite answer, but in reality I was grasping at

straws. And while I didn't expect any answers from the spare contents of the professor's desk—amounting to pencils, paper, clips, and other small items—I couldn't cut corners.

"He must have kept a calendar," I finally said, pushing back the chair in frustration.

The dean gave me a perplexed stare.

"Or an appointment book, for meetings with students?"

"Yes, yes, of course." She indicated that I should follow her to the small secretary's office at the end of the hallway. I did, leaving Isabella to the task of searching the set of cabinets below Professor Hartt's bookcases.

"Our secretary is home ill today, but she keeps all of the professors' appointment books. Most, you see, spend more time in the classroom or the research library than they do in their offices. So we have someone on staff to handle student requests for appointments."

She ushered me into an office just large enough for a desk and chair, bookshelf, and telephone table. I managed to squeeze myself between the desk and the wall, with barely any room to turn around, while the dean ran her finger along the pile of appointment books.

"Allan Hartt. Right here."

She passed me a flimsy cardboard book, which I immediately flipped open to October 1906. Two different kinds of handwriting were inside: one was fine and close, with perfect penmanship; the other was so heavy and bold that the black ink often smeared. My instinct—one that Dean Gill confirmed—was that the secretary had entered the former, and the professor himself the latter. Most of the professor's days had been filled with student appointments, judging from the names and class references the secretary had marked. The professor himself used initials—and I immediately saw that Monday the twenty-second had been marked "HJ." Hugo Jackson?

This could be the connection I was looking for. Had Allan Hartt joined in the meeting with Alistair and the two murdered judges this past Monday? But that meeting had presumably been about the Drayson case. While I'd learned from Dean Gill that Professor Hartt was a native New Yorker from a well-known family and would have run in the same social circles as Alistair, there must be some other reason why the history professor would have joined in a discussion ostensibly about Drayson.

I flipped through prior months and saw similar notations: sometimes "HJ," but other times "AP" or—even more troubling— "AS" initialed on the pages. Alistair Sinclair? It was another confirmation of what Isabella had discovered in Judge Porter's calendar: evidence that these men had met regularly for months.

The final confirmation of a link came from Isabella, who approached the doorway with a worried face. "I finished searching his office and found this, Simon." She passed me a folded letter. "It was tucked between one of his history books and the rear wall of his bookcase."

My fingers pulled the letter apart, though I knew what it was before I opened it: music. Two bars only, but in the same style as the others.

An uncomfortable thought took hold of me. Four men had been meeting regularly. Three were now dead—the same three who had received musical ciphers in the days before their deaths. If Alistair was the fourth, then he was in danger. And given the murder of Professor Hartt, more so than he would imagine.

"You need to see this." I handed Isabella the appointment book, directing her to the relevant dates.

From the odd expression on Isabella's face, I had no doubt that the same thought had occurred to her. She bit her lip and tugged on a curl of her hair, as she often did when worried about something.

"What's wrong?"

"I've figured out how they knew each other," she said. "Come." She motioned me back down to the professor's office, with Dean Gill following close behind.

Once there, she pointed to the framed diplomas on the wall, hidden behind the door. We had not noticed these when we initially entered his office. One from Columbia, the other from Harvard.

"Look," she exclaimed, pointing at the Harvard diploma. "It's not just Harvard. It's Harvard *Law*. And the date is 1877."

I stared at the large piece of parchment. Most of it was in Latin.

"I'm not positive," she said, "but I think that's the year Judge Jackson, Judge Porter, and Alistair graduated. It means the four of them were classmates."

I turned to Dean Gill. "Is that right? I didn't know Professor Hartt had legal training."

She nodded, puzzled that we were so interested.

"Why did he turn from law to history?" Isabella asked.

"I never knew," the dean replied. "Perhaps he loved history more. He certainly completed his history doctorate in record time."

Isabella and I exchanged a worried look. Allan Hartt had

been a classmate of Alistair's—and that meant there was no question that Alistair was hiding something significant. And there was no good explanation for it: either he was involved in something he ought not to be—or his own life was in danger.

We needed to figure out what the two remaining ciphers said—for there were two, including the one Isabella had retrieved from the Porter household. We'd not yet had the opportunity to decode it.

"You must have music rooms where students practice," I said to Dean Gill.

"With pianos," Isabella added.

"Of course. I'll escort you across the quad to the music building." Dean Gill's answer was stiff, but her face wore a look of relief that we were leaving Professor Hartt's quarters.

A cacophony of sounds filled the third floor of the music building where the practice rooms were located. An accomplished pianist was playing something that reminded me of falling raindrops—Isabella told me it was Chopin. With the exception of a high soprano singing her scales, for me the other music blended into indistinguishable notes and sounds. We finally found an empty room, right next door to the music library, and settled in at the piano bench. I placed both ciphers, the code Judge Porter had devised, and a blank sheet of paper in front of us. While we knew that the piano was not essential to unraveling the cipher, I thought it was important to hear the melody played out loud. I wanted to be sure we missed nothing.

"Should I start at the first bar?" Isabella asked, playing a few tentative notes.

"No," I said, "we should start at the white rose." I pointed to the third bar on the page where the image of a rose replaced the clef symbol.

"F—low A—low C . . . B—G." Isabella said the notes intermittently as she began to play.

I cut her off. "This makes no sense. Am I misreading the substitutions?"

"It's the key of A, just like the others," she said, puzzled.

Angus Porter had laid out for us the key to Porta's cipher, based on an A major scale. It was a simple substitution cipher in which pitch and rhythm governed the correspondence between letters of the alphabet and specific musical notes and values. Thus, *A* correlated with the written half-note "low A," then the alphabet ascended to "high E" where the half-note indicated *M* and the quarter-note indicated *N*, with all quarter-note values then descending until quarter-note "low A" indicated *Z*.

Porta's cipher had easily unraveled the embedded code in the music sent to Judge Jackson. But here it revealed nothing but a garbled series of letters.

Isabella's fingers floated over the keys, trying to make music of the notes on the page. "Simon, why do you think the killer uses a musical cipher?" A frown crossed her face. "I mean, there are plenty of ways to hide a message. Why music?"

"No idea. Unless . . ." I stopped myself.

"What is it?"

"He's obviously confident that his recipients can decode what he sends. That may mean something in itself."

"Maybe he sent them instructions," she said.

"Instructions would be useful right now," I muttered, staring at the page in front of me. "You're good at puzzles," I finally said. "Can you think of some variant of Porta's cipher that might have been used here?"

"Maybe. Let me check something in the library."

She left me for a few moments to visit the small music library room, then returned with a biography of Michael Haydn. After grabbing her pencil and notepad, she began to work, flipping through the book's pages, then writing feverishly.

"The goal of these is to make the music as realistic as possible," she said. "A lot of composers—Bach and Schumann among them— became masters of embedding names in their music using more complicated correspondences. But I remember reading about Michael Haydn's cipher, and I'm wondering if it might help us. He devised a cipher that, while presumably for communication, also helped him to compose his music."

Utterly transfixed, I watched her write a series of notes and letter correspondences. "How is his system different?"

"It's more complex than Porta's. His correspondences begin with low bass clef G; that corresponds with the letter *A*. Then G-sharp is *B*, A-flat is *C*, and so forth. He even incorporates punctuation, aligned with rests."

With interest, I noted that what Isabella called a half-note rest—it looked like a man's hat on top of a line—corresponded with a question mark. "And I think this one makes sense. Look: we read it as bass clef high G, high A, E-flat, high G, low B-sharp . . ."

We continued to match each note to the cipher until we had a message:

Two thousand more or you meet the same end.

"Do we assume 'two thousand' refers to money?" Isabella asked.

"I think so. And the word 'more' implies that this wasn't the first request."

She tapped the musical score. "Is this the one delivered to Judge Porter?"

I nodded. "Should we move on to Professor Hartt's?"

"It begins with a white rose," Isabella said, pointing, "and look—these are the same notes. High G, high A, E-flat, high G, low B-sharp, and so forth."

"The exact same message," I said aloud. "Except that Professor Hartt seems unlikely to have two thousand dollars in the bank."

"The dean mentioned that he came from a well-off New York family, though. Perhaps he had family money."

"It's possible. If he did, his manner of living certainly didn't reflect it. Either way, it's blackmail," I said.

"But if the writer wanted money—and had been getting paid—then why kill off the source? It makes no sense." Isabella sat back, dropping her pencil on the table.

"I don't know," I said. "Maybe he'd gotten enough money from his victims. Maybe in the end, revenge was better than payment. But right now we have a different concern—"

She cut into my thoughts. "Alistair—"

"Exactly. We've got to find him, get a message to him."

"But he *must* already know. I don't like thinking this—but he's probably been receiving the same ciphers. Paying the same blackmail money."

"He doesn't know Professor Hartt has been killed," I said, my voice tight with worry. "He doesn't know he could be next."

CHAPTER 22

The Dead House. 10 A.M.

We sought proof of Hartt's murder—solid proof that only science could provide—at the Dead House. It towered above us,
casting gloomy shadows along Centre Street as Isabella and I
approached. Sometimes, when superstition got the better of me,
I thought of the many departed souls whose violent, untimely
deaths led them to pass through this house. And even when my
rational mind kept superstition at bay, I still entered with no
small amount of trepidation.

Dr. Jennings himself would be quick to call this a house of
learning and knowledge, not death. He believed that science
yielded truth, and truth ensured justice. Yet I'd learned otherwise: everyone has a different truth, and science itself is vulner-
able to interpretation. But in a given case, the hard facts that
Dr. Jennings offered—gleaned from massive soapstone tables

where steel instruments cut into flesh and blood and coaxed out their secrets—provided me with the closest approximation of certain knowledge I could hope to find. And if this particular evidence didn't always lead to justice, well—that wasn't the coroner's fault.

Isabella leaned in closer to me as we entered the building and made our way up the marble staircase to Dr. Jennings's office on the second floor. According to the station house secretary, Mulvaney had managed to make it downtown despite his injury and was meeting with the coroner now. Sure enough, we heard the sound of Mulvaney's thick Irish brogue even before we reached Dr. Jennings's door, which was open a crack. Mulvaney was being typically stubborn.

"You're telling me that the path of the bullet alone indicates that it wasn't suicide? Since when did you become an expert on ballistics, Doctor?"

"I've learned a thing or two from doing hundreds of autopsies on gunshot victims." There was a pause. "It wasn't suicide, Mulvaney," Dr. Jennings said, his tone emphatic. "Ziele is right about this one."

I took a breath, made a loud rap on the door, and opened it before the invitation to come in could be issued.

"Speak of the devil," Dr. Jennings said with a broad smile. His eyes rested on Isabella. "I don't believe we've had the pleasure, Miss . . . ?" He half rose out of his seat to greet her.

"Mrs. Sinclair. Professor Sinclair's daughter-in-law."

"Ah." His eyes lit with recognition. "And where is the professor? I'd have thought he'd be eager to help out with a high-profile case like this."

"Unfortunately, he's not."

My response was short, and Jennings interpreted it the wrong way—as I intended him to.

"You need my help, then," he said, self-satisfied. "Take a seat." He motioned for us to pull over two chairs from the corner of his office. "And if you have the stomach for it, help yourselves to something to eat."

A pile of tired, soggy turkey sandwiches rested on a plate between them—right next to several pages of what appeared to be Allan Hartt's autopsy report. I helped myself to one. Despite the subject matter we were about to discuss—not to mention the two skulls that stared down at me from the bookshelf next to the coroner's desk—I was famished.

"I believe you were saying that the bullet trajectory clearly rules out suicide," I said.

"And he doubted me." Jennings passed me a section of his report. "But if bullets don't fall within the expertise of a pathologist like myself, then I don't know what does. No one is more expert at evaluating the damage bullets do to the body—and the trajectories they take when they snuff out a life. And the great city of New York has given me ample opportunity to study the subject."

He waved his left hand toward a glass jar at the top of his bookshelf, filled to its top with small, shiny gold pellets.

"Bullets?" Isabella asked. "There must be at least fifty in that jar."

"Each one is from a victim I autopsied. And I've got two more jars just like it in the lab."

Of course, his lab also contained specimen jars of the sort I'd learned to avoid examining too closely. He collected it all for his research, from tissue samples to liver extracts.

I scanned his autopsy report. "So it was the lack of tattoo-ing around the bullet wound that led you to believe suicide was inconsistent?"

"Exactly." Dr. Jennings pointed to the relevant section of the autopsy with his pen. "If Allan Hartt had committed sui-cide, then the gun would have discharged within inches of his head. That leaves powder marks that we describe as 'tattooing' around the wound. But Hartt's wound showed no sign of that, nor did the pillowcase on his head, indicating that the gun was fired from at least a foot away—physically impossible."

I let Isabella explain the details of what we had discovered at Barnard this morning.

"So blackmail is involved—and Alistair is somehow mixed up in it. Why am I not surprised?" Mulvaney asked with a roll of his eyes.

"The four men are connected. Now three of them are dead," I said simply.

"Have you spoken with Alistair?" Mulvaney asked.

Isabella shook her head. "I can't reach him. I have contacted all of his close friends and colleagues. No one knows where he is, including those friends with whom he often stays while in Boston."

"You've got to try harder," Mulvaney said, sitting up in alarm. "Not just for this case; for his own good."

"We plan to look through the papers in his study. He may have left a record of his itinerary," I said. Not to mention anything else that would help me figure out what he was mixed up in.

"Perhaps Mrs. Sinclair can do that, without your help. I need you back on Drayson," Mulvaney said.

"No one has reported seeing him?" I asked.

Mulvaney shook his head. "Plenty of other developments, though. We located the print shop that created the pink flyer found in the aftermath of the Tombs bombing. And guess who had the flyer made up?" He grinned. "China Rose. We had her picked up yesterday for questioning. And while Funke hasn't yet made a positive identification, I'm guessing that she's also the exotic-looking woman with our Swedish friend the day he bought the Browning pistol used to kill Angus Porter. Looks like the commissioner was right: it's one large conspiracy."

"A large conspiracy where the pieces don't fit together," I said.

"And where the murders of these other three men are playing a role we don't understand," Isabella added.

"I gave you a morning. It's all I can spare." Mulvaney made a hard square of his jaw.

"And in just hours," I countered, "we found compelling evidence linking Allan Hartt to both murdered judges. All three men were in the same Harvard Law class. All three were being blackmailed."

Isabella interrupted me. "And probably Alistair, too—though both of you are too polite to say so in front of me. He's like a father to me and I'm worried about him. I need Simon to solve this case, or Alistair will never be safe."

A flash of sympathy crossed Mulvaney's face, for he genuinely liked Isabella. "I guess we can spare a little more time. Ziele, why don't you put together a comprehensive evidence chart? Maybe organizing our evidence will help us to see the gaps in our knowledge."

"Use my chalkboard," Dr. Jennings urged. "You can erase my own notations."

I walked to the board and picked up an eraser and piece of chalk. After I cleaned the space, I wrote at the top:

VICTIMS
Judge Hugo Jackson, presiding over Drayson trial
    Killed by knife; throat slit
    White rose and Bible by body; hand posed on Bible as though
        taking oath
Judge Angus Porter, expected to take over Drayson trial
    Killed by gunshot, specifically a Browning pistol
    White rose and Bible nearby
    Hands bound
Professor Allan Hartt
    Killed by gunshot, weapon unknown, no bullet found
    White rose and Bible nearby
    Head covered by pillowcase

"These are important differences between the victims," I said, sounding like Alistair. "We've spoken before about how most criminals don't vary their behavior from crime to crime. We're in agreement on that point, so I'll only remark that it's odd that this killer switched from a knife to a gun. And given the likelihood of anarchist involvement, it may simply indicate that more than one person was involved."

"In which case, someone who was comfortable with a knife might have killed Jackson, but someone who preferred guns may have killed Porter and Hartt," Dr. Jennings said. "Makes sense."

"There are other differences besides weapon," Isabella said, studying what I had written. "Each victim was posed—whether with a hand on a Bible, hands bound, or head covered. I believe that has significance, as well."

"And we think the Bible and the flowers are a message from the anarchists?" Mulvaney asked.

"Or something else. It's the blackmail that makes me think of it, since blackmail implies some wrongdoing," Isabella said, her voice becoming animated. "Alistair spoke earlier about how the white rose has often been used to signify betrayal. So since Judge Jackson was posed as though taking an oath, with the rose beside him, it could suggest he broke his oath."

"From his killer's point of view, yes," I said. "Go on."

"Judge Porter's hands were tied. So he may have known about this wrongdoing but done nothing to stop it. So literally, he may have been killed because his hands were tied."

I followed her train of thought. "Hartt was involved, as well, but he didn't—or wouldn't—see the wrongdoing. So whereas I first thought the covering over his head was the act of a suicidal man, trying to spare his wife the sight of his wound, it was actually a message from the killer."

"Sort of like 'see no evil,'" Mulvaney said. "Maybe our killer has a sense of humor."

"Then what was Alistair's role?" I asked.

No one could answer me, not even Isabella.

After some moments, I wrote: *The Killer—what we know.*

"He likely has anarchist connections," Mulvaney said. "Certainly the judicial murders suggest it."

"Agreed," I said, continuing to write.

POSSIBLE ANARCHIST CONNECTIONS
Timing of Jackson (eve of Drayson jury deliberations)
Timing of Porter (verge of taking over case)
Timing of Hartt (day of Drayson escape)

POSSIBLE SUSPECTS
The Swede at the Breslin and Funke's gun shop
He posed as elevator attendant at the Breslin Hotel
He bought and returned a nickel Browning at Funke's
He was seen with an "exotic-looking" woman, possibly Mei Lin
  (China Rose)
Paul Hlad, anarchist leader
Jonathan Strupp
Drayson himself, if masterminding it all from jail
China Rose
An unknown with anarchist leanings . . .
Any combination of the above

"You've mentioned how angry Jonathan was with the directors of the Knickerbocker Company," Mulvaney said. "Were either Judge Jackson or Porter slated to play any role in future *Slocum* trials?"

I raised a skeptical eyebrow. "You mean *if* there are to be additional *Slocum* trials, which I doubt. And to my knowledge, neither judge played—or was expected to play—any role in Captain Van Schaick's trial or appeal."

"Don't forget the repeated references to Leroy Sanders," Isabella instructed me.

I added to the board:

"LEROY SANDERS"
Name referenced in musical cipher
Name signed in register at Breslin Hotel, where Judge Porter
    was killed
Name signed in registry at Funke's gun shop, when second
    murder weapon was bought and returned

PROBLEMS
What do different weapons and crime scene choices indicate?
    More than one killer at work?
    A message about each victim's role in some wrongdoing
No witnesses
No indication how victims were connected, other than Harvard
    Law 1877
Leroy Sanders is unknown. Is he an anarchist or in any way
    related to their cause? Or is he in some way connected to the
    three victims? Or both?
How is Alistair involved?

"I just thought of something," Isabella said, suddenly animated. "What if Professor Hartt didn't turn to history because he
preferred it, as Barnard's dean believed? What if something happened that soured him on the law? Something related to these
blackmail ciphers."

"Maybe," I said. "Alistair maintained that he and the judges
had grown apart in recent years. If there were reasons for that . . ."

"It's a mess," Mulvaney said, tapping his cane against the
floor. "And I'm telling you now: what the commissioner wants is
a clean solution that will yield solid convictions. *That's* our job.
Not this endless speculation."

"I realize the commissioner would like an easy solution. But as we know too well, the easy solution isn't always the right one. Remember the theater murders last spring? You were firmly convinced—"

Mulvaney cut me off. "I know, I know. You needn't remind me . . ."

Dr. Jennings pushed his chair back and stretched his arms behind his head as he glanced at the chart. "When I autopsied each of these men, I did so with the hope that what I would learn would help us to understand how and why they died. It's all I can do for them. But my science can take us only so far." He made a sweeping gesture toward the chart. "Why not let Ziele finish the job?"

Mulvaney hesitated—and in that moment I knew he would agree.

"I need you to trust me," I said, adding with a wry half-smile, "and give my excuses to the commissioner."

"I'll cover for you," Mulvaney said, grumbling. "But tell me, do you honestly think that this case goes beyond the anarchists and their political goals?"

"Yes—in ways I don't yet understand," I said.

One possibility came to me in a flash—and when it did, I wondered why I'd not thought of it before. "Maybe it's the money. Remember what I told you earlier: in recent years, more anarchists have gone to jail because of robbery convictions than dynamite conspiracies. They need money, just like everybody else."

Isabella frowned. "That explains the blackmail, Simon— but not the killings. If the blackmail generated a much-needed source of cash, then why put an end to that source?"

"It's a good question," I admitted. "When we know the answer, we may know who the killer is."

Mulvaney struggled to his feet with the aid of his cane. The meeting was over. "You'd better make quick progress. Every officer in this city is needed for the Drayson hunt. I won't be able to justify this for long."

"You won't need to," Jennings said, chuckling. "Ziele seems within striking distance of a solution." Then, more soberly, he added, "I'd say the main worry is how well the truth he uncovers will suit the commissioner's agenda."

Mulvaney's reply was gruff. "The truth rarely does. But we'll worry about that later."

Isabella said a polite good-bye and left the room first.

Before I followed her, Mulvaney took hold of my left arm. "One word of advice for you: find Alistair and you'll find your answers. I'd bet money on it. Because one thing's for certain—I was right about Alistair Sinclair. I never trusted that man."

I left, saying nothing.

But if I were perfectly honest, I'd admit it: I'd never trusted him, either.

CHAPTER 23

The Dakota, 1 West Seventy-second Street. 12 P.M.

Isabella, now blind to everything except her own purposes, rushed us uptown as fast as the hansom cab would take us. Before I knew it, we were inside Alistair's apartment, and Isabella set to work gaining access to Alistair's private study. Our first obstacle was Mrs. Mellown—for despite her vociferous complaints about Alistair and his habits, she was fiercely protective of him. That also included his work, as it was the thing he considered most important.

Isabella forced a smile, saying, "We've just had a major development in the case, and we need to reach Alistair. He must have left you a number where we can reach him?"

Mrs. Mellown, taken aback, made a large frown. "Why, no. It's not like the professor, of course. But this trip he forgot."

Isabella lifted her chin, and her voice was firm when she

said, "Then I'll need to look through his papers to find it. It won't take but a minute."

Mrs. Mellown crossed her arms. "You know how the professor feels about that, Mrs. Sinclair. Even for you—"

Isabella didn't let her finish. With a dazzling, confident smile, she added, "It's his own fault this time, isn't it? He *always* leaves a number so we can reach him. But he was in such a rush, he forgot to leave it with either of us. And we must reach him immediately." She took off her coat and hung it on the massive walnut and brass coat rack in the entry hall, motioning for me to do the same.

"There's something important you could do," she said, turning back to Mrs. Mellown. "You know the usual places Alistair stays when he visits Boston. Would you help us by placing calls to each of them? If you can locate Alistair by telephone, it will save us some time."

It was unnecessary as a means of finding Alistair because Isabella had already made those calls. Not a single friend had expected Alistair or even been aware that he was in town. It was a fool's errand she was proposing.

But it was a brilliant request all the same, for now Mrs. Mellown had something to do other than worry about her current predicament. As she scurried toward the telephone Alistair kept in his library, Isabella and I made our way to his study at the end of the hall.

I'd rarely been there, for this room was Alistair's private space—his inner sanctum, so to speak. Few guests ever made their way in—through heavy oak French doors with double-paned glass into a room filled with the finest of materials. A thick blue-and-gold-patterned carpet covered the floor, the desk was a

high-gloss mahogany with leather trim, and luxuriant velvet draperies framed the window—which itself offered sweeping views
of Central Park, today a stunning expanse of orange, yellow,
and red treetops.

"I'll take the desk; you take his file cabinet," Isabella said,
crossing to the oversized burgundy leather chair behind the
desk. She pulled open the top drawer and began flipping through
papers.

The file cabinet was near the window. It was locked, so I
pulled out the small steel file I carried with me and made short
work of picking the lock. The cylinder released within a minute—
and I silently thanked my father, a professional con artist, for
teaching me this skill. It came in handy more often than I cared
to admit.

"Remember, we're also looking for anything that might help
to clarify the link among these four men," I said to Isabella.
"Yearbooks and newspapers are just as important as letters,
datebooks, and calendars."

She nodded but didn't look up from her search. Her every
movement was tense as she worked her way through Alistair's
desk, then turned her attention to his bookcases.

Alistair was not a man who saved things, I soon realized.
His most extensive records were financial—but those I barely
scanned, so great was my discomfort in viewing such information. I couldn't justify viewing details I didn't need; after all, my
goal was only to discover his whereabouts and understand his
connection to the three murdered men.

The other file drawers were devoted to individual case studies
he had put together on his research subjects—the various criminals he had interviewed over the years in an effort to learn what

compelled them to behave in the manner they did. There were murderers and arsonists, most of them repeat offenders. I paid particular attention to the notes of his correspondence and conversations with various judges. But neither Porter nor Jackson was ever mentioned—nor was Leroy Sanders, the other name I hoped to find.

I moved to the opposite end of the bookcases from Isabella, pulling over a small ladder to allow me to reach the top shelves, where piles of papers and folders were stacked high. I went through them methodically, one by one, until Isabella motioned for me to join her.

"Look at this, Simon," she said, gesturing to the contents of a crimson leather book.

I climbed down and peered over her shoulder at the Harvard Law School classbook from 1877.

"I marked every page where something connects the four of them together. There are several illustrations and written pieces describing them," she said, flipping between her bookmarks to show me. "The four were inseparable."

"It's a good find. Keep looking—especially in the signature pages at the back where friends write messages."

I returned to my search, pulling down a pile of newspaper articles. I took them to the round table and chair in the corner of the room to review—and flipped through what felt like a news snapshot of Alistair's life. There was a write-up of Isabella and Teddy's wedding in the society pages; of Alistair's joining the faculty at Columbia Law School; and of important trials and criminal cases in which he had played a role. Conspicuously absent were two items.

Teddy's obituary.

And Alistair's own wedding announcement.

The latter I could understand, perhaps, in light of his separation from his wife. But the former struck me as odd, and I dared not ask Isabella. Especially not today.

I had almost made it through the entirety of the stack of papers when I found the item I'd sought. It was from the *Tribune* in September 1877.

> *The District Attorney of New York County, Benjamin K. Phelps, is pleased to announce that six newly minted lawyers have answered the call to public service in this great state of New York.*

I skipped down past the description of one hire from Yale and one from Columbia, until I read:

> *The remaining four new hires are Harvard Law men, graduates of this year's class. Allan Hartt, Hugo Jackson, Angus Porter, and Alistair Sinclair come from New York families of the highest pedigree. It is always a boon to our society when the brightest and most talented of men choose public service over other options they would surely have at their disposal.*

They had begun work together in September 1877—but how long had they continued? I flipped quickly through other papers until I found it: another article detailing Alistair's departure from the district attorney's office. Apparently he had gone from there to clerk for a Criminal Court judge in January 1880. He had spent just over two years with the district attorney, at least some portion of that time serving side by side with the three other men who were murdered this past week.

I made a note of the Yale man and Columbia man who had likewise served in that office. It would be worth a telephone call, at least, to ask whether they had any idea why three men from that office would be brutally murdered almost thirty years later.

Isabella interrupted my thoughts, saying, "Simon, I found something else in the back notes, as you said. Are you familiar with what a final club is?"

"No idea."

"Well, I know from Teddy—" She bit her lip. "I know they're sort of like secret societies. They've got initiations and meetings, and I think their selection process is fraught with secrecy and drama."

"You mean like Yale's Skull and Bones?" That was one society even I had heard about.

"Harvard's groups are different in their focus and scope, but you could think of it that way. The main thing is," she said with a deep breath, "their membership isn't secret. They publish it here." She passed me the classbook.

Before I could examine it, Mrs. Mellown knocked at the door, then opened it. She cast a suspicious look at the stack of newspaper clippings I'd been reviewing, saying, "I've had no success locating the professor. He's not staying at his usual places."

"Thank you, Mrs. Mellown. I wonder if you would help us with one more favor. Are you familiar with these men?" I passed her the names of the Yale and Columbia men who had served with Alistair at the district attorney's office.

"I don't know them," she said, offering the paper back to me.

"While we finish up here," I said, "would you telephone the central operator and try to get a number or address for them?"

She gave me a dubious look but agreed. "And just five more

minutes in here," she said as she left us. "I know the professor's not going to be pleased with this."

We ignored her, turning our attention to the membership lists that Isabella had found published in the classbook. We saw the Delphic Club, the Fox Club, and others with Greek-lettered names. But the one under which Alistair's name appeared— together with the names of Jackson, Porter, and Hartt—was the Bellerophon Club.

"Bellerophon? I assume it has a meaning?"

"In Greek mythology, he is a hero—a slayer of monsters. He tamed Pegasus and killed the Chimera. Alistair appears to have been a founding member, along with the other murdered men . . . and there are references to the club as representing Order triumphing over Chaos."

"Heroes triumphing over monsters," I said. "But perhaps not in this killer's view . . ."

"And you'll find this even more interesting. Look at the signatures in back. There's a page where the members of Bellerophon have written notes to one another."

She flipped the pages to a section at the back.

I took a sharp breath.

I didn't quite trust what was before my eyes—for the page was entirely covered in musical notations. It was just like the ciphers we'd seen, except that there were real signatures beneath the bars of music so carefully hand-drawn. And they matched the list of names we'd just seen under the Bellerophon Club.

"All musical ciphers?" I asked her.

She confirmed it. "I deciphered the first several bars, as you'll see here." She passed me her notebook, explaining, "The ciphers are filled with the usual sentiments: good wishes upon graduation, have a nice summer, and keep in touch. My guess is that to make the club feel more like a secret society, they used the musical ciphers to communicate. So *that* is how they all were able to interpret the blackmail notes they received."

"Which raises the question: How did the killer know this?" I asked, thinking aloud. "Maybe he had some association with Harvard himself, to know about the cipher's connection to these four men."

"Or—imagine if he figured it out later and then used it to his advantage. It would be an effective way of telling them: I know exactly who you are and what you've done."

Mrs. Mellown's knock on the door was brisk—and I knew we'd not be permitted much more time in this room. We'd found what we needed, anyway. I swept the classbook and relevant newspaper clippings into my satchel, then returned the other items to their home on Alistair's top shelf.

Mrs. Mellown stared at us. "Did you discover the professor's whereabouts?"

"Not exactly," I replied, "but we did find some information that may help us. Were you able to locate the men whose names I gave you?"

"Just one. The other, unfortunately, has passed on."

Isabella gave her a horrified glance. "How did you find that out?"

"The family told me. I went ahead and called both men—because I think there's more going on with the professor than you've told me." She shot me a knowing look. "The Yale man died in a train accident fifteen years ago. But the Columbia man is here, still practicing law in New York. I have his number and he's willing to talk with you, if you'd like to telephone him."

I started to thank her, but she cut me off as she tightened her apron.

"Now, along with the both of you. I need to straighten up this room so the professor doesn't find out you've been here. Else he'll have all of our heads."

"Call him from my apartment," Isabella said the moment we left.

I agreed, now almost as worried about Isabella as I was Alistair.

Across the hallway, we opened Isabella's door to find not Isabella's housemaid but her rambunctious golden retriever, Oban. His leash in his mouth, he circled us repeatedly, refusing to be ignored.

Reaching down to rub his head, I attached his leash and passed it to Isabella. "I'll make the call. Take Oban to the park, and I'll catch up with you there. A walk will do you good."

She gave me a look of protest.

"I promise to tell you everything," I said, giving her my most reassuring smile.

Her eyes were pools of worry, but with only one backward glance, she went into the hallway and pressed the button to call the elevator operator.

Closing the door behind me, I went into Isabella's library, picked up the earpiece of her candlestick telephone, and waited for the operator.

"Columbus eight-fourteen," I said—and waited again for her to make the connection. It was several moments before I heard a booming baritone voice on the other end of the line.

"James Ford, here. Who's calling?"

I introduced myself as a colleague of Alistair Sinclair's and explained what I wanted.

"Are you a historian or a detective, Mr. Ziele?" he asked, amused. "You're asking about a time almost thirty years ago."

"It does feel a bit like a history exercise," I said. But I went on to explain how I was interested in Alistair's time working in the district attorney's office—especially in light of the fact that three attorneys who began work there in 1877 had been killed just this week. "I'm wondering if you could tell me about these men—specifically, anything you remember about working with them there."

Sobered by the mention of murder, Mr. Ford took some time composing his thoughts. "I didn't know them well. They were a tight group, at least in the beginning. They'd gone to school together for so long, they'd formed strong bonds. Howie—the other entering attorney that year—and I didn't ever join them."

"Socially or at work?"

"Neither," he said, his answer making clear that he'd never before thought about it.

"They worked cases together?"

"They partnered often—not all four, of course, but in groups of two or three."

"How long did you work for the district attorney?"

"Nearly seven years. I went into private practice from there. Great experience, of course."

"Were the four Harvard men still working there when you left?"

"No. Only Hugo, I think. The other three had drifted away to their own careers."

"But they remained a tight-knit group the entire time they were there?"

James Ford thought for a long moment, then finally said, "I'm not sure. It's been a long time, but I seem to remember they had a falling-out. They split in two, literally. Alistair and Allan left quickly afterward. Angus stayed on a while and continued to be friendly with Hugo."

"Any idea why it happened?"

"No. But your colleague Alistair was always very opinionated. Extremely sure of himself. When others disagreed with him, he didn't tolerate it well. So I always assumed that their falling-out had to do with that."

I smiled in spite of myself. Alistair had changed little during the past thirty years.

"Just one more question: Can you read music, Mr. Ford?"

"I enjoy music—especially a Sousa band," he replied. "But I can't read a note of it."

"So you've never received any music in the mail?"

"You mean concert tickets?"

"No. Actual music that a pianist might play."

"Why would I? It would be preposterous."

The note of truth in his voice led me to believe him—so I thanked him for his time.

"There's just one last thing," I said. "Do you know a law clerk I might hire for a couple of hours to help me look through old cases?"

Isabella sat, looking very small, on a park bench near the open green field. She tossed a ball repeatedly, and Oban dutifully retrieved it. When I appeared, Oban dropped the ball and nuzzled my hand. I picked it up and threw it long—sending Oban hurtling after it.

"Did you learn anything?" she asked, her voice dull.

I took the seat beside her. "Enough to want to look deeper into Alistair's time with the district attorney's office. The four men were close when they entered, but their friendship had splintered by the time Alistair left."

"Mr. Ford himself . . . do you think he's involved?"

"No. He sounded genuinely surprised by most of my questions."

"So maybe nothing happened at the district attorney's office," she said, brightening.

Oban returned the ball, and I threw it again, even farther. "Not necessarily. James Ford didn't work often with the Harvard men; they were too close-knit."

Her face fell.

"I just don't understand," she finally said, her voice cracking. "Alistair is a good man. I *know* that from every interaction I've had with him over the years. How is it possible that we've come to this—searching among his private things? Wondering why he's being blackmailed?" She paused. "You can only blackmail someone if there's some wrongdoing they want to hide."

I turned to face her. "What we're searching for is rooted deep in Alistair's past. It changes nothing about who he is today—or how he has treated you over the years."

"It makes me wonder: how well do I know him really?" She whispered the question as though she was afraid to ask it.

Oban returned, this time collapsing at our feet, deciding to chew the ball.

"Everyone has secrets, Isabella," I said. "Alistair's secrets matter because they're placing his life in danger—and they're thwarting our investigation into three murders."

"What if we discover something that changes things?"

There was no good answer to that, so I didn't try. "Alistair has always been willing to bend the rules, if you will, for his professional goals. But he's remained loyal to you and all his family."

It was a polite lie, for I'd never seen him with family other than Isabella.

She shook her head vigorously. "I understand that family was important to him. He loved Teddy; no one could love a son more. He even stood up for me when no one else did. You see, no one approved of me as a match for Teddy, at first."

"Why?" I held my breath, wondering if she'd answer.

A curious expression crossed her face before she said, "My mother was Italian."

She was matter-of-fact, as though that admission should explain everything. And perhaps it did—at least, in the Sinclair social circle.

But it had not mattered to Alistair, and I found myself admiring that about him.

"But now he's disappeared without saying anything. What problem could be so terrible that he wouldn't confide in me?"

"I don't know." I'd asked myself the same question—and I had yet to come up with a good answer.

"The problem is, I depend on him."

There was nothing I could say, so I put my arm around her

and held her as she cried quietly, grieving for something precious, now forever lost. To depend on someone, you have to be able to trust him—or her. And Isabella would never manage that with Alistair again.

CHAPTER 24

The Legal Archives Office. 1:30 P.M.

I'd had no luck tracking down Alistair himself—but at the Legal Archives Office that afternoon, I believed I was close to discovering part of his past.

"Do you know what you're looking for, sir?" Jeremy Jacobs, the twenty-four-year-old clerk at James Ford's law firm who would be helping me, looked at me with earnest eyes. "What you told the records keeper made it sound as though we're searching for the proverbial needle in a haystack."

I grinned. "We are—though I do have more information than I shared with the records keeper."

I'd spun a general tale about Judge Jackson's anarchist cases to gain entry here, into the vast building that housed the district attorney's nearly one hundred years' worth of archival records.

With Drayson still at large, no one questioned any undertaking related to the anarchists.

Jeremy gave me a blank look—and I worried whether he would be up to this morning's task.

"We don't typically do criminal work," Mr. Ford had said, "but Jeremy is my brightest clerk."

"Has he been with you long?" I'd asked, worried about his lack of experience.

James Ford had laughed at me. "Three years. But don't worry: In law, it's not what you know. It's how well you discover the things you don't know. And Jeremy's research skills are superb."

I could only hope that Mr. Ford was right, now that Jeremy and I had descended into the bowels of the archive building. We stood in a dusty, ill-lit basement storage room, where hundreds of boxes were stacked on metal shelves, representing thousands of old case files.

"We're lucky," Jeremy said, "that the more recent case files are right over here." He gestured to an area by the window that was noticeably brighter and cleaner than other sections.

"Unfortunately, I don't need recent materials. I'm looking for case files from almost thirty years ago: September 1877 to January 1880, handled by one of four attorneys." I recited their names.

His jaw dropped. "Excuse me, Detective—but you can't be serious. Thirty years ago? I thought your research was related to the Drayson matter."

I ignored him, saying only, "Judge Jackson and three of his close friends began working in the district attorney's office in

September of 1877. I need to know what they were working on. And I believe the name Leroy Sanders will come up somehow."

"Was he the defendant in a case they were prosecuting?"

"I'm not sure."

"Have you tried looking up *People versus Sanders*?"

"I would if I knew how. I'd asked a colleague of mine to check, and he claimed there was no such case. It's possible that he lied."

Jeremy adjusted his black-framed glasses. "I'll check for you now, Detective."

"Meanwhile, could you direct me toward the case files for September 1877?"

"Of course, sir." He consulted his map. "We'll need to find stacks section number three hundred thirty-five."

"These case files should include their personal notes, am I correct?"

"Yes, sir—to the extent there are any."

He directed me to the relevant area of the stacks before he went upstairs in search of *People v. Sanders*.

I opened the box nearest me and began thumbing through papers. The files made clear that Hugo Jackson had pursued center stage in the courtroom—and by December 1877, he was being permitted to run a handful of easy cases as lead prosecutor. Angus Porter had similar early success; he served as lead prosecutor on smaller cases by 1878.

Alistair had played a different role in the district attorney's office. He had been expert, I soon realized, at building strategy for the most challenging parts of a case—instinctively understanding what pieces of evidence would be most compelling to a jury. From the trial notes, it seemed everyone wanted Alistair's advice. He had often sat in the second chair at the prosecutor's table.

But he hadn't served as a lead prosecutor himself. In fact, it looked as though he hadn't even sought the role—and I wondered why. It wasn't typical of Alistair to embrace a supporting part.

Then again, looking at a newspaper sketch artist's illustration that depicted Alistair's younger self at twenty-five, I realized how odd it was to observe Alistair through the lens of so many years. If I didn't truly know the present-day Alistair, then how could I pretend to know his much younger self?

Out of nowhere, Jeremy's voice startled me. "Here you are, Detective. It's the opinion of the appeals court on the matter."

I'd not expected him back so quickly—and yet, a quick check of my pocket watch showed me that he had been gone nearly an hour. It was a reminder of how easily one could lose track of time down here.

Jeremy practically beamed with pride when he handed me a file in a tattered brown file folder. *"Appeal in the Matter of People versus Sanders."*

"Thank you. But what about the original trial?" I asked. That was the trial Alistair and the others would have worked on—and thus what interested me most.

"It's the oddest thing, sir. The transcript is entirely missing. Several people have looked for it over the years, according to the records keeper's log sheet. But it's been missing since the mid-1880s. I'm afraid the appellate court opinion will have to do, sir."

So Alistair hadn't lied, exactly—but I couldn't help wondering whether he'd had anything to do with the trial transcript's disappearance. I wouldn't put it past him.

I glanced at the multiple stacks of boxes around us. "I'll want to see the case notes surrounding it. Does the appeal tell us when the case was originally tried?"

"November 1878, sir. I'll locate the box while you review the case."

I muttered my thanks and read.

The People of the State of New York, Respondent,
V
Leroy A. Sanders
Court of Appeals of New York
Argued June 17, 1879
Decided October 15, 1879
Opinion of the Court
Laskey, J.

In various forms the indictment herein charges the defendant with the crime of murder in the first degree. The substance of the charge is that defendant killed one Sally Adams, age ten, by strangulation and other violence done upon her body. The legal question, which it is our duty to consider upon this appeal, cannot be intelligently discussed without a clear understanding of all the complicated facts and circumstances upon which the prosecution seeks to sustain the judgment of conviction against the defendant.

I skipped through several more paragraphs of legal language until I finally reached a concise summary of the case. The facts were that Leroy Sanders, a carpenter, had done work on the Adams family home in Fordham. Shortly after his project for the family was completed, their youngest child, Sally, had disappeared. After a week, her battered, violated body had been discovered in an outhouse a half mile away. Suspicion had fallen upon Leroy Sanders almost immediately, but it was the testimony of his own partner that had convicted him. Harry Blotsky had testified that Leroy gave undue attention to the girl, and that he had seen him take the girl and walk with her some distance from the house. The appeal challenged the trial judge's decision that had admitted Blotsky's evidence at the last minute; the appeal was denied and the conviction sustained.

"These two boxes should do it, sir," Jeremy said, struggling under their weight. "Would you like me to help you look for anything in particular?"

"Thanks," I said, motioning for him to put them on the floor. I eased myself into a sitting position between the two stacks of bookcases. "I'll start with this box, and you with the other. Please look for anything that strikes you as unusual."

"In what way?" A puzzled look crossed his face. "I'm not sure I'd recognize anything unusual about a criminal case."

"Just use your common sense," I said, trying to sound encouraging. "The legal background is less important than what the attorneys working on the case discussed."

For the next hour at least, we read and reviewed dozens of notes about the case—many of them written in Alistair's precise hand, now so familiar to me. As before, he had orchestrated the legal strategy that Hugo and Angus had presented in court as co-counsel. Alistair and Allan Hartt had served as research counsel—a role they evidently preferred. Both had an instinctive eye for what evidence was most compelling. But I saw nothing untoward. In fact, according to all evidence in the box, Leroy Sanders's eventual conviction had been entirely justified.

It was Jeremy who brought up the only aspect of the case that might be considered odd.

"Look at the date when Leroy's partner, Harry Blotsky, surfaced to testify against him: December 1878. The trial was just wrapping up, and they needed the judge's special permission to allow him to testify so late in the proceedings."

"Why?" I asked.

"Well, it seems he had changed his testimony from when the police first interviewed him. That's always a problem for the prosecution. But attorneys Jackson and Porter presented good reasons as to why the witness's testimony changed, and so the judge permitted it."

"What did they argue?"

He flipped back through the pages in his hand. "Based on Alistair Sinclair's research, they claimed that Harry had been so intimidated by Leroy that he didn't feel safe telling the truth. Until he was assured that the truth would keep Leroy behind bars for life."

"That makes sense, doesn't it?" I thought it did. It was the reason why my own precinct sometimes had difficulty gathering the evidence that would convict our most violent offenders: no one wanted to risk testifying against them.

"Perfect sense," Jeremy said—but he didn't sound as though he believed it.

I considered the question again. Leroy was accused and convicted of violating and killing a child. As awful as that was, there was no suggestion anywhere in his file that he posed a threat to other adults. Alistair himself had written a memo concluding that Leroy had a high potential for recidivism—in other words, for repeating his crime. But in Alistair's own words, the threat Leroy posed was to minors. And in the sketch artist's rendering, Leroy was a slight man. Harry Blotsky towered over him. Would Harry truly have been afraid of Leroy?

I continued to puzzle over that oddity as I thanked Jeremy for his help.

The records keeper gave us both a satisfied look as I signed out of his registry. "I'll bet you boys haven't heard the good news, since you've been stuck in the archives all morning."

"What news?" I set the pen back into its inkwell.

"They captured Drayson. Found him hiding out in the basement of some opium den in Chinatown. Now we'll have justice and order in this city again," the records keeper said with a vigorous nod. "The anarchists will pay for what they've done."

Drayson and Jonathan Strupp and the other anarchists would certainly get their due. The commissioner would see to that. But I couldn't help wonder: Would it come at the expense of the truth?

There was no doubt that the murder of Judge Jackson lay at the center of a hotbed of anarchist conspiracies and political malcontent, but I was now convinced that the murders of Judge Porter and Professor Hartt were connected, as well. Their murders extended this matter far into the past, touching on hidden secrets and issues so deeply personal that vengeance must be sought in blood. And if I didn't find him soon, not only did I fear that Alistair's blood would be the next to spill—I somehow knew that we would never uncover the truth.

CHAPTER 25

The New York Times Building, Times Square. 3 P.M.

"Hop to it, boys. We got thirty minutes till press time—and we don't want to get scooped by the *Tribune* like last week." Ira Salzburg, the stout managing editor of the *New York Times*, swaggered across the room as he barked instructions. Dressed in his trademark yellow and green suit, he stopped to check on first one reporter, then another, before retreating into his office and closing the glass door. There were nearly fifty reporters in the room, punching keys furiously on Hammond typewriters along long rows of tables. But not one reporter looked up.

I had come to see Frank Riley, the crime beat reporter who had been instrumental in helping me to solve a series of murders in the theater district last spring. He'd impressed me then with his tenaciousness as a crime beat reporter—and if anyone had the determination to look for the story that Commissioner Bingham was determined to quash, it was Frank.

I'd just left Mulvaney at precinct headquarters and he'd confirmed what I knew all along: the commissioner planned to charge Drayson and other anarchist leaders, including Jonathan, with the murders of Judge Jackson, Judge Porter, and the guards who were victims at the Tombs bombing. The commissioner's edict had been to gather proof by any means necessary. And I knew what that meant: scapegoating an anarchist conspiracy would be more important than uncovering the truth.

I soon spotted Frank, a wiry man with dark hair slicked back, working at the first typewriter on the left. No one even gave me a second glance as I made my way toward him.

"Got a minute, Frank?" I asked, my voice quiet.

He looked up, and his expression of annoyance turned to surprise the moment he recognized me. "Your timing's bad, Ziele. Things are crazy here. We're printing a special edition. I've got half an hour to pull together my piece on Drayson and the Tombs bombing."

"I don't have much time, either—and I need your help. If I'm right, you'll be typing up a whole different story." I nodded toward his typewriter.

He shoved his chair back. "That important? Then let's find a quieter place to talk."

"How about the archive room?"

He raised an eyebrow. "Guys around here call it the newspaper morgue. Follow me."

He led me out of the City Room to shouts of protest from

other reporters. "Helluva time to grab a smoke, Frank," and, "Tryin' to get fired, Frank?"

Flashing a grin, he quashed their remarks, saying, "You fellas worry about your own job."

He led me to the stairwell, where we descended six flights. The morgue itself was a cavernous room, dimly lit, and filled floor to ceiling with file cabinets and bookcases.

"We got everything here. Photographs. News clippings. Everything we've done since 1851, with major story clippings from the competition, too." He gave me a hard stare. "Want to tell me what's up?"

"There's a second story here—one that's far more complicated than just the anarchist conspiracy." I briefed him on the major evidence I'd found, omitting Alistair's name for now.

When I finished, Frank only shrugged. "Sounds interesting. But the commissioner won't be interested in hearing about a more complex plot."

"Politicians like things simple. I realize that."

He gave me a curious look. "Then why are you so keen to figure out the truth? It will make no difference to you."

I thought of Alistair and, more importantly, of Isabella, but I said only, "Because Allan Hartt deserves justice. His murder—because it *was* murder—should be formally connected to the others. He's as deserving of justice as Judge Jackson or Judge Porter. There is a deeper motive at work, one that I do not yet understand, but I am confident it connects the murders of these three men."

"So what's here in the morgue that will help?"

"Any old write-ups you have of *People* versus *Sanders*. The trial began in November 1878 and continued until a verdict was reached in January 1879. It was appealed in June of the same year."

Frank raised another eyebrow as he ran his hand over slicked-back hair. "Forgive me for saying so, but if you're trying to tell me a modern-day anarchist conspiracy is connected with a thirty-year-old trial, I'm not sure you're thinking straight."

"You may be right. I won't know until I find those files."

He inclined his head. "I'll pull them for you. And if there's anything in them that leads to a story . . ."

I nodded. "You'll be the first to know."

"You always did keep your promises, Ziele. That's why I'll help you. But be quick, 'cause I gotta get back to work."

Frank Riley had kept his word before, too; it was the main reason I had sought his help. Unfortunately, at this point in the investigation, men I could trust were in decidedly short supply.

Two hours later, I stepped into Artuso's, an Italian coffee and pastry shop where glass shelves filled with cannoli and colorful cookies competed for customers' attention with a selection of Italian coffees in hand-painted ceramic canisters. But the crown jewel of the shop was an espresso machine imported from Italy—a shiny silver device that whistled and chugged as the steam pressure forced the hot water through finely ground coffee. I ordered a double espresso and cannoli from the gruff man behind the counter, then settled at a table by the window. Outside, the crowds converged onto Longacre Square—or rather, Times Square as it had been renamed in honor of its major tenant, the *New York Times*. Salzburg's reporters had made their deadline, and I watched as newsboys sold papers like hotcakes to passersby.

I downed my espresso, savoring its rich aftertaste, ordered

another, and began to go through the files Frank had lent me. Article by article, I soon pieced together the story in more detail than the legal archives had allowed.

By all accounts, Leroy Sanders was an expert carpenter who had found ready work up until the day of his arrest. As a tradesman in the Adams family home, he had almost immediately come under suspicion after young Sally Adams first disappeared, then turned up dead, "discarded like a used doll in an outhouse," as the paper had said. It was the evidence that Harry Blotsky had provided at the last moment—that Leroy went walking with the girl away from the house—that had convicted him. The final article mentioned that only Mrs. Leroy Sanders had been present at his sentencing; he had been lucky to escape a death sentence in favor of a life term at Auburn Prison. Mrs. Sanders had left the courtroom in tears, insisting that Leroy's conviction was wrongful. "My Leroy is a peaceful man," she had said. "He loves his family and his music."

Reading that, my breath caught and the pit in my stomach grew larger as I thought of the musical ciphers each victim had received. Remember Leroy. A lover of music. They now had added significance in my mind.

I turned my attention to my cannoli, which I'd not touched. I devoured it so fast I barely tasted it. The three murders had to do with the killer's belief that Leroy had been wrongfully convicted of murder; that motive was now clear. But who cared so deeply about this case from long ago? Who had the means and opportunity to plan and execute these killings? And what connection was there to the anarchists?

I scraped my plate with my fork, watching as an electric cab drove past on the street in front of me.

I sat up—and dropped my fork—for it immediately came to me.

The electric cab at the Dakota.

It had taken Alistair's luggage to its destination. And while Alistair's horse-drawn hansom cab had been hailed off the street, the electric motorcar had been ordered in advance. The company no doubt had a record of the fare.

I pushed back my chair, got up, and ran to the counter. "Do you have telephone service here?" I asked the gruff, whiskered man who ran the coffee machines.

He turned his back to me. "Not for customers."

I pulled out my detective badge. "For official police business."

"Well, in that case." He motioned me toward a small back office where a black candlestick telephone sat on the desk.

I picked up the receiver. "New York Transportation, please."

I drummed my fingers in anticipation, waiting for the operator to make the connection.

The moment she did, my words tumbled out in a rush. "On Wednesday, you picked up a fare at the Dakota—a luggage trunk, billed to Alistair Sinclair. I need to know where that trunk went."

The woman on the other end must have recognized the urgency in my tone; she didn't bother to ask for my credentials. She disappeared from the line for several minutes and returned.

"Sir, that cab took the trunk to Fifth Avenue and Thirty-fourth Street. The Waldorf Hotel."

I wasn't sure I'd heard right. "Are you sure?"

"Yes, sir. We noted it clearly in our log."

I thanked her, called Isabella to meet me, and then grabbed my files before sprinting the eight blocks downtown to where Alistair was apparently in hiding.

I had to admit the irony of it: in dire straits, Alistair had turned not to friends or family, or even to one of the seedy hotels downtown where my own father often sought anonymity after a bad night at the tables. Alistair had chosen the Waldorf as his place of refuge. It was an absurd choice. But leave it to Alistair to manage a course of action that was both foolhardy and at the same time brilliant—simply because no one in his right mind would ever think of it.

CHAPTER 26

The Waldorf-Astoria Hotel, Fifth Avenue and
Thirty-fourth Street. 6 P.M.

"There's no one here by that name, sir." A young man with tousled brown hair frowned after examining the register. "Definitely no Sinclair registered here. Perhaps you have the wrong hotel?"

"He would have checked in Wednesday," I said, insistent. "Late afternoon, between four and five o'clock. He may not have used his own name."

The clerk's hazel eyes grew wide. "But I can't possibly check the record of every guest who checked in Wednesday afternoon. We're the largest hotel in the world; we register over fifteen hundred guests a day."

I didn't move.

He scratched his chin. "Of course, I can try. Maybe you'll recognize one of the names."

"Try the Astoria section first," Isabella said, adding for my benefit, "It's newer and more luxurious."

He rustled through his register, then began reciting names.

Jacques Rimes.

Anthony Black.

Hugh Stowe.

John Rhys.

We shook our heads. Maybe this just wasn't going to work. I scrambled to think of other options—from questioning the maid staff to tracking down the specific bellhop who delivered his luggage—as the clerk ran through more choices.

Edward Graham.

James Warble.

Hans Enrico.

Isabella grabbed my arm with excitement. "That's it."

"Are you sure?" I asked. The name meant nothing to me.

She nodded. "It's the perfect alias Alistair would choose. The names of his two criminology mentors."

"What room is Mr. Enrico in?" I asked the clerk.

"Number sixteen twenty-one. The Astoria section of the hotel. To reach the elevator, you'll pass through Peacock Alley." He pointed. "The passageway to the left."

Isabella thanked him, then rushed with me to the elevator, explaining on the way. "You see, they were two hotels until recently—the Waldorf and the Astoria, owned by two Astor cousins, William and John Jacob. Now they're connected into one large hotel."

"By this passageway?" I asked, glancing at the blue and gold decorations around us—no doubt the inspiration for the term "Peacock Alley."

"Exactly. Now, let's hurry."

At the elevator bank, an impassive attendant in a stiff blue and gold uniform pressed the buttons that would take us up to the eighteenth floor. The small elevator, stuffy with hot air, seemed to move at a snail's pace before finally lurching to a stop.

We raced down the hallway until we reached the cream-painted door at the end adorned with number 1621 in brass.

I rapped three times, then called out, "Alistair! Open up."

No response.

I knocked again, louder this time. "Alistair."

Two doors down, an elderly lady in a stiff pink satin gown opened her door and stared at us. "Sir, really," she said with an imperious glance, "the concierge downstairs is available to help you with any problem." Then she closed her door with a slight snap.

"Let me try," Isabella said with a nervous glance farther down the hallway. "You're just going to generate noise complaints."

She knocked on the door herself: a series of short, brisk raps. "Alistair, it's me, Isabella. You've got to let us in. We know you're in there; we're here to help you."

We were rewarded with only more silence.

"It's no good," I said. "We're going to have to find someone on staff with a key."

Isabella held up a finger, continuing to talk. "We have information you need to know. About Allan Hartt. About why you and other members of the Bellerophon Club have been targeted."

We heard heavy footsteps approaching the door.

Alistair swung it open and stared, angry and belligerent.

"How the hell did you find me? And what do you know about the Bellerophon Club?"

His words were slurred and he was a disheveled mess— unbathed and unshaven, stinking of liquor, and wearing a stained, untucked shirt. He blocked the doorway, but I pushed my way inside past him. Isabella followed, and I caught her sharp intake of breath when she saw the room itself—for Alistair had managed to transform one of the Waldorf-Astoria's finest suites into something that resembled a pigsty.

The plush blue-and-gray-patterned carpet was littered with scotch bottles. Though most were now empty, a handful contained liquor that had spilled and created dark stains on the carpet. At least ten silver trays, stacked with dirty plates of half-eaten food, were strewn about the room. Alistair's luggage trunk sat to the left, closed and untouched. But newspapers and his personal writings were everywhere.

"What is going on?" I asked, my eyes blazing in anger. "You sit here, holed up, while we are searching all over for you. You left word at Columbia that you would be at a legal conference in Boston. Why did you lie?" I kicked an empty scotch bottle out of my path as I made my way into the room. "Why didn't you say anything to us?"

He leaned in close and his breath was foul with stale liquor. "I trust no one. They're trying to kill me."

"You might have trusted *me*," Isabella said. "Family doesn't do this to each other. Or, at least they shouldn't."

Alistair's clear blue eyes momentarily clouded. "I didn't want you to worry."

"Never mind our worrying; think of the progress we'd have made if you'd only talked with us," Isabella said, her voice rising. "Instead, we wasted days figuring out your predicament for ourselves."

"You might have saved yourselves the trouble," he said, grumbling. "I don't want you involved. I can handle this on my own."

"Just like Hugo Jackson thought he could?" I demanded. "Or Angus Porter? Or Allan Hartt?"

Alistair blanched, sinking onto the bed. "Allan Hartt's not—"

I didn't mince words. "You're the only one left. This killer is coming for you. And if we're going to stop him, we need your help."

"But I don't *know* anything." He got up yet again and started pacing back and forth. "If I did, I wouldn't be holed up here."

I removed a pile of papers Alistair had set on an upholstered ottoman, then I sat and spoke to him more calmly. "Alistair— what, exactly, are you doing here?"

He collapsed into the high-backed paisley chair next to the desk. "Trying to figure out why someone wants to kill me."

"And you have no idea?"

He hung his head. "None whatsoever."

I gave him a sharp look. "Then let's put together what all of us know. I'll start." I went on to detail all I'd uncovered about Leroy Sanders, saying, "The root of this murder plot seems to originate in the Sanders trial. Someone believes the four of you are responsible for what was—in the killer's view—an erroneous conviction."

He sat back, deflated. "I'm impressed, Ziele. You discovered more than I ever thought possible about a decades-old case."

"All of which you might have told me, instead of wasting my time and endangering your life."

"As I said, I didn't want you involved."

"Blast it, Alistair," I said, "you involved me the moment you brought me into the Jackson investigation. For that, you might have trusted me more."

I forced my rising anger back under control, then said, more calmly, "Now tell me about the musical ciphers. You used them in law school as part of your final club."

"Yes," he said with a sigh. "A form of secret communication for club members. We concocted it . . . I don't even remember why. We were young and wanted to prove how smart we were by inventing a secret language."

"How could the blackmailer know this?"

His face flushed with embarrassment. "You know about the blackmail?"

"We do," I said.

He dropped his face into his hands and was silent for several moments. "I've no idea," he said, his voice hoarse with frustration. "I figured it was his way of proving how smart *he* was. He wanted us to know he knew all about us."

"We thought of that, too. How much did he ask for?"

"Five hundred dollars, usually. Sometimes more. The latest request was for two thousand dollars."

I whistled. It was over two years' salary for me. "How often?"

"About twice a year for me. But Hugo apparently received letters more often."

"And you continued to meet as a group in New York, even after you graduated?"

"We did. The four of us—you've already learned that Hugo, Angus, Allan, and I went to the district attorney's office together— met at the Lawyers' Club once a week."

"Why bother, when you weren't in school?"

He shrugged. "We thought we had all the answers. That we understood the latest in criminal thought, unlike anyone else around us. So we met to discuss the cases we were handling in our offices, with an eye to how we'd do it better."

"When did you stop?"

"Just before I left the DA's office. There was no point any longer. Besides, we'd argued—and our friendship had deteriorated because of it."

"When did the blackmail begin?" Isabella asked, breaking into our conversation.

"It was five years ago," Alistair replied. "The four of us began receiving letters from someone angry about the Leroy Sanders case. The writer—who signed every letter 'Avenge Leroy'—knew all about the case."

"What did he threaten if you didn't pay up?" Isabella's voice was crisp.

Alistair made a wry half smile. "What do blackmailers ever threaten? Exposure of something embarrassing. Something you'd rather the world not know."

"A real misstep in the Sanders trial," I said, finishing for him.

"Exactly. And the four of us were at points in our professional lives where admitting our mistakes would be publicly humiliating. Whoever the blackmailer is, he correctly surmised that we'd rather pay up than have our past mistakes scrutinized." His face flushed, filling with embarrassment, and then something resembling relief as he admitted it.

"Prosecutors get it wrong all the time," I said. "I don't understand why you would give in to a blackmailer—not over this."

He shrugged. "Hugo had just been elevated to the bench. I'd just published a major paper. We wanted to avoid any embarrassment. And we didn't want to revisit the past. Even if what happened wasn't entirely our fault. The evidence was there."

I let forth a deep sigh, frustrated that Alistair still wasn't being completely honest. But rather than argue the point now, I decided to move on. "You mean the evidence offered by Leroy's partner," I said. "His testimony is what convicted Sanders."

"Yes, but there was more, as well." Alistair's cheeks flushed again, and he sat up straighter. "We'd all studied under an eminent criminologist at Harvard who believed you could ascertain a man's propensity for crime. He had tested his research and the results were astounding. Based on his methodology, no man had a greater propensity for crime than Leroy Sanders—particularly the sort of crime he was accused of committing. He shared all the common characteristics and behavioral patterns of others who have committed similar crimes."

"You mean those who have violated and killed young girls," I said.

"You're rather blunt, Ziele," he said with a glance toward Isabella, "but yes, that's what I mean."

"And in Sanders's case, you were wrong." I got up, crossed to the window, and opened the drapes. It was a cloudy day, but at least some light now entered the room.

"It turns out we were, yes. But we didn't know it at the time." He let forth a heavy sigh as he ran his hands through unwashed hair. "We found out years after the fact. A series of murders happened that were eerily reminiscent of the Sanders case. They caught the man responsible—and he admitted he had been killing young girls for years, first in New York, then in his native

Canada. They caught him when he returned to New York after a fifteen-year hiatus."

"So you worked to clear Leroy Sanders's name."

A guilty expression crossed his face. "There was no point."

"Why not?" I pivoted away from the window to face him. "It seems the least you would owe an innocent man!"

Alistair's voice grew rough. "By the time we understood everything, Sanders was dead. You see, he died in prison. We were too late."

We remained silent.

Alistair finally spoke again. "You have to understand that we were absolutely convinced of Leroy Sanders's guilt at the time. Especially Hugo Jackson—and no one knew the case better than he did."

"But none of you ever had the slightest inkling who the blackmailer was?"

"Never," Alistair said.

"Did you ever find Leroy's next of kin?"

"I'm ashamed to say, I never tried to find out," he said with a sheepish look.

"That would be a place to start," I said, and suggested to Isabella a number of sources where she might look. "Begin with the death records at Auburn Prison," I said. "I'll check the newspaper archives."

She nodded, making a note of it.

"We need to look seriously at the Swede," I said, and explained how his use of the name Leroy Sanders—at both the Breslin and Funke's gun shop—connected him firmly to Angus Porter's murder. "There was a matching ballistics test, as well," I added, explaining the results.

We talked more of different theories and possibilities but always came back to the Swedish man and his likely connection to Sanders.

"We need to go," I finally said, exchanging a look with Isabella.

"Not me. I'm staying here." Alistair planted himself in the desk chair, almost gripping its sides.

"Only if you take care of yourself," I warned, my voice stern. "You're staying in a world-class hotel and believe me—no one except us would think of looking for you here. I'm sending a housekeeper up to get rid of this mess." I made a face of disgust as I gestured to the liquor bottles and food trays that surrounded us. "And no more scotch. You should eat a decent meal and take a bath."

He started to interrupt me, but I wouldn't hear him. "If you do these things—then we will keep your whereabouts a secret." I let out a heavy sigh and glanced at Isabella. "Just one more question. Why didn't you confide in one of us?"

He glanced out the window at the view of Fifth Avenue and its slow-moving traffic. "I told you already. I didn't want you to worry."

I stepped closer to him. "No. I'm asking for the *real* reason."

He caught my eye briefly, then looked away. "You've never been blackmailed, Ziele. There are no words to describe—" His voice cracked. "It makes you feel trapped. Completely helpless."

"But we could have helped you, from the beginning," I said.

"I didn't want your help." He looked down at the floor. "I couldn't bear you seeing me this way. Weak." His voice shook with disgust.

I nodded. At least I now understood. It wasn't the mistake

from his past that had shamed him. He was proud, and the humiliation caused by the blackmail had been too great.

He looked up, his eyes filled with concern. "Are you sure you weren't followed?"

"We weren't," I said, my voice flat. "We'll stop by tomorrow to check on you. Meanwhile, try to help us think of the best strategy for solving this matter."

"Good night, Alistair," Isabella said, her voice a whisper.

Alistair didn't answer—but his expression was one of complete remorse.

And the look of disappointment on Isabella's face was unbearable, so I turned away.

I escorted Isabella back to the Dakota, buying three papers along the way: the *Times*, the *Tribune*, and the *Post*. Each paper was filled with stories about Drayson's capture, together with that of "masterminds" Paul Hlad and Jonathan Strupp.

I inwardly groaned, though I was careful to give Isabella nothing new to worry about. This case seemed destined to end badly. And I was becoming convinced that there would be no satisfactory conclusion for any of us.

Not for me, with my investigation running counter to the commissioner's designs.

Not for Isabella, with her trust in Alistair broken.

Certainly not for Alistair, least of all.

Saturday,
October 27, 1906

CHAPTER 27

Green's Printing Shop, Hudson and Leroy Streets. 8 A.M.

It was the crack of dawn on Saturday morning when Mulvaney telephoned to summon me downtown. "We have a lead. Remember those pink flyers we found after the Tombs bombing?"

I remembered; they had been everywhere outside the building, and their message was ingrained in my memory. *Our acts of destruction will rid the world of your institutions.*

"Turns out the Swede works for the print shop we traced them to," Mulvaney said.

"Which one?"

"Green's Printing Shop on Hudson Street off Leroy, if you can believe it. Meet you there in twenty minutes?"

"What about the Swede himself?"

"I've sent six men out in search of him; we have a list of rooming houses where he's stayed. You and I ought to talk with the owner of Green's Printing. He makes it sound like there's a treasure trove of evidence at his shop."

Mulvaney had been misinformed on that count, for there was scant physical evidence at Green's Printing Shop. But Lew Green and his son, Richard, were anxious to help: they welcomed us into their family business with open arms and shared what information they had about the Swede.

"Lars Halver was his real name—or so he said," the print shop owner explained.

He was a large, affable man with a ready smile beneath a bushy salt-and-pepper mustache. He sat in a spacious room with the high ceilings required to accommodate two mammoth printing presses. His son, a gangly boy of about seventeen, all arms and legs, was occupied at a table filled with what resembled black bricks. Tools in hand, he was at work creating new cuttings to go into the machine.

"Lars was a good worker, an expert at working my Chandler and Price job press." Lew Green patted the side pole of the black press machine. "We print note cards and small flyers, and cut the occasional advertisement for the newspapers, as Richie is doing now."

I took a step closer and saw that Richie was crafting the imprint that would advertise Hood's sarsaparilla. Based on his paper model, it would be an elaborate creation, showing a lady toting an umbrella and box of medicine leaving a pharmacy. Underneath, the text of the advertisement read:

If you suffer from any disease or affliction caused by impure blood, or from dyspepsia, headache, kidney or liver complaints, or that tired feeling, take Hood's sarsaparilla. It purifies the blood, creates an appetite, makes the weak strong. Sold by all druggists.

"This ad is typical of your work?" I asked.

The boy nodded. "We do a lot of advertisements for Hood's and other medicines. See, we make the cutting here." He gestured to the black, bricklike box on which he worked. "Then we put it in the machine, there." He showed me how.

"But no official work for anarchists," I said, giving him a smile.

He shook his head in embarrassment. "Lars must have come in overnight to do it. We work long hours and keep busy during the day."

"How long had he worked for you?" Mulvaney asked, walking the perimeter of the room with some difficulty, for he still leaned heavily on his cane. The place was large but spare, comprising only windows, machinery, and tables filled with black cuttings.

"Lars worked here the better part of two years," Lew replied.

"You knew he was an anarchist?" I asked.

"Of course not. But I don't ask many questions of the men who work for me so long as they do a good job." He frowned. "Maybe I should. I'd no idea Lars was running his own side operation at night, printing anarchist newsletters and flyers. I'd have fired him, had I known."

"And you never saw any indication of it, either?" I turned back to Richard.

The boy flushed as he looked up from his work. "No, I didn't.

The only thing is, he did carry a heavy bag filled with papers. Now that I know, I wonder if that's where he kept the cuttings he stole from us."

"As you look back now, were there any warning signs that you missed?" Mulvaney asked.

Lew thought for a moment. "I don't think so. He was a man who came on time, did his job, and said little. He was a recent immigrant, and I just assumed his command of English was weak."

I recalled that on the elevator ride at the Breslin, I'd assumed the same thing. I now realized that I might have been wrong.

"Any of his friends ever come around?" Mulvaney asked as he continued to hobble around the perimeter of the room, surveying everything.

"Just one," Lew said with a broad grin. "A lady—and a real looker. Always dressed up. And exotic-looking. Made me remember the Creole women I used to see down in New Orleans."

"She reminded you of a Creole woman—or she was Creole?" Mulvaney demanded.

"She never came in, so I never heard her say a word or got a good look at her. But from the street . . . Well, that was my assumption."

Funke the gun seller had mentioned a similar woman, I recalled. "Exotic-looking" had been his phrase, as well.

"How often did she come by the shop?" I asked, walking back toward the machine that Lars had operated.

He shrugged. "Twice a week maybe. Always near quitting time." He paused. "I wish I could tell you more, but he was a regular worker who gave me no cause for concern. It's why I'm shocked," he said, rubbing his forefinger over his chin, "absolutely shocked that he used my shop to create such a vile message."

"So no unusual habits?" I surveyed Lars's workspace as I listened. "Nothing at all that might lead us to find him?"

Lew's son piped up. "Just this: I don't think he liked it here much. He might have come to America to earn a living, but he was a Swede through and through. He only ate Swedish food. Only read Swedish newspapers and stayed in Swedish rooming houses, so far as I could tell. So if he's not at the rooming address we gave you, then check out the other places in this city that cater to Scandinavian immigrants. I'd wager you'll find him at one of them."

I registered that for a moment and decided it made sense—except for one thing. "Then why take up with the Creole woman rather than a fellow Swede?"

The boy exchanged a look with his father, then gave me an odd stare. "Sir, that is *exactly* what my father and I have always wondered."

Before leaving the print shop, Mulvaney had called ahead to check in with his secretary for messages. To our surprise, he was informed that Lars Halver had been captured and was waiting for us in a holding cell at police headquarters on Mulberry Street. Richard Green's assessment of the Swede had been uncanny in its accuracy: Lars had been arrested at a boardinghouse run by a Swedish woman named Anna Brundige. All we had to do was identify him as the man we'd seen at the Breslin Hotel and question him about the recent killings.

We were so close to wrapping up this case—for surely the questions we would ask of Lars Halver would generate the answers we wanted. We'd figure out how—and why—he had targeted Jackson, Porter, and Hartt in the name of achieving justice for Leroy Sanders. We'd learn why Sanders was important to the anarchist cause. And just maybe, the answers we found would satisfy Commissioner Bingham.

Of course, it wasn't to be that simple.

Our first intimation of trouble came when we arrived at the grand lobby at Mulberry Street and heard a booming bass voice from the hallway, launching a series of profanities. I recognized the voice as that of Big Bill Hodges, the commissioner's right-hand man.

Mulvaney and I exchanged a worried glance.

"See what's going on," he said, leaning heavily on his cane. Normally he'd have been first to see for himself, but his broken leg continued to slow him down.

I entered the hallway and saw Hodges himself, apoplectic with rage. "This is beyond belief. Just what kind of incompetent louts are running our jails? This man was valuable to us—"

"We know, sir." A man in a black suit took his arm. "Don't worry; General Bingham remains satisfied. As he puts it, dead men cause no trouble. There'll be no trial now; no defense. We'll frame the story we give the press to suit our purposes."

Hodges, somewhat mollified, said something incomprehensible as they rounded the corner and descended the stairs.

"Ziele!" Mulvaney called out.

I stuck my head into the first office door to our left, where a young man sat alone, nervously drawing on his cigarette. I recognized him as one of the department secretaries.

"Captain Mulvaney and I are here to question Halver, the man you just arrested. Can you tell me what's going on?"

The man's eyes grew wide. "You mean no one's told you? He's dead."

"Who? Not Halver." I hoped I had misunderstood.

He gave me a sober nod.

"But how? You just picked him up. No one told us he was injured during his arrest."

"He wasn't." The young man ground his cigarette into an ashtray. "That's why everyone's upset. Someone managed to knife him in the gut, right in his holding cell."

I stared at him, incredulous. "Where?"

"Downstairs in the basement. Within the last half hour."

I returned to Mulvaney's side, helping him along the corridor and into an elevator where the attendant took us down to the basement, which swarmed with men in blue.

Commissioner Bingham was at the center of it all, gazing down at a crumpled man lying in a pool of blood. He caught sight of us. "Ziele. Mulvaney. Is this the Swede you saw at the scene of Angus Porter's murder?"

The other men broke ranks and made way for us to draw closer. When we did, I immediately recognized the white-blond hair and broad face of the man in the elevator.

"It's him," I said. "What happened?"

"One of us?" Mulvaney added, his voice low.

"What do you mean?" The commissioner's eyebrows furrowed.

"Who else had access to this man other than the police?" Mulvaney asked with a shrug. "Surely not another anarchist?"

The commissioner ignored the question but seized upon a thought that occurred to him. "That's exactly how we'll play this one, boys. A hated suspect—an anarchist ringleader—meets his deserved end. Never mind that his landlady thinks he was a choirboy."

"What if the reporters ask how, General?" one officer said.

General Bingham's lips curled into a self-satisfied smile. "We'll distract them. If we give 'em what they need to make their story a sensation, boys, they'll never ask. Now, let's put this case to bed."

But was Lars Halver the real criminal mastermind or the perfect scapegoat? Had he sent the blackmail letters that killed the judges as well as Professor Hartt? Would his rooms at Anna Brundige's reveal any answers? Mulvaney opined that he was certain all evidence necessary would be found there, and he would personally take charge of the search.

I looked one last time at Lars Halver's lifeless, bloody form. Was this case over?

Or not.

CHAPTER 28

The Tombs. 10 A.M.

For my part, I returned to the Tombs. I owed it to Mrs. Strupp, who had left me multiple messages asking that I check on Jonathan. I owed it to the investigation, for I believed that Jonathan possessed the answers I sought regarding Lars Halver's role in this conspiracy. But most of all, I owed it to myself. All around me, stories were being manipulated and framed for public consumption; tales told that would satisfy politicians, judges, and the masses alike. I'd no use for polite fictions. I wanted the truth.

Jonathan's cell was at the end of the second-floor corridor. He had been isolated; no one occupied the cells immediately surrounding his. His only company was the guard who sat, silent and wooden, charged with ensuring that Jonathan would neither escape nor cause further trouble.

I motioned to indicate that I wanted privacy. The guard got up from his metal chair and stretched. "Time for my cigarette break anyhow. Just call if you need help," he said.

I muttered a quick thanks, grabbed the metal chair, and placed it opposite Jonathan's cell. Then I waited.

He sat at the foot of his bed, staring at the wall of his bare cell. There was scant light. And, presumably because they believed he had been involved in the bombing that had taken two of the department's own, he had even been denied the usual courtesy of a washbasin and bucket. He looked frail and small, in prison clothes at least two sizes too big for him.

It was a long time before he finally spoke. "What do you want?"

"Answers," I replied.

He let out a long sigh but did not turn. "You always wanted to *understand* everything. As though that would make things better. It doesn't."

"Maybe not for everyone." I waited some more, then said, "Jonathan, you're going to be charged with conspiracy to murder."

A brief pause, then, "I know."

"Is it true? Did you help plan the bombing?"

"Individual responsibility doesn't matter anymore," he said, turning wearily. "They say if one of us did, then all of us did. We're all co-conspirators."

"It matters to me."

He looked toward me for the first time, sizing up my colorful bruises. "You don't look so good."

I didn't miss a beat. "Neither do you." Jonathan's guards had been none too gentle transporting him to his cell; there was a large purple contusion near his left eye.

"I know what you think, but it wasn't me who ordered it." It was as close to an apology as he was going to offer.

"I can help you, if you help me. I need information."

He raised an eyebrow. "Don't promise what you can't give. The commissioner intends to make an example of all of us. There will be no room for leniency."

"I'm well aware of the political complications," I said, keeping my voice even. "Even so, there are many who want to see justice done. I have contacts in the newspapers and the law—and I will see to it you have the best defense available."

He made a wry face. "In my case, that may mean little."

He was silent for a few minutes, then finally gave me the opening I'd been waiting for. "What can I tell you?"

I leaned in to see him clearly, placing my elbows on top of my knees. "What do you know about Lars Halver?"

"Ah, the Swede," he said, his face lighting with recognition. "One of our most reliable members, who handled all our news-letters and flyers, among other tasks. We could always count on Lars."

"We know about the flyers," I said quietly. "Was he the man commissioned to murder the judges?"

Jonathan grew pale. "I don't know about that."

"There's evidence that he was. I myself saw him at the scene of Judge Porter's murder."

"Look," Jonathan said, beads of sweat beginning to form on his brow. "Al Drayson and Paul and the others all talked a good game. They constantly had plans going on for one thing or another—and I'm not going to lie to you and say I wasn't part of it sometimes. I knew about Drayson's first scheme, and I also knew there was a plan to break Drayson out. God knows I've no love for anyone here; they got what they deserved," he added, his voice bitter. "But I didn't know about any plan to kill the judges."

"Tell me about the woman who kept company with Lars Halver. She's been described as 'exotic-looking' and possibly Creole. Did you know her?"

"Of course. She was a true comrade. Paul liked her and relied on her, giving her a good deal of work."

"What was her name?"

"Her real name? I don't know."

My voice grew hard. "How could you possibly not know? You just told me one of your highest-level members gave her a good deal of work."

"Sometimes we make it a practice not to know. Especially for those comrades who want to keep their true identity a secret . . . those who would risk their livelihood if they were discovered. Anyway, we called her Allison. Whether that is her true name is anybody's guess."

"So what do you know about her?" I asked.

"I first met her when she came to a meeting with China Rose. They worked together for a while on feminist issues, and both of them were close with Al Drayson, Paul, and other higher-ups."

"Did you ever personally work with her?"

"No. Paul tended to use women for one kind of work and men for another."

"But someone apparently assisted Lars—"

He cut me off. "You discovered that, not me. She never helped me with any project. I just saw her regularly at meetings."

"Any idea where I might find her?"

A curious look crossed his face. "Normally, I'd say to check out the next meeting. Assuming you haven't arrested her by then."

"But you don't know where she lives?"

"No. I never knew that. Paul might."

Tired of sitting, I stood—and took a step closer to Jonathan's cell, leaning on the cold iron bars. "There's one more thing. There was blackmail involved in this case. I take it you knew nothing of that?"

He shook his head.

"I wouldn't misplace your loyalty," I said, keeping my tone reasonable. "If I wanted to follow the money, where would I begin?"

He gave me a guarded look. "What do you mean?"

I was thinking again of something I had told Mulvaney at the beginning of this investigation: more anarchists have done jail time for robbery than dynamite.

"Whatever the citizens of New York may think of your group, the fact is, you *are* an organization," I said. "You sponsor activities—some legal, some admittedly not. All of them require money."

"So you're asking me where we keep our books?"

I nodded.

"I can't tell you that," he said, sitting straighter. "They'll have my head if I do. Paul especially—he'd pin every action our group has taken in recent months on me. If I managed to escape the electric chair, he'd ensure I never saw the light of day again."

"Paul Hlad has never had your best interests at heart."

"Yes, he has," Jonathan said, setting his jaw. "He has done nothing but good for me."

"I'm sure that's why he's turned evidence against you," I said, my voice sarcastic.

He stood and walked toward me. "What do you mean?"

"I guess they don't tell you guys much. Paul Hlad is providing evidence against Drayson, you, and others in exchange for immunity from prosecution. He was released this morning."

"You're bluffing me." He caught hold of the bars that caged him, and I'd no doubt that he would have grabbed me instead if he could.

"I wouldn't bluff, Jonathan. If you like, I'll call the guard and you can ask him yourself."

He glowered. "If I find out later that you lied . . ."

"Where do you keep the books?" I asked again. "Not the money itself. Just your financial records that show cash flow coming and going."

"If I tell you . . ."

"Then I will help you to the best of my ability."

With a sigh, he walked away. Crossing to the opposite side of his cell, he banged his fist into the wall, hard.

I simply waited.

The words, when they came, were wrenched out of him as though against his will. "China Rose," he said. "She keeps the books—and the cash—at her parents' restaurant. But she won't help you; you'll have to break in."

"You can't be serious."

"Do you want the books or not?" he said with a growl. "Now, in the cellar, you'll see a wall filled with bags of rice. One bag will look deflated compared to the others; that one contains our records as well as the money. And there's one more thing."

"What's that?"

"If what you told me about Paul Hlad is true, then you'd better hurry. Because he is certain to run the moment he's out, no matter what they promised him. And those books—not to mention the money we have on hand—will be among the first things he'll go for upon his release."

"All right." I gave him a final look before I left. The sadness I felt was almost unbearable; I'd have done a lot to spare him the ordeal that lay ahead of him.

"You'll help?" he asked in a whisper, suddenly drained of all bravado.

"I promised I would."

"Because of what I just told you?" His voice caught in his throat.

I shook my head. "No. For your daughter."

And although I didn't say it out loud . . . *for Hannah*.

It would have been better to wait for nightfall, but I didn't dare. I couldn't risk Paul Hlad getting to the information I wanted before me.

It was now almost noon. It was a good window of opportunity; lunch service would demand everyone's attention upstairs— or so I hoped.

The streets were as crowded as ever. I shadowed a man carrying a giant basket of fish on top of his head, on the theory that it would somewhat disguise my presence. When he rounded the corner of Mott Street, I ducked into the alleyway behind. Slinking past garbage containers and wooden crates, I found a second back alley leading to the rear of most buildings on Mott.

I counted carefully, five buildings from the corner.

But no rear entrance to the cellar. How was I to pass unnoticed if the only entry was from the cellar door in the front sidewalk?

I crossed back through the alley to the sidewalk and decided: there was no help for it. I'd enter through the front. So long as I looked like I knew what I was doing, chances were no one would question me.

Head held high, I walked to the cellar door, flung it open, and descended the staircase into the dank space below the Red Lantern. No one shouted at me or followed me; there, I was lucky.

I found the shelf of rice bags exactly as Jonathan had described. With my left palm, I punched each in turn until I came to one that deflated the moment I touched it.

I reached to grab it—then froze, for somebody had shouted.

The voice was male—guttural and Chinese. I tucked into the shadows so that I was hidden from the view of anyone peering down from above. Of course, if anyone descended the stairs, then I had no hope of avoiding discovery.

Another shout from above—female this time.

Then the metal doors clanged shut and all went dark. So long as they didn't lock them . . .

I made my way to the burlap sacks containing rice as my eyes readjusted to almost total darkness. I felt rather than saw the deflated sack—and reached in. I first came across a stack of bills but left them for now. I'd tell Mulvaney to send a pair of officers to retrieve the anarchist funds later. My focus now was on the records ledger, which was at the bottom of the sack.

Grabbing it, I shoved the ledger inside my coat flap, replaced the sack on the shelf, and felt my way back to the ladder that would take me to street level once again.

I reached my hand up, prepared to lift open the door, when it was flung open wide.

Blinded by the sudden light, I could barely make out Mei Lin—her face livid with anger. "What are you doing here?"

"Must have taken a wrong turn," I said without a hint of humor on my face.

Her eyes narrowed. "The others will find out. You will not be safe."

"Are you threatening a police detective?" I replied.

"I'm responsible for what's down there. You cannot take. They will blame me and my family." She crossed her arms, blocking my way.

"I only want the ledger," I said in my calmest voice. "The money is still there. You can check."

In answer, she began to clamber down the ladder herself, forcing me to retreat into the small basement space.

She immediately went to the rice sack, opened it, and began counting the bills and coins. I stayed near the afternoon sunlight and opened the ledger, scanning their list of donations. Most amounts were small, given by members themselves: a nickel here, a penny there. Larger donations in dollars were given by organizations, including the UAW. Given their close association, I wondered if a portion of union dues was regularly diverted to the anarchist coffers.

I continued to look for signs of blackmail. Alistair had said the requests usually came in five-hundred-dollar increments, sometimes as much as two thousand. I saw nothing so large, but a series of entries—each for one hundred dollars—made my breath catch in my throat.

They were donated at regular intervals, and the most recent was from last week. The donor listed: *the White Rose Mission.*

"I counted. It's all there." China Rose still regarded me suspiciously. "I guess you tell the truth. Take the book—but please don't come down here again." For the first time I noticed the look of fear on her face.

She watched as I scrambled up the ladder and joined the crowds on the sidewalk, the ledger once again jammed under my coat sleeve.

Who—and what—is the White Rose Mission?

I hurried toward Canal Street, where I knew I'd find a public telephone pay station. I'd get the attendant to check the directory and find out where this organization was. Then I would telephone Isabella.

I had almost reached Canal Street when I caught a glimpse of a tall but slight man with dark blond hair, wearing a black eye patch.

Paul Hlad.

I'd been right not to risk waiting till dark: Paul was planning to run, and he wanted his money.

Would he come after me and his missing ledger?

It didn't matter now. I ducked into an alleyway behind a row of garbage containers, waiting until he passed by.

I counted to thirty, slowly. Then I ran back onto the street and continued, refusing to stop until I'd reached the Canal Street telephone station. There, I flashed my badge and cut the line, giving my instructions to the surprised matron in charge.

"Please connect me to the White Rose Mission. Immediately."

CHAPTER 29

White Rose Mission, 217 East Eighty-sixth Street. 1 P.M.

A cold, cutting rain had begun to fall by the time I reached the White Rose Mission on East Eighty-sixth Street and read the brass plate on the black-painted door.

MRS. VICTORIA EARLE MATTHEWS. FOUNDER.

I had just rapped the knocker when a hansom cab pulled in front of the building. A figure emerged under a large black umbrella, paid the driver, and then dashed up the stairs to join me. *Isabella.* I had called her the moment I'd finished speaking with the lady from the White Rose Mission.

"I can't believe you got here first, coming all the way from Canal Street," Isabella said in a rush. "I only had to cross Central Park, but it was impossible finding a cab in the rain."

"Mrs. Matthews is expecting you," said the young woman

who swung open the door. "She's in her office; I'll show you the way."

"Thank you," I said, passing her our coats and umbrellas.

After she put them away, she led us down a bare but clean hallway covered by a solid green rug. The walls were lined with hooks upon which hung girls' coats, and we passed by a library where at least a dozen young African ladies sat reading in front of a roaring fireplace. Over the telephone, Mrs. Matthews—the founder and superintendent of the mission—had described it as a cross between a home and a school. Now I could better see why: it was more comfortable than an institution, and yet obviously a large number of young women called it home.

We were led into a large office at the back of the hall, where daylight streamed in through floor-to-ceiling windows and multiple bookcases were filled with leather-bound volumes. A handsome woman, tastefully dressed in a cream and peach silk dress, looked up from her mahogany desk when we entered.

"Detective Ziele. Mrs. Sinclair." Mrs. Victoria Earle Matthews rose to greet us. "You made it here quickly. Do sit." She indicated the two leather-cushioned chairs across from her desk. Her face, lined with worry, was kind as she regarded us.

"You wished to see me because you have concerns about our finances?" She pushed her wire-rimmed glasses back into place from where they had fallen down her nose.

"We do. As I mentioned earlier, your organization appears repeatedly among the list of donors to a major anarchist group in the city. In fact, you're recently listed as having given hundreds of dollars. But you say you know nothing of this?"

She met my gaze with a forthright expression. "Absolutely not. I personally oversee the finances of the White Rose Mission.

And I assure you, not a penny of our funds has gone to anarchist organizations."

"Then perhaps you can help us figure out why someone listed you as having made these donations," Isabella said. "Perhaps one of your employees made donations in the mission's name?"

Mrs. Matthews rested her chin on her hand, thinking. "It's possible," she finally said, adding, "How much do you know about the work we do here?"

"Very little," I said. "I'd never heard of your organization until its name appeared on the donation list I just mentioned."

Mrs. Matthews nodded. "I thought not. There are a number of homes like mine for new immigrant girls, Detective Ziele. I'm sure you're familiar with some of them."

"Some, yes." There were a number of charitable organizations devoted to helping young women new to the city—some geared to the Irish, others to the German—not to mention those connected with churches of every denomination. Their goal was simple: to help these women obtain gainful employment and protect them from unscrupulous men who would take advantage of them and ensnare them in disreputable employment.

"I took them as my model—but my primary concern has always been for those girls of my race who are already here. Many are born into poverty and come to this great city seeking a better life. Should they have no protection? No education? No guidance or training to help them learn to support themselves in respectable positions? I decided they should—and that's what I offer."

"The girls live here—or just train here?" Isabella asked.

"Both," Mrs. Matthews said with pride. "We are a school,

essentially. We offer classes in sewing and dressmaking, cooking and nutrition, hygiene and other skills. I also make sure the girls learn to read—and read good material. There is no better education than from books. And I personally teach a class in race literature because I want them to be proud of who they are."

In later years, I would hear Mrs. Matthews described as "a great reader and thinker, one of the best-read women in the country," and I would remember this very conversation. But even now, she impressed me as a woman of great energy and intellect. And I believed her when she insisted she had not made donations to the anarchists in the mission's name.

"How many girls are here at any given time?" I asked.

"As many as fifty. We moved here from our original, smaller building on Ninety-seventh Street so we could help even more girls."

I wanted to understand more. "So they live here and take classes; then what?"

"We help them find suitable employment—but only after their education is complete. There is no greater advantage I can give them. What they learn here can never be taken from them."

"But none of them have shown anarchist leanings, to your knowledge?"

Mrs. Matthews's reply was firm. "No. Why would they? As I understand it, anarchy is born of discontent. But my girls here are comfortable and happy."

Of course, I was curious about the origins of the name of the mission. The fact that a single white rose had been left next to the three murder victims I was investigating could not be a coincidence. But Isabella beat me to the punch.

"Why did you decide to name your mission after the white rose?" Isabella asked.

Mrs. Matthews explained. "The white rose is a symbol of purity and innocence. The goal of the mission is to preserve these characteristics in my girls for as long as possible. The young ladies that come through the White Rose Mission are lucky. They are spared the real world for a period of time. Yet it is inevitable that they will eventually face the vices and dangers of being a young African woman in this city."

"And you've been helping girls for how long?" I asked.

"Since 1897."

My hopes fell. If she had been educating classes of girls for almost ten years, then many students had passed through here. Too many.

I tried anyway. "I'm wondering if you remember one girl—a girl who may have turned to the anarchist cause after leaving you. She had taken up with a Swedish man, though of course she may not have known him at the time she was with you. *If*, that is, she was ever with you." My question sounded desperate even to my own ears.

It was an assumption to associate the "exotic-looking woman" who accompanied the Swede with the White Rose Mission and I knew it. But she was a known anarchist, and who better to fake a donation from the mission? And to make use of a white rose at three different murder scenes?

Mrs. Matthews shook her head. "I don't permit my girls to have gentlemen callers while they're with me. It's a distraction they shouldn't have until they are better settled. So if the girl of whom you speak was one of mine, she did not take up with this man until later."

"Then I suppose we've no choice: we must focus on your list of students," I said, exchanging a demoralized glance with Isabella. "We can search the names against our list of known anarchists."

"Very well. I keep all my records over here." Mrs. Matthews gestured to four large file cabinets in the back of the room. "I'll ask my assistant to help me, but nevertheless it will take time to compile a list."

I knew she was right; the sheer number of files would take a large commitment of time to examine—time we didn't have, given the commissioner's rush to judgment.

Mrs. Matthews began pulling files from the cabinet closest to her, carrying them over to her desk. "I should be able to compile a list for you by tomorrow morning."

"Thank you. We'll return at eight o'clock," I said, standing.

I had no difficulty hailing a hansom cab heading west on Eighty-sixth Street. Soon Isabella and I were traveling south on Fifth Avenue heading toward the precinct station.

"What's next?" she asked.

"To be honest, I'm out of ideas," I said, rubbing my brow. "I suppose we can check whether there's an anarchist behind bars who has information about the White Rose Mission. The offer of a reduced sentence may entice someone to talk." I sighed. "But with the commissioner and other top brass believing the case is wrapped up now . . ."

"You're unlikely to get their cooperation," Isabella said, finishing for me.

We rode in silence for several blocks.

"Is it possible they're right?" she finally asked. "Maybe it was the Swede. Maybe the person we're looking for died this morning at Mulberry Street headquarters."

"Perhaps. But if so, I'd like to know for sure."

The driver reined in his horse, narrowly avoiding a motor-car ahead of us that was swerving back and forth. As we slowed to a stop, passing a row of limestone town houses, I watched as a service door opened and a maid in starched black and white exited the building.

I bolted straight up and turned to Isabella. "Where do you think the White Rose Mission places most girls?"

She made a frown. "The more educated ones may get work in a hospital or school, even as a ladies' companion."

"What about in service?"

"Probably. Why?"

I leaned forward and called out to the driver. "Turn around! We've got to get back to Eighty-sixth street."

"What is it, Simon?" Isabella turned. "Why are we going back?"

We were going back because I now knew where Mrs. Matthews should begin her search. Because of the donation list, I'd been preoccupied with finding an anarchist connection—and so I hadn't asked the right questions.

"I have an idea. . . ." I said, my excitement building. "What if the White Rose Mission placed a girl in service inside one of our victim's homes? This may be the break that we've been waiting for."

"Like a maid or a ladies' companion?" She raised her eyebrows. "But I thought we were looking for a man."

"I thought so, too. But it would make sense if it were a maid," I said, continuing. "Who else could have known so much about these men? Someone inside their home would have had unfettered access to everything about them: their current habits, their papers, their telephone conversations, even their personal history."

"Someone inside the home . . ." Isabella said, giving me a thoughtful look.

We were back at the mission house on East Eighty-sixth Street within moments, brushing past the young maid who answered the door again, making our way back to Mrs. Matthews's office.

She sat at her desk, surrounded by files; when she noticed us, she looked up in surprise. "Detective, you forgot something?"

I leaned both hands on her desk "Do many of your girls go into service after leaving you?"

"Of course," she replied.

"Can you check your files quickly? I have four names, and I'm wondering whether you ever placed a maid at one of their homes."

"Yes," she said, taking out a pencil, "if you have specific names, I can check my employer files."

Isabella cleared her throat. "Try Judge Hugo Jackson first."

I turned to stare at her. "Why?"

"Just check, quickly. It may be nothing." Her mouth settled in a tight line.

A chill went down my spine. "What may be nothing?"

"Here's the file for the Jackson household," Mrs. Matthews said, returning to us with a small stack of papers. She handed me her top file, saying, "Nettie Harris worked for Judge Jackson from 1897 until 1901, when she married a Samuel Taylor and moved to a farm in Albany."

"Who else?" Isabella asked, her face turning pale.

"The next one is Sarah Barnes. She has been with them for eight years, I believe, having risen from housemaid duties to cooking." Mrs. Matthews laid that folder on her desk, as well.

I scanned her file. She was indeed still with Mrs. Jackson and had doubtless been interviewed last week. But the picture in the file showed a chubby girl with plain features. I didn't want to rule her out entirely, but she didn't resemble the description of the woman with Lars Halver.

Mrs. Matthews then displayed the next file. "This is Mary Flanders. She joined the Jackson household in 1901."

She showed us the file, and I recognized the maid I met the night of the judge's murder. The same woman I had seen again at Beau's.

"The name is wrong," I managed to say. "She goes by Marie. And I hadn't placed her as African, exactly."

"If you look in her file," Mrs. Matthews said, "you'll see she's of mixed race. It's not uncommon, especially in our girls from the South. Slavery left its mark in more ways than one." She pressed her lips tightly together. "It's a shame, but girls like her are often easier to place. Like me, they can pass, quite often, for European. Especially southern European. It's not always to their advantage—"

She was exotic-looking, the man at Funke's—and the Greens at the print shop—had said. In my mind's eye, I'd remembered her only in formal housemaid dress—and I'd not seen it.

"Simon!" Isabella grabbed my arm in a viselike grip. She looked like a ghost, as though she'd taken suddenly ill. "Marie may know Alistair's whereabouts. You see, I'd told Mrs. Mellown that Alistair was at the Waldorf so she wouldn't worry.

But she was indiscreet: this morning, I overheard her sharing that information with someone from the Jackson residence. Someone who wanted to send Alistair more of the judge's private papers. She swallowed hard. "I said nothing because I didn't think any harm had been done . . ."

"In telling her to send it to Alistair at the Waldorf," I finished for her.

She nodded, now at a loss for words.

In that instant, I realized we had no time to waste. "We've got to go," I said, choking on the words as I whisked Isabella out the door.

"Thank you for your help," I called back to Mrs. Matthews, who remained behind—bewildered but aware that something important had just happened.

Just outside, I was able to hail another hansom cab.

"To the Waldorf-Astoria," I said, "as fast as you can."

The driver cracked his whip high above the horse's head. Isabella sat beside me, stiff—her fingers locking together, then unlocking in her lap.

For her sake—as well as Alistair's own—I prayed that we were not too late.

CHAPTER 30

The Waldorf-Astoria, Fifth Avenue and
Thirty-fifth Street entrance. 3 P.M.

We scrambled out of the cab and into the lobby of the Astoria building, heading straight for the elevator past a number of astonished bellhops, concierges, and hotel guests.

"Sir, really!" one of them protested when we raced past the elegant Palm Court dining room in our haste.

I didn't bother to apologize but kept moving as quickly as Isabella could manage. I was out of breath by the time we squeezed ourselves into the cramped elevator beside two ladies with voluminous dresses. "Sixteenth floor. It's an emergency."

The two ladies openly gawked and the elevator attendant said nothing in response, but he flipped the elevator into gear and sent us to the top of the building first.

I didn't wait for Isabella the moment the elevator doors opened. I ran down the hallway on thick carpet that muffled the sound of my feet, reached number 1621, and gave a sharp knock at the door.

"Alistair! Open up!"

I pressed my ear to the door and heard muffled sounds.

"Alistair!"

I thought I heard something that resembled a moan. Leaning my shoulder into the door, I gave it a shove.

Nothing. It was bolted.

"Can you break it down?" Isabella asked.

I shoved again.

At the end of the hallway, the service elevator opened, and a heavyset man in a crisp white suit pushed a room-service cart into the hall.

"Can you help us?" I shouted. "It's an emergency. We need access to this room."

He hesitated for a moment, then something in Isabella's expression caused him to reconsider. "I got keys," he said. "Let me open it."

He pulled out a large skeleton key, put it in the door, and turned it.

Nothing happened.

"That's odd," he said, frowning. "Skeleton keys always work. Maybe they stuck something in the lock." He leaned over, peering into the lock cavity.

I pulled out my set of picks, chose one, and maneuvered it into the lock recess. Felt for the catch, leaned into it, and—nothing.

"Something's blocking it," I said.

"Then we gotta break it down," the man said. He grabbed his room service cart, lifted the silver platter onto the floor, and wheeled the cart until it was positioned in front of room 1621. "Lean into it with me on the count of three. One, two . . . three."

Both of us shoved into the door with every ounce of our strength.

"I felt it give a little," he said. "Same thing again. One, two . . . three."

This time the door cracked open a fraction, and we pushed it the rest of the way down.

I heard Isabella's scream before I managed to process the sight in front of us.

Alistair sat in a leather chair in the middle of the room, his hands and feet bound by a thick white rope. He was gagged with a long red silk scarf—expertly tied enough that he was able to make only muffled noises, though I could tell by his facial contortions that he was doing his best to shout.

And above him—a pistol trained at his head—stood Marie Flanders, the woman I'd recognized as Mrs. Jackson's maid. Her face was like steel when she warned us, "If you come one step closer, I shoot him now."

"Isabella, stay in the hall!" I said—and breathed easier the moment she retreated.

"What the hell are you doin', lady?" The employee helping us was angry, about to charge into the room toward the woman holding the gun.

I placed my hand on his arm. "I've got this. Go get help," I managed to say. "Take Isabella."

He looked for a moment as though he'd refuse to back down—then changed his mind when Marie pointed her gun toward him.

"You don't need to do this," I said, taking a step closer into the room. I noted the single white rose lying in the middle of the bed. "Untie him. Let him go."

Her eyes narrowed. "That's not what's going to happen, mister."

"It's what needs to, if you want this to end well." I took another step closer.

"This was never going to end well. Don't take another step or I'll shoot."

I motioned to the desk chair to my left. "May I sit?" I wanted to appear relaxed; it was my best chance of keeping her calm.

She nodded. "Put your hands on the desk where I can see them."

"Very well," I said.

I regarded her as though seeing her for the first time—which, in truth, I was. She had an attractive, dusky complexion—and I saw how her features, depending upon dress and circumstance, would mark her as either very light-skinned African or dark European. I hadn't noticed before. Other officers had interviewed her extensively following Judge Jackson's murder; I'd read their report. But there had been nothing suspicious in her answers, and Mrs. Jackson had vouched for her in the strongest terms.

She regarded me with serious, intelligent brown eyes—filled not only with hate but with resolute purpose.

"You should take off his gag. He's having trouble breathing." I cast a worried glance toward Alistair.

She laughed—a harsh, guttural sound. "Why? He had every opportunity to speak earlier. But he didn't."

"What would you have wanted him to say?" I asked. My voice was calm.

She began twirling the gun as her voice rose. "I wanted him to admit that he was wrong. That he and his friends did a stupid thing. And that my family suffered because of it."

"You mean Leroy Sanders."

Her lips curved into a smile. "You've been doing your homework. But I'll bet you still don't know the half of it. After all, he's spent the better part of the last thirty years keeping this truth hidden." She jabbed her gun at Alistair's head. He winced.

She was distracted, I could see.

"Tell me more," I said. If she kept talking, she wouldn't shoot. And the more she talked, the more time I would have until help arrived. Or until I figured out a way to disarm her.

"Tell me about the white rose," I said when she remained silent. "It seems to me you left it as a sign; you must have *wanted* us to catch you. Because if any one of us had associated it with the White Rose Mission, we might have gone to Mrs. Matthews and found you much earlier."

It was something Alistair might have said—for he believed that the choices a criminal makes at any crime scene reveal something important about motive.

"Don't be ridiculous," she retorted. "It was a message to *them*. To my victims. There were white roses at my father's funeral. They make me think of death." Her eyes glazed over. "They also remind me of the White Rose Mission, which ruined my life. I ended up there, because of these men and what they did to my father."

"I spoke with Mrs. Matthews myself," I said. "She seems to want to do nothing but good."

Marie swore softly. Then, her expression cold, she said, "Like many, she claims to mean well. The truth is different." She walked to the other side of the room, glanced outside the door. Reassured, she turned back to me. "The White Rose Mission offers nothing but a different kind of slavery. Girls are trained, but for what? To be servants, toiling and scrubbing, never paid a decent wage. To be abused by men of the house who think you're there for the taking. Like a prostitute." Her voice was savage as she finished. "The White Rose Mission ruined my life when they sent me on my first assignment. I wanted to cause them some trouble."

"Was your first position at the Jackson home?"

She shook her head. "The Jackson position was my second job; I begged Mrs. Matthews for it. And after what happened to me, she'd have done anything I asked. It was the perfect opportunity to take revenge for my father's death and my family's suffering."

"But you can't have done it alone," I said, keeping my voice low and calm. "Three large men. And different methods of killing them. Besides, we know that Lars helped you. He purchased the gun, and he was at the Breslin."

Her face softened for a moment. "Yes, Lars was a sweet, helpful man. I was sorry to have to kill him, as well."

"But he was knifed to death in his cell," I said, raising an eyebrow.

She smiled sweetly. "No one ever questions the cleaning lady. The men charged with protecting him never even noticed."

They had actually suspected one of their own. In truth, I suppose they hadn't cared about the anarchist that they believed was responsible for so much suffering.

"You are one woman," I said, shaking my head. "I don't believe that you had the strength—or the knowledge—to kill three grown men without help."

"I never said I didn't have help," she said, annoyed enough to enunciate the words slowly. "I said that I killed these men personally."

"All right," I said, encouraging her to go on.

"I started with the blackmail—and it worked better than I had expected." She looked amused for a moment. "They were terrified when I sent them my first demand—not just because I knew about Leroy Sanders but because I knew about *them*. I made use of their old habit of using musical ciphers to send messages."

"How did you even figure the code out?"

A smile flickered across her face. "I went through the judge's old papers. I was looking for evidence, you see? And when I found his old letters and classbooks, I had a decent enough knowledge of music to figure out their code."

"So if this was personal revenge, then why involve Lars and the anarchists?"

"I needed them," she said simply. "I joined their cause because I shared their overall goal: they wanted to improve working conditions for people like me. But I soon discovered I had a better use for them. They offered me the training I needed to execute my revenge. They taught me how to make a bomb, use a gun, and wield a knife." She nodded. "Yes, even a woman like me. It's all about technique and confidence, not strength. And when I needed a little help—mainly so I wouldn't be recognized—they gave me Lars. They all believed I was working for the cause, not my own goals. But that was fine."

"You gave them part of the blackmail money, saying it was from the White Rose Mission," I stated.

"Yes," she said with satisfaction. "I brought them donations, which convinced them that I was a true comrade. So they helped me, without question."

It was a relationship that had profited both of them, apparently.

"Judge Jackson and this man"—she jabbed at Alistair—"together with the other two are responsible. Now they must pay."

Alistair grunted and twisted vigorously under his restraints.

"What did they do?" I asked. "You said that it was because of them that you ended up at the White Rose Mission . . ."

"As I wouldn't have, had I grown up with my mother and father. Girls with families don't have to come to this city looking for work when they turn eighteen. They don't end up in mission homes, training to do slave labor for rich folks." she said. "These men planted the evidence that sent my father to Auburn Prison for life. They destroyed his life," she hissed, "which in turn destroyed mine and my mother's. There was never any future for us after he went to Auburn. Never!"

She held up her hands, forcing them within my line of sight. "My family was musical. My mother taught me to sing and play piano. I dreamed of a future as a pianist before all the scrubbing and toiling made a wreck of my fingers. This world filled with capitalist evil and greed destroys us all."

"You said they planted evidence . . ."

She inclined her head. "I'll bet your friend didn't tell you that, did he? That's how they managed to send Leroy away. My innocent father."

"What if they didn't know the evidence to be wrong? What

if it was just a mistake?" I realized I was asking the questions of myself as much as of Marie Sanders.

"There was no mistake," she said coolly. "You forget: I gained access to Judge Jackson's private files. I *know* what they did. It's why your friend will die with this gag in his mouth. Because he had the chance to say something at the time and chose not to."

"He could still clear your father's name."

Another harsh laugh. "It's too late. For my father—and for me." She crossed the room. "Now it's time." She checked her gun, locked the trigger in place.

"Help will be here any moment. Don't add to the crimes you've already committed," I begged.

"Don't worry," she said, her face steeled with resolve, "you won't take me alive. I refuse to suffer my father's fate."

She picked up the gun and pointed it at me. I dove for the floor, narrowly missing the shot she launched in my direction.

I lifted my head just in time to see her point the Browning pistol at Alistair's heart and pull the trigger.

"No!" I screamed.

The bullet hit its mark. Alistair's body jolted from the impact, then relaxed, limp in the chair.

My mind numb, I scrambled to my feet.

She was heading for the window. She reached for the latch, opened it.

I got up and bounded across the room, determined to stop her. She would pay for what she had done to Alistair.

But I was just within reach of her, ready to grab her, when she spoke. And her words were so shocking that I paused for a split second—just long enough, it turned out, for her to get away.

"Tell Jonathan to take care of our daughter," she said.

Then, with no hesitation whatsoever, she stepped through the open window and flung herself out into the night.

CHAPTER 31

3:30 P.M.

I pulled Alistair's limp frame off the chair and onto the bed, untying the ropes that bound him. Then I ripped open his cravat, sending it flying, for I needed to stem the flow of blood.

There was no blood—and yet I had seen the shot strike his chest!

I felt for his pulse—and found it. I tapped his face, first the right cheek, then the left. He stirred, then moaned softly. He was still with us.

"Alistair!" I felt his chest, searching for a wound. "Alistair, can you hear me?"

Groggy, he opened his eyes with effort. "That hurt like the dickens," he murmured.

"Where?" I undid his shirt to expose his chest—then stopped

and whistled. For underneath his crisp white shirt, I saw the brass bullet itself exactly where it had stopped.

And what had caught its trajectory—and prevented it from entering Alistair's chest—was the most beautiful woven silk vest I had ever seen. Strands of gold intermingled with royal blue and vibrant red in a shimmering pattern.

I could only stare at Alistair.

"Help me sit up," he said. "My chest feels as though I've just lost a boxing match with Philadelphia Jack O'Brien."

"But you're alive," I said quietly.

He coughed, and it was clear the movement sent tremors of pain throughout his body. "I'm alive thanks to the Reverend Casimir Zeglen of Chicago—and the best eight hundred dollars I ever spent."

"Zeglen?" Something about the name sounded familiar.

"He's the Polish priest who discovered that he could weave silk in such as way as to create a bulletproof vest. I'd read the article about his invention in the *Brooklyn Eagle*. He had experimented for years with steel shavings and moss, but nothing worked until he got the silk weave right."

I'd known the technology existed; in fact, bulletproof vests in some form had been around since the early 1800s. But they were far too expensive for anyone on the detective force to make use of.

"It's so thin." I felt the material, marveled at it.

"Only an eighth of an inch thick." Alistair coughed again. "It literally catches the bullet and spreads its force. No wonder my chest is killing me."

"You bought it because you were worried . . ."

"After Angus was shot, yes," he replied.

I nodded. "I have a lot of questions for you. But they can wait."

For Isabella stood in the doorway—and I watched as her expression of horror turned to immense relief when she realized that Alistair was unharmed. As the room filled with police detectives, I extricated myself, promising to meet up with the Sinclairs later on.

On Thirty-fourth Street, Marie Sanders's limp corpse still lay at odd angles in a pool of blood on the sidewalk where she'd fallen. A group of policemen attempted to block the sight from horrified passersby as enterprising journalists snapped photographs.

Alistair had always said there was no such thing as a born criminal. They were created, generated by circumstance and environment. I could think of no better example than that of Marie Sanders. For if she had spoken the truth, then Alistair and his three associates had sown the seeds that had turned a young woman into a tortured soul bent on revenge.

Downtown at Mulberry Street headquarters, the commissioner stroked his handlebar mustache while he stared at me in disbelief. "So you're telling me that a dame called Marie Sanders was responsible for murdering two judges and a Barnard professor, not to mention the attempted murder of Alistair Sinclair. *Not* the anarchists."

"She personally committed each murder," I said, "with help from the anarchists. They trained her and provided her support because they believed she was working to further their goals. But she was out for personal revenge."

"And she used the Swede?"

"She manipulated him, yes. She told him that she needed his help to destroy the capitalist enemy."

The commissioner only grunted.

I went on to tell him everything, excluding no detail as to how I had discovered everything and emphasizing that many of the anarchists locked up had played no specific role whatsoever.

"Jonathan Strupp in particular," I said, "played no part in either the murders or the bombing itself."

"No matter," the General said with a sweep of his hand. "We've reclaimed this city at last—and found sufficient evidence to put away all those who would have destroyed it. As Strupp would have," he said with a sharp look, "given half the chance. You see, I'm not looking to parse out the details of individual responsibility. As far as I'm concerned, they're all guilty."

"But our justice system is based on personal culpability," I said in protest. "It's not right for someone to pay for what he didn't do."

"What he didn't do?" The commissioner slammed his hand down on the table. "He conspired to destroy this city and all the hardworking people who make it great. He and his 'comrades' did so every meeting they attended, with each word they spoke and every dollar they gave to their cause." He leaned in close to me and spoke in a fierce whisper. "I've got a story here that will play—to juries and judges, as well as the press and the public. Drayson and the anarchist ringleaders are going down. The lot of them have enough crimes on their conscience that I feel no guilt whatsoever."

He leaned back again. "Marie Sanders and the Swede are dead. We'll fix the early blame on them as worker bees who executed their superiors' orders. But the ringleaders will pay, too.

They'll go to trial for the killing of the guards in the Tombs bombing, as well as ordering the murders of the two judges and the professor. Now," he said, fixing me with a glare, "I don't want to hear another word."

And I didn't say another word to the commissioner. But I said plenty to Frank Riley, who came right away to meet me in the small Chinatown noodle shop where we spoke in complete privacy.

"What do you think?" I asked him when I finished talking.

He twirled his chopsticks through a half-empty bowl of noodles. "You've spun quite a story. I'm not sure they'll let me print it." He paused a long moment. "I'm not even sure I want to. If I do, people may go free who don't deserve it."

"Because of what they think?" I asked. "We don't lock people up in this country because of that. It's what they *do* that matters."

"Do you really believe there is that much of a separation?" He gave me a hard look. "Take your friend Jonathan Strupp. Now, I understand why you want to help him. But think hard before you answer my question. Do you truly believe he's a decent man who just got in over his head? Or—is this your guilt interfering with your better judgment?"

I waited a long moment before I answered. "I don't know. But if we don't give men like him a chance, then what kind of people are we?"

He pushed the bill toward me, saying with a grin, "All right, Ziele. I'll see what I can do."

I explained exactly that to Jonathan half an hour later. "It doesn't look good," I said to him. "There's going to be a trial. But the lead crime beat reporter at the *Times* is going to ensure that your side of the story is heard."

Jonathan could only shake his head. "What will become of my daughter now?" he said. "Marie was a passing acquaintance of mine, and I knew she had no interest in being a mother. It would have endangered her livelihood, which she'd protected at all costs by hiding her pregnancy."

"Your parents will care for her as best they can," I said after his words faded away. "I've seen that already. And there's one more chance for you I can think of."

"What's that?" he asked, his tone morose.

"His name is Alistair Sinclair, and he's a criminal scientist," I said. "He's a preeminent researcher—and he's also got connections to some of the most influential people in this city's legal system."

"And why would he help me? People like him don't care about people like me."

"Personally, no. But he'll care very much about what you have to say. You've just got to talk with him."

Jonathan was dumbfounded. "Talk with him?"

"Exactly," I replied. I didn't tell him that Alistair would try to spin his story into groundbreaking research about how an anarchist is formed . . . about how the criminal mind and the terrorist are related. I'd leave all that to Alistair.

I got up. "He'll help you get as light a sentence as possible. It will be worth your while: talk with him and tell him everything he wants to know."

It was all Alistair would demand of Jonathan.

And exactly what I would demand of Alistair myself in coming days.

Friday,
November 2, 1906

CHAPTER 32

The Dakota, 1 West Seventy-second Street. 5 P.M.

My rift with Alistair was serious, and the chasm between us grew wider each day. Neither Isabella's efforts—nor the time we spent together helping Jonathan plan his defense—served to resolve it.

To his credit, Alistair helped Jonathan in every way possible. He secured a top defense attorney, paid for out of his own pocket. And he did it for the reasons I had suspected: he found Jonathan to be a fascinating subject. Alistair had quickly become obsessed with figuring out why this studious young man had abandoned his passion for science in favor of anarchist violence. He understood Jonathan's anger following the *Slocum* disaster, and how easily the anarchist leaders had manipulated it to persuade Jonathan to join their cause. But that didn't completely explain why Jonathan had done it.

"After all," Alistair had said to me, "the *Slocum* disaster was the greatest tragedy ever to strike our city. A thousand victims, and each one left behind a grieving, angry family. Yet others didn't turn to the anarchists and embrace their talk of violence and dynamite. Jonathan did. I have to ask, 'Why?' What made him susceptible to their cause, when others were not?"

Alistair insisted that the answer would not only be the foundation for an award-winning paper, but it would also revolutionize how the justice system dealt with terrorists of the kind the Russians and French had long known. Terrorists were, he insisted, a unique kind of criminal that our existing legal system didn't provide for.

He was expounding his ideas in that regard as we walked home together from Angus Porter's memorial service on a crisp November evening—the kind where the wind whipped around corners with sudden ferocity and dry leaves danced somersaults on the sidewalk.

We had reached the entrance to the Dakota and exchanged brief good-byes when he turned.

"Winter's coming," he said. "You can feel it tonight."

I breathed in sharply, appreciating the way the cold air cut into my lungs.

"Why don't you come up for a dram of scotch? I've a new bottle of Glenmorangie."

I hesitated for a split second, then agreed.

We rode up the elevator in silence, as Alistair made small talk with the attendant about the New York Giants and their prospects with Christy Mathewson come spring season. I had never known Alistair to be interested in baseball.

Then again, everybody was talking about the Giants since

they'd won the World Series last year. And there was plenty about Alistair that I didn't understand.

We soon settled into Alistair's library with a fire roaring in front of us, and the vast expanse of Central Park forming a bleak picture outside the window. It was—almost—like old times. But the memory of something lost added a bittersweet quality to the evening.

I finally spoke. "I want to know if Marie Sanders was right."

"About what?" he said, refilling his glass of scotch. "I've already told you that we made a mistake. Her father was indeed innocent of murdering young Sally Adams, though I didn't discover that fact until he was in his grave."

I leaned in closer, warming my hands by the fire. "When Marie made the attempt on your life, she claimed that the four of you had conspired against her father. She said that you planted evidence."

Alistair sat silent, drinking.

"I'm asking you straight-out if she was telling the truth!"

He returned my gaze with tired eyes. "You assume there's a simple answer."

I stared at him in amazement. "Yes, I do. Either you manufactured the evidence that convicted him. Or you didn't."

He was silent, so I continued talking. "I'm inclined to agree with Marie Sanders. Because from what I've learned about Leroy's trial, it was the testimony—the *last-minute* testimony—of Harry Blotsky that convinced the jury to convict."

"I know how it looks," Alistair snapped. He sniffed his glass of scotch, swirled it, but did not drink. "I'm not proud of the way we handled the Sanders case. We could have done better. I'd like to think I would have, anyway, if we'd been more seasoned in the practice of law." He stared into the flames. "But the circumstances are more complicated than you might imagine."

I took a sip from my own glass, savoring the liquid's slow burn. Then I gave him a steady look. "I've got no other plans tonight."

He sighed before getting up and putting another log on the fire. It crackled in response, spitting flames high into the chimney's recess.

Finally, he returned to his seat and began talking as though determined to get it over with. "As much as I regret my failures with regard to Leroy Sanders, I can say that his case is responsible for changing my life—at least its professional direction. You see, he is the reason why I first became interested in—obsessed, really—with the criminal mind."

But I didn't want to hear a treatise that would make no sense. "I think you ought to start at the beginning. Tell me about how you started the Bellerophon Club."

"That was so long ago." His lips curved into a rueful smile—and though I knew it was only the way the light cast shadows that accentuated his graying hair and lined forehead, I thought suddenly that he looked old.

As if he knew my thoughts, he began by saying, "We were impossibly young—not very mature and no doubt far too pleased with ourselves. We were full of our own knowledge and learning, believing that we knew things that nobody else did. That was why we formed Bellerophon. Final clubs were popular, and we thought it was a way to leave a lasting influence on the classes behind us."

"Why Bellerophon? I meant to ask you earlier and forgot."

He shrugged. "I came up with it. Took it from Greek mythology, where Bellerophon was a slayer of monsters—including the Chimera, arguably the greatest monster of them all. It symbolized how we viewed ourselves: we were going to slay the criminal monsters of our society and put them away."

"That doesn't sound like you," I said, shaking my head.

"It was at the time. As I said, the mistakes I made with the Sanders case changed me." He paused a moment, collecting his thoughts. When he spoke again, I could almost imagine him as he must have been, thirty years ago. "We didn't want to grow up and leave school, I suppose. Even after we had graduated Harvard and taken jobs at the district attorney's office, we decided to continue meeting at the Lawyers' Club. We talked about the cases we were working on and complained about our superiors. And we had impossible goals. We knew that every legal case set a precedent for the future, so we thought we could revolutionize our outdated legal system. All foolish dreams—for who were we, that we knew better than all the legal thinkers who had gone before us?"

He stopped again, and this time I noticed his gaze had fallen on the memorial service program from Hugo Jackson's funeral just two days earlier.

"Tell me about Sanders." I was almost afraid to breathe, for I didn't want to disturb his focus.

"Leroy Sanders offered us the perfect opportunity to demonstrate what we had learned. He was—quite literally—the monster we would defeat with the law as our weapon. Sanders was the worst sort of criminal: he had brutally murdered a child. A little girl."

"Go on." I leaned forward, listening.

"The case was assigned to Hugo, who almost immediately became frustrated with the limits of the law. Sanders's propensity for crime was clear. From interviews with his family and friends, we established that he had a long history of unnatural interest in young girls."

"What do you mean by 'a long history'?" I asked. "That's too vague for me to understand."

Alistair looked at me with somber eyes. "It means that we believed he had killed before. We also knew that he had raped before. I spoke with the victim myself."

"Impossible! He would have been tried and made to answer for earlier crimes."

But Alistair slowly shook his head. "The girl that we believed he murdered prior to our case was considered a runaway. She'd had troubled relations with her family, and the police were not inclined to treat her disappearance as anything out of the ordinary. And the girl that he had raped was from a poor immigrant family; they were not up to the task of seeking justice through the courts."

"You could have brought this up at trial. As prior history, it would be relevant."

He gave a harsh laugh. "You think we didn't try? The judge wouldn't allow it."

"At sentencing, then."

"But to get to sentencing, you first have to obtain a conviction." Alistair rubbed his hands together. "His guilt for the Sally Adams murder was circumstantial, but it seemed unquestionable. Still, hard evidence was lacking. And Hugo was worried." Alistair reached for the judge's memorial program and stared at it—then pulled Angus's program out of his pocket and joined the two together.

"Hugo and Angus didn't have to do much," he said. "Juries *want* to put away men like Leroy Sanders if you only give them the ammunition. I suspected what Hugo had done, with Angus's help, the moment Leroy's partner appeared out of the blue, ready to testify. Mr. Blotsky's testimony was too perfect. And the jury believed him." He gave a deep sigh. "The judge sentenced Sanders to life imprisonment at Auburn and you know the rest."

"Not exactly," I said, sitting on the edge of my seat. "To clarify, you're saying that Hugo Jackson manufactured Mr. Blotsky's testimony?"

"No need to put too fine a point on it," Alistair said, his voice dull. "Hugo and Angus bribed Harry Blotsky to testify as he did."

"When did you find out?"

"For certain?" He looked at me, one eyebrow raised. "Not for years."

"But you were suspicious at the time. And did nothing."

He nodded. "Allan Hartt and I were suspicious. We argued with Hugo about it."

I sat straight up, for I saw it: the truth was evident in his attitude—his arrogance even. "You didn't argue with Hugo because you disagreed with him," I charged. "You were angry that he hadn't involved you. You were the architect of his case, yet he hadn't consulted you."

"Hugo was clumsy. That's why, after all this time, Marie Sanders was able to figure out what had been done. If he'd talked to me, we might have planned better." Alistair was angry, even now, at this perceived slight from years past.

I stared at him in disbelief. "You're not upset that an innocent man went to prison. You're concerned that your misbegotten efforts to put him there weren't better orchestrated!"

"He wasn't innocent." Alistair slammed his fist on the table. Then, recovering himself, he tempered his tone. "You've got to understand, Ziele. You'd have done the same thing, given the chance. It was a child. A little girl. How could we not take advantage of our chance to remove this worst sort of monster from the streets?"

"Except that he was innocent," I said.

"Of this particular crime, yes. But only this one." Alistair ran his tongue over his lips. "I need water."

Wordlessly, I got up, crossed the room to the carafe that always sat above his bar, and poured him a glass. He drank greedily when I gave it to him.

"How can you possibly know what he'd done?" I asked.

"Because I believed the earlier evidence before my eyes," he said. "Later on, it became clear that another man had committed the Adams murder. Years after Sanders was sent to Auburn Prison, a similar killing occurred. Followed by another, and then another. I knew then for certain: Hugo and Angus had overreached with the Adams case—and we'd gotten it wrong."

"But you did nothing to restore Sanders's good name?" I looked at him quizzically.

"By then, Sanders was dead. And still—I truly believe that while he was guiltless in the Adams girl's murder, he was not an innocent man. He had blood on his hands. Just not *her* blood."

SECRET OF THE WHITE ROSE

My own mood was now black. "I'm as much for protecting our streets as anyone. But not when it means convicting a man of something he didn't do."

"Sometimes the law fails us." Alistair drained his glass. "Our actions with Sanders weren't the answer, either. My failure led me to think, how could we have done better? So what if Leroy Sanders was predisposed to this sort of criminal behavior? Was there no room for rehabilitating that impulse? I resolved to find out—not with Sanders, for it was too late, but with others in similar circumstances."

And I realized: that was how Alistair's research interest into the formation of the criminal mind was born. Out of misplaced guilt and mistaken judgment.

"What did Hugo and the others say when it became clear that you'd made a grave error with Sanders? They obviously demanded that you keep quiet."

"They believed, like me, that the end justifies the means," Alistair said, giving me a cool glance. "Sometimes extraordinary situations require extraordinary solutions. Leroy Sanders would have killed again, given the chance. Someone had to intervene."

I looked at him with great sadness. "The law would never condone your way of thinking."

"Which is why I conduct my research outside the bounds of the law," he said. "For my own purposes, I operate just beyond its parameters."

"The end justifies the means," I said, echoing his words.

Alistair's tone was cutting. "We all believe that at one point or another. You, most recently, when you invaded my private quarters."

I had only to think of Alistair's handling of the Michael Fromley matter in our first case together . . .

Or Jonathan, when he had explained to me why he had embraced the violence of the anarchists . . .

Or the commissioner, whose actions placed the security of his city and its population above all else . . .

Or myself. Because Alistair was right: when the stakes were high enough, more than once I'd convinced myself to cross an ethical line.

I would have asked more, but there was a knock at the door. It opened, and Mrs. Mellown immediately began to apologize. "I'm terribly sorry, Professor. This man has just barged in. I can't imagine why the attendants downstairs didn't stop him," she complained.

A rail-thin blond man with a black patch over his eye pushed his way past her and crossed the room toward us.

"Who are you and what the hell do you think you're doing?" Alistair stood.

The man merely smiled. "Mind if I take a seat? Detective Ziele will explain who I am."

"Paul Hlad," I said, my tone subdued. "Why are you here?"

He pulled an envelope out of the black satchel slung over his shoulder before taking the hard-backed chair between us. He looked around the library, taking in the foreign artifacts as well as the expansive view. "Nice place. But I suppose there's no need to waste time on pleasantries. I have something for the professor."

He gave the brown envelope to Alistair.

"What's this?" Alistair asked, his voice rough with anger.

"Open it." Hlad flexed his fingers.

Alistair ripped it open and stared at the single sheet of paper within.

"My creative work," Hlad said with a half smile. "I hoped you might appreciate it."

Alistair stared, lines of worry deepening across his brow.

"Marie Sanders was a true comrade," Hlad said. "Even though her devotion to the cause was compromised by personal motives, she was a dedicated worker."

"You knew . . ." I said.

Paul smiled in a way that told me he knew everything, but his answer was disingenuous. "Who's to say what a man like me really knows?"

"You need to explain yourself." Alistair sat again, this time at the edge of a chair.

"It's quite simple. I made a few interesting discoveries." His one good eye surveyed us. "I want you to appreciate that fact."

A chill ran down my spine.

"Appreciation can take many forms," Alistair said. "What do you want?"

I watched as Paul's lips curved into a smile. "I've been granted immunity by the state of New York in exchange for my valuable testimony," he said. "I'm likely to be deported thereafter. But I've no plans to disappear."

That was the moment I knew that we had not fully realized the role Hlad had been playing throughout.

Al Drayson. Jonathan Strupp. Marie Sanders. His henchman Savvas.

All individual actors, loosely linked by their association with the anarchist movement. But each one had been manipulated by Hlad—a virtual puppetmaster behind it all. His words went on to confirm it.

"I make it my business to know what those in my organization are doing. Marie may have thought she was using me," Paul Hlad said, "but the best leaders are those who can exploit the goals of their followers to accomplish their own. Marie was a brilliant find in that respect. She confounded the police and helped cover our plan for Drayson. Without ever knowing she was doing it," he added with a short, brittle laugh.

"Because everyone believed the murders were connected to Drayson," I said.

He nodded, then turned to Alistair. "When you founded the Bellerophon Club . . . when you designed strategy for your friends at the district attorney's office . . . when you plucked those criminals from jail cells who best served your research goals . . . You have always been expert at manipulating other people's desires to accomplish your own ends. No?"

Alistair's face blanched. "No matter what you think, I'm not—"

Paul interrupted Alistair. "I know all about you. Let's leave it at that, Professor."

Alistair slumped back into his chair as though the lifeblood was drained from him.

The sheet of paper he had held fell to the floor—and on it, I recognized a familiar image, albeit now written in an unfamiliar hand.

A musical cipher.

I picked it up as Paul Hlad slipped through the door.

Isabella was waiting for me in the hallway when I left.

"You spoke with Alistair?" she asked.

I nodded.

"Who was that man who just left? I remember him from the anarchist meeting."

I only shook my head. "He's not important."

She eyed me suspiciously for a moment but then seemed to understand. It wasn't a conversation I wanted to have tonight.

"Come walk with me." Her tone brooked no disagreement.

She disappeared into her own apartment for a moment, re-appearing wearing her coat and with Oban leashed. His golden tail cut a wide swath, moving the entire back portion of his body to and fro.

This night, we walked the city streets. She seemed to understand that I found comfort in the bright lights and bustling activity of Broadway—the Boulevard. A few grocers and pharmacy shops remained open, even though the evening was growing dark.

"Did Alistair tell you what you needed to know?" A curious expression crossed her face.

"He did." I didn't elaborate.

Dry leaves crunched under our feet, and in the moonlit sky, the trees stretched craggy limbs high into the bleak November night.

"I've often thought that sometimes those with the greatest gifts are cursed with the most serious flaws." Her expression was unreadable as she added, "I saw something of that even with Teddy: those qualities that made him an intrepid explorer and archeologist also made him a less than ideal husband. Much as I loved him."

"I suppose most people disappoint, given half a chance," I said. Like my own father, who meant well—except when he held a pair of aces in one hand and a roll of coins in the other.

"Even you, Simon?"

I deflected the question. "So do you want to know what Alistair said?"

"I don't." A sober look crossed her face, and her eyes filled with an intense sadness. "Sometimes it's better not knowing."

We walked in silence until we reached the intersection of Eighty-second and Broadway. Then Isabella stopped. "What do you think, Simon? Should we turn back or keep going?"

Ahead of us, the night stretched long and dark—for this uptown section of the Boulevard lacked the restaurants, shops, and street lamps that illuminated the streets below. Given the city's insatiable appetite for expansion, that would come. But tonight, all was quiet and the path ahead beckoned.

I took Oban's leash from Isabella. "Let's walk a few blocks more."

She settled her arm comfortably into mine and—if only for the span of that walk—I was content. People would disappoint. The lies and half-truths, the betrayals and double-dealings, that I had witnessed were simply part of life.

But perhaps not always.

Perhaps not tonight.

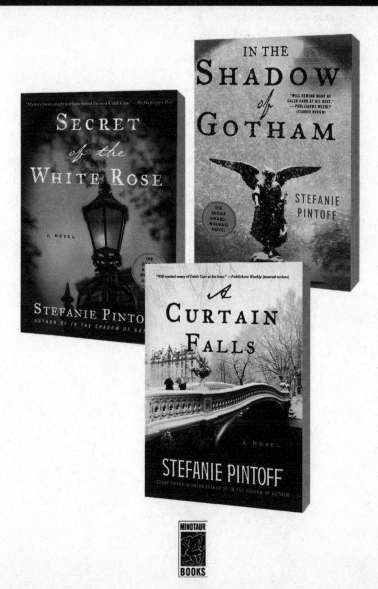